P9-DCD-191

DREAMS MADE FLESH

Weaver of Dreams

The magic of the Darkness is passed from one race to another as new caretakers for the Realms are chosen in this tale of the origin of the Jewels of power. . . .

The Prince of Ebon Rih

Under the cold eye of his aristocratic mother, Eyrien Warlord Prince Lucivar Yaslana struggles with his feelings for his housekeeper, the hearth witch Marian. . . .

Zuulaman

The Queens of Zuulaman believe they can coerce Saetan into doing their bidding by threatening the life of his child—only to unleash the High Lord of Hell's incalculable fury. . . .

Kaeleer's Heart

Daemon fears Jaenelle will never recover from sacrificing her Black Jewels to purge the Realm of the corrupt Queens. He desires nothing more than to heal her, body and soul—and help her unravel the secret of Twilight's Dawn, the Jewel Jaenelle now possesses. . . .

Praise for *The Black Jewels Trilogy*

"A terrific writer . . . the more I read, the more excited I became because of the freshness of [her] take on the usual high fantasy setting, the assurance of [her] language, all the lovely touches of characterization that [she slips] in so effortlessly."   —Charles de Lint

"Rich and fascinatingly different dark fantasy, a series definitely worth checking out."   —*Locus*

"A darkly fascinating world . . . Vivid and sympathetic characters, a fascinating and fully-realized magical system, lavish and sensuous descriptions, and interesting world building. . . . Many compelling and beautifully realized elements. A terrific read."   —SF Site

"Lavishly sensual . . . a richly detailed world."   —*Library Journal*

"Vividly painted . . . dramatic, erotic, hope-filled."   —Lynn Flewelling

"Intense . . . erotic, violent, and imaginative. This one is white-hot."
                                                      —Nancy Kress

"Mystical, sensual, glittering with dark magic."
               —Terri Windling, coeditor of *Year's Best Fantasy and Horror*

"Dark, intricate, and disturbing."
                        —Josepha Sherman, author of *Forging the Runes*

"A high voltage ride through a new realm. Bishop draws her characters with acute emotion [and] leaves the reader lusting for her next novel."
               —Lois H. Gresh, coauthor of *The Termination Node*

"[Anne Bishop's] poignant storytelling skills are surpassed only by her flair for the dramatic and her deft characterization . . . a talented author."
                                                 —*Affaire de Coeur*

"Daemon, Lucivar, and Saetan ooze more sex appeal than any three fictional characters created in a very long time . . . a fascinating world consisting of three realms peopled with interesting and nearly always dangerous characters."   —*The Romance Reader*

"When I first read *Daughter of the Blood* by Anne Bishop, I was blown away by the vividness of her writing. Dark, morbid, sinister, and yet it holds you completely fascinated and spellbound by its beauty. Once I'd begun reading . . . I couldn't bring myself to put down the book and leave the world that Anne Bishop had magically spun around me . . . Rich in both positive and negative emotions and intense in its portrayal of human behavior and human desires. At the same time, it also has many humorous moments. . . . One of the most original and readable books in the fantasy genre."
                                                        —The 11th Hour

"Has immense appeal for fans of dark fantasy or horror. Most highly recommended."
                                                        —*Hypatia's Hoard*

Praise for *The Invisible Ring*

"Plenty of adventure."   —*Locus*

"[An] entertaining otherworlds fantasy adventure with battles and dangers and chases."
                                                        —*Chronicle*

"Plenty of adventure, romance, dazzling wizardly pyrotechnics and internal workings of Bishop's unique and fascinating hierarchical magic system. The plot strands' convergence is skillfully handled, building tension and suspense right up to the end. . . . Bishop's world is rich in strongly dark elements balanced by a firm belief in ideals like loyalty and love.

Bishop is also superb at depicting the essence of her characters through dialogue, which can often be quite witty or emotionally heartwarming or chilling at just the right moments. Then there's the author's overall sublime skill as a writer, blending the darkly macabre with spine-tingling emotional intensity, mesmerizing magic, lush sensuality, and exciting action, all set in a thoroughly detailed invented world of cultures in conflict, based on ingeniously reversed genre clichés. *The Invisible Ring* will serve as an enticement, whetting the appetite to explore more of the realms in the Black Jewels trilogy."
                                                        —SF Site

"Anne Bishop has an awesome knack for characterization, used to great effect in this novel. It's a bittersweet story, and you'll love every word of it. Readers of fantasy and romance will love this book, and of course it's a must-have for Bishop fans. Most highly recommended."
                                                        —*Hypatia's Hoard*

ALSO BY ANNE BISHOP

The Black Jewels Trilogy
Daughter of the Blood
Heir to the Shadows
Queen of the Darkness

The Invisible Ring

The Tir Alainn Trilogy
Pillars of the World
Shadows and Light
The House of Gaian

ANNE BISHOP

Dreams Made Flesh

RoC

A ROC BOOK

ROC
Published by New American Library, a division of
Penguin Group (USA) Inc., 375 Hudson Street,
New York, New York 10014, USA
Penguin Group (Canada), 10 Alcorn Avenue, Toronto,
Ontario, Canada M4V 3B2 (a division of Pearson Penguin Canada Inc.)
Penguin Books Ltd, 80 Strand, London WC2R 0RL, England
Penguin Ireland, 25 St. Stephen's Green, Dublin 2,
Ireland (a division of Penguin Books Ltd.)
Penguin Group (Australia), 250 Camberwell Road, Camberwell, Victoria 3124,
Australia (a division of Pearson Australia Group Pty. Ltd.)
Penguin Books India Pvt. Ltd., 11 Community Centre, Panchsheel Park,
New Delhi - 110 017, India
Penguin Group (NZ), Cnr Airborne and Rosedale Roads, Albany,
Auckland 1310, New Zealand (a division of Pearson New Zealand Ltd.)
Penguin Books (South Africa) (Pty.) Ltd., 24 Sturdee Avenue,
Rosebank, Johannesburg 2196, South Africa

Penguin Books Ltd., Registered Offices: 80 Strand, WC2R 0RL, England

First published by Roc, an imprint of New American Library,
a division of Penguin Group (USA) Inc.

First Printing, January 2005
10   9   8   7   6   5   4   3   2   1

Copyright © Anne Bishop, 2005
All rights reserved

ROC REGISTERED TRADEMARK—MARCA REGISTRADA

LIBRARY OF CONGRESS CATALOGING-IN-PUBLICATION DATA:
Bishop, Anne.
Dreams made flesh / Anne Bishop.
p.   cm.
"A ROC book."
ISBN 0-451-46013-8 (trade pbk.)
1. Witches—Fiction. 2. Love stories, American. 3. Occult fiction,
American. I. Title.
PS3552.I7594D74   2005
813'.92—dc22
2004015957

Set in Bembo
Designed by Ginger Legato

Printed in the United States of America

Without limiting the rights under copyright reserved above, no part of this publication may be reproduced, stored in or introduced into a retrieval system, or transmitted, in any form, or by any means (electronic, mechanical, photocopying, recording, or otherwise), without the prior written permission of both the copyright owner and the above publisher of this book.

PUBLISHER'S NOTE
This is a work of fiction. Names, characters, places, and incidents either are the product of the author's imagination or are used fictitiously, and any resemblance to actual persons, living or dead, business establishments, events, or locales is entirely coincidental.

The scanning, uploading, and distribution of this book via the Internet or via any other means without the permission of the publisher is illegal and punishable by law. Please purchase only authorized electronic editions, and do not participate in or encourage electronic piracy of copyrighted materials. Your support of the author's rights is appreciated.

for

Debra Dixon

and

Annemarie Jason

ACKNOWLEDGMENTS

My thanks to Blair Boone for continuing to be my first reader, to Debra Dixon for being second reader, to Laura Anne Gilman for giving me the go-ahead to do these stories and to Anne Sowards for seeing the book through to completion, to Kandra for her continued patience in keeping up the Web site, and to Pat and Bill Feidner for the dinners and laughter and all the other things that make them special.

CONTENTS

JEWELS

WHITE
YELLOW
TIGER EYE
ROSE
SUMMER-SKY
PURPLE DUSK
OPAL★
GREEN
SAPPHIRE
RED
GRAY
EBON-GRAY
BLACK

★Opal is the dividing line between lighter and darker Jewels because it can be either.

When making the Offering to the Darkness, a person can descend a maximum of three ranks from his/her Birthright Jewel.

Example: Birthright White could descend to Rose.

BLOOD HIERARCHY/CASTES

MALES:

landen—non-Blood of any race

Blood male—a general term for all males of the Blood; also refers to any Blood male who doesn't wear Jewels

Warlord—a Jeweled male equal in status to a witch

Prince—a Jeweled male equal in status to a Priestess or a Healer

Warlord Prince—a dangerous, extremely aggressive Jeweled male; in status, slightly lower than a Queen

FEMALES:

landen—non-Blood of any race

Blood female—a general term for all females of the Blood; mostly refers to any Blood female who doesn't wear Jewels

witch—a Blood female who wears Jewels but isn't one of the other hierarchical levels; also refers to any Jeweled female

Healer—a witch who heals physical wounds and illnesses; equal in status to a Priestess and a Prince

Priestess—a witch who cares for altars, Sanctuaries and Dark Altars; witnesses handfasts and marriages; performs offerings; equal in status to a Healer and a Prince

Black Widow—a witch who heals the mind; weaves the tangled webs of dreams and visions; is trained in illusions and poisons

Queen—a witch who rules the Blood; is considered to be the land's heart and the Blood's moral center; as such, she is the focal point of their society

Places in the Realms Mentioned in These Stories

TERREILLE

Askavi
Black Valley—valley that is the Keep's territory
Blood Run
Ebon Askavi (aka the Black Mountain, the Keep)
Khaldharon Run
Dhemlan
SaDiablo Hall
Hayll
Draega—capital city
Zuulaman Islands

KAELEER (THE SHADOW REALM)

Arachna
Arceria
Askavi
Agio—Blood village in Ebon Rih
Blood Run
Doun—Blood village in Ebon Rih
Ebon Askavi (aka the Black Mountain, the Keep)
Ebon Rih—valley that is the Keep's territory

Khaldharon Run
Riada—Blood village in Ebon Rih
Dea al Mon
Dharo
Dhemlan
Amdarh—capital city
Halaway—village near SaDiablo Hall
SaDiablo Hall (the Hall)
Fyreborn Islands
Glacia
Nharkhava
Scelt (shelt)
Maghre (ma-gra)—village
Sceval (she-VAL)

HELL (THE DARK REALM, THE REALM OF THE DEAD)

Ebon Askavi (aka the Black Mountain, the Keep)
SaDiablo Hall

AUTHOR'S NOTE
The "Sc" in the names Scelt and Sceval is pronouced "Sh."

WEAVER OF DREAMS

Long, long ago . . .

1

Her web shook with the violence of the storm. AboveWorld roared and flashed, turning dark-time to light-time. But there was something more, something *different* that trembled through the strands of silk. Something she'd never felt before.

AboveWorld roared and flashed again. Then something screamed—a terrible shuddering in her web—and a piece of AboveWorld crashed into World, ripping, tearing, roaring, shrieking.

Dark Wet splashed her, splashed her web, at the same moment something struck the web near the center. Prey?

Hunger overcame hesitation. She hurried along the threads, intending to secure her meal before heading back to the safer, more sheltered edge of her web.

But the *something* was hard and had no meat. As she tried to sink her fangs into it, she ingested some of the Dark Wet, and that . . . filled her, flowed through her, sang inside her.

Changed her.

After cleaning off every bit of Dark Wet, she discarded the *something* and hurried back to the sheltered edge of her web to wait out the storm.

2

Light. And a hunger. For meat, yes. But also for something more.

Leaving her web, she traveled along the Rough that stretched out over World until she reached a place where the piece of Above-World had crashed into World. The Dark Wet still sang inside her, almost too quiet to feel, but it was enough to guide her to more of the Dark Wet.

Fixing an anchor thread to the Rough, she spun out silk. The World trembled with anger. The air quivered with grief and despair . . . and longing.

Her legs touched the piece of AboveWorld. Hard, like the *something* that had struck her web. Moving cautiously, she found a place where the Hard was torn away, revealing meat—and the Dark Wet.

After consuming as much of the Dark Wet as she could, she sank her fangs into meat and pumped her venom into the spot. It would only liquefy a tiny bit of meat, but that tiny bit would feed her well.

So she spun a web as close as she could to the meat—and the Dark Wet that seeped over the meat.

3

In dreams, she unfurled her wings and sailed through the Darkness—a vastness that was outside the body, and yet the body became its vessel; a power reached by heart and mind and spirit. Through it flowed the whispers of creation . . . and the silence of destruction. Her race had spiraled down its chasms and canyons and strange abysses for years beyond memory—and had understood that they would never understand this place that was, and wasn't, a place.

In dreams, the vision of webs shining in the Darkness hadn't dazzled and overwhelmed her mind, hadn't blinded her to the danger of the storm, and she had reached the caves on this island that she had chosen as her final resting place. But the wounds received because of the storm were fatal, and the caves were too far away.

No. Not quite true. She could have used her power to shift her broken body to the caves, but she felt a small tug, a small promise that her unique gift would not be lost if she remained where she was.

So in a dream that was more than a dream, she sent her last vision to her mother, Draca, showing her Queen how the new caretakers of the world would be able to travel safely through the Darkness: shimmering, colored webs of power stretched through that vastness—pathways that could be reached from the Realms.

She could not say why the beautiful symmetry of the web resonated so strongly inside her, but the image didn't fade from her mind, despite the agony that clawed at her flesh. Nor could she say why, as she drifted between visions and dreams, she felt certain there was something nearby, something small and golden, that would be able to hold her particular gift.

She would have enough time. Just enough time. If this potential Weaver wanted what she had to give.

4

Light-time . . . day. Dark-time . . . night. AboveWorld . . . sky. Rough . . . tree. Hard . . . scale. Dark Wet . . . blood. Meat . . .

Sorrow. Pain. Longing. Need. Hope.

. . . dragon.

She . . . spider. Small. Golden.

Momentarily distracted by the strange thoughts, the spider returned to her housekeeping, rolled up the tattered remains of her old web, along with the discarded prey, then spun a fresh web. She did not spin in order to catch prey. She spun to keep other things away from the flesh that not only fed her body but sang to her about things she had never known existed. The World kept shifting as she absorbed the Weaver, showing her new things in the familiar.

Showing her ancient things in the familiar.

Showing her a Need for Weavers who could spin dreams into shapes that could walk in the World, for Weavers who could spin dreams into flesh.

She did not understand this Need, but it flavored the flesh her venom liquefied for her to ingest. So at night, when she was safely tucked beneath the scales in the hollow created by her feedings, she drifted on the tangled, silken threads of the dragon's longings and dreams—and began to learn how to weave a different kind of web.

5

Perhaps the other Seers were right. Perhaps her particular gift was too dangerous to give to the new caretakers of the Realms. Perhaps there was no other race that could, or should, take the deepest heart-dreams and provide a bridge for those dreams to become flesh.

But those dreams would be needed in the world. She knew that with unshakable certainty. They would be needed—and it was unlikely even the simplest of those dreams would ever exist because she hadn't reached the caves as she'd intended. She wouldn't make the same transition as the rest of her race, transforming her scales into Jewels that would serve as a reservoir for the power the new caretakers could not contain in their smaller, weaker bodies. The Jewels that came from her should have been the vessels that contained her gift and would have changed the wearer into a Seer that could shape dreams into flesh. Now . . .

Did her mother know she was trapped on this island, exposed and dying? Did her sire, the great Prince of the Dragons, sense her fading presence in the world? Would they feel disappointment in her that, during moments of despair and heartache and hope, she was trying to pass her gift to a small, golden spider?

She should have stayed in the dark mountain that was the lair of the Prince and the Queen. She should have curled up in one of the deep hollows within that mountain and followed the rest of her race into the forever sleep. Instead she had followed a vision of a cave filled with dreams—a vision that would never come to pass.

Soon now. Soon. Her body was failing. Her power was fading. Soon she would be free of the world. Soon.

Closing her gold eyes, she drifted on dreams.

So much sorrow gave the flesh a bitter taste, but the spider remained, burrowing deeper beneath the scales for meat that still seeped blood, was still fresh. And it wasn't all bitter. When the daring male had approached her and indicated his willingness to mate, Dragon's flesh had been tastier that day, as if the mating had drawn sweeter memories to the surface.

Since she wanted her hatchlings to feed on this flesh that was making her more than just a spider, she worked to find a way to reach the memories, to see the dreams.

Dragon had shown her before. Why wouldn't Dragon show her now?

Frustrated, she climbed up to Dragon's jaw, anchored a strand of silk, and began to build a web. But as she built the web, she . . . felt things. So she spun them into the web, ignoring instinct and placing the threads where they needed to be. Sorrow. Pain. Longing. Need. Hope.

As she cautiously traveled the strands of the completed tangled web, warmth flowed through her. She paused, absorbed the feel of this sensation, and added one more small thread. Joy.

Suddenly she saw the caves, the place Dragon had intended to go to do the finest dreaming. And in those caves, she saw golden spiders, much larger than herself, spinning tangled webs.

Sound, faint and fading, filled her.

You have learned well, Dragon said. *But heed me, little one. You must guard the webs you weave that make dreams into flesh. Many beings will cherish those webs because they are spun out of magic that lives in the heart. But there will be others who will want to destroy that heart-magic before it can touch the world. Guard the webs . . . Weaver of Dreams.*

Dragon's breath came out in a long sigh . . . and then there was silence.

7

The golden spider spun out the last thread of the web that filled the space between Dragon's jaw and shoulder. Most of her offspring had gone away, just ordinary spiders who would spin ordinary webs and catch ordinary prey. But the few who were different, who were like her, had stayed nearby, learning how to spin the tangled webs.

Despite the size of her web, she had caught only one small dream, but that one held a deep well of yearning . . . and a taste of sorrow that was, somehow, connected to Dragon. So she plucked the thread of yearning, sending it back to the heart it had come from.

As day turned to night, she settled into the most sheltered edge of her web—and wondered about the dreamer.

8

Day had barely touched the sky when she sensed a Presence that resonated with her tangled web. She waited, feeling the faint tremble of footfalls on the earth, the change in the air.

Sso. My daughter wass able to passs on her gift after all.

The voice that flowed through her felt like Dragon, but wasn't quite Dragon.

The Presence approached her web. Her offspring plucked the strands of their own webs, trying to ensnare the Presence's mind. But the Presence didn't respond, didn't give any sign that it had felt the tugs and whispers in those webs.

Blood singss to blood, the Presence said, leaning over the spider's tangled web. *Remember me.*

A drop of blood fell on a knot of tangled threads, a glistening bead of power.

The spider waited until the Presence went away before hurrying over to devour the offering.

Power flowed through her, a power even stronger and richer than Dragon's had been.

Draca.

Dragon's Mother. Dragon's Queen.

Remember me.

For hours that day, the spider stroked the strands of her tangled web, remembering Dragon, remembering the feel of Draca. Not shaped like Dragon, but still a dragon.

This dream web had done what it was meant to do. Draca would not sorrow for Dragon anymore because she had seen that, in the most important way, Dragon was still in the world. Small now, and golden, but still in the world.

The spider carefully cut the anchoring threads and just as carefully rolled the web into a cocoon. She traveled down Dragon's neck and shoulder until she reached the hole in the chest.

Perhaps it was the way of Dragon's kind, or perhaps it was some last bit of magic that had changed Dragon's flesh into porous rock covered with hard stone scales. Inside Dragon were several chambers where she could spin the first stage of a web, then listen, quiet and protected, while the strongest heart-dreams drifted over her, guiding her as she created her web.

The time would come when she and her offspring would make the long journey to the caves where the golden spiders would protect the webs of dreams that would become flesh. But not yet.

She squeezed through the opening that led to a small chamber and pulled the cocoon in with her.

Dragon's body was hollow stone now, but the heart hadn't rotted like the rest of the organs. It had changed to smooth stone. Whenever the spider came to this chamber and brushed a leg over that stone, the chamber filled with warmth, and she felt Dragon's joy that the Weaver's gift had not been lost.

The day would come when she no longer felt that warmth, and the stone would be no more than a stone. When that day came, she would leave. But even then, whatever bit of heart-memory might remain wouldn't be alone.

Before leaving the chamber, she spun out some silk and attached the cocoon of Draca's dream to Dragon's stone heart.

THE PRINCE OF EBON RIH

*This story takes place after
the events in Heir to the Shadows*

ONE

Lucivar Yaslana stood at the far end of the flagstone courtyard of his new home, enjoying the early morning sunlight that had begun warming the stones beneath his feet. The mountain air felt chilly against his bare skin, and the freshly made coffee he sipped from a plain white mug tasted rough enough to make him wince. Didn't matter. The coffee might not have the smooth potency that Mrs. Beale produced for his father's table, but it wasn't any worse than what he made when he went hunting and spent a night out on the land. Couldn't be any worse, since he'd made it the same way.

He looked over his shoulder at the open door that led into the warren of rooms that made up the eyrie. Some of the rooms had been carved out of the living mountain; others had been built from the extracted stone. The result would have been a nightmare for any race that needed predictable lines and angles in a structure, but for anyone born of the Eyrien race, it was perfect.

And this particular eyrie was now his.

Smiling, he closed his gold eyes and tipped his head back to feel the sun on his face. Slowly opening his dark, membranous wings, he savored the feel of sunlight and chilly air playing over his wings and light-brown skin.

In all of his seventeen hundred years, he'd never had a home until three years ago when he'd been reunited with his father—the man who, through the machinations of Dorothea, Hayll's High Priestess, had had his two younger sons taken from him. The man who had never forgotten or forgiven the betrayals that had left scars on all of them.

He'd been happy living in the suite of rooms at SaDiablo Hall, but the Hall was still his father's house. This place was his. Exclusively, totally his.

Yas?

Well, maybe not exclusively his.

Sipping his coffee, Lucivar watched the adolescent wolf trot toward him. The youngster had been ready to leave the pack that lived in the north woods of his father's estate but hadn't wanted to go back to the Territory most of the kindred wolves called home. Tassle had grown up near humans and wanted to learn more about them, but there still weren't many places where the wild kindred could safely live in human Territories—and there still weren't many humans beyond Jaenelle Angelline's court who felt easy about living around an animal who had the same power as the human Blood. Since he now had plenty of land for a wolf to roam in, it was easy enough to share the space.

Tassle, Lucivar thought, raising the mug to hide his smile. *What kind of name was Tassle for a Warlord wolf?* "Good morning. Smell anything interesting?"

Yes. Yas, you aren't wearing your cow skin.

"It's called leather." Which Tassle knew perfectly well. Humans had prejudices, but so did the kindred. If something could be described by referring to the animal it came from, they ignored the human word for the end result. They viewed the world from their own furry perspective, which was fair, he supposed, since no two people, let alone two species, would view the world around them in quite the same way. "I don't need clothes right now. It's a fine morning, we're alone up here, and it's not like anyone living in the valley is going to see me."

But, Yas—

He sensed it then. Someone coming up the stone stairs from the landing area below had passed through the perimeter shield he'd placed around the eyrie. The shield wasn't meant to keep anyone out, just to alert him if someone approached his home.

As he turned toward the intruder, Helene, his father's housekeeper, hurried up the last few steps, then stopped abruptly when she reached the flagstones and saw him.

"Good morning, Prince Yaslana," she said politely.

"Helene," he replied with equal, if forced, politeness—especially when a dozen maids who worked at the Hall came up the stairs and gave him a quick, and approving, glance before going into the eyrie.

Well, Lucivar thought sourly, *they all got an eyeful to perk up their morning.* "What brings you here, Helene?"

"Now that all the workmen are done with the renovations the High Lord felt were necessary to make Prince Andulvar's old eyrie livable again, we've come to give it a good cleaning."

"I've already cleaned the place."

She made a sound that told him what she thought of his ability to clean *anything*. But that was a hearth witch for you. If it didn't sparkle, shine, or gleam, it wasn't clean. Never mind that stone walls weren't supposed to sparkle, shine, or gleam.

"Fine," Lucivar said, knowing he was cornered and arguing was a waste of breath. "I'll get dressed and show you—"

Helene waved her hand dismissively. "You were obviously enjoying a fine morning. There's no reason why you should do otherwise. I'm sure we can find everything. What there is of it," she added under her breath.

He bared his teeth in what he hoped would be mistaken as a smile. "I wouldn't want to be a distraction."

She gave him a fast sweep with her eyes. "You won't be."

Lucivar just stared at her, too stunned to think of anything to say.

Helene sniffed delicately. "I won't say I've seen better, but I've seen just as good."

Who? He could think of one man Helene could have walked in on and surprised.

As she headed for the door, another woman's voice, coming from the stairs, said, "Come along, ladies. We don't want to interrupt too much of the Prince's day."

Helene turned toward the stairs, the light of battle in her eyes, as Merry bounded up the last few stairs and saw him. Along with her hus-

band, Briggs, Merry ran a tavern and inn in Riada, the closest Blood village in the valley.

"Oh, my," Merry said with approval. Then she noticed Helene, and
the glint in her eyes didn't bode well for a peaceful morning.

"Ladies," Lucivar said, wondering if he was going to start his day
breaking up a brawl outside his door.

"We're going to clean up the eyrie for the Prince," Merry said stiffly,
indicating the women crowding the stairs behind her. "As a welcome to
Ebon Rih since he'll be living here now."

"I'm sure Prince Yaslana appreciates the gesture, but I've brought
some of my staff from the Hall to take care of things," Helene replied.

"Ladies."

"There's no need for you to be taking time away from your own duties. We can look after him. He *is* the Warlord Prince of Ebon Rih now,"
Merry said.

"Which doesn't make him any less his father's son—" Helene said,
raising her voice.

Hell's fire! They were squaring off like two bitches ready to fight over
a meaty bone—and he was *not* going to become the prize of whoever
won this battle.

"—and I won't have it said that any of the High Lord's children are
living in squalor," Helene continued.

Lucivar gritted his teeth. Squalor? *Squalor?* He'd moved to the eyrie
two days ago. There hadn't been time to accumulate *squalor. "Ladies."*

They turned on him, and after studying them the way he'd study any
adversary, he wisely swallowed his rising temper. Helene worked for his
father, and since he would, no doubt, continue to spend time at the Hall,
telling her to leave would be an insult he didn't want to live with. And
Merry made the best steak pies he'd ever tasted. If he told *her* to go, it
might be years before he had another slice of steak pie.

Finally Helene turned to Merry and said, "While yours is the more
recent claim, it is equally valid. And there's more than enough work for
all of us."

Merry nodded, then clapped her hands. "Come along, ladies. We've
work to do."

Four of the women who'd come with Merry were married or, at least, had acknowledged lovers. The other seven were younger and unattached—and would have dawdled a lot longer if Merry and Helene hadn't herded them into the eyrie.

When he'd been a slave in Terreillean courts, he'd been stripped down and displayed for the enjoyment of the Queen who controlled the Ring of Obedience. He'd never felt the need to smile politely while he was being ogled. But here he was, smiling—showing his teeth, anyway—as Helene pushed the last witch inside and closed the door.

Rage danced in his belly, twisting it into knots. He closed his eyes and tightened the leash on his temper. He had an explosive one, and it had served him well when he'd lived in Terreille, but this wasn't the same. He hadn't been forced to strip down. He'd been standing outside of his own free will, and if the women who had suddenly appeared appreciated the view he provided, he couldn't blame them for it.

Thank the Darkness none of them had tried to touch him. He wasn't sure what he would have done if any of them had tried.

No. That wasn't true. He *knew* what he would have done. He just didn't know how he would have explained breaking a woman's arm for a touch they'd all think of as harmless or, at the very worst, an invitation.

Yas? Tassle's sending on a psychic thread sounded hesitant, a little fearful.

Turning, Lucivar looked at the young wolf. "Women are a pain in the ass."

Confusion replaced fear. *Pain? They didn't nip you. Why is there pain?* After a pause, Tassle added, *I could lick it to make it better.*

Maybe it wasn't just for Tassle's sake that he'd offered to share his home with a wolf, Lucivar decided as amusement eased the knots in his belly. You could never tell what the kindred would pick up from human behavior and decide to make their own. Obviously, Tassle had decided the wolf version of "kiss it and make it better" was the appropriate response to this situation.

"No, thanks," Lucivar said, moving away from the eyrie to walk in the rock-strewn grass that might have been a lawn or a garden once upon a

time. He swallowed a mouthful of coffee and swore. Not only rough
enough to bite but now it was also cold.

Noticing the way Tassle sniffed the air, Lucivar made a "go forward"
gesture with one hand. "Go on. Go explore. If you stay around here,
you'll end up getting washed and polished."

You come too?

He hadn't had a chance yet to really walk the land around the eyrie
and get a feel for it, but leaving right now felt a bit too much like running away—and it went against his nature as an Eyrien Warlord Prince
to run from a battleground. "You go on. I'll keep an eye on things here."

As he watched Tassle trot off to mark the home territory, he felt the
weight of the eyrie at his back and wondered if it *really* would be running away to get out of sight while all of those women cluttered up his
home. Besides, if his presence wasn't a distraction from the allure of
buckets and mops, his absence wouldn't be noted either. Which should
have pleased him. The fact that it didn't was an annoyance he'd think
about later.

"I'd wish you a good morning," a deep, amused voice said, "but I'm
not sure that's appropriate."

Turning, he watched the slender, brown-skinned man cross the rock-
strewn ground with feline grace. The movement lifted the edges of the
knee-length black cape, revealing the red lining and providing slashes of
color to accent the black tunic jacket and trousers.

His brother Daemon moved with the same feline grace.

He tried not to think about Daemon too much, tried not to wonder
too often if his brother had found a way out of the madness the Blood
called the Twisted Kingdom. There was nothing he could do for Daemon, wherever he was.

He pushed those thoughts aside and focused on the man settling on
a stone that time and the elements had weathered into a natural seat. He
looked like a handsome man at the end of his prime, his black hair sil-
vered at the temples and faint lines around his golden eyes—an aristo
Hayllian male who would be in his element at a dinner party and
wouldn't know what to do on a killing field.

Looks could be deceiving. This was Saetan Daemon SaDiablo, a

Black-Jeweled Warlord Prince who was the Prince of the Darkness, High Lord of Hell, Warlord Prince of Dhemlan, Steward of the Dark Court at Ebon Askavi . . . and his father.

It was the last title that made Lucivar wary. There weren't any clear rules when it came to sons dealing with fathers. Not that he paid much attention to rules, but it would have been nice to know when he was about to do something that would stomp on Saetan's toes and end with them yelling at each other. Which he did know, actually. Every time Jaenelle said, "Lucivar, I have a wonderful idea" and he went along with it, he could pretty much count on ending up in Saetan's study to receive a blistering lecture. Too bad he enjoyed squaring off with his father as much as he enjoyed getting into trouble with the golden-haired, sapphire-eyed witch who was Saetan's adopted daughter—and, therefore, his sister. The fact that Jaenelle was the Queen of Ebon Askavi and they both served in the First Circle of her court just added spice to their shouting matches.

"It's none of my business, but I am curious," Saetan said. "Why are you standing out here displaying your assets?"

"I'm standing out here because my home has been invaded by two dozen women with brooms and buckets—"

"Two dozen? I wasn't aware Helene brought that many from the Hall."

"She didn't. Some of the women from Riada showed up right after Helene did. And this is how I was dressed—"

"—or not dressed," Saetan murmured.

"—when they showed up." Lucivar took another gulp of coffee and shuddered. "And getting dressed after I'd been assured I wouldn't be a distraction seemed like . . . bragging."

"I see. Who told you this?"

"Helene. She said she'd seen just as good." Lucivar eyed his father.

Saetan shook his head. "No. I will not indulge in a pissing contest with you to appease your curiosity. Besides, you've seen me naked."

True enough, but he'd only noticed Saetan looked damn fit for a man who'd seen over fifty thousand years. He hadn't paid attention to particulars.

"So Helene said you wouldn't be a distraction," Saetan said, looking more amused. "And you believed her because . . . ?"

"Well, Hell's fire, she's your *housekeeper*."

"She's also a woman in her prime who is, in fact, only a few centuries older than you."

Lucivar stared at Saetan. "She *lied* to me?"

Saetan's gold eyes gleamed with suppressed laughter. "Let me put it this way: Your floors won't be swept, but you'll have the cleanest windows in Ebon Rih—at least on this side of the eyrie."

Lucivar spun around. Female faces were pressed against every window, watching him. Oh, there were cleaning rags pressed against the windows, too, but nothing was being done with them—until the women realized he'd seen them. *Then* there was a lot of vigorous polishing.

Swearing under his breath, he used Craft to vanish the coffee mug and call in a pair of leather trousers. As he pulled them on, he snarled, "It was easier when I could use my fists. If this was Terreille, I would have thrown the lot of them off the mountain."

"You still can."

It surprised him that the words hurt.

"You're the Warlord Prince of Ebon Rih," Saetan said quietly. "You are the law here and answer to no one but your Queen. If you want to use your fists, there's no one who will stop you. No one here who *can* stop you since you wear the Ebon-gray Jewels."

"What happened to that code of honor you live by and insist is followed in the court?" Lucivar snapped, letting temper ride the crest of wounded feelings. "What happened to the lines that are drawn for what a Blood male can and can't do? If I hurt them for no good reason, what does that say to every other man? That he can strike out for the least little thing? *We serve.* We're the defenders and protectors. I've hurt women, and I've killed women. They were the enemy and the court was the battleground. But I will *not* be the kind of man women cower from because they're afraid of being brutalized."

"I know," Saetan said. "You'll decide what is and isn't acceptable in Ebon Rih, and you'll stand as defender and protector. As volatile as your temper is, as physical as your responses are most of the time, I've never worried about you hurting the coven. If you're pushed, you push back. That's not a bad thing. I'm sure there were times in the past three years when something scraped a nerve and reminded you too much of what it was like living in Terreille, but you didn't lash out automatically. You won't now."

The temper faded, but his feelings were still raw. "Then why did you say that?"

Saetan smiled. "Because you needed to hear yourself draw the line. You're the strongest living male in this valley. The strongest Blood, regardless of gender, when Jaenelle isn't at the Keep or staying at her cottage. Having that much power isn't easy."

He would know, Lucivar thought. Saetan wore the Black Jewels. Until Daemon made the Offering to the Darkness and came away wearing the Black, Saetan had been the *only* male in the history of the Blood to wear that Jewel. If anyone knew the price that came with that much power, it was the High Lord.

Lucivar glanced at the eyrie. "What should I do about them?"

"Hire a housekeeper."

He winced. "Hell's fire. Then I'll have a female underfoot all the time."

"From where I'm sitting, your choice is one hearth witch who works for you or dealing with this lot two or three times a week."

Lucivar felt his knees weaken. "Two or three— *Why?* How many times can they polish the same few pieces of furniture?"

Saetan just looked at him pityingly. "If you hire a housekeeper, your home is her domain, and if she's worth what you pay her, she'll be territorial enough to take care of any unwanted help without you having to do a thing."

That didn't sound bad. But he sighed. "I don't know how to hire a housekeeper."

Saetan stood up and arranged the folds of his cape. "Why don't we go to the Keep and discuss it over breakfast?" He looked back at the eyrie. "Or were you planning to stay here and get in the middle of the tussle over who would cook it for you?"

"I can cook my own damn breakfast."

"You could try, boyo, but the odds are against you."

Oh, yeah. If he walked back in there now, *somebody* would be pissed

off at him before he even got close to a piece of toast, let alone something more substantial. "Let's go to the Keep."

"A wise choice."

As they walked back to the eyrie to inform Helene that they were
leaving, Lucivar said, "If I'm so wise and so powerful, tell me again why
I have to hire a housekeeper I don't want?"

"Because you're not a fool," Saetan replied. "And given your choices,
only a fool would put up with this any longer than he had to."

"This is more than I bargained for when Jaenelle appointed me the
Warlord Prince of Ebon Rih."

"Everything has a price. This is yours. Deal with it."

Lucivar sighed and gave up. So he'd have to put up with having one
little hearth witch underfoot. How bad could it be?

TWO

Saetan stepped out of the carriage and walked away from the Hall, wanting a few minutes to savor the sweet night air. It had been a pleasure escorting Sylvia to see her oldest son's debut theater performance. Watching her play the role of "Queen enjoying an amateur production put on by her village's theater group" had been more entertaining than the play. No one would have guessed she was a nervous mother—unless she'd been grabbing that person's hand and squeezing his fingers numb every time Beron came onstage.

He enjoyed spending time with Sylvia. They'd clashed sometimes, but she'd offered support and understanding—and, occasionally, a caustic tongue—while Jaenelle was an adolescent, and they'd become friends in the process. So it gave him pleasure to stand as her escort when she needed the company of a friend who wouldn't expect her to act like Halaway's Queen.

But it also had produced a dull ache inside him to watch Sylvia's face while she watched her son, to see her eyes shine with pride and remember the times when his wife, Hekatah, had sat beside him during an amateur performance, her face set in bored tolerance, or when the seat beside him had been empty because she wouldn't make an appearance at something so common—not even for one of her sons.

When he'd first met her, Hekatah had given a performance to rival any actress on the stage. She'd made him believe she loved him. But she'd never loved the man, just the dark power he wielded. She'd never loved her sons. She'd never loved anything but herself and her ambition.

He locked those thoughts away, as he locked so many away. He didn't want to think about Hekatah and a past that was long gone—and still had the power to hurt.

It was for the best that he and Sylvia could never be more than friends. Being a Guardian, he was one of the few Blood who straddled the line between living and dead in order to extend their lifetimes into years beyond counting. But everything had a price, and the sheer weight of the years he had lived had silenced the craving for sex.

Just as well. He could protect his heart while he and Sylvia were friends. If it had been possible for them to become lovers . . .

Too many years between them. And he was who and what he was.

It was better this way. He would continue to tell himself that. One day, he might even believe it.

Any thoughts of Sylvia fled when he walked into the Hall and found Beale, his butler, waiting for him. That wasn't unusual in itself, except . . . something didn't feel quite right. Something was missing.

He opened his psychic senses, searching, probing. It took a moment because her dark psychic scent permeated the walls of SaDiablo Hall, but he knew what was missing. *Who* was missing.

And yet the anticipation in Beale's gold eyes didn't seem anxious in any way, so Saetan removed his cape and used Craft to vanish it before making the opening statement in this game of verbal chess. "Good evening, Beale."

"High Lord," Beale replied. "You had a pleasant evening?"

"Yes, I did. The play was charming."

"And the dinner?"

Ah. "It was quite good. Not up to Mrs. Beale's standards, of course."

"Of course."

Now that he had given Beale the expected—and only acceptable— response, his butler was ready to move on to what he found a trifle more important—like the whereabouts of his daughter and Queen.

"The Lady went to the Keep about an hour ago," Beale said. "She left a message for you on your desk in the study."

"Thank you."

"If there is nothing else you require, High Lord, I will lock up and retire."

Saetan shook his head. "There's nothing. Good night, Beale."

He walked to the end of the great hall and paused at his study door to watch Beale lock the front doors. Not really a necessary precaution since there were other ways of safeguarding the people and things he treasured. Even with those protection spells, it was simple enough to get into the Hall. Getting out was another matter.

He went inside his study, flicked a thought at the lamp on his desk. The candle-light inside glowed softly. He picked up the half sheet of parchment that had been folded into thirds and sealed with a few drops of black wax, called in his half-moon glasses, opened the note, and read.

Saetan,
Meet me at the Keep at dawn. The High Lord's expertise will be required.
Jaenelle

Vanishing the paper and glasses, he stared at nothing for a moment before extinguishing the lamp and leaving the study. As he crossed the great hall to reach the informal receiving room and climbed the stairs that led to the family wing, a chill spread through him. He knew what kind of expertise Jaenelle might require from the High Lord of Hell. What he didn't know was why.

When he reached her suite of rooms, he knocked on the sitting room door. He didn't expect an answer since she wasn't there, but the knock was a habit—and a precaution, since some of the kindred Warlord Princes who served her were fiercely protective.

As he opened the door, the cold rage filling the room stopped him before he'd taken the first step. He gritted his teeth and moved forward, each step a test of will, until he stood in front of the worktable and stared at the reason Jaenelle had declined Sylvia's invitation to see the play.

The curtains were still open, and the moonlight was enough to make the spider silk look silvery in the dark room.

A tangled web. The kind of web Black Widows used to see dreams and visions. Besides being a Queen, Jaenelle was a natural Black Widow and Healer. That rare combination of gifts made her an extraordinary witch. The Ebony Jewels she now wore—Jewels that indicated power he couldn't begin to estimate—made her the most powerful—and lethal—witch in the history of the Blood.

She hadn't cut any of the threads. Hadn't destroyed the web. She'd left it intact, knowing there was another Black Widow living at the Hall who could look into that web and see the same vision. Him.

Not quite an invitation to look, but the tacit offer to let him see what she had seen was the reason he turned and walked out of the room. It was enough to know whatever she'd seen had produced the cold rage that lingered in the room.

As he retraced his steps through the corridors and down the stairs, he called in his black cape and settled it over his shoulders, hooked the silver chain that held it together in front, and flicked the material so that the front edges folded back to reveal the red lining. He didn't bother unlocking the front doors. He simply used Craft to pass through the wood.

A few moments later, he reached the stone landing web in front of the Hall, caught the Black Wind, and was riding that psychic roadway through the Darkness to Ebon Askavi.

It didn't take him long to reach the Keep, despite the distance between the Hall in Dhemlan and the Keep in Askavi. He dropped from the Winds, appearing on the landing web closest to the residential section within the mountain. Not the area that housed scholars when they came to study the books in the library, but the part of the Keep set aside for the Queen and her court.

He wasn't surprised to see Draca waiting for him by the time he reached the first common room. She was the Keep's Seneschal. Had always been the Keep's Seneschal. And a very, very long time ago, she had been the dragon Queen who, when her own race's time in the world had finally come to an end, had shed her power along with her scales. The females those scales touched had become the first Blood, inheriting an old power in order to become the new guardians of the Realms. She looked human now, and ancient, but the reptilian cast to her features intimidated most people.

Even as he walked toward her, his mind was reaching out, searching, probing. Not finding what he sought honed his temper. But this was the Keep, and this was Draca, so he tightened the leash on his growing rage . . . and fear.

"Draca," he said, bowing slightly when he stood before her.

"Ssaetan," she replied, inclining her head in a mark of respect she rarely gave anyone.

"Jaenelle told me to meet her here. Where is she?"

"Sshe iss expecting you at dawn, High Lord."

"I'm here now. My daughter is not."

"The Queen hass gone to the Keep in Terreille."

Anger flamed, then turned icy. He understood the distinction she made, heard the warning in it, but he still turned away, intending to go to the Dark Altar within the mountain—one of the thirteen Gates that linked the Realms of Terreille, Kaeleer, and Hell.

"High Lord."

He stopped and looked over his shoulder. "No. Terreille is enemy territory. She shouldn't be there, and she certainly shouldn't be there alone."

"The Keep iss protected."

He knew that, but the need to protect—a need that was part of what made a Warlord Prince so deadly—was swelling in him until he couldn't think past it, couldn't feel anything but the drive to defend his Queen.

"Ssaetan."

Centuries of training made him hesitate.

"Sshe doess not expect you until dawn."

He fought a vicious internal battle, instincts warring with training.

"Come," Draca said, her voice gentled with understanding. The door of the common room silently opened, untouched by any hand. "I will have yarbarah brought for you. When you are needed, you will be nearby."

He closed his eyes. Breath by breath, he pulled himself back from the killing edge, that state of mind that stripped Warlord Princes of the veneer of civilized behavior—and was an intrinsic part of their nature. When he was sure he wouldn't respond by striking out with lethal intent, he opened his eyes, and said, "Thank you. Yarbarah would be welcome."

He walked past her and entered the common room, feeling as if he'd stepped into a cage. In a way, he had. But he had made the choice to obey. That was the only thing that made staying in that room tolerable.

Removing the cape, he dropped it over a chair, then walked to the windows that overlooked one of the many gardens. He heard a servant enter and set the blood wine and a glass on a table, but he kept his eyes focused on the garden . . . and the night sky. And waited for the long hours to pass until dawn.

THREE

Listening to the voices just beyond the kitchen, Marian watched batter drip from the wooden spoon back into the mixing bowl, nervous that even the quiet sound of a spoon against a bowl might call attention to herself. It wasn't likely anyone would notice sounds in the kitchen if she continued making breakfast. No one in her family noticed she was around unless there was some hearth-Craft they wanted done. But there was something about the anger and desperation edging her father's wheedling voice and the strained annoyance in her mother's that made her draw her wings in tight to her body in a defensive gesture and want to play least-in-sight.

"Hell's fire, woman," her father said, his voice rising. "It's not so much to ask. I need the errand done, and I need it done now."

"Why can't it wait until after breakfast? One of the girls—"

"No." A pause. "A Priestess-in-training and a Healer-in-training can't take valuable time away from their studies for something simple like this. Besides, Marian isn't doing anything important. She won't be missed."

Marian pressed her lips together as she looked at the biscuits ready for baking. She wouldn't allow her father's words to cut her this morning. She wouldn't. Besides, she'd been hearing that sentiment in one way or another her whole life—more in the past few years since her younger sisters had been accepted into training. A hearth witch was a convenience, but her skills wouldn't enhance the status of a family who wasn't aristo, wouldn't aid her father's ambition to be more than a Fifth Circle guard for a light-Jeweled Queen.

She heard her mother's exasperated "Very well, then" and went back to mixing the batter as Dorian entered the kitchen. Her mother hesitated, then moved briskly to the table where Marian was working.

"You heard," Dorian said.

"Hard not to," Marian replied, keeping her attention on the mixing bowl.

With a huff, Dorian pulled the bowl and spoon out of Marian's hands. "Well, go on then. Take care of this errand that's got him so bothered and get back here as quick as you can."

"To do more things that are unimportant?" Marian asked, surprised to hear the resentment that had been building inside her for a long time actually color the words.

Dorian's face flushed with temper, but she kept her voice low. "Don't you use that tone with me, girl. I won't put up with you getting snippy and acting above yourself."

Marian swallowed the lump in her throat. Yes, this had been building for a while now. It might as well be said. "If I'm going to be treated like hired help instead of family, I should at least get a wage for the labor."

Dorian dropped the spoon on the table. Her hand swung back. Then she regained enough control to press her hand against the table. "You've got a roof over your head and food in your belly. You shouldn't have to be paid to help me provide those things."

"My sisters get those same things—and spending money besides—without doing any of the work."

"Marian—"

"What's the delay?" Her father's voice boomed from the kitchen doorway.

"We'll finish this later," Dorian said.

She disliked confrontation, couldn't hold on to anger. She'd end up doing more work to make up for her show of defiance—and nothing would change.

As she walked through the kitchen doorway, her father raised his hand as if to cuff her, but she hurried past him and stayed ahead of him until they were outside the eyrie. Then he caught up to her and grabbed her arm hard enough to bruise.

She saw temper in his face, but it made her think of a scared bully rather than a dangerous Eyrien Warlord. Still, a scared bully could become dangerous if he needed to convince himself that he was strong.

He started to speak, then held back, clearly deciding to ignore a household squabble since it wouldn't interfere with what *he* wanted.

Using Craft, he called in a thick envelope and handed it to her. "Messenger's waiting for that. Needs it before the day begins at court, so don't be dawdling."

"If it's so important, why don't you deliver it?" Marian said.

His fingers dug into her arm. "Don't sass me, girl. Just do as you're told." His other hand pointed at a small wood in the valley below. "He'll be waiting for you there. You fly down, then take the path through the woods."

"And if I don't find him?"

"He'll find you." He released her arm with enough force that she staggered a couple of steps to keep her balance. "Get on with it."

Vanishing the envelope, she moved farther away from him before she spread her wings and launched herself skyward. She forgot him as she pumped her wings to take her up into the pale dawn sky, dismissed the troubles waiting for her at home as she focused on the joy of soaring over the land. She loved flying—loved the feel of it, the freedom of it. When she was in the air, she could almost believe her dreams were possible. A home of her own, with a garden big enough to grow food, flowers, and the herbs and other plants she could sell to Healers for their special brews. A place of her own, where her hearth-skills wouldn't be dismissed and she wouldn't have to tiptoe around male temper and moods.

It was nothing more than a dream. Her Purple Dusk Jewels didn't give her enough power or status to keep her safe from stronger males if she were on her own. She didn't have the temperament to cope with the cruelty and vicious games that were played in the courts and in aristo houses, so there was no point thinking she could work in one of them. If her mother turned her out, she'd end up working somewhere for room and board and little else. Or, worse, she could end up begging for a place in one of the large eyries that stabled the warriors who served in the Eyrien Queens' courts. She'd seen some of the women who did the cooking and laundry in those eyries—and who were expected to take care of other needs as well. She wouldn't survive long in one of those places. So it always came back to accepting that she would be her mother's unpaid help.

But she still wished for something better.

Blinking back tears—and telling herself it was the wind that created them—she looked up . . . and saw the Black Mountain in the distance.

Ebon Askavi. The Keep. Rumors had been flying recently that there was a Queen there now—a powerful, terrible, Black-Jeweled Queen. But no one had actually seen her. No one could say for certain.

She paused, moving her wings to hover, unable to look away from that mountain. Unable to shake the feeling that something was aware of her, watching her. From that mountain.

Heart pounding, she shook her head to pull her gaze away from the Keep, folded her wings, and did a fast dive toward the woods in the valley. She was an unimportant hearth witch. There was no reason for anyone to look in her direction.

Unless it had something to do with the envelope her father wanted delivered to a messenger without the court he served in being aware of it.

Pulling out of the dive, she glided to the edge of the woods, then backwinged to land lightly on the path. She'd deliver the envelope and go home. Once she was safely back in her mother's kitchen, she'd convince herself that the uneasiness growing in her was her own doing, that there wasn't something in the woods that made her want to turn and run, that she wasn't sensing ripples of dark power far, far, far below the strength of her Purple Dusk Jewel—ripples of power that were rising up from the abyss and coming toward her.

She kept to a fast walk, afraid to run because that would incite a predator's instinct to hunt. And there were predators out there, somewhere. She was certain of it.

She'd almost reached the other end of the small woods when an

Eyrien Warlord stepped out of the trees and spread his wings to block the path. Four other Warlords stepped out of the trees behind her.

"You have a message for me?" the first Warlord asked.

They were all wearing clothes that were old but of good quality. The kind of quality only aristo families could afford. That didn't make her feel easier.

"Well?" he demanded.

Calling in the envelope, she walked toward him until she was close enough to hand him the envelope by extending her arm its full length.

He snatched it from her, tore it open, read the first page quickly, then tossed all of it aside. When he looked at her, his smile was amused and cruel.

"The message wasn't meant for you?" Marian said, backing away from him.

"Oh, it was for me. You're the payment, witchling."

"I— I don't understand."

"You don't have to."

She felt the other men moving closer, surrounding her. "If you hurt me, my father—"

The Warlord laughed, a vicious sound. "He sent you here, didn't he? He knew well enough what's going to happen. But nobody is going to miss the likes of you."

She leaped skyward. There wasn't much room to maneuver under the trees, but she was only a few wingstrokes away from open land—and open sky. If she could get past the Warlords, she might be able to stay ahead of them long enough to catch one of the Winds and . . . head where?

The Black Mountain. If she could reach the Keep, she could beg for sanctuary, and the Warlords couldn't hurt her.

She'd almost reached the open land when she heard the crack of a whip, felt the leather cut her skin as it wrapped around her ankle. They hauled her back under the cover of the trees—and they were on her, flying around her, letting her flail and struggle and try to fly while their knives and war blades sliced her. Blood flowed from dozens of shallow cuts. When they sliced her wings, she managed a rough landing, but there was nowhere to run, no way to escape.

Ripples of dark power coming closer. Closer.

"Help me!" she screamed. "Please! Help me!"

Laughing, the Warlords grabbed her arms and legs and flipped her over on her back, holding her down. The fifth man dropped to his knees between her legs and ripped her torn, bloody clothes to expose her.

"Hurry up," another Warlord said, "or the bitch will bleed out before we all have a chance to use her."

"She'll last long enough," the Warlord kneeling between her legs replied as he opened his trousers.

No, Marian thought. *No.*

"You want to play with a witch?" a midnight voice said quietly. "Then play with me."

The last thing Marian saw before her vision blurred was the fear on the face of the Warlord in front of her. Then a wave of freezing black rage washed over her, pulling her under. She thought she heard muted screams of agony and terror, then the sounds were gone. Everything was gone . . .

. . . until she felt a hand close over hers, felt power that wasn't hers flowing into her. She forced her eyes open and stared at the golden-haired, sapphire-eyed woman kneeling beside her. Stared at the Black Jewel that hung from a chain around the woman's neck.

"You're the Queen," Marian said, barely able to draw enough breath to shape the words.

"Yes, I'm the Queen," the woman replied.

"I don't want to die."

"Then don't." The woman placed her other hand on Marian's forehead.

The dark power closed in around her again, but it was warm now, gentle, a cocoon of soft blankets. Power not her own kept her heart beating, kept her lungs moving.

Her last thought before she surrendered to it was, *I've seen the Queen of Ebon Askavi.*

As soon as Saetan stepped through the Gate, he knew Jaenelle wasn't in the Keep in Terreille. A moment later, when her psychic scent flooded the corridors, he knew she'd returned—and the control on his temper frayed a bit more.

That she was his Queen didn't matter. That her power eclipsed his didn't matter. By the time he was done explaining things, his Lady would be in no doubt about how her Steward felt about her entering Terreille, which was the enemy's territory, without even one escort going with her.

Then he stepped out of the room that held the Dark Altar and saw her moving toward him, one hand under the blankets wrapped around . . .

He smelled the blood, noted the dangerous, feral look in Jaenelle's eyes, and felt the heat of his temper chill to cold rage as he rose to the killing edge.

Jaenelle stopped in front of him. She said nothing while he carefully pulled aside a part of the blankets and looked at the young Eyrien woman, while he studied the torn clothing and the slices in her skin that still seeped blood despite the healing web he sensed Jaenelle weaving around her.

"Why?" he asked.

Jaenelle turned her head. "Ask them."

Five bodies appeared in the hallway. Saetan used Craft to probe the bodies. He felt equally chilled by and approving of what Jaenelle had done. From neck to toes, the bones of the Eyrien males had been crushed into small pebbles, making the bodies look like oddly shaped sacks. The muscles and internal organs had been ripped apart, as if claws had slipped beneath the skin, leaving it untouched while they tore through everything else in long, leisurely strokes. Which, he imagined, is exactly what she'd done. And for the few seconds it took her to do it, the pain would have been exquisite . . .

He looked at the Eyrien woman.

. . . but not enough to pay the debt.

"This is what you saw in the tangled web last night?" he asked too softly.

"I saw emptiness where something bright and joyful should have been. I saw happiness wither like a plant that couldn't find the right soil to take root in. And I saw the terrace where I was standing at dawn, but it was empty—a warning that my presence, or absence, would make the difference in what would come."

"I see." He looked at the bodies again. "Now I understand what kind of expertise you need from me."

Jaenelle nodded. "Find out why this happened, High Lord . . . and settle the debt."

"It will be a pleasure, Lady."

He stepped back, watched her hurry into the room that held the Dark Altar and the Gate that would take her and the woman to Kaeleer.

He waited a few minutes, studying the bodies that flopped in unnatural positions. Then he raised his right hand. His Black-Jeweled ring flashed with the reservoir of power it held. The bodies rose from the floor and floated toward him. Turning, he walked back to the Dark Altar, lit the four black candles in the candelabra in the proper sequence, and walked through the misty Gate, the bodies floating behind him.

When he walked out of the Gate, he felt the difference between this Realm and the two Realms that belonged to the living. Hell was the land of the demon-dead Blood who still had too much power even after the body's death to return to the Darkness. A cold, ever-twilight Realm. He'd begun ruling here while he still walked among the living. He'd been ruling the Dark Realm ever since.

Turning to look at the bodies floating behind him, he smiled a cold, cruel smile. He accepted that executions were sometimes necessary, and he performed them with exacting skill when duty required it of him. He'd never developed a taste for them, but he suspected finishing what Jaenelle had begun was truly going to be a pleasure.

Walking through the corridors of the Keep, he went to the closest landing web, caught the Black Wind, and took the five bodies with him to the Hall he'd built in this Realm. There, he would have everything he needed to make sure the debt owed to the Eyrien woman was paid in full.

The sun had set by the time Saetan returned to the Keep in Kaeleer and entered Jaenelle's suite of rooms. She was on the couch in her sitting room, reading one of those romances that was as close as she was willing to get when it came to experiencing intimacy with a man. With Lucivar as her First Escort, she didn't need a man just to fill the position of Consort, and when Daemon finally . . .

He wouldn't allow himself to travel down that road. He would defend Jaenelle's choice not to have a Consort—and he would hope that, with the right man, someday her interest in sex would go beyond the pages of a book.

Jaenelle closed the book and looked at him with sapphire eyes that still held a touch of feral rage. His daughter hadn't come back yet. Not completely. He was still dealing with Witch—and his Queen—and he needed to tread carefully.

"How is the woman?" he asked quietly.

"Marian will be all right," Jaenelle replied just as quietly.

Marian. Saetan tightened the chain on his temper. The bastards hadn't known her name, hadn't cared who she was. Finishing the kill shouldn't have taken more than a few minutes for each of them. It was *why* they'd done it that had spurred him to prolong their suffering with a viciousness that wasn't a side of himself that usually surfaced. But they had deserved everything he'd done after he helped them make the transition to demon-dead— and then proceeded to rip their minds apart before he drained what was left of their psychic power, finishing the kill so they could become a whisper in the Darkness.

"She lost a lot of blood," Jaenelle continued, "but all the wounds were shallow. Her wings were sliced in several places, but they were easily repaired. A couple of days of bed rest and good food will rebuild her strength. There won't be any permanent damage to her body."

Yes, Jaenelle would make the distinction between body and heart. Her body had healed from the brutal rape that had almost destroyed her when she was twelve years old, but she carried the emotional scars . . . and always would.

"Have you eaten?" Saetan asked, noticing the decanter of yarbarah on the table in front of the couch.

When she gave him a wary smile, he knew his daughter was back.

"I was waiting for you." Shifting her legs, Jaenelle poured a glass of yarbarah, warmed it over a tongue of witchfire, and offered it to him.

Accepting the glass, he sat on the couch, and tipped his head to read the title of the book between them. "Are you going to loan that to me when you're done?"

"Why?"

Oh, yes. His daughter was back. "A father should be aware of his children's interests."

"Then why don't you ask Lucivar what he's reading?"

"Because Lucivar rarely picks up a book, let alone reads any of it. If he showed an interest in one, any comment from me would more than likely embarrass him into putting it down and not picking up another for at least a decade."

"You could point out some of the stories have sex in them," Jaenelle said.

A topic his son found even less interesting than his daughter did.

A quiet chime sounded. Moments later the small table on one side of the sitting room held a basket of fresh bread, a small bowl of whipped butter, and two steaming bowls of soup.

Grateful for the interruption, Saetan offered his hand and led Jaenelle to the table. As a Guardian, he really didn't need more than yarbarah and a token amount of fresh blood once in a while, but he could eat and enjoy food again, thanks to the tonics Jaenelle made for him, and she'd eat more if someone joined her than she would alone.

She settled into her meal with a healthy appetite that relieved him— and enforced the decision not to tell her why Marian had been attacked by those five Eyrien males unless she specifically asked him.

They'd finished the soup and were halfway through the prime rib that followed before Jaenelle spoke again.

"I was thinking," she said with enough hesitation to make him watch her sharply. "If Marian doesn't want to return to Askavi in Terreille, she'll need a place to stay. So I was thinking she could stay with Luthvian for a while. Help out a little with small hearth-Craft things while she regains her strength."

"Why Luthvian?" Saetan asked, keeping his voice painfully neutral.

"She's the only Eyrien female in Ebon Rih. She could help Marian adjust to living here. And she's a Healer, so she could keep an eye on how well Marian is recovering."

He focused his attention on his meal, biting back all the comments that were ready to spill out if he wasn't careful. His relationship with Luthvian, who was Lucivar's mother, was too tangled and adversarial, and any response he made would reflect that. But he understood why Jaenelle would think staying with another woman would be easier for Marian right now, and she could be right. So he offered no opinion.

"If it doesn't work, I'll find another place for her," Jaenelle said.

"Then it's settled." He didn't feel easy about it, but he let it go. For now. "In that case, witch-child, tell me about this book you're reading."

She evaded, he pursued, and they ended the evening with a delightful hour of haggling over the value of various kinds of stories that helped them both step back from the blood and the fury that had started the day.

FOUR

As twilight softly deepened into night, Marian stood behind Luthvian's house, relishing a quiet moment with nothing to do. Her back was sore, and it worried her because Lady Angelline had been very insistent that she take things easy for a fortnight and not overwork muscles that still needed time to fully heal. But every time she mentioned feeling strain in her back or legs, Luthvian dismissed the concern and implied—when she didn't say it outright—that Marian was just trying to get out of earning her keep. The criticism stung. Since arriving at Luthvian's, she'd done nothing but wash, scrub, polish, and mend. And everything she did was adequate but not good enough that she should even dream of looking for a position in another household. Luthvian was letting her stay as a favor to Jaenelle.

It didn't matter, she told herself, feeling despair rise up before she choked it down again. She was alive, and she was living in Kaeleer, the Shadow Realm most people had thought nothing more than a myth until a few years ago. She didn't have to go back to Terreille, didn't have to trust her life to the whims of male temper.

Not as much, anyway.

Luthvian had also made it very clear that anything that displeased her would also displease her son, the Warlord Prince who ruled Ebon Rih.

Marian understood the threat. What had been done to her in Terreille would be a slap on the wrist compared to what an enraged Warlord Prince who wore Ebon-gray Jewels could do to her.

She carefully spread her wings as far as she could until she felt her back muscles pull. Gritting her teeth, she counted to five, then slowly closed her wings and waited a few seconds before beginning the exercise again.

She would find other work—*paying* work—and she would work hard and save and one day have that place of her own. And she would soar again, riding thermals over land that was more beautiful than anything she'd ever seen back home. She would—

"Did you hem that dress?" Luthvian's voice stabbed out of the dark.

Marian winced, wondering how long the Black Widow Healer had been watching her. Reminding herself that she had nowhere else to go—yet—she turned. "As I explained, Lady Luthvian, I can't hem the dress until you have the time for a fitting so that I can make sure the length is correct."

"I told you how much to take it up."

Her younger sisters had said the same thing to her in the same sneering voice—and complained bitterly to their mother when the hem fell too long or too short because they insisted she should be able to hem something without wasting *their* time.

"Nevertheless," Marian said, fighting to keep her voice respectful, "I would feel more confident about the length if I pin the dress while you're wearing it."

The silence that followed made Marian uneasy. A Black Widow was too dangerous a witch to antagonize, and Luthvian could do far more than hurt her body.

"They don't work. You know that, don't you?" Luthvian said.

"I don't understand." A ball of fear settled in her belly.

"The wings. They were damaged too severely. You'll never fly again."

The fear sharpened into pain. "No. Lady Angelline said—"

"Jaenelle is a decent Healer, but she has little knowledge or experience when it comes to Eyriens. I have both. And I'm telling you those are only for display now. You'll never fly again. If you try, you'll only end up damaging your back so badly you won't be able to work enough to earn your keep, and *then* where will you be?" Luthvian's voice softened. "You'd be better off having them removed. If they're gone, you won't be tempted to do something that would cripple you."

No, Marian thought as tears filled her eyes. *No!*

"I can do it for you." Luthvian's voice was quiet and persuasive. "In a month, you won't remember what it felt like to have them."

"No!"

Luthvian's voice turned cold. "Please yourself. But if you do something that makes you useless, don't expect to remain *here.*"

She didn't hear Luthvian walk away, but she heard the kitchen door close. She stayed outside for a long time, hunched over to try to ease the pain that twisted her up inside.

She'd hoped being in Kaeleer meant a promise at a new life, a better life. But nothing had changed for the better. If anything, the life ahead of her was worse than the one she'd left behind.

FIVE

Lucivar glided toward the courtyard in front of his eyrie, glad to be home. He'd spent the past week visiting the villages in Ebon Rih, meeting with the Queens who ruled the Rihlander Blood villages of Doun and Agio, and talking to the council members who ran the larger landen villages. The non-Blood Rihlanders were afraid of him—with good reason. The Blood might be a minority among any race, but the power that lived within them made them the rulers and guardians of the Realms. For the most part, the Blood ignored the landens and the landens kept away from the Blood. Reminding village council members that they were now answerable to an Ebon-gray Warlord Prince wasn't going to make them sleep easy for a while.

Hell's fire. It didn't make *him* sleep easy. He'd spent most of his life ignoring or defying anyone's claim of authority over him. Now he *was* the authority who was going to draw the line and stand against anyone in his territory who dared step over it.

He wasn't sure he liked being on that side of the line, but he'd adjust to the formality directed at him from the Queens' courts in Doun and Agio. At least in Riada, which was the closest village to Ebon Askavi and was also his "home" village, the informal respect the villagers had shown him since he'd arrived in Kaeleer hadn't changed. Not much, anyway. There was a proprietary interest in him now. What he did affected all of them.

Which made him wonder why Merry had looked so uneasy when he'd stopped by The Tavern to see what she was serving that night that he could take home with him.

"A dinner for two, Prince Yaslana?" Merry had asked.

"Or one hungry man," he'd replied, grinning.

Why hadn't she smiled back when she'd prepared the basket of food for him?

As he landed lightly on the flagstone courtyard, he sent a thought out on a psychic spear thread. ★Tassle?★

★Yas.★

The wolf sounded sulky, almost edgy.

★What's wrong?★

A pause. Then, ★I don't like that female. I don't want to be friends.★

Lucivar felt his temper unsheath as he studied the front door of his home. An Ebon-gray shield formed a finger-length above his skin, an instinctive response to walking into a situation where it was safer to guard against a potential attack. The fact that he was reacting that way before entering his home honed his temper until the slightest push would have him riding the killing edge.

He pushed the door open and stepped inside. The female psychic scent hit him the moment he crossed the threshold. He knew that scent. Loathed the young witch it belonged to.

Roxie.

She'd been one of Luthvian's students when he'd first come to Kaeleer—a Rihlander witch from Doun whose family was aristo enough that she thought she could do anything she pleased. She used lovers the way other women used handkerchiefs. She soiled them, then tossed them aside. But from the first day she'd met him, her goal had been to corner him and force him into bedding her. The bitch had never understood that if she *had* managed to corner him, bedding her would have been the last thing on his mind.

And now she was here. In his home.

He moved silently until he reached his bedroom door. The wide corridor reeked of her.

As he pushed the door open and walked into the bedroom, Roxie raised her bare arms over her head and smiled at him, her body clearly defined under the sheet that covered her.

He usually had a hot, explosive temper. As he approached the bed, he felt chillingly calm.

"Get out of my bed," he said softly.

She shifted a little, the movement uncovering more of her breasts. "Why don't you join me? You want to. You know you do."

The revulsion that washed through him almost sheared his self-control.

A triumphant look filled her face when he stepped up to the bed. A moment later, the look changed to terror.

He hadn't consciously made the decision to call in his Eyrien war blade. But the edge of that blade, honed so sharp it could make air bleed, suddenly hovered just above Roxie's neck. If he relaxed his hand, the blade would slide through skin and muscle until it gently came to rest against bone. He wouldn't have to do anything, wouldn't have to exert any force. Just relax his hand.

"If I ever find you in my bed again, I'll slit your throat," he said, his voice still calm and soft.

Roxie swallowed. The movement was enough to push her skin against the blade.

Lucivar watched the blood trickle from the shallow wound, becoming seduced by the heat of it, the smell of it. He stepped back before the temptation to let the war blade sing became too great. As he stepped back, the cold inside him broke and hot temper flared.

Vanishing the war blade, he scooped up her clothes in one hand, hauled her out of bed with the other, and dragged her through the eyrie, ignoring her squeals and protests. He flung her and her clothes out the door and slammed it shut, not knowing or caring if she got hurt when she landed.

Then he stood with his teeth clenched and his hands curled into fists, fighting the urge to open that door and purge the memories of all the witches he'd known in Terreille who were just like her. He wanted to pound those memories into her flesh, exorcising them from his own.

Minutes passed, but the feelings didn't. He still rode the killing edge.

Violence still sang in his blood. He had to purge that violence—or have it purged out of him. There was only one person who could do that for him.

Roxie was gone when he left the eyrie. That spared him the inconvenience of killing her and taking the bitch's mangled body back to her family. He *would* have killed her if she'd still been there. He couldn't have stopped himself. A Warlord Prince was a born predator, a natural killer, and the "training" he'd received under the hands of the witches in Terreille had honed that killing instinct instead of providing a sheath for it. Right now, he was a danger to everyone.

With one exception.

He opened his psychic senses, searching until he brushed against the dark power that eclipsed his own.

Launching himself skyward, he flew to the cottage beyond the outskirts of Riada. He landed close enough to the porch that two steps and a leap had him standing in front of the door of the neat little cottage Saetan had built for Jaenelle as a place where she could spend solitary time when she needed it. Not that she was ever really alone. There was always a kindred male with her, but a wolf or dog was content to nap for hours while she got lost in a book or would walk with her for miles without wanting conversation.

He hesitated a moment, then opened the door and entered the cottage's main room. Jaenelle stood near the hearth as if she'd been expecting him. She probably had. She would have felt that flash of temper, would have sensed him coming toward her.

He stood close to the door, wanting to go to her, *needing* to go to her. He couldn't do that. Not yet. Not until he'd smoothed some of the jagged edges off his temper.

"Lucivar," Jaenelle said quietly.

He stared at her, focused on her sapphire eyes.

She walked up to him and placed one hand against his cheek. "Lucivar."

He closed his eyes and breathed in the physical scent of her and the dark psychic scent that was both a balm and an enticement. He didn't want her sexually—had never wanted her that way—but the hugs and sisterly kisses kept him balanced in a way nothing else had ever done.

Hold the leash, he silently pleaded. *Choke me into obedience if that's what it takes.*

She just stood there, her hand against his cheek, until those jagged edges of temper receded—and made him aware of something that brought a different edge to his temper.

"Where's your escort?" he demanded.

"It's been a warm afternoon," Jaenelle replied. "Jaal is sprawled in the stream out back."

Lucivar snarled. "He didn't even rouse himself to find out who had entered the cottage."

Jaenelle lifted both eyebrows to express surprise. "You wanted to be pounced on by a wet tiger?"

Being near her had restored enough of his balance that he took a moment to consider that. "No."

"Didn't think so. That's why I told him to stay where he was." She stepped back and turned toward the archway that led to the kitchen. "I have a small keg of ale."

"I have half a steak pie, cheese, and a fresh loaf of bread."

Jaenelle grinned at him. "In that case, you can stay for dinner."

He waited until they'd eaten and were sitting on the porch, watching twilight smudge the land into soft shapes.

"I need help, Cat," he said quietly, using his nickname for her to indicate he needed help from his sister, not his Queen.

"Still being overrun by helpful ladies?" Jaenelle asked.

"No. Well, yes, but . . ." He took a deep breath, knowing he was about to walk the crumbling edge of a sheer cliff. "I found Roxie in my bed when I got home today."

"Roxie," Jaenelle said in that midnight voice that chilled her court.

Roxie didn't like Jaenelle, and Jaenelle didn't like Roxie. The difference was Roxie didn't have enough power to do anything with that feeling. Jaenelle disliking someone was out and out dangerous.

Lucivar rubbed his hands over his face and sighed. "I need a housekeeper. I need a dragon who will—"

Jaenelle cocked her head and looked at him.

"No." His nerves jumped, making him feel like he had tiny bugs skittering all over his skin. "Not a real dragon." Not that he didn't like the dragons who lived in the Fyreborn Islands. He did. He enjoyed wave whomping with them whenever he and Jaenelle visited the islands. But the last thing he needed was a dragon the size of a pony—not including the tail—waiting by the door to flame anyone who crossed the threshold.

"It would solve the problem of uninvited guests," Jaenelle pointed out.

"No."

She got that half-puzzled look on her face that always made him think of a kitten puzzling over a large, hoppy bug. "I wonder if any of the kindred have witches with a gift for hearth-Craft. What would they use it for?"

"It doesn't matter." His voice sounded firm, didn't it? Hell's fire, he *hoped* it sounded firm. "I need a human with enough housekeeping skills that Helene and Merry will be satisfied that the eyrie is being tended and whose presence will keep any other females from thinking that—" He bit back the words. Best not to mention Roxie again.

Jaenelle hesitated. "There is a hearth witch who has come to Kaeleer recently."

"Through the service fairs?" Lucivar asked, wondering about Jaenelle's hesitation. The twice-yearly service fairs in Little Terreille had been set up to deal with the flood of Terreilleans fleeing the cruelty of the courts and Territories under the influence of Dorothea SaDiablo, the High Priestess of Hayll.

"No," Jaenelle replied. "I brought her in."

What in the name of Hell were you doing in Terreille? He knew better than to ask *her* that question. He'd just visit the Hall in the next day or two and ask his father.

"She may be . . . content . . . where she is," Jaenelle said, "but I can ask if she'd consider being your housekeeper."

"All right."

Jaenelle nodded. "I can—" Her mood turned grumpy, and she rolled her eyes. "No, I can't. I have to do Queenly things tomorrow, and there's a formal . . . something . . . late in the evening."

Lucivar grinned. "Something that requires getting all polished and dressed up?" Jaenelle hated fancy dress.

"Yes," she growled, "it's dress-up. But there will be time to come back here after your usual dinner hour."

"That won't give you much time to get ready."

The look she gave him could have frozen blood.

"I could still see if there are hearth witches among the dragons," Jaenelle said.

Feeling more relaxed than he'd felt all week, Lucivar stood, stretched, then bent over to give Jaenelle a kiss on the top of her head. "Don't threaten your older brother," he scolded mildly. "Especially after I took the brunt of Father's snarling over the raft."

Wincing, she looked up at him. "Was it bad? He just kept gritting his teeth when he saw me and refused to talk about it."

Lucivar straightened up and leaned against one of the porch's supporting posts. "No, it wasn't bad. He was actually quite calm about our making a raft out of what he called 'twigs and kindling'—"

"Which is what it was," Jaenelle said.

"—and holding the whole thing together with nothing but Craft."

"Which is what we did."

"And he *said* he understood why we felt we needed to be standing on the thing when we put it in the river to test it."

"How else were we supposed to find out if it worked?"

"He even managed to sound calm about our not abandoning the raft after we hit the rapids. And he didn't yell about our going over the waterfall." Lucivar scratched his neck. "Although, I still haven't figured out how he could speak so clearly with his teeth clenched like that."

Jaenelle leaned forward. "You didn't tell him the raft started breaking up before we went over the waterfall, did you?"

"Do I look like a fool?" Lucivar demanded. "Of course I didn't tell him that. Besides, what threatened to pop a few blood vessels was his finding out that we went back to the starting point and did the whole thing all over again."

"Oh, dear," Jaenelle said. "I'm surprised the walls of the Hall didn't shake when he started yelling."

"He didn't have a chance to yell." Lucivar smiled that lazy, arrogant smile that always signaled trouble. "Before he got started, I ended it."

"How?"

"I told him he was jealous."

Jaenelle's mouth fell open. "*Lucivar!* You told Papa—"

"That the only reason he was mad at me was because you'd invited me to go with you to try out this idea instead of inviting him."

Her silvery, velvet-coated laugh rang out over the land. "Oh," she gasped. "Oh, that was mean. What did he say?"

Lucivar laughed with her. "He just gave me that stare that will burn holes through bone, then threw me out of his study. He hasn't said a thing about it since then."

"Poor Papa." Jaenelle sighed. "I guess I'll dress up special tomorrow to make it up to him."

"You do that, since my wearing a dress won't do anything for him."

She looked at him and howled with laughter—which brought an answering roar from behind the cottage.

Great. Any moment now, he'd be trying to explain to a baffled feline Warlord Prince why their Queen was making those funny noises.

"I'll see you tomorrow." He leaped off the porch, spread his wings, and launched himself skyward.

"L-Lucivar!"

Nope. Fair was fair. He'd dealt with Saetan on his own over the raft, so she could explain her behavior to the "kitty."

He didn't let Roxie's lingering scent spoil his mood when he returned home. Besides, by tomorrow evening, all his female problems might be solved.

SIX

As she set the brass basket next to the woodpile, Marian felt her back muscles protest and threaten to seize up. Again. Studying the woodpile, she raised one hand and used Craft to lift the pieces of wood and set them in the basket.

Luthvian would criticize and sneer, saying—again—that it was laziness to use Craft for simple things, but Marian didn't care. Using Craft instead of straining muscles wasn't laziness, it was practical—especially since her back had seized up once today while she was scrubbing the kitchen floor.

Odd how gentle Luthvian had been when she'd come into the kitchen and found Marian on the floor, unable to get up. At that moment, she had been all Healer, skilled and efficient. But the quiet words she'd said as she eased the pain were the same ones she'd been saying— the useless wings were causing the back pain. Removing them was the only way Marian would fully heal.

Since she wouldn't let Luthvian remove her wings, she couldn't say anything about the chores that made her back hurt. She *knew* the wounds had been healed, but when she ached, she could close her eyes and mentally trace every knife slash the Warlords had inflicted.

Gritting her teeth, Marian reached for the handle of the brass basket.

The basket vanished before she touched it. It reappeared a moment later, waist high and just out of reach. Then it fell to the ground with a heavy *thunk*.

"Perhaps I wasn't clear enough when I told you to take it easy for a few days." The voice didn't quite hide the ripple of anger beneath the mildly spoken words.

Marian turned. Jaenelle stood a few feet away from her.

"Lady Angelline." Marian swallowed hard, unable to look away from those sapphire eyes. She felt as if fingertips were passing over her body, just above her skin.

"You haven't done any permanent damage," Jaenelle said, "but—"

"Marian!" Luthvian's voice lashed out through the open kitchen windows. "Are you going to dawdle all night over a few pieces of wood? You have chores to finish."

Something deadly flashed in Jaenelle's eyes, gone so fast Marian wasn't sure she'd actually seen it.

"Pack your things," Jaenelle said quietly. "You're leaving."

"But—"

"Now."

She wasn't going to argue with *that* voice. Moving as fast as her stiff legs could manage, she reached the cottage's far corner just as Luthvian stepped out of the kitchen door.

"Hell's fire, girl," Luthvian snapped. "Where's the wood? Can't you do anything—" She froze for a moment. "Good evening, Jaenelle."

"Good evening, Luthvian." Jaenelle moved forward until she stood next to Marian. "Marian is leaving. Her skills are required elsewhere."

Luthvian looked as if she'd been slapped, but she recovered quickly. "We need to discuss this."

"Fine," Jaenelle replied. "We'll discuss it while Marian packs her things."

The air crackled with suppressed temper. Marian stepped back and swung around both women, too nervous to step between them. As she entered the kitchen, she heard Luthvian say, "She's adequate, but anyone who pays wages for her work will be disappointed."

She didn't wait to hear Jaenelle's reply. She simply hurried up to the small, second-floor room Luthvian had given her. There wasn't much to pack. When Jaenelle had brought her to Luthvian's cottage, she had only the trousers, tunic, and underthings she'd been given at the Keep since her own clothes had been destroyed in the attack. Luthvian had given her a skirt and two tunics the Healer no longer wanted and had grudgingly purchased two sets of underthings for her. Her only other possessions were the things that, through Craft, she always carried with her—her moontime supplies, the hairbrush and hair ornaments her sisters hadn't permanently "borrowed," the book she'd asked for last Winsol and had actually gotten as a gift from her mother, and the small loom and cloth bag of yarns.

She vanished the clothes, since she had no other way to carry them, and had just walked out of the room when thunder shook the cottage. Her heart pounded as she rested a hand against the wall to steady herself. There had been no sign of a storm when she was outside a few minutes ago. Where had the—

A different kind of thunder.

A chill went through her. Her heart pounded harder.

The kind of thunder that happened when a witch revealed enough of her temper to be a warning to those around her.

Biting her lip, Marian gave herself a few seconds to gather her courage before going downstairs to the kitchen. Luthvian sat at the kitchen table, her gold eyes full of resentment and fear. Jaenelle stood in the doorway, not actually in the kitchen but also not waiting outside.

Marian hesitated. She should say something to Luthvian, but she didn't know what it would be. She couldn't thank Luthvian for the hospitality since she'd more than earned her keep while she'd stayed at the cottage—and hadn't felt welcome in the first place. And she was afraid that no matter what she said right now, Luthvian's response would be brutal and heart-shattering. So she looked away and walked to the outside kitchen door.

Jaenelle stepped back and to one side to let her pass. The door closed behind them with a gentleness that was worse than a bad-tempered slam.

"Can you walk a bit?" Jaenelle asked when they reached the gate in the low stone wall that surrounded Luthvian's land.

Marian nodded.

They walked in silence for several minutes. Then Jaenelle said, "I'm sorry things were difficult for you. I thought—" She shook her head. "It doesn't matter what I thought. It was an error in judgment, and you paid the price for it."

There were things Luthvian had hinted at, reasons why enduring work she knew was harming her was better than being told to leave. But now that she'd been *taken* from the cottage . . .

"I don't want to go back to Terreille," Marian said, the words bursting out of her.

"No one said you had to," Jaenelle replied.

"But if I don't serve Lady Luthvian—"

Jaenelle swore. Marian didn't know the language, but she understand the vicious way the words were said.

"You don't serve Luthvian," Jaenelle said tightly. "You serve in *my* court."

Marian stopped walking, too stunned to keep moving. "I— *Your* court?"

Jaenelle turned to face Marian. After studying the hearth witch, she said, "Eighth Circle. Don't you remember signing the contract after I explained that you needed to serve in a court for eighteen months if you wanted to stay in Kaeleer?"

She remembered Jaenelle handing her a piece of parchment and explaining *something* about her needing to sign the document in order to stay in Kaeleer, but she'd still been feeling too weak and woozy to take in anything except that signing would let her stay. And when Luthvian had implied that staying or being sent back to Terreille rested on *her* decision . . .

"What do I have to do?" Marian asked.

Jaenelle shrugged. "Service in the Eighth Circle? A meal once in a while when I'm staying at my cottage in Ebon Rih would cover the requirements."

A meal. Would Jaenelle supply the food for her to cook, or would she be expected to provide it? *How* would she provide it? "Where are we going?"

Now Jaenelle smiled. "Your skills really *are* required elsewhere. I know someone who needs a housekeeper."

Marian relaxed a little. If wages were included as well as room and board, she could fulfill her obligation to the Lady's court.

Jaenelle looked up at the sky and winced. "Come on. We'd better ride the Winds and get there. If I'm late getting back to the Hall, Papa will give me that patient look. I really hate that patient look—especially when I deserve it."

Before Marian could wrap her mind around the idea that the Queen of Ebon Askavi had a papa who would dare criticize her, even if it was just with a look, Jaenelle took her hand and launched both of them onto the Purple Dusk Wind.

A few minutes later, they dropped from the Winds and landed on a flagstone courtyard in front of an eyrie. Marian winced when she saw the rock-strewn, overgrown mess on one side of the eyrie, but she didn't have time to decide if it had once been a garden or had always been a wild, overgrown tangle before Jaenelle opened the door without knocking and pulled her inside.

"Lucivar!" Jaenelle called.

A sharp whistle came from another room in the eyrie.

Lucivar? Fear rushed back into Marian as Jaenelle pulled her toward the archway on one side of the big empty room.

"I thought you—" a male voice said.

One last tug and Marian was in the kitchen facing an Eyrien male. A Warlord Prince. Who wore Ebon-gray Jewels.

The room spun. Her knees weakened. *Hell's fire, Mother Night, and may the Darkness be merciful. Not him.* Please, *not him.*

"Marian," Jaenelle said, "this is Lucivar Yaslana, the Warlord Prince of Ebon Rih. Lucivar, this is Marian—your new housekeeper."

No. No no *no*. She'd heard of Lucivar Yaslana. Who in Askavi *hadn't* heard of Lucivar Yaslana, even though it had been centuries since he'd actually lived in Askavi. *He* was Luthvian's son? The ruler of Ebon Rih? She couldn't possibly stay here. She *couldn't*. When Luthvian complained to him about her leaving . . . He could do anything he wanted to her and no one would mutter a word. Warlord Princes were a law unto themselves. Even in Terreille the ones who weren't kept on a tight chain were treated cautiously, and everyone knew the rules that applied to every other male didn't apply to them. *Couldn't* apply to them.

"Lady Marian," he said.

Had she already done something wrong? Was he already angry with her? She couldn't stay here.

Jaenelle huffed. "I'm sorry. I really have to go." Her hand brushed Marian's shoulder. "I'll be back in a day or two to see how you're doing."

Then she was gone, and Marian was left facing a man who, even doing nothing, was a hundred times more dangerous than the five Warlords who had tried to kill her.

"Why don't you sit down?" Lucivar said, tipping his head to indicate the nearest of four chairs that were on either side of a large pine table.

Not knowing what else do to, Marian pulled out the chair and sat down.

"Would you like some coffee?" he asked.

She nodded, but kept her eyes focused on the table. She flinched when he set a white mug in front of her, but he stepped back, putting enough distance between them that she could breathe again.

"Did my sister explain anything on the way here?"

Startled, Marian looked up. "Sister?" Luthvian hadn't mentioned a daughter.

"Jaenelle," Lucivar said. "She's my sister."

That should have been comforting. It wasn't. But there was one thing she had to know. "Does anyone else live here?"

"Tassle lives with me. He's—"

She heard the click of nails on stone a few seconds before a wolf appeared in the archway. Yaslana kept a wild animal for a *pet*?

The wolf came forward slowly, the tip of his tail waving as he sniffed her hand. She didn't move, didn't dare even twitch when he stepped closer to sniff her feet and legs, his tail waving with more enthusiasm. But she jumped when he suddenly pushed his muzzle between her legs. That's when Yaslana stepped forward, grabbed the wolf by the scruff of the neck, and pulled him away.

"Go outside, Tassle," Lucivar said, his voice, although quiet, demanding instant obedience.

With a whuffle-whine, the wolf left the kitchen.

Lucivar stepped away. The move brought him to the archway rather than moving back into the kitchen. "Relax for a few minutes and finish your coffee. Then I'll show you to your room." He left, not waiting for her answer.

Just as well. She wasn't sure she *could* have answered. Her hands trembled as she lifted the mug and took a large swallow of—

She shuddered. He'd said this was coffee. She wasn't sure what it was, but she was *certain* it wasn't coffee. At least, she hoped it wasn't. Setting the mug down, she braced her head in her hands. She was alone with an Ebon-gray Warlord Prince and a wolf. Sweet Darkness, what was she supposed to do?

Lucivar wound his way through the rocks, needing to put some distance between himself and the witch trembling in his kitchen. Tassle danced beside him, a furry bundle of excitement.

Can we keep her, Yas? Tassle asked. *She can be the female for our pack.*

Since he didn't think Marian wanted to be part of their "pack," he answered the question with a question. "Why all the tail wagging?"

Ladvarian says dogs wag their tails to let humans know they want to be friends.

Ladvarian was a Sceltie Warlord Jaenelle had brought to the Hall when he was a puppy. Since dogs had more experience living with and around humans, the wild kindred who were part of Jaenelle's court considered Ladvarian an expert on human behavior and looked to him to explain the bewildering things humans did.

So I wagged my tail, Tassle continued happily. *I want to be friends. I like her smells.*

Lucivar's feet rooted to the ground. *This* was a statement he couldn't ignore . . . no matter how much he wanted to. He scrubbed his hands over his face and sighed. "Tassle . . . Don't sniff her crotch."

But . . . Yas—

"I know it's acceptable among wolves, but you cannot do it with human females. It makes them snarly."

★But—★

"*No,* Tassle."

Tassle hung his head and looked up at Lucivar with woeful eyes. ★Would she snarl at you if you sniffed her crotch?★

The picture formed in his mind before he could stop it. Marian, sitting in the chair in the kitchen. Him on his knees in front of her, his arms around her waist, his face pressed against the juncture of her thighs, breathing in the smell of her as her scent changed from warm and quiet to hot and aroused.

He turned away from Tassle, not sure if he should curse himself, curse Marian, curse Jaenelle, or curse the wolf for asking the question.

Because that was the question, wasn't it? One look at Marian and everything in him had sharpened with interest, had churned toward desire. If he'd met her in any other way, he would have staked a claim. That was Protocol. That was permissible.

Warlord Princes weren't like other men. They were passionately violent and violently passionate and far more territorial than other males. And when a particular woman intrigued a Warlord Prince sexually, he had a simple way of dealing with potential rivals: He killed them.

Because that lethal response was part of the nature of Warlord Princes, the Blood had long ago established Protocols to give other males a chance of survival. When a Warlord Prince indicated interest in a female, the other males stood back, giving him time to get to know her—and for her to get to know him and consider if she wanted that formidable temper and driving sexual hunger focused exclusively on her. Because it would be exclusive. But the choice was always hers. When she'd spent enough time with him to make a decision, she would either accept him as a lover . . . or tell him to go. And if she told him to go, he didn't argue, didn't try to persuade her—he had to walk away. That was part of Protocol, too.

But *he* couldn't even follow Protocol because *she* was his damn *housekeeper.* She had every right to expect him to protect her from any male's unwanted sexual attention—and that included *him.*

But . . . Hell's fire, she was pulling at him in too many ways. Her fear spiked his temper because his instincts demanded that he defend and protect—and destroy whatever was causing that fear. He couldn't do that because *he* was the cause. And underneath that fear he sensed a warm, quiet strength that intrigued and aroused him, that made him want to wrap himself around her and breathe in her psychic scent as well as her physical smells. Oh, he'd been stirred by a few women over the past three years, and there had been times when the hunger inside him had been fierce, but never enough to give in, never enough for him to forget the rage and bitterness that had flavored most of his sexual experience. So it had been easy enough to turn away from that stirring, to chain that hunger. Until Marian had walked into the kitchen. Now he *wanted,* and he wasn't sure if he could keep that hunger chained.

Lucivar looked toward the eyrie. Maybe, once she was settled in the housekeeper's room, her fear would ease a little. Maybe it would ease enough that she would stay, although he wasn't sure if her staying would be a torment or a boon.

He sighed, then turned back to look at Tassle. "I'm going to get her settled in for the night. You stay here. I don't think she can handle more than one male at a time right now."

Tassle whined but didn't follow him when he went back to the eyrie. She was still in the kitchen, her eyes too bright with fear.

"I'll show you to your room." His voice was as calm as he could make it, but there was a hint of a growl that was a response to her fear.

Silent, she followed him to a room that was on the opposite side of the eyrie from his bedroom. She shuddered when he opened the door and she realized she had to walk past him.

Watching her look around the room, he said, "My father's house-keeper brought over the furniture and set up the room. There's a private bathroom through that door. I expect you'll find everything you need." *At least for tonight.*

She still didn't say anything. She looked bruised and exhausted, and the only thing he could do to help her was to leave her alone.

"Good night, Lady." He closed the door and stared at it for a few moments. *Damn you, Cat. You really kicked me in the guts this time.*

But as he went back outside to tell Tassle it was all right to come in, he had a bad feeling it wasn't his guts that would feel the pain.

★   ★   ★

Marian stared at the door. No lock. No way to prevent someone from coming in during the night to . . .

She could put a Purple Dusk shield around the room, but that would probably just insult him—or amuse him. It certainly wouldn't stop him if he . . .

She shuddered, then clenched her hands until they ached. She couldn't think like that. Fear was already a living thing crawling inside her. If she was going to survive staying here, she had to beat it back, not feed it.

She called in her nightgown—another piece of clothing Luthvian had been ready to discard and had given to her instead. She wouldn't think about that either. Just wouldn't think anymore. Couldn't think anymore.

After changing her clothes, she settled into bed and called in her book, sure she wouldn't get any sleep.

Later, she roused enough from a deep sleep to realize someone was gently pulling the book out of her hands and turning off the lamp on the bedside table, but not enough to wonder who it was.

SEVEN

Marian jolted awake, her heart pounding. She kept her eyes closed, feigning sleep to give her scrambled brain a few precious seconds to catch up and identify what had ripped her out of a deep sleep.

There. Warm breath against her hand. Someone was in her room, next to her bed. Someone who would know by the change in her breathing that she wasn't asleep, and pretending only kept her blind to the danger.

She opened her eyes . . . and stared at the wolf who was watching her intently.

You are awake. Yas told me not to wake you and I didn't wake you but now you are awake. The wolf stretched his neck so that they were nose-to-nose. *You can pet me.*

She raised her hand to obey. Then her brain identified what was wrong with this "conversation."

A breathless shriek, a wild kick to free herself from the bedcovers, and a hasty scramble had her standing on the opposite side of the bed from the wolf, who looked equally startled.

The bedroom door was open. She was closer to it. If she could reach the door . . .

She shuffled sideways, never taking her eyes off the wolf—until he put one paw on the bed as if intending to spring over it and reach her.

She bolted through the doorway, sprinted down the corridor, turning the corner so fast she almost hit the opposite wall, and ran down the wide main corridor of the eyrie. Seeing the archway of the only room she recognized, she grabbed at the stone wall and swung into the kitchen, startling Yaslana enough that he almost dropped the mug he was holding.

"What in the name of Hell—" he began.

"The wolf talks!"

"I know," Yaslana replied. "He's kindred. Since you're up, do you want some coffee?"

Marian stared at him. Maybe he wasn't awake enough to understand what she'd said. "The wolf *talks*. In *sentences*."

"I know." He studied her for a moment, then added, "He's kindred. Blood."

"Blood?" She suddenly felt a bit weak and woozy.

"The Blood from the nonhuman races are called kindred." Yaslana scratched his cheek. "Tassle is a Warlord, as a matter of fact. Wears the Purple Dusk Jewels."

Marian groped for the nearest chair to keep from sinking to the floor. Blood? Warlord? Purple Dusk Jewels?

A whine.

She turned. Standing in the archway, the wolf gave her the most woeful look she'd ever seen.

He whined again and slunk away—and she felt as if a small boy had tried to give her something he thought was a wonderful present . . . and she'd smacked him for it.

Confused and feeling guilty, she focused on the familiar sound of sizzling meat—and frowned. "What are you doing?"

Turning back to the stove, Yaslana picked up a fork and flipped the two steaks sizzling in a skillet. "Making breakfast. You want some? There's plenty." He poked at something else in the other skillet.

Marian slumped in the chair. "But . . . I should be making breakfast."

He shrugged. "You were asleep."

She quailed at the implied criticism. Then she bristled at the unfairness of it. "I'm sorry, Prince Yaslana. You didn't tell me what time you expected—"

"I woke up early and decided to make breakfast," he said testily. "It's not important."

Not important. The words cut into her, telling her clearly enough what he thought of the skills that usually gave her such pleasure.

He picked up a pot, poured dark liquid into a mug, brought the mug over to the table, and plunked it down in front of her.

She looked at the mug—and shuddered.

He stiffened as if she'd slapped him, then grabbed two plates from the counter, returned to the stove, and started dishing out the food. Every move he made radiated temper as he put the plates of food on the table, then dug out silverware from a drawer and dropped it on the table.

As he pulled out his chair, she gathered her courage to ask, "May I have some cream and sugar?"

He paused. "You didn't use any last night."

True, but last night she hadn't known how bad this stuff tasted.

A sugar bowl and a small glass bottle appeared above the table. They hovered for a moment before gently coming to rest within easy reach.

She added two teaspoons of sugar—then added a heaping third when he turned away from the table for a moment—and as much cream as she could fit into the mug without having it spill over the rim. She stirred carefully and tasted cautiously. It was lighter and sweeter—and it was still terrible.

He sat down, chose some silverware from the pile on the table, and said, "Eat."

She stared mournfully at what could have been a very fine steak if it hadn't been slapped into a skillet with no regard for its potential. Suppressing a sigh she was sure would only irritate him further, she selected her silverware and began to eat. The fried potatoes were quite good, the scrambled eggs were bland but not bad, and the steak, despite its treatment, was still tender. But every bite she chewed and swallowed was an effort of will. She was too aware of the annoyed man sitting across from her, too aware that she hadn't yet performed her first task in her new position and he was already displeased with her.

After a few bites, her aching stomach threatened to rebel if she forced another mouthful of food into it, so she pushed the food around, wishing the meal would end—and afraid to consider what might happen when it did.

Suddenly, Yaslana set his knife and fork down and pushed back his chair, his half-eaten meal another silent criticism.

"I have to go out for a few hours," he said. "I should be back by midday."

As he moved toward the archway, she half turned in her chair but couldn't look at him. "What— What would you like me to do?"

"Whatever hearth witches do."

Defeated, she said, "Nothing important."

She thought she'd said it quietly enough that he wouldn't hear, but he stopped in the archway and stared at her for a long moment. Then he was gone.

She sat at the table for a long time, trying to convince herself that she had work to do. The dishes to wash at the very least, and the remains of the meal to store, and the midday meal to plan once she'd taken a look at what was available. The task of exploring her domain should have de-lighted her. Instead, she sat.

She was a hearth witch whose Jewels weren't dark enough to give her any status worth mentioning, and her skills had no value. So what was the point of trying, always trying? The only time anyone had valued her was when those five Warlords wanted to kill her. What did that say about a woman who, being from one of the three long-lived races, had already lived thirteen centuries and would live many more—and would never do or be anything important?

Maybe Lady Angelline didn't do me a favor when she rescued me. Maybe it would have been better if—

Marian shook her head. No. This was just another rough patch of road, just another part of the journey that she had to get through before she could turn the dream of having a place of her own into a reality.

A whine made her turn toward the archway. The wolf was back, still looking woeful.

Kindred. Blood. Warlord. Young.

She finally realized why he made her think of a small boy. He was still young.

"Good morning, Lord Tassle." When he didn't respond, she tried again. "I'm sorry I reacted badly. I— I've never talked to a wolf before."

★We do not talk to many humans. Only friends.★

She raised one hand. "Would you still like me to pet you?"

★Pet?★ He came forward, slipping his head under her hand. ★Pet.★

So she petted—and the wonder of touching a wild animal who was more than a wild animal began to fill her.

She glanced at the unfinished meals. "Would you like some steak, Tassle?"

★Burned meat?★

"No, it isn't burned—" Oh. Wolf. "—but it is cooked."

He sighed. ★I will eat it anyway.★

She gave the meat to Tassle, ignoring the fact that she could have made a nice steak pie out of it, and began to clear the table.

"After I wash up and get dressed, could you show me around?" she asked him.

★I can show you,★ Tassle replied. ★You do not have to mark territory. I mark our territory. Even Yas cannot mark territory as well as I can.★

She thought about that for a moment, then bent her head so her long black hair fell forward and hid her grin. Even if nothing else was what she'd hoped for, learning about the kindred was going to be interesting.

Lucivar stormed into Saetan's study at the Hall and slammed the door behind him. Saetan didn't even flinch, just set the documents he'd been reading aside and leaned back in his chair.

It figured that the High Lord wouldn't have much reaction to that kind of entrance. After all, he'd been dealing with Jaenelle, the coven, and the boyos for the past five years, and the combination of adolescence, power, and those particularly agile minds when it came to using Craft would have shattered the nerves of a less strong-willed man.

But that lack of reaction annoyed Lucivar. He needed a battleground on which to vent the emotions churning inside him, and his father wasn't being accommodating. So he shaped the battleground himself.

"This isn't going to work," he snarled as he paced in front of Saetan's desk. "It just isn't going to work."

"What isn't?" Saetan asked.

"Marian."

Saetan sighed, but there was exasperation underneath the sound. "The woman has barely had time to unpack. What has she——"

"I can't stand this!" Lucivar shouted. "This is my home. I don't want this in my home." He stopped pacing and raked one hand through his hair. "She's bringing out everything that's savage in me."

"Why?"

"Because she's afraid! She's afraid of Tassle and——" It burned him to say it. "——she's afraid of me."

"She has good reason to be afraid of you."

Oh, now. *Here* was a battleground and an opponent who wouldn't flinch at his temper. His voice became quiet and deadly. "Meaning what?"

"Do you know how Marian came to live in Kaeleer?" Saetan asked.

"Jaenelle brought her in." Another battleground. "And what in the name of Hell was Jaenelle doing in Askavi Terreille?" he roared.

"Rescuing a hearth witch."

He heard it then. It wasn't anger under Saetan's calmly spoken words; it was rage. So he chained his temper, no longer sure if he was dealing with Saetan, his father, or Saetan, the High Lord of Hell. He didn't understand why Andulvar Yaslana, the Ebon-gray Eyrien Warlord Prince who had been Saetan's closest friend for more than fifty thousand years, made a point of warning him to be careful when he dealt with the High Lord, but the fact that the Demon Prince felt the need to make the distinction was reason enough for him to be cautious.

Saetan rose, came around his desk, and leaned against the front of it. That informal stance, rather than his remaining behind the desk, usually signaled a discussion between equals.

"Marian's father is a Warlord serving as a Fifth Circle guard in a Queen's court," Saetan said, his voice still quiet—and still filled with suppressed rage. "From the information I gathered, he doesn't have the brains, the backbone, or the balls to advance any higher, but he deludes himself by thinking it's his lack of the proper social connections rather than his lack of abilities that keeps him from being in the First or Second Circle. He likes to rub elbows with the aristo males in the court, and he likes to gamble—and some of them tolerate him because they find his expectations amusing and they like winning the quarterly pittance he earns whenever they consent to let him gamble with them. But they wouldn't let him play on credit because they'd quickly realized he had no way to pay them back.

"But one night, a few weeks ago, they let him play beyond the marks he'd brought to the table. They kept refilling his glass, and they let him play because he had something they wanted. He'd been bragging recently about his younger daughters and how he expected them to become prominent witches once they completed their training as a Healer and a Priestess. But the eldest daughter was an embarrassment to him. A witch whose skills would never provide the family with any status, a witch who did—"

"Nothing important," Lucivar murmured, remembering the defeated way Marian had held herself when she'd said those words.

Saetan nodded. "That was exactly what those aristo males wanted— a witch who did nothing important, a witch whose disappearance wouldn't draw the attention of anyone in the court." His hands curled around the edge of the blackwood desk. "So they let the bastard gamble until he was so far in debt he would never be able to repay them. And when he sobered up enough to realize his standing in the court would be ruined if he didn't repay them, they offered him a trade—and he took it.

"He didn't even have the courage to take her to the meeting place so she would know why she was being sacrificed. He just sent her there. Five Warlords with knives and Eyrien war blades. One terrified hearth witch, tethered so she could fly, since that made it more interesting, but couldn't escape. Shallow slices to prolong the pain and fear. And when she couldn't fight anymore, they pulled her down, intending to rape her while she bled out under them."

Feeling sick, Lucivar closed his eyes. "So they raped her."

"No. Jaenelle arrived before they began that part of their entertainment."

Lucivar shuddered. Jaenelle had been brutally raped when she was twelve. Her body had healed, but she, and those who loved her, lived with the emotional scars. There was nothing that turned Jaenelle lethal and merciless faster than rape.

He opened his eyes, needing to see Saetan's confirmation. "She killed those Warlords." Then he shook his head. "If she intended to begin the healing in order to save Marian, it would have been a fast kill." Which meant they hadn't suffered nearly enough to repay the debt of pain and terror they'd inflicted.

"A fast kill," Saetan agreed. "Although, considering the condition of their bodies, it was sufficient for the initial payment."

Lucivar said nothing, just waited for the rest.

"Jaenelle gave them to me to extract the rest of the payment," Saetan said too softly. "And they paid the debt in full."

The knowledge of what Saetan could do to one of the Blood after the physical death should have frightened him, but he took a grim satisfaction in knowing every wound Marian had received, every moment of terror she'd experienced, had been accounted for. While Saetan ripped their minds apart, piece by piece, he would have found out everything there was to know about why and how Marian had ended up being attacked by those men.

"What about her father?" Lucivar asked.

"I have no authority in Askavi Terreille. I can't touch her father."

Yet.

The word hung unsaid between them, and Lucivar knew with absolute certainty that it didn't matter how many more centuries Marian's father lived. The day would come when his body died, and he would make the transition to become one of the demon-dead. He would end up in the Dark Realm—and the High Lord would be waiting for him.

"So you have a choice, Lucivar," Saetan said. "I can appreciate, quite well, what it means to have Marian's fear scraping against the instincts that bring out the best, and the deadliest, side of your nature. If you can't tolerate it, then you should dismiss her. Between Jaenelle and me, we should be able to find her another position. Or you can grit your teeth for a while and endure it, giving her time to settle and regain her balance. Giving both of you time to find out if it's you she really fears."

Lucivar turned away. He couldn't dismiss her. Not just because of what he'd learned from Saetan, but because it would confirm that she did nothing important, that her skills had no value. That she believed it, *accepted* it, chafed as much as anything else.

But having her stay wasn't going to ease the other part of his frustration—especially now that he knew there were five—the bastards!—more reasons why she'd run from him.

Lucivar started pacing again.

Saetan watched him for a while, then cocked his head. "Something else?"

He tried to think of a delicate way to say it, but in the end, he blurted it out. "She makes me hungry."

"She —" Saetan paused. Crossed his arms over his chest.

Lucivar glanced at his father, expecting to see criticism or anger in Saetan's expression. Instead, he saw . . . interest.

"I know it isn't possible," he said.

"Why not?"

Lucivar stopped pacing and stared at Saetan in disbelief. "For one thing, she works for me. If she thinks that's part of what I expect from her—" He raked his fingers through his hair. "I couldn't stand it if she came to my bed because she thought she had to."

"If she worked for someone else?"

Where he couldn't protect her, especially now that he knew she *needed* protecting? Not while he was breathing. But the question made his temper soar. "I'd follow Protocol and stake a claim," he snarled.

"There's no reason why you can't do that," Saetan said.

"She *works* for me."

Saetan made an exasperated sound. "There's just the three of you. If she worked somewhere else and you expressed interest in her, she'd be scrutinized by everyone in that household because your interest would be public knowledge. This way, you can get to know her—and she can get to know you—in private. The end result will be the same. If she wants to be your lover, she'll make the choice."

"She still might think—"

"If I ever have so much as an inkling that you're doing anything that makes her feel cornered, I will kick your ass from one end of Kaeleer to the other and back again."

The threat, which was sincere, shouldn't have cheered him up, but it did.

"You want advice about how to deal with Marian?" Saetan said. "Treat her the same way you treat the coven."

Lucivar clenched his fists. The coven could take anything he dished out, but . . . "She's too fragile to be handled that way."

Saetan just looked at him for a long time, then said quietly, "I saw her when Jaenelle brought her to the Keep. The woman who survived that attack has strength she's never tested, strength she probably doesn't even realize is inside her. Give her the chance to find it. Give her a reason to test it."

Marian stared at the open kitchen cupboards. The *empty* kitchen cupboards. The man had two skillets, a pot, a chipped mixing bowl, four mismatched dishes, two coffee mugs, three glasses, two kitchen knives, and an odd assortment of silverware. No baking dishes, no baking sheets, no measuring cups. No coffee pot or coffee grinder. He didn't even have *wooden spoons*. How was she supposed to prepare decent meals for him without any tools?

And the pantry. The size and design of it thrilled her, but the barren shelves made her want to cry. There was a small keg of ale and a wine rack that held three bottles labeled "yarbarah," which she assumed was the name of a vineyard somewhere in Kaeleer because the only other "yarbarah" she knew about was the blood wine warriors drank at special ceremonies, and Yaslana wouldn't have three bottles of *that*. But the flour, sugar, and coffee beans were just left in their sacks without so much as a light shield to keep the bugs out, and they were the only food items.

The cold box was a delightful discovery, especially when she realized the top third of it was a separate freeze box, but leaving hunks of meat wrapped in nothing more than brown paper was just . . . scandalous. The only other things in the cold box were a half-full butter bowl, the glass bottle of cream, and one egg.

Marian slumped in a chair. There had been no mention of wages last night, and she'd been too frightened to ask, but now she was glad she hadn't.

The pine table and chairs in the kitchen were new. So was the stove, the cold box, and the furniture in Prince Yaslana's bedroom. The furniture in her room was not, but it was good quality.

The rest of the rooms were empty.

Which made her wonder if Prince Yaslana was just getting by until it was time for the next tithe. After all, Luthvian had said he'd just recently become the Prince of Ebon Rih, so he wouldn't have received any of the income yet that came with the title. Maybe he couldn't afford anything more yet. Maybe that's why he hadn't mentioned wages.

Dark power washed through the eyrie, warning her that he'd returned. She jumped up and quickly shut all the cupboards and drawers so he wouldn't wonder what she'd been doing. Then she stopped and looked around. Better if he found her doing something useful, but . . . what?

Yaslana walked into the kitchen, checked his stride, then advanced toward her more slowly, almost warily.

Marian's heart leaped into her throat. It was midday, wasn't it? He was expecting a meal, and she didn't have anything to serve him.

Three dishes suddenly appeared on the counter—two large glass baking dishes with covers and a brown crock.

"Mrs. Beale sent these, with her compliments. She said it wasn't likely that you'd get to the market today since you'd need a little time to settle in and—" He made a face. "And since she doubted I had more than salt and pepper on hand for spices, you'd want to make a list before you went shopping."

Mrs. Beale, whoever she was, was an optimist, Marian thought as she eyed the dishes. She hadn't even found salt and pepper when she'd gone through the cupboards and pantry.

"So this should take care of today's meals," Yaslana said.

While she was grateful for the meals, Marian really wanted to know how long she could keep the dishes.

"And there's this." He took another step toward her and held out a thin stack of papers.

She took them, fanning them out before she actually looked at them. Her heart leaped into her throat, and she had to bite back a squeal.

Silver marks. A *lot* of silver marks. More than she'd ever seen in her life.

"This—" She had to clear her throat before she could get the words out. "This is the housekeeping account?" Oh, the meals she could make with these kinds of funds.

Frowning, he shifted his weight. "I have accounts set up at all the shops in Riada. When you do the marketing, just tell the shopkeeper to put it on my account." He tipped his head toward the marks. "That's for you. An advance in your wages. Since you haven't been in Kaeleer very long, I figured there were things you'd need to buy for yourself."

She felt the blood draining out of her head as she stared at the silver marks. "You're advancing me a month's wages?"

His frown deepened. "Half a month."

Now she did squeal as she thrust out her hand. "I can't take this!"

He took a step back. "Why not?"

"It's too much." Too agitated to think about what she was doing, she took a step toward him, still holding out the marks.

He took another step back.

"Who says it's too much?" He sounded testy. "Besides, I can afford it."

Marian shook her head. *If you can afford it, why don't you have any furniture?* "It's too much."

"Look," he said, a snarl rising in his voice. "My father suggested that as an acceptable wage for a housekeeper, and he should know. Hell's fire, woman, there are enough servants at the Hall to populate a small village."

She finally looked at him—and realized he was defensive . . . and nervous. It suddenly occurred to her that he'd never done this before, never had to decide things like wages or define the duties of household staff. So she folded the silver marks, put them in her skirt pocket, and said, "Thank you, Prince Yaslana."

He looked as relieved as a man walking off a battlefield. "Fine. That's settled." He took another step back toward the archway. "I'll go out and chop some wood."

Marian glanced at the dishes on the counter. "Don't you want to eat?"

"Sure. I'll be out there. Just yell when it's ready."

The man could certainly move, Marian thought as she stared at the empty archway.

It was rather sweet, the way he got all testy and nervous about giving her wages. And it was considerate of him to realize there were things she would need to buy for herself.

She pulled the silver marks out of her pocket, fanned them out again—and smiled.

It was still excessive for a half-month's wages, but if she kept half of it for herself, the other half would give her a good start on buying the basics she needed for the kitchen.

EIGHT

Marian sipped her coffee, looked around her clean kitchen—
and sighed. It was barely midmorning, and she'd already
made a casserole, cleaned up the kitchen, stripped the beds
and put on fresh linens, had all the laundry washed and hanging in the
drying room, dusted the furniture, and swept the floors. There was
nothing left to do—and Prince Yaslana would be gone for the next
two days.

She still wasn't sure how service in Lady Angelline's court worked. It
all seemed so . . . casual. She knew Prince Yaslana went back to SaDiablo Hall one or two days each week for a few hours, but she wasn't sure
if he went there for court business or just to visit family. He'd explained
that since all the males in the First Circle had other responsibilities, his
father, as Steward of the Court, worked out a rotation so that each male
fulfilled his obligation to Queen and court by being on duty for two or
three days twice a month.

So he'd left before sunrise, and she had the next two days stretching
out in front of her. She could read, but reading was the reward after the
day's labor. She'd finished the weaving she'd started on her small hand
loom and had made a decorative mat for the kitchen table. She didn't
feel like making something just to fill up time. So what . . .

Turning to look out the window, she studied the mess of rocks and
weeds. It had been a garden a long time ago. She'd found herbs growing

wild among the weeds and suspected there had been an herb bed and a kitchen garden on this side of the eyrie.

Why hadn't Yaslana done anything to at least clean it up? For a man who was always aware of his surroundings, he seemed willfully blind to the fact that a natural meadow, which had its own kind of beauty, wasn't the same as the tangled mess she was staring at now.

Besides, it would be so nice to have a little kitchen garden to tend.

Marian refilled her coffee mug and took a moment to admire the coffeepot she'd bought with part of her wages. Yaslana hadn't said a word about the pot's sudden appearance in his kitchen, but he'd definitely approved of the taste of the coffee she could brew in it.

She walked down what she'd labeled the "domestic" corridor, since it provided entry to the pantry and the laundry and drying room—and the small area between the pantry and laundry that had a door to the outside and a purpose she was still puzzling over. Opening the door, she studied the land in front of her.

The growing season was already well along, and she wasn't sure what kinds of plants might be available. But the women in Riada would know—or she could ask Lady Angelline the next time the Queen stopped by for a brief visit. A few vegetables, a few herbs. Maybe some flowers. Yaslana wouldn't mind if she cleared a little ground. At least, she was almost certain he wouldn't mind.

He was, and wasn't, what she'd expected, based on the things she'd heard about Warlord Princes and him in particular. She had no doubt he was a trained warrior and a born predator whose temper could turn deadly in a heartbeat. She could see it in the way he moved, the way he looked at everything around him. But she hadn't actually seen a display of temper. Well, not much of one. The only time he'd snarled at her since she'd arrived was when he'd come home early one afternoon, taken a long look at her, and decided she needed something to eat. When she'd told him she wasn't hungry, he informed her that anyone who worked as hard as she did was not going to deprive her body of food. Then he marched her into the kitchen and rummaged through the cold box until he put together a plate of food that he considered sufficient. His idea of sufficient was vastly different from hers, but her token effort at eating had satisfied him enough that he'd eaten what was left on her plate.

Since he didn't seem to care what she did as long as *she* was pleased with the result, she didn't think he'd mind her clearing some ground and having the pleasure of a little garden of her own.

After vanishing her coffee mug, then calling it back in so that it would reappear on the kitchen counter next to the sink, Marian pushed up her sleeves, stepped outside, and got to work.

As she stepped back into the eyrie, Marian understood the purpose of the little room. If it had pegs in the wall or a coat tree, wet or muddy outer garments could be hung in there to dry. Boots could be removed instead of tracking dirt or mud through the rest of the eyrie. And it was close to the big sinks in the laundry room for a quick wash if it was needed.

If there was a bench in here, it would make removing boots so much easier, Marian thought, groaning softly as she bent over to unlace her boots. At least Tassle was off doing his daily trot around the land surrounding the eyrie and hadn't heard her groan. He'd just start howling again.

Wolves had a very effective way of nagging. When he'd started telling her around midday that it was time for her to rest and eat, it had been easy to tell him she would do that in a few minutes, or after she'd moved a couple more rocks. But after she'd done that several times . . .

That howl rising up over the land was *not* something that could be ignored. He wouldn't hush, she couldn't catch him, and she suspected everyone in Riada could hear him. Since there was no way to shush him except to do what he wanted, she warmed up a piece of casserole and spent an hour reading at the kitchen table. When she came back out, he was pleased enough by his success in taking care of a female that he'd used Craft to help her move rocks until the game bored him and he went off for a while to do something wolfie.

So it was just as well that she'd announced it was time to quit for the day before *he'd* decided it was time for her to quit. One howling experience was quite enough.

She closed the door and touched the stone in the wall that had been spelled to engage the Ebon-gray locks Prince Yaslana had put on all the doors. He'd worked out a way for the spell to recognize her and Tassle so that they could come and go, but he'd been adamant about the doors being locked whenever he wasn't home, especially the front door. He'd been equally adamant that she not allow anyone but his family to enter the eyrie when he was gone.

The command had baffled her, but it was his home, his business. As she hurried along the domestic corridor to the kitchen, she dismissed all thought of the locks, her focus now centered on a long, hot bath to ease the deep ache in her muscles. Those aches, and the shivers of pain that occasionally came with them, worried her sometimes, but she hadn't said anything to Jaenelle whenever the Lady asked how she was feeling. Luthvian had warned her that removing her wings was the only way her back would completely heal. But she didn't want to lose her wings, didn't want to lose the hope that, someday, she might fly again—even though she was too afraid of crippling herself to even try.

She pushed those thoughts away by focusing on the pleasure of soaking in a hot bath, eating a big piece of casserole for dinner, reading her book, and turning in early so she could get back to her garden at first light tomorrow.

As she stepped through the kitchen archway, she was concentrating so hard on not thinking about her wings that she let out a breathless shriek when the front door suddenly rattled.

With a hand pressed against her chest, Marian stared at the door. There were two solid bolts that provided physical locks for the door as well as the Ebon-gray lock, so even if a "visitor" managed to destroy the front door, he or she still wouldn't be able to get into the eyrie.

The rattling stopped. The pounding of fist on wood started.

Tassle? Marian called on a Purple Dusk psychic thread.

Marian!

There's someone at the front door. They sound quite . . . insistent.

I should call Prothvar?

Marian hesitated before saying, *Not yet.*

I am coming back to our den.

That was good. She'd feel easier if Tassle was within shouting distance.

Yaslana had told her his cousin Prothvar, whom she hadn't met yet, was staying at the Keep while he was gone and would respond if she needed help for any reason. Knowing one cry for help would bring a Warlord wolf and an Eyrien warrior to her defense gave her the courage to go to the front door and draw back the bolts. Besides, it was possible that it *was* Yaslana's cousin, just stopping by to check on her. It would be rude not to open the door.

The woman on the other side of the door was *not* Yaslana's cousin. She was young, a Rihlander, a stranger, and was dressed . . .

Marian couldn't think of a polite way to describe how she was dressed.

"Who are you?" the woman demanded.

"I'm Prince Yaslana's housekeeper," Marian replied courteously.

The woman looked at her sweaty, dirt-smeared tunic and trousers, and said, "Oh" in a way that clearly indicated that Marian had been dismissed as unimportant. "I'm here to see Lucivar. He's expecting me."

Not likely, Marian thought, shifting slightly to block the doorway. "Prince Yaslana is not at home."

"Then I'll wait for him."

The woman took a step forward. Marian didn't step back.

"That won't be possible," Marian said, working to remain polite. "He may not be back until quite late."

"He won't mind if I make myself comfortable," the woman insisted.

Where? There were only three rooms in the eyrie that were furnished, and Marian didn't think this woman intended to sit in the kitchen.

It probably would be easier to say she wasn't permitted to let anyone enter the eyrie. After all, a servant had to obey her employer. But it wasn't Yaslana's order that kept her blocking the door; it was her own dislike of the woman that kept her from stepping back. There was something calculating about this stranger, and there was meanness lurking in the backs of her eyes.

"If you would like to leave a message," Marian said, "I'll give it to Prince Yaslana as soon as he returns."

The meanness filled the woman's face for a moment before she shifted her hips, pushed out her chest, and smiled in a way Marian supposed was meant to be sultry.

"The message I have for Lucivar isn't something I'd leave with *you*."

"In that case, good evening, Lady," Marian said. As she closed the door, the woman shouted, "I won't forget this!"

Neither will I, Marian thought as she slid the bolts back into place. She'd bet a month's wages that she'd just met the reason Yaslana had Ebon-gray locks on his doors.

NINE

Lucivar strode over the rock-cleared ground, working up from annoyance to being thoroughly pissed off as he watched Marian set herself to try to lift a rock that weighed more than she did. One slashing look at Tassle was enough to prevent the young wolf from announcing his presence. The fact that his little hearth witch was so focused—or so exhausted—she wasn't even aware of him coming up behind her just made his temper more volatile and his control more slippery.

But he would stay calm.

She groaned a little as she tried to get a better grip on the rock.

He would be reasonable.

She braced herself to try again.

He was on her in a heartbeat, his arms going around her, his hands clamping down on her wrists to keep her from jerking upward. Not that she could move much, with his arms locking her wings against her body, his chest pressed against her back, and his legs bracing hers.

Even though he'd expected her to react to being restrained by a male, her instant panic still screamed at his instincts to defend and protect. He fought a quick, nasty battle with himself to keep from rising to the killing edge since that was the last thing that would ease her fear.

So he would stay calm.

"Marian," he said quietly.

She panted, trembled. But after a few painfully long seconds, she said, "Prince Yaslana?"

"Yes, it's Lucivar. Let go of the rock now."

He waited while she fought her own internal battle. On one level, she knew holding the rock wasn't a defense against an attack, but it still took a while before she managed to convince her body. When her hands finally relaxed, he drew them away from the rock. Sliding his hands up to her shoulders, he straightened up, bringing her with him.

Being attracted to her made him aware of her body in ways he'd had to pretend he didn't notice, but he wasn't going to ignore this. No, he was not.

But he would stay calm.

He led her over to the stone that had weathered into a natural seat. As he helped her ease down to sit on the stone, he noticed the Rose Jewel she wore. Her Birthright Jewel. He could think of one reason why she was wearing the Rose instead of her Purple Dusk, and he didn't like it.

But he would be reasonable.

"What in the name of Hell are you doing?" he roared.

She shrank away from him as he towered over her, but seeing her so tired made him too angry to care that he was scaring her.

"I—I—" Marian stammered.

"You what? Wanted to see how many rocks you could move before you ruined your back? I know it still bothers you occasionally, so don't bother trying to deny it."

She winced. "I used Craft to take most of the weight."

"Oh, I can see that," he said, pointing at her Rose Jewel. "And you needed to draw so much power to lift things you couldn't possibly lift otherwise that you drained your Purple Dusk Jewel doing it. Isn't that why you're wearing the Rose?"

When she just stared at him mutely, he swore and started pacing to work off the sharpest edge of temper. Problem was, the movement also gave him time to notice more of what she'd done.

He snarled at her. "In order to get this much cleared, you must have started the minute I was out of sight and kept at it for the past two days."

"I got my work done," Marian protested.

Oh. Well. *That* certainly made him feel better. And the tears in her eyes and defeated way she held herself ripped at him. He didn't want her defeated. He didn't want her afraid. But he'd be damned if he was going to let her hurt herself in order to do . . .

"What is this, Marian?" Lucivar waved his hand to indicate the cleared land. "Explain."

She looked at the ground, a tear sliding down her face. "A kitchen garden," she whispered. "Some herbs. A few flowers. I didn't think you'd mind."

His temper had eased back from true anger to just being pissed off again, but that comment came close to snapping the leash. He hauled her to her feet, certain her back and leg muscles were now tight enough that she couldn't have gotten up by herself, and pulled her toward the eyrie.

Her emotions battered at him—fear that he was going to punish her for doing something without his permission, fear of what a man of his temper and power would do to her as punishment. The fact that she expected punishment told him more about the males who had been part of her life than he wanted to know.

"If you wanted a kitchen garden, you could have spent the past two days figuring out where you wanted it and what you wanted in it," he said, keeping his voice as level as he could manage. "I could have cleared the ground for you when I got back. Did it even occur to you to ask me?"

"No," Marian said in a small voice.

No. Well, that was a kick in the balls. Even the coven knew better than that. Blood males served. That was something so deeply ingrained in the males even the cruelty in Terreille couldn't extinguish it completely. In Kaeleer, where the Blood still lived by the Old Ways, males considered it their right and privilege to serve—and got pretty testy when a witch they knew personally denied them an opportunity to be helpful.

If Marian didn't know that yet, it was something she'd better figure out. Fast.

He pulled her into the eyrie, through the laundry room, and wound his way through curving corridors until he reached the pool Andulvar had built long ago as a place for a warrior to sit back in heated water and ease tired muscles.

She hadn't openly fought him in an attempt to get away, but from the first step, she'd been silently resisting like some stubborn puppy tethered to a leash. That was fine since he had the rhythm of this little dance and knew how to use it.

Treat her like the coven, Saetan had said. Well, he knew exactly what he'd have done to Jaenelle or any of her friends if they'd upset him over something like this.

When he got near the edge of the pool, he propelled Marian forward. Her automatic step back gave him time to switch hands so that one now gripped her arm and the other held a fistful of her tunic. A hard shove forward, a swinging lift up, and—

"No!" Marian yelled. "My boo—"

—*splash*.

He used Craft to control her drop so she wouldn't slip and damage a wing. Now she stood in heated water up to her waist, with a look on her face that was closer to grumpy than fearful.

Grumpy was fine. Grumpy was good. He wondered just how grumpy he could make her.

"Boots," he said. He'd vanished them off her feet just before she hit the water. Now he called them in, dangling them over her head before he vanished them again. "Which you'll get back if you do what you're told."

She stared up at him. "If I do what I'm told?"

Pointing at her, he said sternly, "You're going to sit your ass down and let that hot water soak out some of the soreness in your muscles. And you're going to stay there until I come back and fetch you." He turned and walked to the entrance.

"Fetch me?" Marian said, sputtering. "*Fetch me?* What do you think I am? An addlebrained *puppy*?"

He turned back. "No, you're female. And I don't think it's wise to discuss your brains right now."

He walked out of the room, stopped as soon as he was out of sight, and listened.

Mutters. Then the slap of wet cloth on stone.

Lucivar grinned. So there was a little temper under that quiet disposition. He'd have to work on that. Shouldn't be too difficult. He excelled at getting witches riled up.

When he got back to the side doorway, Tassle was waiting for him.

I tried, Yas, but she wouldn't listen.

"No, she wouldn't have."

Tassle hung his head. *Because I am kindred.*

"Nope. Because you have a cock instead of breasts. She probably patted you on the head and promised to stop soon."

She did. Tassle looked at Lucivar with interest. *Did she pat your head?*

"No, she didn't." If she'd been capable of lifting another rock, she would have tried to brain him, but patting any male wasn't exactly on her mind at the moment.

The daylight was almost gone, so he couldn't see the full extent of what she'd done in the past two days, but what he could see was enough to make him shake his head.

Hell's fire, Mother Night, and may the Darkness be merciful. The woman was insane.

That was the only explanation he had for Marian trying to clear close to half an acre of land in order to plant a few vegetables, herbs, and flowers. Of course, being a hearth witch meant having a tidy streak that went down to the marrow, so she'd never be content with seeing weeds beyond her little beds. Which meant she'd be out here working too hard every time he turned his back.

She'd drive him up the walls inside of a week—and she was already doing that on a regular basis just by being where he could see her.

He understood her wanting the garden. Besides the practical reasons of growing some of their own food, it would be hers. Her work, her accomplishment, her . . . claim.

He looked at the land again, turning that thought over. Everyone needed something to call their own. She lived in it and took care of it, but she thought of the eyrie as his place. But the garden . . . Something of her own, apart from him. Something she would want to see change with the seasons. Which meant she intended to stay, even if she didn't re-alize it yet.

She'd never be able to clear all of this and have the pleasure of seeing vegetables ripen and flowers bloom this year. And if he tried to help her now, she might see it as his way of reminding her that the land didn't re-ally belong to her.

Moving away from the eyrie, Lucivar stopped when he reached a place where he could look down at Riada—and smiled. He had a way he could prepare the ground for her. Now he just needed a reason to get her away from Ebon Rih for a couple of days—and a little help doing it.

"My fingers are shriveled," Marian complained, clutching the towel she'd wrapped around herself.

"But you can almost stand up straight," Lucivar replied as he led her to her bedroom. "All right. On your belly."

"What?"

A slash of fear.

Gritting his teeth, he gave her a little push toward the bed. "The soak was the first part of the treatment. A rubdown is the second."

"No, that's all right. I can—"

He didn't say anything, he didn't touch her. He just looked at her. The coven never argued with him when they were on the receiving end of that look. Marian didn't either. She stretched out on the bed.

After flipping the sheet up to her waist, he straddled her. She jerked up when he vanished the towel. Her shriek of protest turned into a dif-ferent kind of shriek when he called in a bottle of liniment and poured some on her back without using a warming spell on it first. Leaving the bottle of liniment floating on air freed both hands to push her down and rub her tight muscles.

"It stinks," Marian said.

"It's supposed to smell like that," Lucivar replied. "It's a reminder not to do stupid things that make you need it."

She didn't answer him. Just as well.

When he finally worked most of the stiffness out of her shoulders, she said, "You had a visitor."

"Who was it?" He poured more liniment into his hand and used a warming spell on it since she wasn't resisting the rubdown anymore.

"She didn't say."

Lucivar stiffened. After a moment, he smoothed the warm liniment over Marian's back, giving the area around her wings special attention. "Probably Roxie. Did you let her in?"

"No. Didn't like her." Marian's eyes were closed. Her voice had the slur of someone half asleep. "That's why you have locks on the doors."

"That's exactly why."

"Thought so." She took a deep breath, let it out in a sigh. "I made stew."

He stopped kneading her muscles and leaned over far enough to see her face. "Are we still talking about Roxie?"

"No. Dinner. Stew. You can eat some."

"All right."

Her messages delivered, Marian fell asleep.

After studying her for a long moment, Lucivar decided nothing short of dragging her into the bathroom and holding her under a stream of cold water would wake her. So he finished her back, then pulled down the sheet and rubbed liniment on her legs. When he was done, he vanished the bottle of liniment, pulled up the bedcovers, and put a warming spell on them to keep her from getting chilled during the night.

He ate a bowl of quickly warmed stew, told Tassle to keep watch, and flew to the Keep, where he'd left Jaenelle a couple of hours ago.

She closed her book and studied him. "What brings you back here tonight, Brother?"

Her knowing he was there as her brother and not as a Warlord Prince who served in her court made this a lot easier. "I need a favor, and I don't want to explain why."

TEN

Tarl, the head gardener at SaDiablo Hall, was the first man to arrive that morning.

Which figured, Lucivar thought as he raised a hand in welcome. Tarl had probably come in the Hall's small private Coach and stayed out of sight until the driver caught the Winds and guided the Coach to the next destination—with Jaenelle and a flustered Marian inside it.

Jaenelle had timed the note commanding Marian's assistance perfectly. Arriving late yesterday morning, it had given Marian enough time to wash out clothing and cook enough food that he could heat up so he wouldn't starve to death in her absence but not enough time to do anything else except get herself cleaned up and pack the small trunk Jaenelle had thoughtfully sent over from the Keep with the note.

Now Jaenelle and Marian were gone for the next two days to do some shopping, Tarl was here, and the other men would be arriving shortly.

"Morning, Prince Lucivar," Tarl said.

"Good morning, Tarl."

"Going to be a fine day." Tarl's eyes lit up with something close to lust when he looked at that half acre of rocky, weedy ground. "Sooo . . . it's a garden we're making out of this, is it?"

"Yes," Lucivar said cautiously.

"And—" Tarl broke off at the sound of other men's voices coming from the stairs leading up from the landing place. "You called in the tithe?" he asked softly.

Lucivar nodded. "From Riada. I need this done in two days."

As part of the tithe owed to the Keep, every adult in Ebon Rih owed five days of labor each year along with the financial tithe. As the Warlord Prince ruling on his Queen's behalf, he received two of those days. He'd spent part of yesterday making sure word was spread throughout the village that he was collecting those two days from the men.

The men began to gather round, talking quietly among themselves.

"Well," Briggs, who ran The Tavern with his wife, Merry, said. "What's to be done here, Prince?"

"A garden," Tarl replied before Lucivar could. "But what kind of garden?"

It sounded like an innocent question until Lucivar realized every man now crowded around them had stopped talking in order to hear the answer. He didn't look at any of them. He didn't dare look at Tarl, whom he could have cheerfully strangled at that moment. There wasn't a man on this mountain who wasn't going to go home tonight and report Prince Yaslana's answer to the women in his life—which, in Tarl's case since he worked at the Hall, was Helene and Mrs. Beale.

Lucivar took a deep breath and let it out slowly. "Lady Marian wants a kitchen garden, a bed for herbs, and some flowers."

A few men grinned. Others nudged their neighbors or exchanged knowing looks. By tonight, everyone in Riada would know Lucivar Yaslana was interested in far more than Lady Marian's housekeeping skills. Which was fine—as long as Marian didn't panic when she found out.

Tarl prowled the ground nearest the eyrie, frowning a bit at one thing, nodding at something else. He made his way through the men, crossed the flagstone courtyard in front of the eyrie, and continued on to the other side. He came back a few minutes later, looking thoughtful.

"Right," he said. "I've got the feel of it. I expect your Lady wants to be doing her own planting on this side of the eyrie, but we can take care of the other side."

"Other side?" Lucivar said, feeling like he'd taken a bad slide on what he'd thought was solid ground.

"Lady Marian's a hearth witch, isn't she?" Tarl said, making the question close to a demand. "She'll spend the rest of the summer fretting if this side is put to rights and the other side is left so untidy. We've got two days and"—he looked around as men shifted to make room for newcomers—"plenty of hands to do the job."

Lucivar closed his eyes and accepted that he'd kicked the first pebble, so he couldn't complain—too much—about the avalanche that came out of it. "Fine."

"Right, then," Tarl said, rubbing his hands together. "The first thing we have to do is move those rocks."

Why am I here? Marian asked herself as she looked around the two-story building packed with furniture.

"Tell me again why I'm here?" the man beside her asked.

Jaenelle looked over her shoulder at him. "Because you're male."

"And I'm being punished for this because . . . ?"

"You're Lucivar's father."

He sighed. "I thought that would be the answer." He paused, then added, "Lucivar wanted to select his own furnishings. He said so. Several times."

Jaenelle turned to face them. "That's what he said. He changed his mind, and he picked me to do the shopping for him. And I picked the two of you to help me." She smiled at her helpers in a way that was not the least bit reassuring.

Marian glanced at the man to see what his reaction would be. Lucivar's father. S. D. SaDiablo. That was how Jaenelle had introduced him when they'd all settled into the Coach for the journey to Nharkhava. It was only because Luci— Prince Yaslana had mentioned it that she knew his father was the Steward of the Dark Court at Ebon Askavi. Being the Steward of the most powerful Queen in Kaeleer made him a very influential man. And yet, here he was, helping his daughter buy furniture for his son.

Of course, his daughter was the Queen of Ebon Askavi and his son was the Warlord Prince of Ebon Rih. But still . . .

So it brought her back to the question of why she, a Purple Dusk hearth witch, was here with them. Surely they weren't interested in the opinions of Prince Yaslana's housekeeper.

"If we're going to select furniture for all the rooms Lucivar intends to use, at least for the immediate future, I suggest we split up," Prince Sa-Diablo said. "We'll be able to look at more of what's being offered."

"Good idea," Jaenelle said. "I'll start over there." As she turned, one of the men who had been hovering nearby leaped forward to meet her. She smiled at him.

"I'll take a look at the dining room furniture," Prince SaDiablo said. His hand lightly brushed Marian's shoulder. "Why don't you accompany Jaenelle?"

"Oh," Marian said. "Wouldn't you rather—"

"Let me rephrase that." Amusement filled his gold eyes. "Age and rank have their privileges. You, my dear, drew the short straw and, therefore, get to deal with Jaenelle."

"That's not reassuring," Marian muttered.

"I didn't say it was."

As he moved past her, the other man waiting to help them said, "This way, High Lord."

Marian watched the two men make their way down the aisles of furniture. High Lord? What an odd title. Maybe it was his official title as the Steward? Although . . . She'd heard it before. She just couldn't recall where or why.

She shook her head and hurried to catch up to Jaenelle.

It took her less than a quarter of an hour to realize Jaenelle Angelline had more energy than a roomful of puppies and less sense than any of those puppies when it came to choosing furniture that was suitable for an eyrie, let alone the home of a Warlord Prince. How was she supposed to tell the Queen—or even Lucivar's sister, for that matter—that the lamp Jaenelle was admiring with the lumpy base and the froofy, fringed shade made her shudder just to look at it? Or that the small table, which would probably look lovely in the drawing room of an aristo house, would look pathetic in rooms that had the weight of stone and were extensions of the mountain on which they were built?

She tried to be tactful, reminding herself that she was just the house-keeper, but when she saw Jaenelle eyeing a hutch with elaborate curlicues . . .

"No," she said firmly.

Eyebrows rising in surprise, Jaenelle turned to look at her. "Why not?"

Because I don't want to spend half a day dusting the thing. Which wasn't an appropriate thing to say, especially when the man assisting them was listening so attentively. "It's just not . . . appropriate," Marian said weakly.

Jaenelle narrowed her sapphire eyes. "So far, nothing we've looked at has been 'appropriate.' "

That was true.

"But I haven't heard *you* make any suggestions," Jaenelle continued.

"Oh, but I'm just—" Those sapphire eyes stopped her—and made her think. She wasn't "just" a housekeeper at the moment. She was Eyrien. She didn't know anything about aristo houses, but she knew Eyrien dwellings. Of the three of them, she probably *did* know best what was appropriate for Luci— Prince Yaslana's home.

Turning away, she began studying the other hutches available. Clean lines. Strong pieces. Lucivar's eyrie had more windows than most, which gave the rooms more light, but the wood always had to complement stone.

Seeing two possible hutches, Marian went over to examine them more closely.

Saetan watched the two women wander among the furniture, amused at the way Jaenelle now meekly followed Marian instead of the other way around.

Witch-child? he called on a Black psychic thread.

Papa?

You weren't really interested in that lamp, were you?

Jaenelle snorted. *Of course not. It's hideous. I didn't think I'd have to find so many things that wouldn't suit before Marian jumped in.*

Saetan pressed a fist to his mouth and coughed to hide the chuckle. The man attending him wouldn't understand his amusement. *I found a dining table.*

A real one?

Yes, a real one. He watched Marian as she opened the doors of a cabinet. Even from a distance, he could see her excitement, almost sense the longing as her fingers stroked the wood—and saw her shoulders slump as she turned away from it. *What is that, witch-child?*

A sewing cabinet, Jaenelle replied, still examining it. *There are shelves for cloth, little pegs for thread, bigger pegs for skeins of wool, all kinds of drawers to hold supplies.*

And the asking price is something she can't afford, even with the wages Lucivar is paying her.

Jaenelle nodded, keeping one eye on Marian while she gently closed the cabinet doors.

Are we adding it to our purchases, witch-child?

She turned and smiled at him from across the large room. *Yes, we are.*

Prince SaDiablo had excellent taste, Marian decided as she looked at the table and chairs he'd chosen for the dining room. High Lord, she reminded herself. The men helping them with their purchases kept calling him High Lord, so she should address him that way, too.

"This is wonderful," Marian said, stroking her hand over the gleaming, dark wood. Big enough to seat eight Eyriens, it would still fit easily into the dining room without feeling crowded if a storage hutch and narrow serving table were also added. Looking past the chosen table, she spotted a small pine table. "Oh, yes, that's perfect."

"Why is this perfect?" Jaenelle said, following her. "It's not even finished."

"That's why it's perfect," Marian replied, giving the table a push to test its sturdiness. "Eyrien males need a worktable for cleaning and honing weapons, doing repairs, things like that. And there's a small room in the eyrie that seems like it was designed to be a weapons room—a storage place for an extra bow, quivers of arrows. There's even pegs already in one wall that would hold bladed sticks, so . . ." She shrugged.

"So you want a table that's sturdy but is going to get rough treatment," Jaenelle said.

"Exactly." Marian smiled.

Jaenelle smiled back. "I'm sure it was a weapons room originally and had a similar table in it. Cousin Prothvar and Uncle Andulvar will be pleased with your choice. So will Lucivar." She brushed a finger over the top of the table. "I noticed some of the other craftsmen are displaying bowls and vases. I'm going to take a look."

"Fine," Marian said. The room was turning slowly, making her feel light-headed.

Lucivar was a common name in Askavi, but Prothvar was rarely used anymore, and Andulvar . . .

No one had used the name Andulvar since the time of the Demon Prince—the Ebon-gray Warlord Prince who had once ruled the Black Valley . . . just as Lucivar now ruled Ebon Rih. Lucivar had mentioned his cousin Prothvar. He'd mentioned his uncle, too, but not by name. And he'd said his family took a little getting used to, but he hadn't said why. If what she was thinking, as impossible as it must be, was true . . .

"Marian?"

A deep, soothing male voice washed over her. The room swayed. She looked at Lucivar's father.

Lucivar Yaslana. Prothvar . . . Yaslana. Andulvar . . . Yaslana.

"Darling, what's wrong?"

S. D. SaDiablo. *High Lord.*

"Aren't you feeling well?"

She was sitting down, looking up at him as he bent over her, concern in his golden eyes, his hand resting lightly against her face.

"You're him," she whispered. "You're really him. The High Lord. Of Hell."

He didn't move, but she could sense the warm man pulling away from her.

"Yes," he said quietly, withdrawing his hand. "I'm the High Lord of Hell."

She didn't know much about the High Lord except that he was more powerful—because he wore a Black Jewel—and supposedly more dangerous than the Demon Prince, but the one thing she *did* know about him from the stories Eyriens told was . . .

"You were Andulvar Yaslana's friend. Almost like brothers."

"We still are."

Still are. Oh, Mother Night. "So, Luci— Prince Yaslana's uncle is . . . ?"

"Andulvar Yaslana. The Demon Prince. Prothvar Yaslana is Andulvar's grandson."

"How?"

"I'm a Guardian. Andulvar, Prothvar . . . and my oldest son, Mephis . . . are demon-dead."

"But . . . Lucivar talks as if he sees them all the time."

"He does."

Marian stared at him. She was looking at a legend. Oh, not one of *her* people's legends, but a legend nonetheless. And one who had known— still knew—the greatest Eyrien Warlord Prince who had ever lived.

Dazzled, she studied him as if she hadn't spent the morning around him. He was wearing the Red, which must be his Birthright Jewel. A courteous man who had made her feel welcome. A widely read man, based on the books he and Jaenelle had talked about on the journey. He had a dry sense of humor she didn't always understand. He obviously loved his children.

And he was the Prince of the Darkness, the High Lord of Hell—and Andulvar Yaslana's friend.

"This is more exciting than learning that some wolves can talk," she said.

He stared at her a moment, then laughed. When he held out his hand, she didn't hesitate to accept it.

"Come along," he said. "If you're feeling up to it, we'd better rescue the poor males who have been trying to deal with Jaenelle."

They were going back to the hotel for the afternoon. Marian could have hugged the High Lord for saying the morning had tired him and he needed to rest. Days spent doing heavy cleaning were less exhausting than a shopping trip with Jaenelle Angelline, and she welcomed the chance to get off her feet. They would have their midday meal at the hotel, and then—

"This evening I'll take you two ladies to dinner," the High Lord said as they waited patiently for a horse-drawn cab that would take them back to the hotel.

Marian's heart sank. They'd made it easy for her to forget she was a servant, that the social status between them was as wide a difference as her Purple Dusk Jewels were to the Black. But those differences would become painfully apparent even before they left the hotel, and she didn't want him to feel ashamed of being seen with her.

"You don't have to include me," Marian said. "I'm sure you and Lady Angelline—"

"You don't want to join us?" His words were gently spoken, but there was an undercurrent she didn't understand. "Why?"

She had an odd feeling that it wasn't their acceptance of her but her acceptance of them that was really being questioned. So she told the truth and hoped he was one of those males who understood female vanity. "I don't have anything suitable to wear." Which was true. She was wearing the skirt and tunic Jaenelle had given her, and they were the best clothes she owned—far nicer than the things Luthvian had handed down to her—but they weren't appropriate for dining out.

The High Lord froze, and Jaenelle, who had been watching the street for a cab, slowly pivoted to face her. The chilly anger in the High Lord's eyes made her nervous, but it was the cold fury in the Queen's eyes that scared her.

The next thing she knew, a cab pulled up, she was bundled into it, and the High Lord was giving instructions to take them to the clothing shops.

Not sure what she'd done to upset both of them, she hunched in her seat, her wings curved around her body since that was the only way she could sit in a cab that wasn't designed for winged passengers. She didn't dare mention that the High Lord had wanted to rest or that she didn't think she could afford a dress from any shop he would choose to patronize. She stayed quiet to avoid having that chilling anger focused on her.

Besides, even though he'd initiated this extra shopping trip, the High Lord *was* a man, and based on her observations of men who had escorted their ladies to her mother's shop, his interest wouldn't last long and they'd be heading back to the hotel in no time, with or without a suitable dress.

*   *   *

Marian stretched out on the bed, trying not to whimper. Who would have thought *any* man would have that much knowledge or interest in women's clothing? And when that man was the High Lord of Hell . . .

They'd walked into a shop that catered to Blood from aristo families. Within minutes, merchants from the neighboring shops came running, and she was tossed into the middle of a storm that made the furniture shopping seem calm in comparison. The High Lord found a green dress that complemented her light-brown skin. While she was in the dressing room being carefully measured to have wing slits made in the dress, the cobbler displayed his selection of shoes, other merchants brought selections of skirts, trousers, shawls—anything that complemented the Eyrien coloring of brown skin, black hair, and gold eyes was presented to the High Lord for inspection. He selected, Jaenelle bullied her into trying things on, and two hours later, when even Jaenelle's energy began to flag and the merchants were looking dazed and exhausted, she had a wardrobe of the finest clothes she'd ever owned.

The door opened and Jaenelle walked into the room they were sharing. "Papa just wants to sleep for a while, but I'm going down to the dining room to get something to eat. What about you?"

What about her? She couldn't raise her head off the pillow. "I'm not hungry."

Jaenelle smiled. "All right. You get some rest."

"Why were you so angry about the clothes?"

Jaenelle came over to the bed and crouched down so Marian wouldn't have to look up at her. "When you were staying with Luthvian, did she take you to any of the shops in Doun?"

There was something under that question, but she was too tired to be cautious. "For some underwear. She gave me some clothes that didn't suit her anymore." And had implied that even those were too good for a lowly housekeeper.

Jaenelle nodded, a mix of sadness and anger in her eyes. "I asked Luthvian to take you to the shops so that you could buy new clothes, and since I know her well enough to know she'd complain about spending any of her income on anyone but herself, I gave her enough gold marks to purchase those clothes. The fact that she chose to do otherwise . . ." She sighed. "Everything has a price. She made her choice, and the rest of the family will make theirs."

"I don't want to cause trouble."

"You didn't." Jaenelle gave Marian's arm a sisterly pat. "Get some rest. We'll have a lovely dinner tonight, and tomorrow we'll go to Dharo."

Jaenelle was at the door before Marian managed to prop herself up on her elbows. "Dharo?"

Jaenelle grinned. "We still have to buy carpets, and there's no one in Kaeleer who makes finer carpets than the weavers of Dharo."

Marian stared at the door long after Jaenelle was gone. Dharo. Carpets. Another day of shopping.

She pressed her face into her pillow . . . and whimpered.

ELEVEN

S narling softly, Lucivar paced the flagstone courtyard in front of his eyrie.

Where in the name of Hell was she? He'd told Jaenelle he needed two days. *Two days.* All right, fine. He understood—eventually— why Marian hadn't come back last night. Maybe they'd finished their . . . whatever—he couldn't remember what he'd suggested Jaenelle do as a way to keep Marian out of Ebon Rih—too late to come back last night. And he wouldn't expect them at sunrise, since Jaenelle wasn't someone you dared talk to until she'd had her first cup of coffee. But it was almost midday now, and his sister *still* hadn't returned his hearth witch.

He missed her. He hadn't noticed her absence too much while the men were working all around him, but at the end of the day, when he went into the eyrie alone . . .

She warmed the place, just by being there. When he stepped inside, he could feel the comfort of her presence. There were days when he thought she was really getting used to him, and they were two people who were interested in each other and moving toward living together instead of living in the same place. And there were other days when she withdrew from him for no reason, when the way she held herself made it clear that he was the Prince and she was the housekeeper.

He'd been careful. He kept a choke hold on his body's response to her so that he wouldn't touch her in a way that made her think he required sex from her. But he wanted an invitation to her bed, wanted to take her into his bed, just . . . wanted. Not knowing what he did that made her turn away from him put a dangerous edge of frustration on an already well-honed temper.

She needed time. He would give her time. She would be skittish until she really trusted that he wouldn't hurt her. So he would be patient.

He. Would. Be. Patient.

He glanced at the empty stairs leading down to the landing place and snarled.

Where was she?

A few moments later, he felt her presence at the landing place, along with Jaenelle and . . .

He glanced up at the sky. What was Sactan doing here at this time of day?

His anticipation of having her home again suddenly tangled with an attack of nerves. What if she hated what he'd done here in the past two days? What if she was disappointed?

Then he saw her coming up the last few steps. She looked tired. She looked wonderful. He wanted to sweep her up into his arms and hold on, just to be close to her. Because he couldn't do that, he stood waiting, motionless.

Marian smiled at him when she reached the flagstones, with Jaenelle right behind her. Since his nerves were fraying, he directed a searing look—and his temper—at his sister. "You're late."

"Marian and I had been talking about books, and since we stopped at the town house in Amdarh overnight, we waited until the book shops opened this morning," Jaenelle replied coolly.

Marian hurried toward him, stopping just out of reach. "It's my fault. There were so many books to choose from, and I hadn't realized you'd expected me back at a . . . particular . . ." Her voice trailed off as she noticed the new stone wall and the wooden gate that opened off the courtyard. Silent, she went over to the gate, opened it, and followed the flagstone path Tarl had laid out around the beds that were bordered by stone or wood. She looked around, saying nothing.

"I don't know what's got you in such a snit this morning," Jaenelle said as she came up beside him, "but whatever it is—" She stopped. Looked. "Oh. Oh, Lucivar."

He watched her follow the same path, watched her touch Marian's shoulder. And he felt a sharp stab in the gut when Marian turned and he saw tears in her eyes.

"You did well, Prince," Saetan said quietly.

Lucivar turned his back on the two women now holding each other. "Yeah. I did so well, I made her cry."

"Underneath her quiet nature, she is a woman of strong emotions. You gave her a gift that means something. Did you expect her to respond with a polite 'thank you'?"

"I didn't expect her to cry," Lucivar muttered. Since he didn't want to deal with weepy females, he studied the man. The pride, and approval, in Saetan's eyes went a long way toward easing his nerves.

As Saetan walked to the other side of the courtyard to look at the walled yard and borders Tarl and the other men had planted, Lucivar noticed the slight limp that marred his father's normally smooth stride. Which meant Saetan's bad leg was bothering him—something it only did when he worked it too hard.

"Why are you here?" Lucivar asked.

"To complete my escort duties," Saetan replied.

Lucivar frowned. "Why were you doing escort duties?"

Turning back to look at him, Saetan said dryly, "Because I'm your father." He gestured toward the eyrie's open front door. "Why don't we give the ladies a few more minutes while we take care of the rest?"

The rest? Lucivar wondered as he followed his father into the eyrie. "The rest of what?"

"The furniture."

"What furniture?"

Saetan just looked at him, his expression equal parts pity and amused irritation. "What, exactly, did you ask your sister to do?"

Lucivar resisted the urge to squirm. "Get Marian out of Ebon Rih for two days."

"And Jaenelle was to accomplish this by . . . ?"

He didn't know where this was leading, but he was certain he wasn't going to like it. He shrugged, trying to find the arrogance that came naturally to an Eyrien male. That he couldn't quite find it while his father stared at him worried him. A lot. But he finally remembered what he'd told Jaenelle when she'd asked him what excuse she should use for commanding Marian's time for two days. "I told her to buy a carpet or a piece of furniture, something that would interest a hearth witch."

"A carpet," Saetan said slowly. "A piece of furniture. I see." He sighed and raised his hand.

The room was suddenly filled with furniture, with barely enough room between the pieces for someone to squeeze by.

Lucivar stared. "What is this?"

"The furniture your sister purchased on your behalf. At your request."

"But—"

"I'll put the dining table and chairs in the dining room," Saetan said, walking down the narrow corridor he'd left open.

"Table? Chairs?" Lucivar hurried after his father. By the time he reached the room, a table and eight chairs were tucked against one wall.

Saetan frowned. "Probably best to leave the carpets in here, too."

"Carpets?"

A stack of rolled carpets appeared, filling half the room.

The prick of disappointment surprised him. While he'd had no real desire to endure the miserable task of looking at furniture, he'd wanted to buy his own so that the eyrie would feel like a home that reflected who he was instead of living in a place someone else had created. Not that he actually knew how to achieve that, but still . . .

"You did want to choose for yourself, didn't you?" Saetan asked with too much understanding.

Lucivar shrugged. Jaenelle had spent the past two days doing this for him—and had dragged Saetan into it as well—so he would never say anything that would dim her pleasure.

"If it helps at all," Saetan said, "Marian selected most of it, and what she didn't select herself wasn't purchased without her approval. With one exception."

The prick of disappointment changed into a hum of interest as Lucivar returned to the front room and studied the furniture more carefully.

Marian had chosen these things. Which meant she'd be comfortable living with them. If she was pleased, that was enough to satisfy him.

Then he remembered the last thing Saetan had said. "What's the exception?"

"Ah," Saetan said. "You're going to have to dig in your heels about this one."

They retreated to an empty room. When Saetan called in the last piece of furniture, Lucivar just studied it, trying to figure out why this was different from the rest.

"What is it?" he finally asked.

Saetan lifted a finger. Doors and drawers opened. "It's a sewing cabinet. To store supplies. Marian enjoys weaving in her free time, and she's used to sewing most of her own clothes. She wanted this but couldn't afford it—"

"She can buy anything she damn well wants to," Lucivar growled.

Saetan nodded. "You know that, I know that, and Jaenelle knows that. Marian hasn't figured it out yet, and I think her status as a lowly housekeeper is being reinforced on a regular basis."

His growl deepened, and he turned on his father. "She isn't a lowly *anything*. She's a warm, caring woman with her own talents and her own skills and just because she earns a wage for using those skills—"

The chilling anger in Saetan's eyes stopped him. Something had pricked the High Lord's temper in the last two days. It simmered below the surface, tightly leashed, but it was going to explode. Soon.

His mind raced, thinking of the way Marian retreated from him some days, using the position of housekeeper as a wall between them. Saetan must have brushed against that same wall, but the High Lord, who had a far keener understanding of women than his son did, had realized what reinforced that wall. Since she lived in Ebon Rih, who would keep telling Marian she was nothing but a lowly—

His eyes locked with Saetan's, and seeing the answer, he swore softly, viciously, while his temper soared.

"I'll take care of it," Saetan said too softly. "You shouldn't tangle with your mother over this."

"Why not?" Lucivar snapped. "She loves me because I'm her son and hates me because I'm an Eyrien warrior, so we're not exactly cordial with each other." And that love, he remembered bitterly, had been skewed enough that she'd given him away and he'd grown up believing he was a half-breed bastard, fighting, always fighting, for a place within Eyrien society.

"I will deal with this, Lucivar."

A father's command. Besides, Lucivar knew with chilling certainty how he'd respond if Luthvian used her particular kind of Craft to harm Marian in any way, and knowing she had already tried to poison with words what he was trying to build . . . It was better if he stayed away from his mother for a while.

When they walked out the side door of the eyrie into the garden, Jaenelle gave them a slashing look.

I shielded her, Jaenelle told them. *Having your tempers wash over her would have spoiled her pleasure, so if it's not already settled, pick another time and place for it.*

It's settled, Saetan replied.

Lucivar nodded.

Turning back to Marian, Jaenelle smiled. "Papa and I have to go now. I'll send over those cuttings in a day or two. You've got enough to plant right now."

"Oh," Marian said. "I'm sorry. I didn't even think. Would you like something to eat before you go?"

"No, thank you," Saetan replied, giving Marian a warm smile.

Not sure how annoyed Jaenelle was with him for letting his temper slip, Lucivar breathed a sigh of relief when she kissed him before accepting Saetan's arm and walking back to the landing place where the Coach waited for them.

Which left him alone with Marian, who gave him a shy smile. He would have taken a kiss from her, too, but suggesting it, even teasingly, would upset her, so he settled for the smile.

"Thank you," she said. "It's wonderful. Better than I imagined it could be."

"You're pleased with it, then?"

"Oh, yes."

He nodded. "It'll look even better when you've got everything in place."

He'd meant it as a compliment, so he didn't know what to think when her eyes widened and she began to look distressed.

"Oh," she said. "The furniture."

"It's fine."

"I know the work in the eyrie comes first, so I won't—"

She stopped when he raised his hand.

They were going to learn to compromise. She might as well start learning now.

"There's a lot of plants here," he said, nodding toward the dozens of clay pots that clogged several of the paths around the beds. "Since they're living things, you have to deal with them first. So we're going to compromise."

She studied him warily. "Compromise."

"Yeah." His mood lightened. He was going to piss her off, and she was just going to have to deal with it. "If you want to stay in the garden from sunrise to sundown until everything is planted, that's fine with me—as long as you promise not to lift one piece of furniture, using Craft or otherwise."

"But the furniture needs to be arranged and—"

"And I'll do the moving, the lifting, whatever it takes to put the pieces where you want them. You try to go around me and do it yourself, you're going to spend a day in bed resting, no matter what else you think you have to do."

He watched her hands curl into fists.

"You call that a compromise?" Her voice almost rose to a shout.

He pretended to consider, then sighed. "All right. You can move the lamps."

"The lamps."

It took effort, but he managed not to grin. If he'd done this to Jaenelle, she'd be hissing and spitting at him right about now. Obviously, it would take a little more effort to get Marian to the hissing and spitting stage.

"Your sister wouldn't have to compromise."

Now he did grin. "Yes, she would."

That threw her off enough to lose the glint of temper. "But . . . she's the Queen."

"She's also a smart woman who recognizes a losing battle when she sees one."

He watched her think it through. If Jaenelle couldn't butt heads with him over something like this and win, she didn't have a chance of winning, either.

"Why don't I heat up something to eat?" he said.

"I can—"

"Compromise."

She frowned at him.

"I'll heat up something to eat, and you can check the tools in the shed to make sure you have everything you need."

Her eyes lit up as she spun around to look at the shed the men had built between two of the border beds. She hesitated a moment, then looked back at him. "We'll compromise."

The happiness that flowed from her as she hurried down the path to the shed made his heart stumble. He wanted this. He wanted her. He wasn't going to think about anything else for the next day or two, giving himself the pleasure of working with her to build a home for both of them, even if she didn't realize it yet.

And he would let his father deal with the obstacle standing in his way.

TWELVE

Saetan watched the students hurry out the front door of Luthvian's three-story stone house. They didn't notice him standing just beyond the low wall that enclosed her land. The shields he'd wrapped around himself guaranteed *no one* would sense him until he wanted his presence known. So he had time to study the house he'd had built for Lucivar's mother, had time to tighten the chains that held his temper under control.

The anger that shimmered through him was a sly thing that had twined around memories he'd pushed aside so long ago he'd felt only the echo of them as he'd watched Marian over the past two days. But the echo had been enough to prick at him, warning him that something wasn't right—that something might happen again that had happened before. When he finally recognized what it was about a quiet, gentle hearth witch that made him edgy . . .

He watched his younger son pace the study, a storm waiting to break.

"Peyton . . . what's wrong?"

It wasn't hatred in the young Warlord Prince's eyes. Not quite. But what he saw twisted a knot in his belly.

"I asked Shira to marry me," Peyton snarled.

Where was the joy that should have accompanied those words? Peyton was in love with the Dharo witch, and her feelings for Peyton ran just as deep. He'd been sure of that during the times when Peyton had brought Shira to the Hall to spend time with the family. His son wasn't a fool. Peyton understood that marrying a witch who didn't come from one of the three long-lived races meant their union would be a lifetime for her and, for him, a few decades in a life that would span centuries. But everything has a price, and loving deeply for a few decades was better than yearning for that kind of love and never having it be part of your life. Wasn't it?

"You asked her to marry you," he said cautiously, wondering what had gone wrong, because it was clear something had gone wrong.

"You don't need to worry about me diluting the SaDiablo bloodline with an inferior woman, Father. She's decided we won't suit."

The insult within Peyton's words stunned him for a moment. "What are you talking about?"

"She won't have me!" Peyton shouted. "I love her with everything in me, and I know she loves me, but she won't marry me because—" He stopped, his hands curling into fists as he clenched his teeth.

He locked his fingers together to hide the trembling in his own hands. "Because . . . ?" he asked gently.

Peyton stared at him, tears and fury in those gold eyes. "Because of you."

A son couldn't choose crueler words to lance a father's heart.

Breathing hard, Peyton came forward, slapped his hands on the desk. "The woman I love won't have me because of you. Because you're the High Lord of Hell. Because she's afraid something will happen to her family if she doesn't take the hints that she's tolerable as a lover to satisfy a Warlord Prince's needs but won't be tolerated if she dares become a wife."

His own temper sharpened but couldn't get past the slicing pain inflicted by the words.

"I've never . . . I've never done anything to indicate she wasn't welcome. Peyton, you know that."

"Do I?" Peyton shoved away from the desk. "Do you think I care about our precious bloodline? Do you think it makes any difference to me that she's a musician and earns her living by using the talents she has? Do you think I give a damn that she doesn't come from an aristo family?"

"How could you think those things would matter to me?" It was a heartfelt cry that went unheard.

Peyton returned to the desk, placed his hands on the glossy surface, and leaned forward. "You got what you wanted, High Lord—"

"It's not what I wanted!"

"—but you aren't going to get everything." Peyton stepped away. "I lost Shira—and you lost me." He turned and walked toward the door.

"Peyton!" His legs were shaking too much to hold him. He braced his hands against the desk.

The Warlord Prince who turned to face him was no longer the son he loved, wasn't anyone he recognized.

"I'm leaving," Peyton said quietly. "The only way you can stop me is by killing me."

He sank back into the chair as his son walked out of the study, walked out of the Hall . . . walked out of his life.

Saetan closed his eyes and concentrated on breathing. Just breathing.

The split between him and Peyton had shattered the family for months. It was Mephis who finally realized who had been whispering the poisoned, honeyed words that had made Shira run away from the man she'd loved.

He'd been so devastated by Peyton's accusations, he hadn't thought of Hekatah. Mephis and Peyton had been children when he'd divorced her after she'd tried to shatter his friendship with Andulvar Yaslana by seducing his closest friend and flaunting the pregnancy that had come from that seduction. Instead, Andulvar had kept the child, and Saetan had severed his marriage to a woman who had loved nothing but the power she thought she could control through him.

When the boys were young, he'd refused to let her see them anywhere except the Hall, where they would be under his watchful eye and protection. But once they'd made the Offering to the Darkness and were old enough—and strong enough—to protect themselves, he hadn't interfered whenever they wanted to spend time with their mother.

So he hadn't thought of her—and he should have. He should have. Hekatah wouldn't have tolerated *her* bloodline being fouled by a musician from Dharo, and once Mephis got him to think past the heartache, he'd realized running had saved Shira's life. Because Hekatah wouldn't have hesitated to destroy anything or anyone who didn't suit her own schemes and ambitions.

And even after Mephis convinced his brother that it had been Hekatah and not Saetan who had slashed love into pieces, even after Peyton began returning again to visit, there was a distance between them neither of them could quite bridge . . . because he was the High Lord of Hell. And because Peyton never loved that deeply again. He'd watched from a distance as Shira made a life for herself, watched her love again enough to accept another man as her husband and the father of her children. Watched those children grow and have children. And when the war came between the Realms of Kaeleer and Terreille, Peyton hadn't stayed in Dhemlan Terreille to help Mephis defend that Territory. He'd gone to Dharo in Kaeleer to defend the family of the woman who had died centuries before—and had taken his heart with her.

Now there was another son who was falling in love—and another mother whose intentions were suspect.

He didn't go around to the gate in the wall at the front of the house. He simply used Craft to pass through the stones and walked straight to the kitchen door. He didn't drop the shields until a thought blasted the kitchen door open and he stepped across the threshold.

Luthvian dropped the dish she was holding when she saw him. He measured the fear dancing in her eyes and felt a grim pleasure in seeing it. At least he wouldn't have to put up with her pretending she didn't know why he was there. But he would give her a chance to defend her own actions. Considering what he was about to tell her, it was the least he could do.

"Why?" he asked too softly.

Luthvian licked her lips. "I don't know what you mean."

"Yes, you do, but I'll be specific since you want to pretend ignorance. Why are you trying to hurt Lucivar?"

She looked stunned, then offended. "I'm *not* trying to hurt Lucivar!"

"Aren't you?"

Fear gave way to temper. "Of course not! He's my son."

"He's *my* son, and I won't tolerate you interfering in his life."

"Interfering?" She stepped over the broken dish, coming closer to him. "I may be protecting him from acting rashly, but that's hardly interfering."

"*Protecting him?*" His temper slipped the leash enough that his voice became thunder. "You think undermining the bond he's trying to build with a woman is *protecting him?*"

"She's nothing but a hearth witch!" Luthvian yelled. "A nobody! Her family isn't even a twig on an aristo family tree!"

"Who gives a damn if she's aristo or not? Lucivar doesn't. I certainly don't. I came from a street whore who wasn't even skilled enough to work in a Red Moon house, so I never had an obsession for bloodlines."

"*You* may have come from a Hayllian slum," Luthvian sneered, "but I can trace my line back to Andulvar Yaslana, and that means something!"

"More to the point, you can trace your bloodline back to Andulvar's son, Ravenar. Which means you can trace your bloodline back to Hekatah—and it's *that* bloodline that seems to be rising dominant in you."

She staggered back as if he'd struck her. It was possible she'd never known that Ravenar hadn't been pure Eyrien, but she had to have realized her *bloodline* wasn't pure Eyrien. That's why there were a few Eyrien women each generation who were born without wings. They were throwbacks to Hayllian or Dhemlan women who'd mated with Eyrien males. In Luthvian's case, that woman had been Hekatah.

"You don't know that," she whispered.

"Oh, yes, I do," he replied softly. As he looked at her, he knew it was time to finish it. She'd been a troubled young woman when he'd seen her through her Virgin Night. She was still a troubled woman—and there was nothing he could do to help her beyond providing her with this house to live in. But he could, and would, protect Lucivar.

"I lost Lucivar once because of you," he said. "I won't lose him again. So listen carefully, Luthvian, because I will only say this once. Stay away from Marian. Don't interfere in Lucivar's life. If they want each other, that is their choice, not yours. If you do anything to try to take her away from him, I will show you the darkest corner of Hell—and I will leave you there."

"You'd—You'd kill me?"

His voice became viciously gentle. "No, my dear. You'll still be among the living when I leave you there."

She sank to the floor, shaking.

Satisfied that she understood he would leave her as prey for everything in the Dark Realm that relished fresh meat and hot blood, he walked out of the kitchen. He waited until he had passed through the low stone wall before he caught the Red Wind and rode it to the Keep. Tonight he needed that dark sanctuary while he wrestled with bitter memories that still had the power to hurt.

THIRTEEN

"N o." Unable to sit a moment longer, Lucivar sprang out of the chair. He didn't like this. Didn't like any of this. Especially the fact that Saetan had chosen the sitting area of his study as the place for this discussion. He wasn't sure if he was talking to his father or the Steward of the Dark Court. Didn't matter. He knew when he was being cornered. "Find someone else."

"There is no one else," Saetan said quietly.

Restless, he prowled from one piece of furniture to the next, never looking directly at Saetan but always keeping him in sight. "Why not ask Chaosti? He wears the Gray, and he's First Circle."

"He doesn't, as yet, have enough experience in bed to handle something like this. And his physical relationship with Gabrielle is still too new for him to respond . . . appropriately. Besides, his feelings toward Karla are too familial."

"And mine aren't?"

"You have the maturity to handle this." Saetan sighed. "I know sex is . . . difficult . . . for you—"

"You know nothing about it!" Lucivar shouted. "You have no idea what it was like, being used that way."

Seeing Saetan flinch, he regretted the words, but not enough to stop himself from using whatever weapon he could to avoid this particular duty.

"Lucivar," Saetan said, his voice painfully calm, "Karla is a Gray-Jeweled Queen. Her Territory is divided between the Blood who supported her uncle and the vile changes he was making in their society and the Blood who have waited desperately for Karla to come of age and stand as Glacia's Queen. Until she has her Virgin Night, she is vulnerable and could be broken, could be stripped of the Gray. Without her strength, civil war could erupt in Glacia and devastate her people."

He knew all of that, but it didn't make it easier. "She doesn't like men," he muttered. "Not that way."

"Which will make this even harder for her, since she doesn't have interest in the male body to quicken her own body's response." Saetan rubbed his forehead. "If I was physically able to do this, I wouldn't have asked you. I would have taken care of it—because it's Karla."

Lucivar stared at his father. When the coven first came to visit Jaenelle here at the Hall, they adopted Saetan as an honorary uncle. But over the five years since then, he'd become an uncle to all of them in heart, the man who had trained them in Craft the way no one else in Kaeleer could have, the man who had helped them with problems, disciplined them for mistakes, taught them about honor. Considering the justifiable fears Karla had had about her uncle by blood, having Uncle Saetan take her to bed for her Virgin Night would have been a nightmarish experience for both of them. But Saetan would have done it, knowing he would lose the young woman he loved like another daughter in order to save the Queen. If Saetan would have been willing to pay that price, could he do any less? He was First Circle in Jaenelle's court. So was Karla. He couldn't turn away from a request to help a First Circle Queen. And, really, wasn't this just another kind of battlefield? Normally, the Virgin Night was a witch's initiation to sex as well as the act that would protect her power, but the likelihood of Karla ever taking another man to bed were slim to none, so bedroom skills weren't as necessary as a warrior's skills. He just had to get her safely from one side of this battlefield to the other.

He closed his eyes, accepting his duty while his stomach churned.

"Everything has a price," he said quietly. He opened his eyes in time to see the hint of disapproval in Saetan's before it was masked.

Saetan hesitated before saying, "I'm sure Karla would be willing—"

"Not from Karla. From you."

No hesitation this time. "Then name your price. I'll pay it."

That simple. Not even the usual, sensible precaution of asking what the price would be in case it was too high to pay.

"After," Lucivar said. "We'll discuss it after I've seen her through this." Because he knew what he wanted. They didn't need it hanging between them while they both needed to stay focused on the task ahead.

Saetan rose gracefully. "I'll inform Karla of your decision and make the preparations. Come up to the room when you're ready."

Lucivar waited until his father left the study before he covered his face with his hands. *Please. Sweet Darkness, please let me get her through this.*

Wishing fiercely that his brother Daemon was there to offer advice, he left the study and headed toward the bedroom that would be a very personal kind of battleground.

Saetan had chosen a guest room in another wing of the Hall. Lucivar felt grateful for that since he wouldn't have to remember whatever happened here every time he looked at his own bed. And neither would Karla when she stayed in the suite of rooms she'd been given as her own here at the Hall. But the lack of personal effects in the room also made him feel a bit . . . dirty. Just another male acting the slut.

Leaning one arm against the mantel, he glanced at the small table that held two goblets and a heavy glass container, its contents being kept warm by a small tongue of witchfire.

Night of Fire. The aphrodisiac brew used for a Virgin Night.

Remembering the kinds of aphrodisiacs the witches in Terreille used on a man, he shuddered. It didn't matter that Saetan had made this brew. The thought of drinking it produced a stab of fear in him. The problem was, he wasn't sure he'd be any use to Karla if he didn't drink it.

"I'm sorry," Karla said. "If there was another way . . ."

He shook his head as he looked at her. Her fair skin had a touch of sickly green. She looked so young, standing there in a simple cotton nightgown, waiting for him to open her body and spill the virginal blood that would protect her power as a witch.

"You didn't want to do this," she said.

"No," he replied honestly.

"Why?"

Would it make it easier for both of them if he explained? "I've only done this once before."

Karla swallowed hard. "And it went badly?"

Lucivar looked away. "Not for her." The memory he'd pushed away so long ago rose up, choking him. "The hunting camp I was in at the time . . . The young males who were deemed ready were taken to the Blood Run to test their strength against it. Once an Eyrien male successfully makes the Blood Run, he's considered a warrior.

"Well, we all survived the Run, which doesn't always happen. We guested at a nearby eyrie to celebrate. Plenty of food, plenty to drink . . . and women who were willing to bed newly acknowledged warriors eager to test their other skills.

"One young witch lavished attention on me—the kind of attention I seldom got in Askavi. When she led me to one of the bedrooms, I was imagining a lusty night of hot sex—and was young enough and stupid enough to want it. Well, after a few kisses it was clear something was wrong. That's when she admitted she was a virgin. She'd been refusing the warriors who lived in that eyrie because she was certain any of them would do his best to break her, and she didn't want to lose what power she had.

"So I put aside my own expectations and saw her through her Virgin Night."

"So what went wrong?" Karla asked.

Shame clogged his throat. He swallowed it, just as he'd swallowed it centuries ago. "The next morning, when I went to join the other warriors for a meal before heading back to the hunting camp . . . She was serving up food with the other women. I went over to her, just to talk to someone who would think kindly of me. But the other women must have told her who I was. What I was. Must have teased her about giving herself to a half-breed bastard. So instead of saying anything or even smiling at me, she . . . spit on me."

The memory swamped him. The disgust in her eyes. The cruel laughter of the men. The reminder that they had to accept his status as a warrior but would never accept him.

"Bitch."

The sudden chill in the air jolted him back to the present. Karla's glacier blue eyes flashed with fury. Her Gray power rolled through the room.

Before he could think of how to respond, there was a sharp rap on the door and Saetan walked into the room.

Great. That was just great. He really needed confirmation that his father was staying so close in case something went wrong.

After looking at him, then at Karla, Saetan asked quietly, "Is something wrong?"

"That bitch spit on him after he got her through her Virgin Night!" Karla shouted.

The room had been chilly before. Now it was frigid as Saetan's eyes glazed with cold rage.

"Who?" Saetan asked too softly.

Oh, no. "It doesn't matter. It was a long time ago."

Karla grabbed a pillow and began shredding it as she stormed around the room. "The bitch deserves having her heart ripped out—if she has a heart."

"Who?" Saetan asked again.

Hell's fire, Mother Night, and may the Darkness be merciful. Maybe he should have known better, but he hadn't expected *this*.

"Can we discuss this outside?" He gestured toward the door.

"You're not going to let that bitch get away with this, are you, Uncle Saetan?" Karla demanded.

That's just what he needed—a Gray-Jeweled Queen goading a Black-Jeweled Warlord Prince to rise to the killing edge.

Saetan walked out of the room. Lucivar followed, closing the door firmly behind him.

"Who?" Saetan asked for the third time.

"I don't remember her name," he lied. He remembered everything about her, everything about that night and the morning after.

"Liar," Saetan crooned.

If Daemon had said that to him in that tone of voice, he'd have braced himself for a terrifying kind of fight.

"You never saw another witch through her Virgin Night because of that bitch," Saetan continued. "Isn't that true?"

He didn't say anything. Wouldn't say anything. Not because he gave a damn what happened to that bitch, but because his father's instant response to a son's pain was as frightening as it was gratifying.

"Let it go," Lucivar said. He deliberately looked at the bedroom door. "This is more important than avenging an old memory."

The fury in Saetan's eyes didn't diminish, but he stepped back, walked down the hallway, and entered a room a few doors down from the one Lucivar stood in front of.

Knowing he'd managed to walk away from one battlefield, Lucivar took a deep breath, opened the door, and prepared to step onto the next one.

Karla was still storming around the room, bits of pillow stuffing stuck in her spiky white-blond hair. When she saw him, she planted her feet in the fighting stance he'd taught her, her eyes fired up for battle.

"What can I do to help you?" she demanded.

He almost laughed, but as he looked at her, he could hear Daemon's voice whispering to him. *She took the bait. Now use it. As long as she's focused on helping you perform, she won't be thinking about why you have to perform. Use what she's offering to get her through what has to be done.*

He sighed, then said hesitantly, "Maybe if we just sat together for a while."

Alarm leaped into her eyes. Had he sounded too uncertain, too hesitant?

There weren't many choices in the room. The armchairs by the hearth weren't made to accommodate a man with wings, but there was one straight-backed chair that had been placed near the window. He led her to it and settled her on his lap.

They stared at each other.

Maybe it would have been easier at night, in the dark, instead of late afternoon with the heat and light of late summer pouring through the open window. Saetan had cleared this wing, so there were no gardeners working outside, no servants in the hallways. But there was still that awareness of people working and moving throughout the rest of the Hall. If Marian had been sitting on his lap, he wouldn't have thought about those people—couldn't honestly say he'd be thinking about anything at all except her.

He pushed that thought aside. It wasn't smart to think of Marian right now. They weren't lovers. He wasn't breaking faith with her by being here. And even if they *were* lovers, seeing a witch through her Virgin Night was a duty to the court, not an act of infidelity.

Thinking about that wasn't helping him either.

He looked at the brew warming in its glass container. No choice.

Using Craft, he lifted the glass container, poured its contents into the two goblets, set the container back on its stand, and extinguished the small tongue of witchfire. When the goblets floated over to him, he handed one to Karla and took the other.

"What is this?" Karla asked, sniffing cautiously.

"Night of Fire. A brew made specifically for . . . this." He braced himself, but couldn't lift the goblet up to drink.

Karla took a sip. Took another. She stared into the goblet. "You only get to have this once?"

He studied her as she sipped again. "I suppose so. Why?"

"Because this stuff is wooonderful."

Wary, he took a swallow of the brew. Nothing happened. The aphrodisiacs he'd experienced in Terreille worked wickedly fast, pumping lust through a man's body before he realized what had happened to him. But this . . . He drank again. Waited. It did taste good. Warm. Ripe. Some kind of brandy or wine as the base, but . . .

His limbs felt warm, relaxed, heavy. His cock felt warm and heavy. Desire softly heated his blood, sharpened his senses to the feel and smell of a female. He drained the goblet, then used Craft to send it gliding on air back to the table. Karla's goblet followed a few moments later.

"What can I do to help you?" she asked, looking at him with lightly glazed eyes.

"Kiss me."

The feel of her mouth on his, hesitant, exploring. The feel of her body as his hands caressed her. Desire, thick and golden, swam in his blood as his hand cupped her breast. Her tongue in his mouth . . . Tart and sweet, just like the woman.

He picked her up and took her to the bed, vanishing her nightgown as he set her down on the sheets. Vanishing his own clothes, he stretched out beside her, putting an Ebon-gray shield around his left hand and forearm before he pinned her wrists above her head. Being a Black Widow as well as a Queen, she had a snake tooth beneath the ring finger of her right hand. He didn't need her pumping venom into him in a moment of panic.

Her body responded to him as he kissed, caressed, and suckled, but he felt a tension rising in her. She'd fight him when the time came. Even knowing he was doing this for her, she'd still fight him—unless she was sufficiently distracted. There were different ways of protecting a witch during that moment when her life hung by a hymenal thread, but this way . . . Yes. If she trusted him enough to let him in, she'd be captured, distracted, and protected.

"Karla," he said, his hand still caressing her. "Will you let me in?"

She panted, but it wasn't excitement that made her breathless. "What?"

A psychic touch. A soft brush against her first inner barrier. "Will you let me in?"

She flinched at that light touch, too aware that he was strong enough to force open those barriers. But she opened herself to him, let him glide through the surface layers of her mind. She began to shake when he got close to her core. In another moment, she would try to push him out.

He moved with a warrior's speed and training, wrapping his power around her so fast, she had no time to evade. In his mind, he held a picture of his arms wrapped around her naked body, her back pressed against his chest as tendrils of power strapped her legs to his, leaving her helpless.

"Hold on," he said—and launched them both skyward.

Wings pumping. Blue sky above them. He turned—and sent them diving toward a canyon in Askavi that he knew well. While he pictured the canyon's physical details, he didn't take her through the experience of making the Khaldharon Run. He had to keep his attention divided between what he was doing in the real world and this fantasy he was building to distract her. Even in a fantasy, the Khaldharon Run was too dangerous to play with. So he changed it to a straight flight down the center of the canyon, flying at the speed of the Red Wind, flying so close to the river below them a miscalculation would end with them hitting the water with bone-breaking force.

She squealed and swore at him, but her body was primed for the taking now. As they approached the wall of stone at the end of the Run, he positioned himself between her legs . . . and waited.

They swung up out of the Run and continued flying up, up, up. Releasing the bonds that strapped her legs to his, he flipped her between one pump of his wings and the next so they were now face-to-face. Her arms locked around his neck as he strapped their legs again. His arms wrapped around her, his hard cock pressed against her.

Up, up, up.

"Ready?" he asked.

"For what?" she yelled.

He laughed, folded his wings, and twisted. For one endless moment, they hung motionless before they plummeted toward the ground far below them. And in that moment when they began the fall, he thrust into her.

The speed and exhilaration of free fall. He spun them, laughing, while in another place, his body thrust into hers, pushing her toward climax.

She squeezed her eyes shut and swore at him as the ground rushed toward them and pleasure burst through their bodies.

He opened his wings, changing the picture in his mind as he glided over treetops to settle them in a glen that was one of his favorite places in Ebon Rih.

As he laid her on the grass near a pool of water, he unwrapped the power that had held her captive while he withdrew from her body.

Fully back in the bedroom now, he settled beside her, pulling the sheet up to their waists. They would deal with the practicalities in a few minutes. It wasn't something she needed to see just yet.

"Mother Night," Karla muttered over and over. She finally opened her eyes. "Is that your idea of a good time?"

He grinned. "Actually . . . it is."

She swore at him.

She looked a little pissed, a little dazed.

"It's done," he said gently.

"What's done?"

He rested a hand on her belly.

She stared up at him. "Done? But . . . . how? When?"

He laughed. "When you were watching the ground come up to meet us."

"Who said I was watching?" She blew out a breath and finally began to relax. "Well, that was a unique experience."

He watched the tension build in her and worried about the grim expression that settled over her face.

"Lucivar," she said, staring at the ceiling. "When I asked Uncle Saetan to arrange this, I wasn't thinking about . . . I wasn't thinking. But it's not my fertile time. I swear it's not."

"It's all right. I've been drinking a contraceptive brew for a few weeks now." He'd never had to think about it when he'd lived in Terreille, never had to wonder if the bitches who had used him could get a child out of him. He'd known that he'd somehow made himself infertile in a way the witches who had wanted him for stud couldn't undo. Just as he'd known within a week of Marian's coming to live in his eyrie that he'd turned the key in that lock so that he could flood her with ripe seed. He wanted a child with her, but not without a bond, not without commitment.

"Why are you drinking a contraceptive brew?" Karla asked. Her eyes widened. "You have a lover, don't you?"

"No."

She moved fast, surprising him enough that he ended up on his back with her on top of him.

"Who is it?" Her mouth curved in a wicked smile. "It's the hearth witch, isn't it? The one you made the garden for."

Just the thought of Marian primed him. He shoved Karla off him and slipped out of bed while he still could. "Let's get cleaned up."

"Cleaned—" Karla flipped the sheet back. "Oh."

When she turned pale, he grabbed her arm and dragged her out of bed and into the bathroom.

"There's no need to get snarly about it," Karla said.

He turned on the shower faucets, waited until there was a hint of hot water, picked her up, and planted her under the spray.

She let out one breathless squeal and tried to punch him when he stepped in behind her.

He soaped one cloth and shoved it into her hands. "Wash." Soaping up another one, he spun her around and started on her back.

"If you've been drinking the contraceptive brew for weeks now, you're safe," Karla said as she washed her breasts and belly. "So why aren't you lovers yet? You want her, don't you?"

"What I want doesn't matter," he growled.

Swiping the hair out of her eyes, she turned to face him. "Does she want you?"

"How in the name of Hell am I supposed to know what she wants?" Gritting his teeth, he began washing himself. He watched for signs of interest, didn't he? If he pushed too fast, she'd run. Hell's fire. He hadn't even tried to kiss her yet because he was afraid she'd run, and he needed her there. He needed to be around her.

His hands curled into fists. He closed his eyes. This wasn't the time or place for anger of any kind. Before he could get his tongue around an apology, Karla nudged him.

"I'm washed," she said. "Trade places. I'll do your back."

Frustrated and miserable, he obeyed.

"It's summer," Karla said as she moved the cloth over his back. "Which means you wear what Eyrien males usually wear during the summer—which is next to nothing, right?"

"What's your point?"

"So maybe you're right about not doing anything obvious. Maybe it would be better to wait until she trips by herself and falls into your waiting arms."

He snorted.

"I mean it." She gave him a light punch. "Look. There you are, flaunting all these lovely muscles day after day—"

"I don't flaunt."

"Sure you do. All the males do. You've just got more to flaunt than a lot of them. You can rinse off now."

He turned to face her to get his back under the spray. "Your point is?"

"Does she ever get a dreamy look when she's doing something simple?"

He stuck his head under the spray. "Sure. When she's planning what bulbs to plant for spring flowers."

"Well, what's she supposed to say? That she's daydreaming about your muscles and it's got her all warm and tingly?"

He considered that for a moment. "Yeah. Why not?"

Karla shook her head and smiled at him. "When she finally gets up the nerve to try to seduce you, don't make her work too hard, all right? And don't scare her with that falling out of the sky stuff."

"She's Eyrien. She'd enjoy free fall."

Karla just stared at him, then looked down. "You know," she said slowly, "since you've got the water so cold, it's hard to tell if it's true about wings being in proportion to—"

"Do you want to find out how cold a mountain lake is even in late summer?" he demanded.

"You've never been in a cold mountain lake until you've been in one in Glacia." She stepped out of the shower. "Taking a swim there will shrivel your assets for a month."

His response as he turned off the water was pungent and succinct.

"That's the Lucivar we all know and love," Karla said, giving him that wicked smile. "Kiss kiss."

Lucivar stared at the study door. *Everything has a price.* He'd wanted this since coming to Kaeleer and being reunited with his father three years ago. Now he would finally get the answer to a question that had haunted him.

Now he wasn't sure he wanted it.

Taking a deep breath to steady himself, he walked into the study.

Saetan rose from the chair behind the blackwood desk and came around the desk so that he could lean against the front of it. "You did well, Prince."

He nodded, warmed by the praise but too edgy to respond to it.

"What's your price, Lucivar?" Saetan asked softly.

"The answer to a question."

Saetan raised one eyebrow and waited.

"Why?" Lucivar asked, thoughts and feelings swelling that one word until he wasn't sure what else to say. But when Saetan just looked at him, he tried to shape the question. "When Daemon and I were taken away from you, why didn't you fight to get us back?"

He watched in amazement as Saetan paled.

"I couldn't," Saetan said after a long pause, his voice rough.

Lucivar took a step toward him. "Why? Even if you couldn't have fought back at that instant, you're a Black-Jeweled Warlord Prince. You could have—"

"*I couldn't.*" A tremor of some strong emotion went through Saetan. He wouldn't look at Lucivar. His deep voice was barely a whisper. "I couldn't. Because of Zuulaman."

Puzzled by Saetan's obvious distress, Lucivar said, "Who is Zuulaman?"

"Not a person. A place." Saetan moved fast and was at the door before Lucivar could raise a hand to stop him. But he hesitated as he opened the door. "If you want to know about Zuulaman, ask Andulvar. In some ways, he remembers better than I do what happened."

Then he was gone, and Lucivar stared at that closed door a long time, wondering what had happened in that place that could make the High Lord run away.

He found Andulvar near the small lake that was part of the estate. He could have pounded on the door of Andulvar's rooms, but the coven had gathered to be with Karla, and he suspected it was better to keep this conversation private. So he'd waited until sundown when the Demon Prince rose from his daylight rest and followed Andulvar to the lake.

"Zuulaman?" Andulvar growled. "Why in the name of Hell are you asking about Zuulaman?"

"I asked my father why he didn't fight to get us back when Daemon and I were taken from him. He said it was because of Zuulaman. He said you'd tell me what that means." Lucivar waited while Andulvar stared at the lake. "Do you remember it?"

Andulvar snorted. "Yeah. I remember Zuulaman." Turning his head, he studied Lucivar for a long time. "Are you sure you want to know this?"

No. "Yes."

Andulvar sighed, went back to staring at the lake . . . and began to talk.

Two hours later, Lucivar walked back into Saetan's study and stopped just inside the door. His father was standing next to the bookcases that filled the wall behind his desk. He held a book open in his hands. He didn't look up, didn't turn a page. Just stood there.

"He told you," Saetan said in a voice stripped of any emotion.

Unnerved and a little queasy, Lucivar worked to keep his voice steady. "He told me."

"So now you know."

Something's wrong here, Lucivar thought as he studied his father. Something about the way Saetan stood made him think of a brittle object that could shatter at the slightest blow.

He shook his head, raked a hand through his black hair. "I don't understand why Dorothea let us live. Once she realized she couldn't use either of us for stud, she should have killed us before we got old enough to make the Offering to the Darkness and come into our full strength."

"She couldn't." Saetan closed the book and put it back on the shelf. "Before I left Terreille for good, I sent Dorothea a message. I told her that on the day Daemon no longer walked among the living, Hayll would become another Zuulaman. I sent the same message to Prythian about you."

Lucivar felt the floor slide out from under him. He took a stagger-step to regain his balance. "But . . . it was a bluff, wasn't it? You wouldn't have done it."

Saetan finally turned and looked at him. "Yes," he said too softly, "I would have."

This wasn't the man he'd come to know over the past three years. He understood now all of Andulvar's cautions about dealing with the High Lord. And yet . . .

He'd seen that look in a man's eyes before. But not in that face, not in those eyes. That was the difference between him and Andulvar, Prothvar, and Mephis. They didn't know Daemon. They had never danced with the Sadist.

He understood the brittleness now. Saetan was waiting for him to turn away. Expected him to turn away. As Andulvar must have done for a while. As his other sons must have done when they became old enough to understand what their father was capable of when provoked beyond rage.

Everything has a price. Carrying the memory was Saetan's price. He didn't have to add to the burden.

"I need to get back to Askavi," Lucivar said, feeling awkward and knowing that what he said now could shatter the bond between them. "I didn't tell Marian I was staying overnight."

"I understand."

No, you don't. You think I'm turning away, and I'm not. "I'll be back in a couple of days." Turning toward the door, he hesitated. "Good night, Father."

He watched the tension seep out of Saetan's body. Saw what might be a shimmer of tears in those gold eyes.

"Good night, Lucivar," his father replied.

It was after midnight when he landed in the courtyard in front of his eyrie. He'd been too churned up to go home when he got back to Ebon Rih, so he'd flown, working his body while he struggled to empty his mind. Now his body was tired, but his mind . . .

There were so many ways he could have died. Accidents happened in the hunting camps when youngsters were being trained to handle weapons. Warriors died trying to prove themselves in the Blood Run or the Khaldharon. There were battles between courts—usually staged as contests and exercises with weapons shielded to do nothing more than bruise, but there were always males who used those contests as an excuse to shed a rival's blood, and there had been plenty of warriors who had resented that a half-breed bastard had fighting skills they could match only in their dreams.

There were so many ways he could have died. And he almost *had* died when he escaped and ended up in Kaeleer. If he had . . .

The door opened behind him. Marian said hesitantly, "Prince Yaslana?"

He turned and looked at the reason his feelings were still churned up. "Come here."

She came toward him, her steps uncertain, trying to gauge his mood. "I could heat up something for you to eat."

He shook his head. "I'm not hungry." He reached out, touched her hair. When his fingers trailed along her shoulder, she started to step back. "Marian . . . Let me hold you. Please. I need to hold you."

She didn't move toward him, but she folded her wings tight so he could wrap his arms around her and draw her up against him. At first, she held herself stiffly, but when he didn't do anything else, she relaxed enough to rest her head on his shoulder and put her arms around his waist.

He brushed his cheek against her hair, savoring the feel of her, the smell of her.

Everything has a price.

He would have to talk to Saetan and reach an agreement. He was an Eyrien warrior and Jaenelle's First Escort. He had to be able to step onto any kind of battlefield and fight to defend his Queen. He had to be willing to die for his Queen. He couldn't do that until he got a promise from Saetan that there wouldn't be another Zuulaman.

His arms tightened around Marian. No Eyrien mattered more to him than she did. So he had to have that promise.

Because if he died without it, the price would be too high.

FOURTEEN

Marian looked at the sugar spilled on the kitchen floor and wanted to cry. Such a little thing. A bobble of the hand that held the sugar bowl. Normally, it would have caused no more than a moment's annoyance before she cleaned it up.

But not today. Not when a taloned fist had curled around her womb and was squeezing hard.

She closed her eyes and braced a hand against the kitchen counter. Maybe once in a year, the physical discomfort that came with her moontime escalated to nauseating pain. When it hit, it made her grateful she didn't wear a Jewel darker than the Purple Dusk because the pain balanced the power that could be wielded the rest of the time, and darker-Jeweled witches always suffered more during the first three days. And no witch could use her Jeweled strength during those first three days without causing herself hideous pain.

Marian opened her eyes and stared at the spilled sugar. The thought of doing any physical labor made her want to curl into a ball and weep, but she knew from experience that even using basic Craft today would increase the pain.

With a shaky sigh, she went to the cupboard in the pantry where she kept her broom and dustpan.

★　　★　　★

Lucivar stopped in the corridor, the scent hitting him with the force of running into a stone wall. His nostrils flared. His lips pulled back in a silent snarl.

Moon's blood.

Some change in a witch's psychic scent or her physical scent triggered that recognition in Blood males once they reached puberty. Maybe it was a trait that had developed long ago as a tool for survival since this was one of the times when the balance of power between the genders swung in the males' favor. A witch who had to defend herself against a male ended up fighting two adversaries: him and her own body.

Which was why the males closed ranks around a Queen during those days when she was vulnerable. Even the mildest-tempered Blood male became edgy and aggressive, but moon's blood drove Warlord Princes to the killing edge. Naturally aggressive and territorial, their response to an unknown male was lethal more often than not. That response was the primary reason Blood males were trained to ignore the scent of moon's blood except for the females in their own family and the Circle of the court they served in.

And that was the problem now, wasn't it? At the Hall, the male servants looked after, and fussed over, the female servants. The family and the boyos took care of Jaenelle and the coven when they were in residence. The boundaries were established, and all the males accepted them.

But there was just the three of them here. He'd gritted his teeth through it the other times, reminding himself that Marian worked for him, so he couldn't yell at her for exerting herself. He couldn't insist that she sit and do something quiet that wouldn't strain her body. He couldn't roar until it brought every male in the area running to find out what was wrong the way he could when Jaenelle got stubborn. There were boundaries and—

Screw boundaries. Marian was *not* going to make him frantic again, seething in silence and trying to keep a slippery hold on his temper while she scrubbed and polished things that could damn well wait a few days before they got scrubbed and polished. They were going to compromise—and if that meant tying her to a chair to make her rest, so be it.

With his temper choked back to simmering—and ready to boil—he strode toward the kitchen to explain a few things to his little hearth witch.

"WHAT IN THE NAME OF HELL ARE YOU DOING?"

The broom jerked in Marian's hands, scattering the sugar she'd just swept into a neat pile. Her heart slammed against her chest. She took a step back as Lucivar stepped through the archway into the kitchen, his lips pulled back in a snarl and a wild look in his eyes.

"You are *not* going to do this again, do you understand me?" he shouted as he walked toward her. "You are *not* going to beat yourself into the ground trying to do more than you should be doing."

The weepy mood vanished. Resentment welled up, hot and bitter. Hearth witches weren't pampered. Other witches might be excused from their work, but hearth witches were expected to grit their teeth and keep going, no matter how they felt. Her mother had worked half days during the first three days of her moontime. Her sisters weren't required to do more than sit quietly and study—and usually complained about doing even that much. She, on the other hand, was expected to prepare the meals and do the cleaning, excused from her work only if the greasy nausea that sometimes accompanied the start of the moon's blood made her too sick.

It had become a matter of pride that she did her work and didn't complain, since that only brought criticism. Now Lucivar was yelling at her for no reason, just when she'd been about to swallow her pride and tell him she really needed to rest for the day. She was even going to ask him to purchase bread at the baker's in Riada so she wouldn't have to make biscuits to go with the stew she was planning to make for the midday meal. Well, she was *not* going to ask *him* for anything now.

"I can do my work," she said, gritting her teeth as she started sweeping up the sugar again.

"You're going to rest if I have to tie you down to make sure you do it."

Oh, she'd love to rest today, but not on *his* terms. Not when he was snarling at her. "What I do is my own business."

"Think again, witchling," Lucivar snapped, moving closer to her. "You live in my eyrie, you're under my protection. And that means protecting you from yourself when you get too stubborn to do what's good for you."

"And you never get stubborn and always do what's good for you," she snapped back. The nerve of the man. Who did he think he was, anyway?

He grabbed the broom handle, his hand closing over it just above her own hands. He tugged. She tugged back, trying to reclaim control. His hand tightened. A fast twist of his wrist and the handle snapped. He took one step back, turned, and threw the piece of wood through the archway.

Marian flinched, expecting to hear a lamp in the other room smashing. Or, worse, the crash as the handle shattered the glass doors that led out to the lawn on the other side of the eyrie.

No smash. No crash. Nothing. Not even the clatter of wood as it fell on the floor.

He must have vanished it before it could hit something.

Before she could react, he yanked the rest of the broom out of her hands, strode to the archway, and threw the broom away.

How could she forget how strong he was? She'd seen him exercising to keep his warrior's body and reflexes sharply honed. She'd seen him chopping wood. Hadn't she watched those wonderful muscles ripple under his skin all summer? He didn't need Craft to be dangerous.

Turning back to the kitchen, he pointed a finger at her, and snarled, "You are not doing anything today."

A wave of temper drowned out nerves. "Don't you tell me what to do! I can do my work!" Irrationally angry and feeling cornered, she grabbed the pot sitting on the stove and threw it at him.

He tucked his wings in at the last second. The pot hit the wall next to the archway and fell to the floor.

Awful silence filled the kitchen.

Lucivar picked up the pot and walked away.

Marian crept to the archway and saw him outside, throwing the pot at the bales of hay he'd set up for target practice. She sagged against the wall. Eyrien males didn't tolerate defiance from a witch who didn't outrank them. Thank the Darkness Lucivar was taking his anger out on a pot and bales of hay. Her father, who didn't technically outrank her since he also wore Purple Dusk Jewels, would have slapped her for arguing with him. Throwing the pot at him would have earned her a fist in the belly, inflicting pain where it would hurt the worst today.

Marian?

She turned and saw Tassle sniffing the spilled sugar.

"Don't step in that. I have to clean it up."

Tassle sniffed the air. *You cannot use Craft.*

She bit back a snappish reply. That furry body made it easy to forget at times that Tassle was more than a wolf. Other times, forgetting that he would respond to some things like any other Warlord would only cause more problems.

"You're right," she said. "I can't use Craft, but—"

I will clean it up for you.

The sugar on the floor vanished. He looked at her, obviously expecting praise.

Even the furry male didn't think she was capable of doing anything today. But she petted him and thanked him. Pleased with himself and satisfied with the praise, he left her to roam the mountain since Yas was there to protect her.

She didn't mention Lucivar might be the very thing she needed protection from. Tassle wouldn't have a chance of surviving if Lucivar decided to punish her and the wolf got in the way.

When she heard Lucivar come back inside, she looked around for something to do. She winced as she bent over and pulled a skillet from the bottom cupboard. He liked her beef stew. Maybe knowing he'd have it for his midday meal would soften his mood.

Trembling, she put the skillet on the stove and stepped back as he entered the kitchen. Throwing the pot hadn't eased his temper. If anything, his mood seemed darker.

He set the pot on the counter beside the sink, and growled, "That won't do it. The balance is off." Spotting the skillet, he picked it up and took it outside.

Returning a few minutes later, he grabbed her arm and hauled her out to the bales of hay.

"What?" Marian said, trying to pull back. "Prince Yaslana—"

He shoved the skillet's handle into her hand. "The pot doesn't have the balance to be an effective weapon. This does."

He moved toward her. She swung the skillet up over her head.

As his hand closed over her wrist, he shook his head. "Not that way. The move takes too long and tells your adversary too clearly what you intend. It has to be fast and unexpected to do you any good." He positioned himself behind her, one hand on her waist, the other still holding her wrist. "You need to attack with a side motion, working from about the same height as if you'd grabbed it off the stove and swung. Your own strength behind the swing would be enough to bruise bone. With a little Craft to enhance it, you can break bone."

"I'm not going to break anyone's bones," Marian said as he moved her arm back and forth in a swing motion. Of course, the thought of denting his head had a lot of appeal at the moment.

"You're not tall enough to make a head shot practical," Lucivar said as if he'd read her thoughts. "But breaking ribs or a forearm would be a good first strike."

"I'm not going to attack anyone with a skillet!"

"Maybe not. But you're going to learn how to do it anyway." He released her and stepped back. "Now swing it and release to hit the target."

She swung it, put nothing behind it, and let it go. It bounced on the ground halfway between her and the target. Satisfied she'd proven her point, she said, "See? It doesn't work."

The skillet flew through the air, straight to Lucivar's hand. He just looked at her until she stepped aside. Moving into the same spot where she'd stood, he swung the skillet in that sideways motion and let it go. It hit the target with enough force to get wedged in the hay. It hung there for a moment before he used Craft to bring it flying back to him.

Saying nothing, he handed the skillet to her.

Having no choice, she swung the skillet. Damn him, this *hurt*. But she knew he wouldn't relent, so she tried to hit the target—and actually came close.

Studying her, he held out one hand. The skillet came flying back to him. "Marian? Do you have everything you want for the kitchen?"

Anger flashed through her. The insufferable prick! Of course she didn't have everything she wanted! It was late autumn now, she'd been working for him for months, and she was still working with the basic tools she'd bought out of her own wages. She'd bought all the canning supplies out of her own wages, was still buying cleaning supplies out of her own wages—and was still waiting for him to broach the subject of a household budget. Oh, he'd told her often enough that she could put anything she needed to buy on his accounts at the stores in Riada, but he only indirectly benefited from her having all the tools she'd like to have, and she didn't feel easy about running up a bill without first getting his consent, and if he wasn't observant enough to see what was going on in his own home, he'd hardly understand why having extra casserole dishes would be helpful.

"The kitchen could use a few things," she said, working hard to keep from yelling at him.

He nodded. "I'll make a deal with you. You hit the target three times out of six tries, you can buy everything you want for the kitchen. If you can't find something you want in the shops in Riada, I'll take you to Amdarh. Buy everything you've wanted but have been doing without and put it on my accounts."

She stared at him. At home, she'd had to beg and plead to get *anything* that would have made her work easier. That was part of the reason she'd been reluctant to say anything to him. She hadn't wanted him to think she was greedy or extravagant, especially when he was so generous with her wages. But now he was *offering* to let her fill the kitchen, like paying off a wager. All she had to do was win and she could buy more casserole dishes so she could make extra meals and store them in the freeze box so she could just heat them up during her moondays.

She took the skillet from him, swung, and threw it. Grim pleasure filled her when the skillet hit the hay bales before bouncing to the ground. It flew back to her, slowing and turning to present the handle to her hand.

More baking sheets so she wouldn't have to waste time waiting for one batch to bake and cool before she could prepare the next. More pie plates so she could make a fruit pie *and* a steak pie to serve at the same meal.

She threw the skillet and hit the hay bales.

A good set of kitchen knives. Utensils that were actually designed for different functions. *More wooden spoons.*

She swung and threw.

When the skillet came back again, she reached for it, her mind full of the useful things the kitchen still needed. But Lucivar just held on to the skillet. He gave her a lazy, arrogant smile, but the unhappiness in his eyes ripped at her.

"That's it," he said, leading her back to the kitchen. "You won. Three out of three. As soon as you feel up to shopping, make your purchases."

Was that why he was so unhappy? Was he worried about the expense? Maybe she should ask him how much she could spend.

He released her arm, set the skillet on the counter, and started to walk away.

"Prince?"

He stopped at the archway and looked at her. "You do what you have to, Marian. If you have to scrub and polish this place when every move hurts you just to prove you can do your work, then that's what you'll do. Short of fighting you to a standstill, I can't stop you. But I can't stay here and watch you do it. We'll work with the skillet again in a few days— and we'll keep working at it until you can use it as a weapon."

He moved fast. She had to dash to the archway to reach it before he reached the front door.

"Are you coming back for the midday meal?" she asked.

"Yeah, I'll be back." He didn't look at her, didn't hesitate. He slammed the front door behind him.

Marian sank down on one of the kitchen chairs and braced her head in her hands. He got mad at her for sweeping up spilled sugar but dragged her outside to throw a skillet at bales of hay. She threw a pot at him and missed, so he was going to teach her how to clobber him with a skillet. Even taking into account that he was an Eyrien male, there was only one explanation for his behavior. The man was insane.

And she'd made him unhappy. She hadn't meant to, but she'd made him unhappy. Of course, she would have told him she'd intended to take things easy today if he hadn't roared at her as soon as he walked into the kitchen, so it was sort of his own fault that he was unhappy now. Which didn't make her feel any better.

Her eyes filled with tears. Not only did she feel guilty for making him unhappy, but now that she was alone, her body was screaming at her and, Mother Night, she hurt.

Marian looked at the roast on the cutting board. It was almost too good to cut up for stew. She looked at the potatoes, carrots, and onions sitting on the counter next to the cutting board and sighed. No, the real reason she felt reluctant to start was that she hadn't considered how long it would take to cut up a roast into stew-size pieces when she had to use a knife. Using basic Craft, she could have done it in a minute. No help for it. If she didn't start now, she'd be very late serving the midday meal.

As she reached for the knife, someone knocked sharply on the front door.

Her heart galloped as she stepped into the front room and stared at the door. Maybe it was that Roxie woman again. She hadn't told Lucivar about the young witch's second attempt to enter the eyrie when he wasn't home. She hadn't mentioned that Roxie had implied she was meeting him in Riada for an afternoon of sex. She hadn't believed the woman for a minute, but it had made her wonder about things she shouldn't wonder about—like how he kissed . . . and what it would feel like to be in bed with him.

A second knock, sharper this time.

She could pretend no one was home—or say she'd been in the laundry room and hadn't heard the knocking if the person mentioned it to Lucivar. No, not the laundry room. That would upset him. She'd say she'd been in her room, resting. Besides, she didn't want to deal with anyone today.

The High Lord walked through the door, passing through the wood as if the Ebon-gray lock wasn't there. Of course, the High Lord wore a Black Jewel, so an Ebon-gray lock was little more than a moment's inconvenience to him.

He stopped as soon as he saw her. His nostrils flared slightly. His expression turned grim, almost menacing.

"What did he do?" Saetan asked too softly.

Marian swallowed to get her heart out of her throat. "What?"

"What did my idiot of a son do?"

If he'd slapped her, he couldn't have surprised her more. "I don't understand."

Saetan moved toward her. "He upset you."

"No. Yes. It wasn't . . ." How was she supposed to think when he was staring at her like that?

He made a quiet sound of disgust and shook his head. The next moment, he was leading her back into the kitchen, the hand on her arm sliding up to rest on her shoulder.

She couldn't say he pushed her into the chair, but she found herself sitting at the pine table without having decided she wanted to sit.

"I'd apologize for him, but there's really no excuse for upsetting a woman during her moontime," Saetan said as he removed his cape and laid it over the back of another chair. "His education in the Terreillean courts was abysmal at best, but he's been in Kaeleer three years now. He should have acquired *some* understanding from dealing with the coven. Idiot."

Marian's hands curled into fists as she watched him rinse out the teakettle, fill it with fresh water, and put it on the stove to heat.

"He didn't do anything," Marian said.

"He upset you," Saetan replied in a tone of voice only a fool would challenge. "He probably walked in here this morning and started roaring, telling you what you could and couldn't do as if you were a simpleminded child instead of a grown woman who has enough sense to know when her body needs rest and care."

The High Lord was on her side. So why did she want to take the skillet that was still sitting on the counter and smack him over the head with it?

Finding the mugs in one of the upper cupboards, he filled one with hot water and slipped a tea ball into it.

"You don't have to tell me what happened," Saetan said. "I've had enough experience with Lucivar to see it all. You have duties and responsibilities that you take seriously. You would have planned for this and wouldn't be doing more than you had to. But then he comes in, snapping and snarling, so what else can a witch do except defend herself and push back, insisting that she's capable of doing more than she knows she can?" He brought the mug over to the table and placed it in front of her. "Here, sweetheart. This is a brew I make for Jaenelle when her moontime is troubling her. Drink it up."

Reluctant to do anything that would please him after he'd insulted Lucivar but not having enough nerve to defy him, she lifted the mug and sniffed. It smelled good. She took a sip. It tasted even better.

"You're making stew?" he asked.

"Yes."

He washed his hands and began moving around her kitchen with a confidence that looked like he was used to being in kitchens. Which wasn't likely.

"His social skills are rough, to put it kindly," Saetan said. "He just smashes through an obstacle instead of considering if there's a quieter way around it."

Maybe Lucivar's social skills were rough compared to a slick Hayllian, but that wasn't saying much. She'd rather have rough and honest than slick any day.

"Here, darling." Saetan returned to the table and placed a cutting board, the carrots, and a knife in front of her. "Do you feel well enough to cut up the carrots?"

"I feel fine." As he turned away from the table, she drank the rest of the brew and put the mug aside. She picked up the knife, then looked at the carrots. They were cleaned and the ends were neatly cut off. She didn't remember doing that, but she must have.

chop

He moved around her kitchen, but she didn't dare look up to see what he was doing since he kept grumbling about Lucivar and she was afraid of what she might say if she actually looked at him right now.

chop chop chop

Who did he think he was, anyway? He had no right to come into Lucivar's home and criticize. She didn't care if he was Lucivar's father and the Steward of the Dark Court and the High Lord of Hell. He had no business criticizing Lucivar in public. Well, maybe not in public, since they were in the kitchen, but he shouldn't be saying these things to Prince Yaslana's housekeeper. It wasn't right.

chop chop

And it wasn't his business, was it? If she and Lucivar had clashed this morning, it had nothing to do with *him*. *He* didn't live here.

She heard a quiet sizzle, but it was gone so fast she wasn't sure she'd really heard anything, so she kept her eyes focused on the cutting board.

chop chop chop

So Lucivar was a little rough around the edges. So what? There wasn't an Eyrien male who *wasn't*. But he was kind, and if he got testy when he thought she was working too hard, wasn't that better than someone who expected her to work until she was exhausted and *still* didn't think she'd done enough? If she hadn't snapped at him this morning, if she'd kept a tighter hold on her own emotions and told him she was planning to rest today, they wouldn't have argued, and he wouldn't have left because she'd made him unhappy.

chop chop

That wasn't the point. The point was his *father* had *no right* to be grumbling about his son, and if she were Lucivar's lover instead of his housekeeper, she'd tell his father a thing or two. Oh, yes, she would.

Slick Hayllian. Bah!

"Finished?"

The amusement in his voice confused her enough that he slipped the knife out of her hand before she realized he'd reached for it. He set another mug down in front of her and took the cutting board away.

She sniffed. There was a lingering scent of cooked meat in the air. She looked at the counter—and frowned at the bowl of cut vegetables. She looked at the stove and saw the big kettle she used for soups and stews, the witchfire beneath it spread in a circle that was perfect for simmering whatever was in the kettle.

"Now," Saetan said as he settled his cape around his shoulders. "Lucivar is what he is. No social skills, or lack of them, can change a Warlord Prince's nature. If you want to punish him for snapping at you this morning, you go do the kind of heavy work that will most certainly cause you pain today. But if he matters enough to show him kindness, you'll let him make the biscuits to go with the stew and you'll tuck yourself in this afternoon and do something that won't make demands on your body. You'll let him fuss over you a little. If he doesn't have to fight you to protect you, it will make things easier for both of you."

She studied him. "What you said about Lucivar. You didn't mean any of it, did you?"

He smiled. "He's physical, demanding, and rough around the edges. In other words, he's Eyrien. I wouldn't want him to be any other way. But it was an effective way of keeping you distracted."

He brushed a hand over her hair, leaned over, and kissed her forehead. There was something so . . . fatherly . . . in the gesture, she felt tears sting her eyes.

After he left the eyrie, she sat at the table, sipping the brew he'd made for her and thinking about what he'd said.

Lucivar quietly closed the eyrie's front door, then stood still a moment, listening. No sounds. No indication of any kind of what he was walking into.

He couldn't stay away. The worry that she'd do something foolish because he'd jumped on her that morning had gnawed at him. He knew witches tended to snap and snarl when they felt the most vulnerable. Hell's fire, he'd slammed his will against Jaenelle's enough times over the past three years to figure out aggression pitted against vulnerability only caused hurt feelings on both sides. Asking for a favor always got better results than making demands. But when he saw Marian sweeping the floor that morning, his temper had snapped the leash. Now all he could do was hope he could repair whatever damage he'd done.

He found her in the kitchen, her hands wrapped around a mug. She glanced up when she saw him, then looked down at the mug.

Feeling miserable and awkward, he leaned against the counter. "I . . . ah . . . picked up some bread at the baker's." When she just nodded, he winced. Still pissed off at him. "I also picked up this." He called in a box, set it on the table near her, then stepped back. When she opened it, her lower lip trembled.

Hell's fire. Being whipped didn't hurt this much. Chocolate fudge was *the* bribe when it came to being forgiven for doing something stupid and male. At least, it usually worked with Jaenelle and the coven. He knew Marian liked fudge because she'd bought some from that same sweetshop in Riada, but she wasn't giving in enough to even taste it.

Looking around the kitchen, he spotted the kettle. "You made stew."

"Actually, your father made the stew," Marian said. "He showed up a little while after you left."

Lucivar clenched his teeth. Well, wasn't that just fine and wonderful? If *he'd* offered to help make the stew, she would have snapped at him. But *his father* could walk in here and make the damn thing without so much as a yip out of her. And, damn it, he was *not* going to be jealous of his own father.

Of course he was.

"You let him make the stew."

"I didn't let him do anything," Marian said, sounding testy. "One minute he was criticizing you for getting me upset and the next he was making the stew. I think."

"You think?"

"I don't care if he's your father, he had no right to criticize you about what you do in your own home. And when he gave me the carrots to cut up—"

"Wait." Lucivar raised a hand. "He gave you the carrots?"

Marian bristled. "What's wrong with that? I'm perfectly capable of cutting up a few carrots."

He held up both hands in a placating gesture. She did get feisty when she was riled. "I didn't say there was anything wrong with it. It's just not the vegetable I would have given a woman who was holding a sharp knife and was pissed off at men."

When she gave him a blank look, he decided to move the conversation along before she figured out what he meant. "So you cut up the carrots and . . . ?"

"And I was so annoyed with him, I didn't pay attention to what he was doing, and the next thing I knew the meat was cooking and the rest of the vegetables were ready to go in when it was time." She frowned at the mug. "And he made this brew for me."

Lucivar waited. "So what did he say about me?"

She shrugged. "Doesn't matter. He didn't mean any of it. He told me so after he made the stew."

He didn't appreciate being criticized, but wasn't it interesting that it had annoyed her enough that she hadn't paid attention to what was going on in her own kitchen?

"But then he said . . ."

Lucivar studied her. She looked so baffled. "What?"

"He said if I wanted to be kind, I would let you make the biscuits . . . and let you fuss over me a little."

"I can make biscuits."

She shook her head. "You bought some bread."

Not sure how she'd respond to him, he moved closer to her and ran a hand over her hair.

She looked up at him. "Why did he do that?"

"Make the stew?" He leaned over and kissed her forehead, hoping she'd take it as a friendly gesture—and wanting to kiss her in ways that had nothing to do with being friends. "He's a Warlord Prince. I guess he couldn't stand seeing you work when you were hurting." He eased back a little to look at her. Her eyes held a female awareness of a male that eased one kind of tension in him and created another. "So. Are you going to let me fuss a little?"

"I've never been fussed over before."

He smiled. "Think of it as an adventure. It will be easier that way." And until someone, like Jaenelle, told Marian the rules about fussing, he was going to make the most of his hearth witch's ignorance.

FIFTEEN

Marian crouched behind the shelves of dishes and glassware. How soon before the shop's proprietor remembered he had another customer and started wondering what she'd been doing all this time?

She wasn't hiding, exactly. She just didn't want to deal with that Roxie woman. Thank the Darkness she'd been examining some plates on the lower shelves when Roxie walked into the shop. There'd been no mistaking that voice, and one quick look had convinced her she didn't want to meet Roxie when she couldn't slam a door in the woman's face. But having spent the past hour carefully making her selections, she was *not* leaving without her cookware, which was stacked on one end of the large wooden counter that ran across the back of the store.

She peeked over the top shelf, then ducked back down out of sight. Poor man. Roxie had been sneering at his merchandise since she walked in the door, proclaiming loudly that the aristo shops in Doun had *much* better fare. But that hadn't stopped her from plunking several items on the counter. And now . . .

"What do you mean I can't put it on the account?" Roxie's voice rose toward a screech. "He *told* me I could buy anything I wanted and put it on his account."

"Unfortunately," the proprietor replied, his voice condemning in its politeness, "Prince Yaslana has not informed me of that fact."

Marian winced. She'd bought a few things at the shops she usually pa-tronized, but then it had occurred to her that *all* the merchants would owe a tithe to Lucivar, so she'd taken one of the horse-drawn cabs over to this side of the village to spread her spending around a little. She'd felt self-conscious about walking into a shop that so obviously catered to the aristo families in Riada. Only the fact that she was buying these things for Lu-civar's home and Lucivar's table had kept her from walking right back out.

That and the books. The merchant's shop she usually went to had a small selection of books, and most of them were used—and there'd been nothing there that she hadn't already read since Jaenelle was very gener-ous about loaning her books. But there'd been so many to choose from in this shop, she'd lost track of time as she browsed the shelves. If she'd simply picked one that had interested her, she would have completed her purchases and been out of the shop before Roxie came in.

"He's hardly going to tell every merchant in the village that we're lovers," Roxie snapped. "Especially since we've tried to be discreet about our liaison."

Marian swallowed wrong and almost choked, so she didn't hear the proprietor's response.

"Oh, very well," Roxie said. "You can open an account for me, and Lucivar will settle it with you later."

"I am sorry, Lady, but I cannot open an account for you on the ex-pectation that Prince Yaslana will pay it."

"I told you, we're *lovers*."

"And it has been my experience that a man who is willing to share his bed may not necessarily be willing to share his purse. If you do not have the funds for the purchases, I can hold the items for a few days."

"Don't bother," Roxie snapped. "The merchants in Doun wouldn't treat me this way."

"Then I suggest you do your shopping in Doun."

When she heard the door open, Marian rose from her crouch. But Roxie hadn't quite left the shop. For a long moment, their eyes met. Then something outside caught Roxie's attention, and she left the shop in a hurry.

Working to steady her nerves, Marian approached the counter.

"Have you found everything you wanted?" the proprietor asked.

"Yes, thank you," Marian replied, trying not to stammer. She swallowed hard. "Prince Yaslana instructed me to have the household purchases put on his account."

"I see." He flicked a look at the door as someone entered the shop.

Why had she come to this part of the village? Why hadn't she kept to the shops where she felt she belonged? Why—

"What's all this?"

Jaenelle was suddenly beside her, looking at the cookware with a gleam in her eyes that was downright scary.

"Lady Angelline," Marian said.

Jaenelle smiled. "You finally informed Lucivar that he wasn't getting another dinner until you had the proper tools to cook with, didn't you?"

"Not exactly," Marian muttered.

"You're Lady Marian?" the proprietor asked.

"Yes." Maybe she shouldn't be surprised that he'd heard her name. After all, she and Lucivar were the only Eyriens living near Riada.

"Are you sure you have everything?" Jaenelle asked.

"Yes, I'm sure. I thought about—"

But Jaenelle was already heading toward the part of the shop that held household goods, and remembering their last shopping trip, Marian rushed after her.

"I don't need the large cheese grater," Marian said a few minutes later, trying to keep her voice from edging toward desperation. It wasn't a question of taste, as it had been when they'd shopped for Lucivar's furniture, it was Jaenelle's unflagging idea that if Marian needed one of something for the kitchen, two would be better.

"Why not?" Jaenelle said. "You only have the little one."

"The smaller one is all I need. Really." She took the cheese grater out of Jaenelle's hands and put it back on the shelf.

Since she couldn't hold Jaenelle back, she tried to steer the direction of that energy and enthusiasm, so it wasn't really her fault that they ended up buying a set of dishes . . . and glasses . . . and silverware . . . and a corner shelf for what use she didn't know except Jaenelle thought it would look nice in the kitchen.

Numbed by the sheer quantity of purchases, she watched the proprietor tally up the cost and wondered how many years of tithes had just been eliminated.

Then the proprietor turned to the smaller stack of items on the counter.

"No," Marian said. "Those don't go on Prince Yaslana's account. Those are my purchases."

As he tallied up her purchases, she called in the wallet she'd bought on her last shopping trip. Most of her wages were tucked in the back of the dresser drawer that held her underthings. The wallet held the funds she allowed herself to spend freely. She opened it and riffled the copper marks just as the proprietor finished his tally.

Heat flooded her face. Not enough. She hadn't come to the village to shop for herself and hadn't checked to see how much was in her wallet before she left the eyrie. And she hadn't expected to find that wonderful, soft wool material that she wanted to make into a robe for Lucivar as a Winsol gift. She could still afford the material, but . . .

After a wistful look at the two books she'd selected, she cleared her throat. "I'm sorry. I didn't bring enough with me."

"Perhaps the Lady would like to open an account?" the proprietor asked.

She just stared at him. Why would he give a housekeeper an account when he wouldn't open one for Roxie, who came from an aristo family?

"That's practical," Jaenelle said.

That settled it—at least as far as Jaenelle and the proprietor were concerned.

"Thank you," Marian said, after she reviewed the neatly written list and had initialed the paper next to the last item.

"It is my pleasure, Lady," the proprietor replied.

"So," Jaenelle said. "Are you going home to play with your new toys?"

"They're not toys, they're tools," Marian replied as she vanished the material and books. Before she could deal with the rest of the purchases, they vanished.

Jaenelle smiled at her. "I'll come back with you. Then you can tell me what all of those things do."

"Do?"

"I'm not allowed in the kitchen at the Hall, so I don't see most of the things you bought."

"You don't know how to cook? Not at all?"

"No," Jaenelle said sadly.

Marian couldn't believe it. Lucivar could put together an acceptable meal, and he'd mentioned a few times that his father was quite a good cook when the High Lord felt inclined. Why hadn't either of them taught Jaenelle how to put together a simple meal?

"I can teach you," Marian said. "But we'll have to start with something very simple."

Jaenelle beamed. "Simple is good."

The proprietor looked amused.

As she and Jaenelle walked out of the shop, Marian wondered how long it would take for the rest of the village to hear that Prince Yaslana's housekeeper was giving the Queen of Ebon Askavi a cooking lesson.

Since he'd been greeted by grinning merchants when he stopped in Riada on his way home, Lucivar expected to find Marian in the kitchen playing with her new toys. The counter was stacked with things, but his little hearth witch was just sitting at the table, frowning at two bowls filled with eggs. After studying the bottle on the table and considering the glazed look in her eyes, he doubted the two fingers of brandy in the glass near her hand was the first drink she'd poured.

Figuring he wasn't going to see dinner anytime soon, he pointed at the eggs. "Are those cooked?"

"Mmm," Marian said.

He took one from the nearest bowl and peeled off the shell. Just as he punched his thumb into the center to break the egg in half, Marian said, "No! Not—"

Raw yolk fountained up and flowed over his hands.

Lucivar looked at Marian. Marian looked at him.

"You let my sister play in the kitchen, didn't you?" Which explained why his little hearth witch had indulged in several glasses of brandy.

Marian stared at the egg dripping off his hands. "She's the Queen of

Ebon Askavi. She's the most powerful witch in Kaeleer. And she can't boil an egg."

"I know. That's why we don't let her play in the kitchen."

Marian shook her head. "How can she not be able to boil an egg? You don't even need Craft for it. All she did was put the eggs in the water." She blew out a breath. "How can you end up with eggs that have the whites fully cooked and the yolks still raw?"

"I don't know. My father thinks it's *because* she's so powerful that some things don't react as expected."

"I thought I'd explained something wrong," Marian said. "So after she left, I cooked the rest of the eggs. They're perfect." She wobbled in her chair. "Jaenelle felt so bad when she left."

"Your offer to teach her was a kind gesture," Lucivar said. "But, Marian? This is a witch who, when she was sixteen, blew up the kitchen at the Hall because she confused the spell she was putting together with the casserole she and her friend Karla were making and put the wrong mixture in the oven. Think about that for a minute. Casserole. Spell. They couldn't tell the difference by looking at what was in the dishes."

"She blew up the kitchen?"

"Destroyed it. Right down to the last wooden spoon."

Marian shuddered.

"So the next time you want to do something kind for Jaenelle, make her a casserole or bake some nutcakes. But don't let her play in the kitchen."

Putting a shield around his hands so he wouldn't drip yolk, Lucivar walked over to the sink and used Craft to turn on the water taps. As he washed his hands, he said, "Do I dare ask what's for dinner?"

Marian hiccuped. "Eggs."

He turned off the water and sighed. "Yeah. That's what I thought."

SIXTEEN

"I have work," Marian said as Lucivar hauled her out of the kitchen and into the eyrie's front room. Tassle followed them, making worried little huffy sounds.

"The work will still be there an hour from now," Lucivar replied.

She looked at the thick drops of rain hitting the glass doors that led to the lawn beyond. If it got any colder, that rain would turn to snow. "You're just doing this because you're bored."

Using Craft, Lucivar moved the furniture against the walls, leaving a large bare circle of stone floor. "If I was bored, I'd go to the Hall and annoy my father. That perks up both our days."

Bet it doesn't perk them up in the same way, Marian thought. "I don't want to do this."

"Whining about it won't do you any good."

Whining? She bristled at the insult. She wasn't *whining*. She was pointing out the obvious to a thickheaded male. Females *did not* use Eyrien weapons. Ask any Eyrien male—except the one standing in front of her—and he'd tell you that.

Since being reasonable wasn't going to work, she lowered her voice and tried menacing. "I've got a skillet, and I know how to use it."

His quick grin wasn't the reaction she'd hoped for.

"That's fine," he said, turning. "Now you're going to acquire skill with a traditional weapon."

"I'm not—"

He spun back toward her, and shouted, "If you get hurt because you're too damn stubborn to learn how to defend yourself, I will beat the shit out of you!"

Goaded by the unexpected verbal shove, she shoved back. "If you ever raise a hand to me, I will gut you!"

They stared at each other. She had that one moment for fear to zing through her as she realized she'd just threatened a Warlord Prince. Before she could move, his hands clamped on her waist. One quick toss in the air. As she came down, he wrapped his arms around her lower back and buttocks and spun her around and around.

"Ha! I knew you had it in you!" He laughed as he spun her.

"Stop!" Marian grabbed his shoulders. "Lucivar, *stop!*"

He stopped. Since the room was still circling, she clung to his shoulders. Her feet didn't touch the floor, which put them eye to eye. With her heart pounding, she dared to look at him, hoping he wasn't too angry with her.

He didn't look angry at all. His eyes were lit with amusement, and he grinned at her as if she'd just done something wonderful.

Giving her a friendly squeeze, he said, "That's my feisty hearth witch. Now give us a snarl. Say *Grrrr.*"

Heat flooded her face. She pushed at his shoulders, wanting to get down, wanting to get away. He just tightened his arms.

"I'm not putting you down until I get a snarl," he said.

She looked away, mortified—and saw Tassle standing to one side, watching them. The wolf curled his lips, revealing an impressive set of teeth. After a moment, the lips relaxed. He waved the tip of his tail, then did the whole thing all over again.

She lowered her head, let her hair fall forward to hide her face. Great. Wonderful. A wolf was coaching her in how to snarl, and the man holding her off the ground . . .

She peeked at him. His grin had changed to that lazy, arrogant smile.

. . . would hold her like this all day if that's how long it took to get what he wanted.

She took a breath. Blew it out.

As soon as she was free, she was going to hide in her room. He could fix his own meals, wash his own dishes. They'd just see how long he grinned about *that*.

She took another breath. Blew it out.

The way she was pressed against him, there was no mistaking his body's response to hers. And there were all those warm, lovely muscles under her hands, just waiting to be touched, caressed . . .

Hell's fire, Mother Night, and may the Darkness be merciful.

Before she could do something stupid, she took another breath, raised her head, and said, *"gr."*

Lucivar's arrogant smile faded. His brows drew together in a frown. "What a prissy little *gr*. But it will have to do." Sighing, he loosened his arms, letting her slide down his body until her feet touched the floor.

As soon as he released her, the rational part of her mind scampered off, leaving her with less sense than a rabbit. So she bolted.

Grab . . . lift . . . swing . . . *plop*. And she was right back where she'd started.

"You're going to learn to defend yourself, Marian," Lucivar said, an unyielding look in his gold eyes. "You don't have to like it, but you're going to learn."

When he called in the Eyrien sticks, Marian sagged with relief. At least these were the sparring sticks and not the bladed sticks used for fighting. Even so, an opponent could take a terrible beating. Her father had done it enough times to young warriors he brought to her mother's eyrie. He'd insist on a sparring session, with his daughters in attendance, so the young warrior could "show off his skills." Even a skilled youth couldn't match a full-grown Eyrien male who had been trained to fight.

And an unskilled hearth witch was no match for an Eyrien Warlord Prince.

She tightened her grip on the stick and set her feet in the stance she'd seen her father take.

Lucivar just looked at her feet. "What are you doing?"

She tensed, wondering where his first blow would hit. "This is the stance for sparring."

"Only if you want to be knocked on your ass."

She lowered the stick. "What?"

"You set your feet like that, you're going to eat dirt unless your opponent is smaller than you are."

So that explained why she'd never seen her father spar with anyone but half-trained youths. The fighting skills her father bragged about were nothing more than brags, just words without substance to justify what he did, and didn't do, for his family.

She hadn't thought about living with a man, hadn't really wanted to. That had never been part of her dream. Now she wondered what it would be like to live that dream with a man who wasn't like her father. With Lucivar.

"Marian?"

She looked at him and realized she had no idea how long he'd been standing there, waiting, while her thoughts had wandered. "Are we going to spar?"

His lips twitched. "We'll get to it eventually. First you have to learn how to move."

Slow. Quiet. As graceful as a dance. He took her through each move, his voice flowing over her as he explained, corrected, praised. The warmth of his hand on her waist or hip as he guided her body. The movement of his own muscles as he demonstrated the next move. The clean male scent of him.

"Now we'll put all the moves together," Lucivar said. "Watch."

She watched. Grace and power. What would it be like to kiss him? Really kiss him? Would he bring all that grace and power to the bed? Would he be a generous lover? She'd only had one experience with sex after her Virgin Night, and that had been disappointing enough that she'd never been interested in trying again. But when a woman loved, wouldn't there be some pleasure from the act even if the body received none?

The thought staggered her, thrilled her, terrified her. Had she been falling in love with him all along? That would be foolish, wouldn't it? He might take a hearth witch for a lover to satisfy his body's needs, but he'd never give his heart to one. Would he?

"That's enough for the day."

She tripped over the sound of his voice, struggled to regain her balance. "What?"

"That's enough." He tugged the stick out of her hands. "I'm not sure where your mind wandered off to, but you weren't paying attention."

Oh, she'd been paying attention, but she'd been focused on the man and not the lesson.

"It's close to midday, and the weather has cleared." Lucivar smiled at her. "Why don't we fly down to the village? I'll buy you a meal."

Pain lanced her heart, fierce and deep. She shook her head and backed away from him. "I can't."

"Sure you can." He sighed. "Marian, eating a meal you didn't cook isn't neglecting your work."

"I can't." He'd mentioned once or twice that he'd never seen her fly, but she'd been able to avoid giving him a reason. Now . . .

"Why not?" Lucivar asked.

Tears filled her eyes. "I can't fly! My wings . . . they were damaged. They're useless."

Grief and understanding filled his eyes. Here was someone who understood what that loss meant to her.

Then his eyes chilled. "Who told you that?" he asked too softly.

"It doesn't matter. I can't—"

"Who told you that?"

Uneasy now, she wiped the tears off her face. She could almost see the temper beginning to burn in him, could almost see it rising from spike to spike until it would reach the explosion point.

"Jaenelle brought you to Kaeleer," Lucivar said, studying her. "She would have done the healing. If *she* told you you'd never fly again, you'd have to accept it. But she didn't, did she? So who told you, Marian?"

She stared at him, not sure if there was any safe ground to stand on.

Lucivar bared his teeth. "Luthvian. She's the one who told you."

"Lady Angelline doesn't have experience with Eyrien—"

"On her worst day, Jaenelle is a better Healer than Luthvian can ever hope to be." He shook his head. "You think your wings were damaged? When I came to Kaeleer, mine were so broken, so destroyed by slime mold there was barely enough healthy tissue left to work with. Luthvian wanted to remove them. Jaenelle rebuilt them, healed them. So don't tell me she doesn't have experience."

Marian's legs trembled. She could have flown? All these months when she'd been afraid to try, she could have soared over Ebon Rih?

Swearing viciously, Lucivar circled the room as if he couldn't stand still a moment longer. Finally, he stopped in front of her. The hand he held out curled into a fist.

"Don't let them win, Marian. Don't let them make you less than you are. Don't let them take away what means the most to you. Not the family who dismissed your strength and your skills, not the bastards who hurt you—yes, I know about them—and not Luthvian. Don't let them win. Fight for what you want with everything that's in you."

"It's not the same," Marian cried. "I'm just a hearth witch and you're—"

"I was a slave!" Lucivar shouted. "A half-breed bastard sold to one court after another, wearing that filthy Ring of Obedience to keep me submissive. But I wouldn't submit, I wouldn't break, and I fought back with every breath I took. I refused to be less than a Warlord Prince, and I made them deal with me on my terms. No matter how much pain they inflicted, I gave it back."

"I'm not like that. I can't fight like that."

"Have you ever tried?" He raked a hand through his hair. "If you give up your wings, what else will you give up because someone tells you you're just a hearth witch?"

Something broke inside her—broke and reformed in a different pattern. She teetered on the edge of a cliff. She could step back to familiar ground or she could leap—and possibly soar.

He'd been pushing her toward that edge. She saw that now. Every time he challenged and she pushed back, he never undermined the sense that she had held her own. She didn't usually win—his idea of compromise was laughable—but she didn't actually lose, either.

He wanted her to win. And he'd throw everything he was behind her to help her do it.

She swallowed tears and gathered her courage. "Could you help me learn how to fly again?"

He approached her slowly. No smile. No light words. He reached out and stroked her hair, watching her. He kissed her forehead, something he'd done frequently since the day she threw the pot at him. Then he kissed her mouth. A restrained kiss that made no demands—and left her wishing he would make a few.

"I'll help you fly again," he said as he stepped back. "Get your cape. We'll still go down to the village for a meal."

Wondering how soon they could start working to restore her flying skills, she hurried to obey. As she reached the steps that led to the rest of the eyrie, he said, "Marian?"

She turned.

He grinned at her. "Learning how to fly again isn't going to get you out of learning the sticks. Just so we're clear on that."

Hell's fire, she thought as she hurried to her room to brush her hair and get her cape. She hadn't thought about doing both. The time it would take out of her daily schedule . . . But he'd already locked the gate on any argument she could make.

Somehow that didn't annoy her as much as it should have.

SEVENTEEN

Marian paused at the side door of the eyrie and looked at the dark, heavy clouds coming over the mountains. No gentle snowfall this time, but a mean storm that would bury Ebon Rih for days. Hopefully, Lucivar would get home before it hit.

Tassle? she called on a psychic thread.

I am returning to the den, Tassle replied.

Good. A kindred wolf would know how to find shelter if he was caught out in a storm, but she'd feel easier having him at the eyrie.

Hurrying into the mud room, she shook the snow off her heavy cape before hanging it on the pegs to dry. She traded her boots for soft house shoes, then went into the kitchen to put away the food she'd bought to last them through the storm.

As she unpacked her cloth market bags, she kept glancing out the window. The snow was already coming down fast. A hard gust of wind turned the world white and blind for a moment. Then she caught a glimpse of Tassle at the far end of her garden and breathed a sigh of relief. One of her males was home and safe. Now if the other one . . .

For the past few days, ever since they'd returned from celebrating Winsol at his father's house, Lucivar had been on edge. He denied there was anything wrong, but the looks he'd given her were close to hostile. Something was putting his back up, and she suspected it had to do with her.

Spending Winsol, the winter holiday that was a celebration of the Darkness, at the Hall had been fun and dazzling. She'd felt disappointed that Andulvar and Prothvar Yaslana hadn't been there, since she'd been hoping to meet them, but meeting the coven almost made up for that. There had been long walks and snowball fights, afternoons when the women had gathered to talk and laugh. During one of those afternoons, it had suddenly occurred to her that the women who were including her as if she were one of them were the Queens who ruled their respective Territories. But they didn't seem to notice that she was just a hearth witch, just a housekeeper. And the looks on their faces the day she'd told them she'd spent the morning with Mrs. Beale, helping prepare the mid-day meal . . .

No one, she was told, was allowed in Mrs. Beale's kitchen.

It was probably for the best that she hadn't mentioned trading recipes with the woman who ruled the Hall's kitchen.

Then there was Lucivar. Seeing him with his family, the coven, and the boyos had been a revelation. Demanding and yielding, stubborn and considerate, arguing with one of them and defending that person in the next breath. He'd insisted on morning workouts, which hadn't pleased her until she discovered the whole coven showed up without grumbling. Watching them move through the warmups, watching them spar with him and each other, she realized how serious he was about witches being comfortable using weapons in order to defend themselves. And watching him spar with Jaenelle . . . Her heart had been in her throat the whole time she watched that violent dance.

But the biggest difference was the way he'd responded to her. Ever since the day when he'd promised to help her learn to fly again, he'd been touching her, giving her easy, friendly kisses. The kisses he'd given her at the Hall made her wonder, made her hungry. They were the kisses of a man who wanted. Except he hadn't asked if he could come to her bed, hadn't invited her to come to his. So she wasn't sure what those kisses meant, but she wondered what it would be like to be with him.

And she *shouldn't* wonder. She was his *housekeeper.* It would be too easy to forget that if she responded to him as a woman.

Had he wanted her to invite him? Was that why he was so testy now?

Marian looked out the kitchen window. The snow was falling so fast now, she couldn't see anything.

Where was he?

Lucivar stood on a mountain ledge on the other side of Ebon Rih, watching the storm come over the mountains. It matched his mood, matched a temper already primed to explode.

Hell's fire! Why had Luthvian wanted to ride out the storm in *his* home? She had plenty of food, and with warming spells on the pipes that ran from the house to the well, she'd wouldn't be without water. And hadn't he filled every damn woodbox in her house? Using Craft, she could call in more wood from the woodpile without going outside. So why did she suddenly want to spend time with him?

Not that he would have her. Not today. Just the smell of her, and the lingering scent of her female students, had been enough to make him want to smash furniture, shatter bone. And the males in the villages . . .

The sight of them had been enough to bring him a heartbeat away from the killing edge. They hadn't done anything wrong, had, in fact, done everything they could to prepare the villages in Ebon Rih to ride out the storm. But he'd wanted to hurt them, had felt something close to blind hatred for all of them.

His father was at the Keep. He could sense that dark power. So tempting to go to Ebon Askavi and test his precarious control against that darker strength.

What in the name of Hell was wrong with him? He wanted to get home before the storm really broke. Wanted to get back to his eyrie, back to . . .

Marian.

Fury avalanched through him. Changed into something violent, hot, and impossible to resist.

Marian.

He knew what this was now. It had never hit him quite this way before, but he recognized it now.

Rut. That time when a Warlord Prince's sex drive overwhelmed everything else. Every male was a rival to be eliminated. Every female but the one he'd chosen scraped a temper turned wild and unpredictable.

Sex or violence. The rut worked itself out one way or the other. Sometimes both. He'd gone into rut several times since coming to Kaeleer and had had no desire to slake that drive in a woman's body. He'd depended on Jaenelle's presence to keep him chained. She had soothed his need to be close to a female and had channeled the violence into grueling physical activity that he'd thrown himself into with vicious willingness.

But Jaenelle was at her house in Scelt for a few weeks, and the woman he wanted, the woman who made his blood burn and sing . . .

He had to get Marian out of the eyrie, had to get her away from him before the storm closed in and made it too dangerous to travel, even on the Winds. Because if she was still in the eyrie when the storm inside him broke, if they were trapped together for several days . . . If that happened, may the Darkness be merciful . . . because there would be no mercy in him.

Giving an Eyrien war cry that was filled with fury and desperation, Lucivar launched himself into the face of the storm.

As Marian pulled the roast out of the oven and set the pan on top of the stove, the front door slammed.

"You made it," she said as she hurried into the eyrie's front room. When she saw him, she took a step back. His teeth were bared, and he stared at her with glazed, wild eyes.

"Get out," he growled.

"Lucivar . . ."

"Get out!" He ripped off his short wool cape and threw it aside.

She couldn't take her eyes off his bare, slick skin. It was freezing out there. Why was he so hot? And why wasn't he wearing a shirt or vest under the cape?

The vicious snarl that erupted from him made her press her back against the wall.

"I want you out of here. Go to Riada and stay with Merry. Go to the Keep. Go anywhere, but go. *Now.*"

Fear shivered through her. She knew what this was. Survival de-

manded that every witch learn to recognize the rut. Warlord Princes
were always violently passionate and passionately violent, but the rut
drove them to a savagery that bordered insanity. Other males were nothing more than rivals to destroy. And women . . .

Her mother had once said that a Warlord Prince in rut had enough
sexual hunger that he could service an entire coven twice over and still
want more. The problem was, he focused on one female and wouldn't
tolerate the presence of any other. His choice became the vessel for all
that drive, all that need.

She'd heard stories about Warlord Princes. She knew what could happen to the woman under him when he was in rut. Tongues partially bitten off. Nipples bitten off. Bones broken or shattered. Any male who
tried to stop him would be killed, and he would turn away from the
slaughter to mount the female again, oblivious to the carnage around
him until the rut finally wore off.

"Marian."

Lucivar wore Ebon-gray Jewels. If she stayed, she could be maimed,
even killed. But if she didn't stay, what would he do? Trapped here by
the blizzard, driven by the violence inside him, he could hurt himself.

"Marian."

She was young, healthy, stronger than she'd ever been. And she was in
love with him. She'd fallen in love with a man who challenged the world
to take him on, sometimes with laughing, boyish enthusiasm and other
times as a warrior born and trained to kill.

She could do this for him. *Would* do this for him.

"No." Her voice quivered with fear, but her heart didn't waver. "I'm
not leaving."

"GET OUT!" Lucivar screamed.

"No." As she stepped away from the wall, she thought of the basic
rules of survival. *Move slowly because fast moves excite the predator instinct,
and he'll be on you without thought, without mercy. Stay passive. Don't refuse
him. Don't offer resistance to anything he wants to do to you.*

Lucivar snarled, his glazed eyes watching her.

Vanishing her undershirt, Marian slowly unbuttoned her tunic and
pulled it open just enough to display her breasts.

His breathing became ragged. His hands curled into fists.

"I'm not leaving," she said quietly.

He was on her so fast, there wasn't even time to draw breath. One hand fisted in her long hair, pulling her head back, exposing her throat. The other hand pressed her against the cock straining to be free of the leather trousers.

"You should have run," he snarled.

He lowered his head. His teeth closed on the spot where her neck joined her shoulder—not hard enough to hurt, but hard enough to make her heart pound.

When she remained passive, he shifted suddenly, his teeth closing on her neck. He licked, explored, until her pulse throbbed against the tip of his tongue.

Moving slowly, she raised her hands and rested them on his waist. His teeth tightened in warning, then he shifted again, capturing her earlobe.

Quiet. Passive. The only way to survive. But she couldn't stop her hands from stroking his hot skin, couldn't slow her pounding heart when every breath rubbed her breasts against his chest, teasing, arousing.

"Give me your mouth." His voice sounded rough, barely human.

She hesitated, then parted her lips. Those wild, glazed eyes stared at her too long before his mouth covered hers.

She was prepared for teeth and pain. Instead, he gave her a long, lazy kiss, his tongue playing with hers. Her hands slid up his back, curled around his shoulders, pressing her tighter against him. The fist that gripped her hair relaxed, opening to cradle her head. And still he kissed her as if there was nothing more to want, nothing more to need.

Then he broke the kiss, yanked her off her feet, and carried her into his bedroom.

He vanished her clothes as he laid her on the bed, then grabbed her hands and pinned them on either side of her head. When he let go, phantom restraints kept her hands locked in position. He spread her legs, using more phantom restraints to keep her open for his pleasure, then lifted her enough so that she could tuck her wings tight to her body.

He vanished his clothes and stretched out beside her.

She expected him to mount her and take his release, fast and hard. Instead, he started with her arms and licked, nibbled, caressed. He suckled one breast while his thumb stroked the nipple of the other. Finally he moved lower, his mouth brushing the hair between her legs, his fingers delicately stroking, slick with her readiness. He moved lower, licking the skin on her inner thighs, nibbling on her calves, his hands always moving.

Finally, he sheathed himself inside her in one slow stroke. His hips pressed down on hers, denying her any movement while he braced himself on his elbows and went back to suckling her breasts, flexing his hips just enough to keep her on the edge but not enough for release. He held her on that edge for a lifetime while he licked, suckled, demanded kisses.

If she could have gotten her hands free of the phantom restraints, she would have strangled him.

Desperate to respond in some way to this tormenting pleasure, she settled for the only thing she could reach. She raised her head, clamped her teeth on his upper arm and bit down.

His snarl mixed pain and fury. He clamped a hand around her throat.

"Get your teeth out of my arm."

Even knowing she was pushing him toward violence, she paused to lick his skin before she let go.

His glazed eyes studied her as his hand relaxed around her throat. "You do get feisty when you're riled." His mouth hovered over hers. Hesitated. Withdrew. "Don't bite me again until you're coming."

He moved then. Deep, strong thrusts that sent her soaring, sent her over the edge. Before she could glide down all the way, he drove her up again.

"Not yet, witchling," he growled. "You haven't flown high enough yet."

Driving her up and up until her world narrowed to the feel of his cock inside her. When he thrust her over the edge this time, her teeth found his arm again, muffling her scream as she climaxed.

This time he laughed, a sound ripe with dark pleasure, as he set his teeth into her shoulder and followed her.

Shivering, Marian eased into the kitchen, wishing she could have put her winter robe on over the flannel nightgown. But the only time Lucivar had turned violent was when she'd offered to get them some food. He'd agreed to that—until she'd put some clothes on. He attacked without warning, ripping the clothes off her before flinging her back on the bed and pinning her down. When she didn't struggle, his temper shifted back to that raging sexual hunger, and he spent the next hour playing with her and feasting on her arousal and climaxes until they were both wrung dry and exhausted. Since then, he hadn't allowed her out of the bedroom any farther than the adjoining bathroom.

The only thing she could figure out was the clothing signaled an attempt to leave him. Coming to the kitchen now might provoke another attack, even though a nightgown was hardly sufficient clothing if she tried to leave the eyrie in this storm, but he'd been gone so long, she'd become worried about him.

Apparently, she'd worried for nothing. He was standing at the stove, tending the skillets filled with food, looking much the way he did on other mornings when he insisted on cooking breakfast—if she discounted the fact that he was naked, half aroused, and didn't seem to notice the warming spells had faded to the point where the eyrie was chilly, almost cold.

Lucivar had put the warming spells on the eyrie the morning the storm started and told her they would last two days before he'd have to replenish the power in the spells. Which meant they were starting the third day of the rut. Maybe it was over, or at least easing. Should she mention the warming spells?

She shifted from one foot to the other as the cold seeping up from the stone floor bit into her bare feet.

Lucivar gave her a slashing look before turning his attention back to the food. "Go back to bed."

"I could—"

He charged. She stumbled back and hit the wall. His hands slapped the stone on either side of her head.

She stared into those wild, glazed eyes. No, the rut hadn't eased.

"You need to eat," he snarled. "I'll bring you food."

She swallowed hard. "I could—"

"You're not going anywhere! There's a damn blizzard out there. *Nothing* is going anywhere until it blows out. And the only thing you're doing is getting back into bed." He pushed away from the wall and went back to the stove. "Get out of here before I take you where you stand."

She recognized a threat when she heard one, so she slipped out of the kitchen while he watched her with eyes that held more cold fury than hot lust. She kept her movements slow until she was on the other side of the wall, out of his sight. Then she ran back to the bedroom.

The fires in the other rooms had burned out, but Lucivar had fed the one in the bedroom. A small table and two chairs were set before the hearth. They usually sat under one of the bedroom windows. He had moved them before going into the kitchen. Had she, on some level, taken that gesture to mean a return of the man she knew? An error on her part. Maybe he had some lucid moments, but the rut was still driving Lucivar—and she couldn't even guess what he would do when he returned to the bedroom.

Chilled inside and out, Marian sat in a chair close to the fire. That helped warm her, but her feet were freezing. Before she could decide if wrapping herself in a blanket would provoke a violent response, he was back in the bedroom, setting two plates of food on the table.

The look in his eyes . . . Any man facing him on a battlefield would look at those eyes and see death. All she could do was hope she would survive whatever mood was riding him now.

"Eat," he said, sitting down in the other chair.

Silverware and two mugs of coffee appeared on the table.

Steak, scrambled eggs, and thick pieces of toasted bread spread with butter and some of the berry jam she'd made.

He made no move to begin his own meal. Just watched her.

Eat, he'd said. The first bite of meat stuck in her throat, but she sensed something in him relax as she accepted the food he'd provided. When she tried the toast, his attention turned to his own meal.

Despite the fire and the hot food, she was still so chilled, she didn't hesitate to scramble back into bed when Lucivar told her to. But even with the covers tucked around her, she couldn't warm up, and she waited impatiently for him to get back from whatever cleanup he was doing in the kitchen.

The moment he slipped into bed, she felt that wonderful heat that pumped out of him and didn't hesitate to snuggle up against him. So warm. So wonderfully warm and—

The sound he made fell between a scream and a roar as he lifted straight up out of bed, flinging the covers every which way. The next moment, he was standing beside the bed, his Eyrien war blade in his hand, his eyes scanning the room.

Marian scrambled to the head of the bed and crouched there, her heart pounding. "I'm sorry," she gasped. "I'm sorry."

"Get over here," Lucivar said. "There's something in the room. Something in the bed."

"There's nothing—"

"Something touched me," he snapped. "Something icy."

"My feet." Her teeth started to chatter. She wasn't sure if it was from fear or cold.

His eyes stopped scanning the room. His head turned slowly until he looked at her. "What?"

"My feet are cold and—"

"Your feet? That was *your feet*?" He swore with obscene creativity as he vanished the war blade, plopped her back down on the bed, pulled up the covers, and got in with her. He sucked in a breath and let it out in a hiss as he wrapped himself around her and pressed her feet against his legs. "Why aren't you wearing socks?"

She didn't want to tell him she'd been afraid of provoking his temper, so she said the first thing that came to mind. "It didn't seem romantic."

He propped himself up on one elbow and looked down at her in disbelief. "You think wearing socks isn't romantic, but putting a block of ice against a man's balls *is* romantic?"

"They weren't close to your balls," she muttered. Although, if he hadn't screamed and leaped out of bed like that, she would have tried to tuck her feet a little higher up. After all, his thighs were a lot warmer than his shins.

Muttering dark things about female logic, he settled down. In a couple of minutes, she was sleepy and toasty warm, even her feet.

"Lucivar?" she said softly.

No response except to try to pull her a little closer.

"Lucivar?"

The arm around her grew heavy. His breathing was slow and even. For the first time since the rut began, Lucivar was sound asleep.

EIGHTEEN

Encouraged by the heat coming from the stone walls, indicating the warming spells had been renewed, Marian made her way to the kitchen the following morning. This time, she wore socks *and* slippers, as well as a heavy shawl over her nightgown. If Lucivar snarled at her, she could point out that he didn't like cold feet, but she didn't think he'd snarl. After he'd slept for several hours yesterday, he'd been just as hungry for her as he'd been the other days, but it had changed as the day wore on. More of their couplings had been leisurely—not a holding back to prolong the moment of climax, just . . . quieter, sweeter. More like she'd imagined he would be as a lover after his initial hunger was sated.

She paused when she reached the front room. The drapes she'd made to cover the glass doors were pulled back, revealing a clear, sunny day, which meant the storm had finally ended. She hoped the snow piled so high against the glass was due to drifts, but she suspected that wasn't the case. Which meant Ebon Rih was well and truly buried.

Buried.

She looked around—and felt shaky relief when she saw the bowls near the front door. One held water, the other chunks of meat that might have come from a package of venison she'd had in the freeze box. She hadn't dared ask about Tassle, hadn't dared try to contact the wolf on a psychic thread to find out if he was all right for fear Lucivar would sense it and think she was trying to summon another male as a rival to him. There was no other sign of Tassle, but Lucivar must have confirmed the wolf was nearby before he put out food and water.

When she entered the kitchen, she found Lucivar, fully dressed, drinking coffee from one of those plain white mugs he preferred to use. He turned away from the window, gave her one quick look, then turned back to study the world beyond the kitchen.

His eyes were no longer wild and glazed, but there was no warmth in them, either. If anything, he seemed . . . uneasy.

Uncertain about what he expected from her, she tried to smile. "Good morning."

"Storm's finally blown out."

She wondered if he meant the blizzard or the storm inside himself.

He moved away from the window, then stopped, as if he didn't want to get too close to her. And he wouldn't look at her.

He took a swallow of coffee, then set the mug on the counter. "Do you need a Healer?"

The abrupt question startled her. She wasn't sure what she'd expected when the rut finally ended, but she hadn't expected him to act like she was a stranger he'd given shelter to during the storm. "No, I don't need a Healer."

He took a step toward her—and she could have sworn he cringed before he backed away.

"I need to check on the villages, make sure everyone got through the storm all right."

"Do you want some breakfast before you go?" she asked.

"No," he replied too quickly. "I don't want—" He hesitated, then shook his head. "I have to go." He gave her one more glance before he hurried down the domestic corridor that led to the side door.

A moment later, she heard the door slam behind him.

Stunned, Marian sank into a chair and wrapped her arms around herself for comfort.

He'd run from her. Lucivar Yaslana, the Ebon-gray Warlord Prince of Ebon Rih, had fled from his own home to get away from her.

He didn't want. That was it, wasn't it? That was the reason for his uneasiness, his embarrassment. He didn't want. What he'd taken out of need, she'd given out of love. But now that the rut was over . . . Was he ashamed that, having no other females to choose from, he'd taken his housekeeper to his bed? Or was he afraid that, having seen him through the rut, she now expected him to reciprocate and accommodate her whenever she wanted a man?

She hadn't asked him for anything, had she? Having fallen in love with him, she'd hoped he would feel some warmth for her when the rut was over, maybe even want to remain lovers, but she hadn't expected anything in return for what she'd given.

Except courtesy. Or some word of appreciation before he drew the line that separated them into servant and employer would have been nice. A line, she thought with growing resentment, that he made every effort to erase whenever *she* tried to maintain that distinction.

"Ask me if I need a Healer," she muttered as she hurried to her own room and dressed in her warmest clothes. "As if I'm some feeble female who will collapse after a long bout of lusty sex. Who does he think he is, anyway? He doesn't want me? Fine. Who asked him to want me? If I have feelings that aren't returned, well, that's my problem, isn't it? I didn't ask him to love me." *But I want him to. Oh, I do want him to—and all he wanted was to get away from me.*

She had to move, had to work. If she didn't do something, she'd curl up and cry until her heart broke. And that would be the worst thing of all. If he knew she'd given him her heart as well as her body, he might feel uncomfortable about her staying even as his housekeeper.

Work didn't cure a bruised heart, but it gave her an outlet for all that fretful energy. Moving quickly, she fetched the snow shovel from the mud room. When she'd found it in one of the merchant shops, she'd been delighted. It was easy enough to use Craft to remove snow from pathways and streets, but Craft couldn't take the place of exercise to warm and strengthen the body. Today she wanted to shovel snow until she couldn't lift another bladeful. Today she'd sweep and scrub and polish the eyrie until she was too tired to think.

She opened the front door and stared at the waist-high snow. If she wanted to get out without shoveling snow *into* the eyrie, she'd have to use Craft to clear a space to stand in. Vanishing a block of snow as wide as the front door and as long as the shovel, she called it back in and let it drop in the yard beside the eyrie. Then she stepped outside.

Marian!

She didn't have to look far to find Tassle. His face filled a rough opening in a large mound of snow.

"Tassle?" Was he trapped under the snow? She lifted her hand, prepared to vanish more blocks of snow to reach him, when his face disappeared from the opening. Moments later, he scrambled out of the mound and bounded to the top of the snowbank next to her, dancing in his delight to see her.

Dancing. On top of the snow.

"How are you doing that?" Marian asked.

I am air walking. Tassle danced a little more to show off his skill.

Well, that explained the times when she'd seen Tassle trot over muddy ground and still enter the eyrie with clean paws.

Yas can teach you, Tassle said. *The Lady taught the kindred to air walk, and she taught Yas and her human friends, too.*

She wasn't sure Lucivar would be willing to teach her anything at this point. She didn't want to think about that, so she focused on the wolf. "Did you manage all right during the blizzard?"

Yas left food and water for me, and he said I could stay in the front room of the eyrie, and I did stay there at night, but Kaelas and the Lady taught the wolves who live with the High Lord how to make dens out of snow. Kaelas is Arcerian, and they make snow dens to live in during the winter. So I made a den. He paused. *Now that you and Yas have mated, are you going to have puppies?*

Mother Night. She hadn't considered that, hadn't done anything to prevent that. After a quick, desperate counting of days, she breathed a sigh of relief. She was well past her fertile time. She couldn't imagine how Lucivar would react to being told a woman he no longer wanted was pregnant with his child. She'd learned enough about his past to feel certain his response would be less than friendly.

Work. Hard labor would keep her thoughts from wandering toward things that wouldn't be.

She dug in and started flinging shovelfuls of snow as far as she could, ignoring Tassle's repeated offers to use Craft to clear the path for her. Why should *he* care if the path was cleared. *He,* and a certain Eyrien Warlord Prince, could just walk *above the snow.*

Marian?

The only person who was trapped in the eyrie by the snow was the female, who was only good for mating and . . . *making puppies.*

Marian!

The whine in that sending finally made her stop and look at the wolf—who looked back at her with woeful eyes, his head and shoulders covered with the snow she'd flung in that direction.

Then someone quietly cleared his throat to gain her attention.

Marian looked to her left—and considered flinging herself into the deepest drift and just staying there.

The High Lord, standing on air, looked down at her A snow goatee hung from his chin, and his clothes were liberally spattered with the snow she'd thrown at him. Unknowingly, to be sure, but still . . .

"Good morning, High Lord," Marian said.

He brushed the snow from his chin and clothes. "Good morning, Lady Marian."

She couldn't tell by his tone if he was amused or annoyed.

"Would you like a cup of tea?" she asked meekly.

"That would be welcome."

Hell's fire, Mother Night, and may the Darkness be merciful. Could the day get any worse?

Of course, watching him walk down the snow as if he were descending stairs only he could see produced a spurt of resentment that she quickly tamped down. It wasn't *his* fault Lucivar hadn't thought to teach her anything as useful as air walking.

Pushing that thought aside, she vanished the shovel and her cape and boots as she hurried to the kitchen. Saetan paused in the front room long enough to hang his cape on the coat tree before joining her.

As she filled the teakettle, she said, "Prince Yaslana isn't here at the moment."

"I know," Saetan replied, leaning against the counter. "I came to see you." He paused. "Do you need a Healer?"

"Do I look like I need a Healer?" she snapped, slamming the kettle down on the stove. Witchfire flared up beneath it. Cursing silently, she pulled the fire back to its proper level.

"Nooo," Saetan replied dryly, "but the question has to be asked."

She turned on him. "I can't be the only woman who spent most of the past three days in bed. Are *they* going to be asked if they need a Healer?"

"Probably not. But they didn't spend that time with a Warlord Prince in rut."

She turned away to get out cups and saucers. "I'm all right."

"Physically, I tend to agree. But you're not all right, Marian. You're upset about something, and most likely, it has to do with the rut."

She kept silent while she made the tea and set a cup in front of him when he took a seat at the pine table. She didn't join him. A week ago, she would have. But right now, she felt more like a paid servant than she'd felt in all the months she'd worked for Lucivar.

"He ran away," she said, feeling her heart ache as she said the words. "He could barely stand to look at me before he . . . bolted out of the eyrie."

"He's afraid," Saetan said quietly.

Baffled, she studied the man watching her. "Of what?"

Temper flashed in Saetan's eyes. "You have no idea what it's like to be caught in the rut, to be driven by something that eclipses everything else, to lose the veneer of civilized behavior that makes it possible for Warlord Princes to live with other people."

"I know what it's like to be with that kind of man," Marian flashed back.

"Do you remember everything that happened from the time the rut began until it ended?"

"Of course I do!"

"He doesn't."

She watched Saetan rein in his temper, watched the visible effort to chain strong feelings.

"He doesn't," Saetan said again. "Warlord Princes are not held accountable for anything they do during the rut, but that doesn't mean we don't have . . . regrets . . . about things that happen."

We. It hit her like a fist. Saetan was a Warlord Prince, too, and had gone through the rut.

Her nerves danced. She licked her dry lips. "How can a woman know what it's like for you if you never tell her?"

He shuddered. The High Lord of Hell actually shuddered. That, more than anything, made her wonder what Lucivar remembered about the past three days.

Setting the tea aside, Saetan rose. "Well. I have things to see to."

Another strong man tucking his tail between his legs and running away because of the rut.

"Thank you for stopping by, High Lord."

He gave her a wan smile. "It was my pleasure, Lady."

She doubted that, but she smiled and stayed in the kitchen until she was sure he was gone. After making a cup of tea for herself, she sat at the table for a long time.

It must have required a kind of steely courage for the High Lord to come to the eyrie, not knowing what he might find, what kind of damage he might have to try to repair. Remembering the stories she'd heard about Warlord Princes, she had to admit he and Lucivar both had a valid reason for asking if she needed a Healer. It hadn't occurred to her that Lucivar wouldn't know she didn't need one.

Maybe Lucivar's bolting this morning hadn't been meant as a rejection. If he hadn't cared, at least a little, he wouldn't have been as concerned about what had happened during the rut, would he?

She sighed. There was nothing she could do to settle things between them until he came back, so she might as well get some work done.

After bundling up again, she opened the front door—and stared. There wasn't so much as a flake of snow on the entire flagstone courtyard except for Tassle's den.

Taking the hint, Marian went back inside. She'd clean Lucivar's bedroom and make some soup. And she wouldn't allow herself to wonder if he was afraid to come home because of things he couldn't remember.

Saetan waited throughout the day, knowing Lucivar would come to him before going to the eyrie. It had been easy enough to keep track of his son. It hadn't been easy to resist summoning Lucivar to the Keep to offer what reassurance he could. But a summons of any kind would be misunderstood, and Lucivar's fear had bordered on panic too many times during the day to dare give him any kind of push.

Finally, as the afternoon waned, Lucivar walked into the room where Saetan waited. He looked exhausted, and his hands trembled a little as he poured himself a glass of brandy.

"You saw her," Lucivar said, staring into the glass for a moment before he gulped the brandy and poured another glass.

"I saw her," Saetan replied.

"Did she need a Healer? I asked, but . . ."

"No, she didn't need a Healer."

Lucivar sagged with relief. "Is she . . . upset?"

Saetan hesitated. He thought he'd taken an accurate measure of Marian's temperament when she'd stayed at the Hall during Winsol, but the woman who had flung snow on him and snapped at him in her kitchen didn't fit that measure. "She wasn't reacting as I would have expected." He frowned. "She'd struck me as a quiet-natured woman, but . . ."

Lucivar shrugged. "She usually is, but she gets feisty when she's riled."

Riled. Yes, that was a good way to describe the woman he'd seen that morning.

Lucivar set the glass down so carefully, Saetan suspected it was taking every bit of self-control to keep from throwing the glass at the wall.

"Is she going to leave?" Lucivar asked. "Should I stay away until she can—" He swallowed hard, unable to finish.

That, Saetan realized, was the root of Lucivar's fear—that the woman he was in love with, the woman he'd been courting so carefully over the last few months, would want nothing from him except the chance to escape. Lucivar wouldn't believe him right now if he said escape was the last thing on Marian's mind.

"May I offer you some advice?" Saetan asked. "Not as your father or as the Steward of the court, but as a man who talked to Marian this morning."

Misery filling his gold eyes, Lucivar said, "What's your advice?"

Saetan smiled dryly. "Get your ass home in time for dinner."

He found her in the kitchen, arranging slices of bread and cheese on plates while something that smelled delicious simmered on the stove. How many times had he come home to find her like this, preparing the evening meal for them, her warm smile of welcome a feast to a heart that had been starving for love for so many centuries? Now he wasn't sure what he should say to her, what he should do.

"Marian."

She looked up, and the unhappiness in her eyes was a twisting knife in his gut.

"I wasn't sure you would come back," she said, turning back to fuss with the bread and cheese.

"I wasn't sure you wanted me to come back," he replied honestly.

She started to speak, then shook her head and picked up the plates. "Have something to eat." The plates clattered on the counter. She hunched her shoulders, as if to ward off a blow. "You didn't have to run away. I wasn't expecting anything from you because of this. You didn't have to run."

Yes, he did. But he hadn't run far. Just down to the orchard, where he would be out of sight of the eyrie while he puked his guts out in sick relief that he hadn't seen any visible wounds on her, hadn't seen any missing limbs. He'd been terrified to look when he woke up that morning, hadn't known how keen an edge panic could have until she'd walked into the kitchen on her own.

"It's difficult to explain," he said, flinching at the tears in her eyes when she turned to face him.

"How can a woman understand if no one will explain?"

"I don't remember!"

Now *she* flinched. Then she whispered, "So I was just a body."

Lucivar shook his head. "Oh, I remember you, Marian. The taste of you, the smell of you, the sounds you made, the feel of you under my hands. The feel of my cock inside you. I remember *you*. But I don't—" He closed his eyes. "I remember bits and pieces, moments that are jumbled together and shrouded in a violent, red haze that needed some kind of release. But . . ."

Hadn't he run from this all day? This one picture in his mind. He'd worked himself to exhaustion because every time he thought of her, desire burned through him, and he couldn't ask her to be with him tonight. He couldn't. Because of that one fragment of memory. But he had to ask. Had to know. She couldn't stay here with him if he didn't know how close he'd come to destroying her.

He opened his eyes and looked at her. "I do remember one thing. Me standing by the bed, holding my war blade. And you cowering in one corner of the bed."

Marian shook her head. Then she paled as his words sank in. "No, Lucivar. No. You weren't trying to hurt me. You thought something had gotten into the room, into the bed. You were trying to protect me."

"Nothing could have gotten into that room, not with all the shields I had around it."

"Nothing did," she agreed. "But you didn't know that. You were startled and—"

"By what?" he snapped, feeling raw—and not sure he really believed her.

She mumbled something and wouldn't meet his eyes anymore.

"What?"

"I didn't know my feet were *that* cold, but then you screamed and leaped out of bed and—"

He looked at her feet.

"I'm wearing socks."

She sounded grumpy. Grumpy was good. Grumpy was *wonderful*.

"You didn't hurt me, Lucivar. Not in any way."

Relief surged through him, but his heart still ached because he'd sensed a lie beneath her words. He tried to smile. "But you don't want me for a lover." He saw hope in her eyes—and maybe something more? "Do you want me, Marian?"

"I—" She swallowed hard. "Yes, I want you."

He held out a hand. "Then take me."

She turned shy and uncertain. Couldn't quite look at him. Another kind of woman wouldn't have hesitated to take what he offered. Marian might, given time and encouragement, initiate sex by giving a quiet invitation, but she would never demand.

He approached her slowly, his fingers linking with hers when he got close enough to touch her. "Take me, Marian." He stepped back, bringing her with him, until he could sit in one of the chairs. A quick tug and a deft move had her straddling him. He brushed her hair away from her face, enjoying the feel of that black silk flowing around his fingers. His lips touched hers, a soft kiss. "Take me."

He remembered her, but now he could savor the sensations of being with her. The way her mouth opened for him. The timid way her tongue stroked his, encouraging him to take what he wanted. Soft. Sweet. The kind of sex he'd never had before.

Her fingers flexed on his shoulders, her only signal that she wanted more.

His mouth drifting along her jaw and down her neck, he undid her tunic lacings and slipped it down her shoulders as he vanished her undershirt. He doubted she was aware of arching her back in an unspoken invitation to suckle, but he took the invitation while his hands slipped under the tunic to caress her back.

He played with her until she squirmed in his lap, looking for what was still caged behind leather. She gasped, startled, when he vanished all of his clothes and all of hers below the waist. His hands kneaded her buttocks, rubbing her against him.

"Take me." He lifted her, sheathed himself inside her. "Take me." She was too focused on the feel of his cock to understand he was offering more than sex, but he knew he was offering his heart as well as his body.

She was ready to ride. He wanted to be ridden. But she didn't have the leverage, so he slid his hands down her legs and cupped her knees, giving her stirrups.

He couldn't touch her, had effectively tethered himself so that he could only submit. Watching a woman ride him to her pleasure had never thrilled him before, but watching Marian lose herself in a sexual haze made him wild to touch her, taste her. But he stayed tethered, helping her ride him, gritting his teeth against the need to explode until she cried out and crested—and took him with her.

She melted against him, limp and trembling, her head pillowed on his shoulder. Feeling his own muscles quiver, he released her knees and wrapped his arms around her, content to hold her. But as the sweat began to dry on his skin, he shivered.

"Come on, sweetheart," he said, giving her a little squeeze. "We can't sleep here."

"Can," she mumbled, rubbing her cheek against his shoulder.

He considered picking her up and taking her to bed, then dismissed the thought. With the way his legs were quivering right now, he'd just dump them both on the floor.

"We can't sleep here. It's too cold." He pushed and prodded until she finally raised her head to look at him. Her eyes were dull with fatigue, and he realized she must have tried to work herself into the ground to run from her own thoughts. "We'll have something to eat and then cuddle up in bed."

"Cuddle?"

Before she could fold around him again, he got her off him enough to dump her in another chair and call in a blanket to wrap around her. After calling in the robe she'd made him for Winsol and putting a light warming spell on it and the blanket, he brought the bread and cheese to the table, then ladled out two bowls of soup. She just watched him, which told him well enough how tired she was.

Even hunger couldn't compete with exhaustion, and neither of them managed to finish the soup. But Marian roused enough to insist on putting the food away properly, then stumbled with him to his bedroom.

It smelled clean. Fresh. He wasn't sure how she'd managed to air the room when it was still so wickedly cold outside, but he was grateful the thick musk of sex was gone.

A few minutes to add fresh wood to the fire, add more power to the warming spells, and get Marian focused enough to call in a nightgown.

Then he bundled them into bed, set his teeth, and shifted his legs until she could warm her feet on him. Damn, they were cold!

She curled up against him and sighed in contentment.

Lucivar brushed his lips against her forehead and smiled. If sex wasn't enough incentive for his little hearth witch to share his bed, having a man who would keep her feet warm this winter would be.

NINETEEN

After a hard winter, nothing lifted the spirits in quite the same way as the warmth of spring thaw, Marian thought as she went from shop to shop to do the marketing. Even Riada's muddy streets couldn't dull her pleasure—especially since Lucivar had taught her how to air walk and she could keep her boots above the mud.

He'd taught her a lot of things over the winter months.

As she considered stopping at The Tavern to chat with Merry and have a quick bowl of soup or stew before going home, she almost ran into the woman who stepped out of a shop directly in her path.

She hadn't seen Roxie all winter. Didn't want to see her now.

"Lady Roxie," Marian said, stepping to one side to go around the other witch.

Roxie stepped into her path again. "You'd better start looking for a new position. When I move into the eyrie, I'm not sharing Lucivar with the likes of *you*." She gave Marian one scathing look from head to toe. "I suppose using you for relief was better than using his own hand, but not by much. Once I'm there, Lucivar won't have any interest in you, and I'm not going to have a servant working for me who doesn't know her place."

A chill went through Marian. "What are you talking about?"

"Lucivar's going to be *my* lover. I'll be moving into the eyrie with him any day now."

Marian shook her head. "He doesn't want you. He'd never invite you to live with him."

Something ugly glinted in Roxie's eyes before she smiled. "He's not going to have a choice. He's going to have to do everything I want."

"He's the Warlord Prince of Ebon Rih," Marian protested. "You can't force him to do anything he doesn't want to do. He doesn't serve you."

"He's going to," Roxie said smugly. Then she leaned close to Marian. "I'm going to tell everyone he tried to force himself on me but came to his senses before it became an actual rape. The Queens in Ebon Rih won't demand an execution—they wouldn't dare, considering who he's related to. But I'll insist that he be made to serve me for a year as the price for the trauma inflicted by his unbridled lust. And they'll give him to me."

Marian stared at Roxie, stunned. Accuse Lucivar of rape? The accusation alone would require going before a tribunal of Queens to determine the man's innocence or guilt, and even if he was declared innocent, the taint of being accused could shadow him the rest of his life. It had happened to a friend of her father's. Despite being falsely accused, the Warlord had been dismissed from the court—and had ended up leaving Askavi because even his closest friends had turned away from him, afraid their own reputations would be smeared if they were seen with him.

Even though it still chilled her to think about it, she understood why the Warlords who attacked her had planned to kill her. If she had survived the rape and accused them, at the very least, their standing in society would have been ruined. If a nobody hearth witch could ruin aristo Warlords in Terreille, what would an accusation made by an aristo witch do to a man in Kaeleer, where the laws and Protocols were upheld far more strictly?

And if the people in Ebon Rih thought Lucivar was freed because of his family connections rather than because he was truly innocent, it would shatter his life. The Blood here would never continue to accept him as the Warlord Prince of Ebon Rih.

"You can't," Marian said. "Even if they believed you, even if they did demand that he serve you, he's an Ebon-gray Warlord Prince. You'd never control him."

"He'd have to wear a Ring of Obedience," Roxie replied. "I've heard those Rings can control *any* male."

Roxie didn't care that this would ruin him. She just wanted to enslave him, wanted to force him back into that pain he'd endured when he'd lived in Terreille. Lucivar would never obey Roxie willingly, so she'd have to use the Ring to hurt him—and because he'd never shown any interest in her, she would enjoy hurting him.

"You can't do that to him," Marian said as something inside her strained to break free.

"Watch me." Roxie turned and started to walk away.

"No!" Dropping her basket, Marian threw herself at Roxie.

Lucivar pushed his way through the crowd, cursing under his breath. A brawl on the main street of Riada. Just what he needed today. He'd hoped to convince Marian to set aside her chores for an hour to go flying with him since it was a lovely day and she hadn't had much of a chance to enjoy her recovered skills during the winter. Although that icy free fall they'd performed one sunny afternoon had ended with an enjoyable evening keeping each other warm in bed.

First he'd take care of this mess, then share a midday meal at The Tavern with Jaenelle as they'd planned. After that, he'd go home and see—

He reached the front of the crowd and stared at the two women rolling around in the mud, punching, slapping, and generally trying to tear each other apart.

"Mother Night, Marian," he said, shaking his head. What in the name of Hell was she doing?

Moving forward, he waited for an opening, then grabbed the back of Marian's belted cape and yanked. He heard cloth rip as he lifted her enough to get his other hand under her and haul her back out of Roxie's reach.

He felt her legs tuck up and had a moment to think she was trying to help him set her on her feet before he recognized the intent. Releasing the back of the cape, he pivoted in time to take that two-footed kick on the thigh rather than in the balls. Since he was still holding the front of the cape, when her feet dropped to the ground his fist became the hinge her body swung on. Straightening his arm at the last second prevented her roundhouse punch from connecting with his face hard enough to break his jaw or her hand, but it would still leave a bitch of a bruise.

And that, he thought, was more than enough.

One fast jerk that ripped more seams and she landed on his shoulder with a *whoof* that knocked the air out of her.

"Bring that one," he growled as he marched toward The Tavern, which was the closest place that had chairs and enough space to deal with . . . whatever this was.

The crowd, he noted sourly, didn't move out of his way. Seeing where he was headed, they stampeded toward The Tavern to get ringside seats.

Great. Wonderful. At least they had sense enough to leave two tables empty.

He dumped Marian in an empty chair. When she popped right up again, he shoved her back into the chair and held her arms down as he leaned over her and said in his most menacing voice, "Sit down, Marian. *Sit.*"

His quiet, gentle hearth witch bared her teeth and snarled at him.

He would have kissed her for finally producing a decent snarl except he was fairly sure she'd bite him if he tried, and then she'd feel bad. Not as bad as he would, but once she came to her senses, she'd feel bad about doing it.

He kept Marian locked to the chair while two men brought a wailing Roxie into the tavern and settled her at the other empty table. Whatever had gotten Marian so riled up was still churning through her, so when he finally stepped back, he made sure she'd have to go through him in order to tangle with Roxie again.

"Now," he snarled as he looked at the people crowded into the tavern's main room, "what in the name of Hell is going on?"

"She attacked me!" Roxie wailed. "Just because I told her she wasn't going to work for us after I moved into the eyrie."

"Since you're never going to move into the eyrie while I'm still living there, that's not a problem," Lucivar snapped. He looked at Marian and shook his head. "Is that what this is about? Didn't it occur to you she was lying?"

"Of course I knew she was lying," Marian snapped back. "But she said—"

"I *am* going to live with you!" Roxie shouted as she continued to sob. "You want me. You know you do. When I was in your bed—"

"I told you I'd slit your throat if I ever found you there again," Lucivar said.

A collective gasp. Then the room fell silent.

"You didn't mean it," Roxie sobbed. "You were bluffing to—"

"I don't bluff."

Roxie stared at him.

Disgusted, Lucivar turned back to Marian. "Was that the whole of it? What else did she say?"

He saw Marian's eyes shift from side to side, taking in all the people waiting for her answer. He watched her temper fade and her usual quiet nature surface.

"Nothing," she said.

There was more. He could tell by the way she wouldn't meet his eyes that there was more. Well, he'd get it out of her after he got her back to the eyrie and checked her over to make sure the minor cuts and bruises he could see were the worst of her injuries.

"What else did she say?" asked a midnight voice from the doorway.

Hell's fire, Mother Night, and may the Darkness be merciful. The last thing he needed right now was Jaenelle stepping into this.

Marian looked at the Black Jewel hanging from the chain around Jaenelle's neck, then looked into those sapphire eyes—and swallowed hard.

"She said she was going to tell people Lucivar tried to force himself on her so that he would have to serve her," Marian said, her voice barely above a whisper.

"He's an Ebon-gray Warlord Prince," Jaenelle said. "How would she control him?"

Marian licked her bloody lower lip. "With a Ring of Obedience."

Lucivar swore quietly, viciously, the memory of the pain that a Ring of Obedience could inflict shuddering through him.

"She's a lying bitch!" Roxie shouted.

"Is she?" Jaenelle asked, her eyes never leaving Marian's face. "There's a simple way to tell. Are you willing to open your mind to me, Marian? Will you let me read your thoughts, your feelings, your heart? Will you open yourself to me, knowing that if what you said here is a lie, I will take you down into the abyss so deep it will shatter you, destroy you? Are you willing?"

Jaenelle, don't do this, Lucivar thought.

Marian sat up straight. "Yes," she said. "I'll open my mind to you."

Everyone in the tavern waited, hardly daring to breathe.

"And you, Roxie?" Jaenelle asked, turning toward the other witch. "Will you open your mind to me, knowing a lie will destroy you?"

Wailing, Roxie shook her head.

Lucivar suppressed a shudder when Jaenelle's eyes pierced him. Her rage was a living thing, and it would take so little right now to set it free—with devastating results.

I will deal with this, Lady, he said.

And you will report to me after you've dealt with it, Jaenelle replied. *If Roxie's taste for manipulating and controlling males has reached this point, it's not just your life that's at risk, Prince Yaslana.*

I'm aware of that, Lady. I'll deal with it.

Jaenelle nodded. Then her eyes narrowed slightly as she studied Marian. *She has no injuries that require more healing skill than you possess, but I can do the healing if you prefer.*

My thanks, Lady, but I'll take care of her. He sent a touch of arrogance through the psychic thread. *Besides, she owes me for trying to kick my balls into my throat.*

I see. Then you must be pleased that she learned the lessons you insisted on teaching her.

She still punches like a girl. He rubbed his sore jaw. *For the most part.*

He felt a hint of amusement from her, which was exactly what he'd hoped for. Her rage had turned aside, but it wouldn't take much to bring it back with lethal results. As much as he loved her, he breathed a sigh of relief when she walked out of The Tavern and caught the Winds to go back to the Keep.

Which left him with his muddy, bruised hearth witch and the sobbing bitch.

"You two," he said, pointing to the two Warlords who had assisted Roxie into the tavern. "Escort Lady Roxie home and inform her father that I'll see him tomorrow."

"I want her punished!" Roxie wailed as the two men hauled her to her feet. "She attacked me! I want her punished!"

And I want you dead, Lucivar thought. *But we can't always have what we want.*

He waited until Roxie was gone before turning to Marian. "As for you . . ."

She shrank back in the chair, her courage gone.

Shaking his head, he hauled her out of the chair. "Come on, witchling. Let's get you home while you can still move. You're not going to believe how sore you'll be by tomorrow."

"Don't you worry about setting a meal on the table, Marian," Merry called. "I'll pack a basket and bring up a few dishes in a little while."

"Basket," Marian gasped. "My carry basket. All my shopping."

Taking the easy way out of this discussion, Lucivar dumped her over his shoulder, walked out of The Tavern, and caught a Wind that would take them home.

"I'm sorry," Marian said, trying not to wince as Lucivar ripped her clothes off. They were past repairing anyway, and since she was the reason he was limping and had a rather impressive bruise blooming on his jaw, she figured she shouldn't argue with him about the clothes.

"You're not half as sorry as you're going to be," Lucivar growled as he knelt to strip off her boots. He led her to the steps at one corner of the heated pool—steps he'd never mentioned the first time he dumped her in there—and kept one hand on her arm to steady her as she descended. Then he stripped off his own clothes and joined her.

"All right," he said. "Let's have a look at you." He called in a washcloth, dipped it in the water, and washed the mud off her face.

Gentle, thorough, grim. She watched his face as he tended each bruise, saw the flash of temper in his eyes when he came to a cut. Then he growled as he carefully checked her hands.

"Didn't remember to put a shield around your hands before you threw the first punch, did you?" He probed her knuckles and fingers. "Of course, if you'd thought to put a shield around yourself in the first place, she couldn't have landed a blow at all."

She raised her chin. "You didn't shield, either, when you waded into the fight."

His eyes met hers. "I wasn't expecting my lover to try to kick my balls down the street."

My lover. The words warmed her more than anything else could. He'd never said he loved her, and she hadn't wanted to spoil the easy way they were now living together by telling him she loved him. But she thought it, felt it, more with each day—and hoped that someday he would feel the same.

Then what she'd done finally sank in. She closed her eyes and hunched her shoulders.

"Marian?" Lucivar's voice was sharp, alarmed.

"I'm sorry."

"About what?"

"I caused a public scene. I'm sorry I embarrassed you by doing that."

His finger rapped her chin hard enough to startle her into opening her eyes. How could he look grim and amused at the same time?

"Sweetheart," he said, "it's going to take more than a public brawl to embarrass me. Especially since I've initiated my fair share of public scenes."

"I've never done anything like that before."

"Why did you this time?"

Anger spurted through her as she remembered the look on Roxie's face, the things the woman said. "She wanted to hurt you. She wanted to take away everything that matters to you. I couldn't let her do that."

She couldn't read the look in his eyes. Soft. Hot. Something more, but she wasn't sure what it was.

"Do I mean that much to you?" he asked quietly.

I love you. "Yes, you mean that much to me."

He smiled, then brushed his lips over hers. "Do I mean enough to you that you're going to let me fuss over you without snarling at me today?"

"I—" She frowned and studied his lazy, arrogant smile. "Do I have a choice?"

"No." He kissed the bruise on her cheek. "But you can snarl at me. I like the sound of it."

His mouth drifted to her neck, and his soft snarl as his teeth scraped over her skin made her float on a wave of desire.

"Lucivar," she whispered, wrapping arms that felt liquid and heavy around his neck. "Lucivar." She closed her eyes, unable to keep them open anymore.

She felt him shift her, felt him sheath himself inside her. Hard. Hot. Something more.

"That's it, sweetheart," Lucivar whispered as he moved inside her. "That's it. Take all of me. I want to give you all of me."

I want . . . Nothing to do but ride the last crest that left her floating.

She was vaguely aware of being lifted out of the pool, of being dried off and tucked into bed, but she couldn't rouse herself enough to shake the warm contentment that was pulling her down to a quiet, deep place.

"You put a sleep spell on me, didn't you?" she grumbled.

"You'll thank me for it later," Lucivar replied, kissing her temple.

I love you.

"That's good to hear, witchling, because I love you, too."

She was dreaming. Of course she was dreaming. But she smiled and let the dream take her.

Lucivar made a pot of coffee, then rummaged through the cold box for something to eat. Ah. There was the rest of the country casserole Marian had made for dinner last night. After putting the dish in the oven to heat, he started to look around for something to go with it, but the garden caught his attention, drawing him to the kitchen window.

Still plenty of snow out there, but where the sun had melted the snow and warmed the earth, he could see the green shoots. She'd been so delighted when she'd seen that her spring bulbs had survived the winter.

Jaenelle had reacted the same way.

Was that why Marian pulled at him the way no other woman did? She and Jaenelle were so different in some ways and so similar in others. Hearth witch and Queen, but the same qualities that made them both exceptional women, each in her own way.

And she loved him.

Lucivar smiled.

Did Marian realize she'd said it out loud? Had she heard his reply?

He called in the jeweler's box, opened it, and studied the two rings inside. When he'd bought Marian the amber necklace for Winsol, he'd also had Banard make these rings. Amber and jade set in a gold band for Marian. A plain gold band for him.

Marriage rings. He wanted to slide that ring on her finger, wanted to wear that gold band that was a symbol of commitment, partnership . . . and love.

They'd been together almost a full turn of the seasons. She'd seen the worst of him—no, not the worst; she'd never seen him walk off a killing field, but she'd gone through a rut with him—and, hopefully, he'd also shown her the best, had shown her she could grow in a marriage with him, that she could be everything she wanted to be.

Maybe it was time to ask her to share her life with him, not just as a lover but as a wife. He wanted, fiercely, to be her husband.

He closed the box and vanished it. Soon. Very soon.

First, he had to decide what to do about Roxie.

TWENTY

Lucivar took a deep breath before knocking on the front door of Roxie's house. The street was too quiet for midday, even in the aristo part of Doun. He could almost feel all the eyes peering at him from behind sheer curtains. They would have heard some version of what happened yesterday, so they knew why he was here. To pass judgment. To draw a line between what would be accepted in Ebon Rih and what would not.

Jaenelle had been right about that. It was more than his own life at stake in this decision. He'd let his dislike of Roxie color his sense of justice, had avoided her because she reminded him too much of the bitches who'd used him in Terreille—and hadn't gone after her for using other men as he'd done when he was a slave because, he'd told himself, those men had had a choice about being with her. He wasn't sure of that anymore, but the Queens in both Doun and Riada had informed him with wary formality that no complaints had been lodged, no man had come forward to say Roxie had mistreated him. Didn't mean much, although the Queens here could be naive enough to believe it did. As long as an aristo witch didn't play with an aristo male whose family would protest if his reputation was damaged, the Queens would never know about the others—youths, now ashamed that lust had overruled common sense, who were considered "sluts." Good enough when a woman wanted a warm body in bed, but too "experienced" to be considered for a public, long-term relationship—or a marriage.

He didn't like Roxie, which is why he'd given himself a full day to think hard about what was just—and, thank the Darkness, his Queen had approved of his decision.

That didn't mean the aristo families in Doun were going to find it easy to swallow. But everything had a price. Males who warmed too many beds sometimes paid dearly. Roxie would be the lesson—and the warning—that witches who used men would pay a price as well. He'd been too passive in dealing with Roxie. He wouldn't make that mistake again.

A servant escorted him into the formal parlor where Roxie's father waited. The man rocked on his heels, all ruffled indignation and puffed-up anger. But there was fear in his eyes.

"Warlord," Lucivar said.

"Prince." Roxie's father bobbed his head sharply. "I hope you've dismissed that servant. Dreadful woman, accosting an innocent girl on a public street and then spreading lies about her."

"If you're referring to Lady Marian—"

"Marian. Yes, that's the name! Your—"

"Lover."

Roxie's father paled. "What?"

"Marian is my lover," Lucivar said softly.

"But— But you promised Roxie—"

Lucivar snarled. "The only thing I ever promised Roxie was that I'd kill her if I found her in my bed again."

The man staggered toward a chair and sank into it.

He loves the little bitch, Lucivar thought as pity stirred in him. But pity couldn't alter what he'd come here to do. In truth, he was showing Roxie more mercy than she probably deserved. "Everything has a price. The price of rape is execution. Falsely accusing a man of rape also has a price—the witch's Jewels . . . or her life."

"But she didn't accuse you of anything! You only have that woman's—that Lady's word on it."

"She didn't have a chance to accuse me," Lucivar countered. He took a deep breath, let it out in a sigh, and shook his head. Better just to say it and be done. "Because she didn't have a chance to play out her game, I can be . . . flexible . . . about the penalty. I can't justify taking her life, but I won't have her putting men's lives at risk in the land where I rule. Therefore, Roxie is exiled from Ebon Rih. You have three days to get her settled beyond the borders of this valley. If she's not gone by then, I'll come hunting. And if she ever returns to Ebon Rih, I'll kill her."

"You can't!" Roxie's father wailed.

"I'm the law here," Lucivar said. "This is as much mercy as I can offer a woman like her. You can accept it and get her out of Ebon Rih"—he called in his war blade—"or I can kill her now. I imagine there will be a fair number of young men who will sleep easier tonight if I do."

Roxie's father clutched his chest. Tears filled his eyes. "Where is she supposed to go?"

"I don't give a damn." He vanished the war blade. "Just get her out of Ebon Rih, or her life is forfeit."

The man burst out crying.

Since there was nothing more to say, Lucivar walked out of the house and down the street. It was tempting to fly away, to let speed and height put distance between him and that house. But he walked down the street so the people in the other houses would see him, would know. He was the law in Ebon Rih, and nothing except his Queen's command could change that.

"Prince?"

Lucivar stopped, turned toward the voice. A young man lingered in a carriageway between two of the houses. Decently dressed, but not from an aristo family. Probably a merchant's son. "What can I do for you?"

"There was some talk . . ." He glanced down the street. "I mean . . . Roxie . . ."

"Has been exiled from Ebon Rih."

The youngster closed his eyes. "Thank you."

Lucivar choked back his temper. So. Here was one of Roxie's victims. "She won't bother you anymore."

"But what about the others?" the young man asked, pleading.

"What others?" Lucivar snapped.

"We . . . Roxie and me . . . we only did it twice. Then she lost interest in me, said I wasn't a good enough tumble for her to keep seeing me. But her friends started coming around to my father's shop, and they wanted . . . expected . . ." Bitterness filled his eyes. "They said they'd heard I was an easy romp, and I should accommodate them the way I'd done for Roxie. But I'd cared for her, and I thought she cared . . ." His voice trailed off.

"Is your family standing by you?"

"Yes, sir. My father says caring enough to be intimate with a girl isn't a mistake. My mistake was in caring for the wrong kind of girl. And Mother says all young men have a trip and stumble somewhere along the way, that I'll be a better man for it."

"But that doesn't keep the other bitches from expecting you to drop your pants," Lucivar said.

The young man hung his head. "No, sir."

He almost told the youngster there was nothing he could do for him. Then he thought about Saetan's rules for anyone staying at the Hall. "This is an order, puppy, so pay attention." He waited until the youngster straightened up and stared at him. "Until I tell you otherwise, you may not have sex with a girl without my permission. That means both of you coming before me and telling me you want each other. I'll let you make the choice about kissing and petting above the waist. You go any further than that without coming to me first, I will beat the shit out of you. And I'll beat the shit out of her, just so it's clear that the penalty to her will be equally harsh if she pushes after you decline. You understand me?"

"Yes, sir. Thank you."

"Get yourself back home. No man with any sense is going to want to be anywhere near this street today."

A restrained smile. "Yes, Prince."

Lucivar watched the young man move down the street and turn the corner, not quite running as he headed back to his own part of the village, but moving with speed. An example he intended to follow.

Spreading his wings, he launched himself toward the clean spring sky, then hovered for a moment before catching the Red Wind and heading for the Keep.

*   *   *

Lucivar watched Saetan sort through books stacked on the large black-wood table in the Keep's library. He wasn't sure why his father needed so many reference books, but if it had anything to do with Jaenelle, it wasn't something he really wanted to know. "Did I do the right thing?"

"Who are you asking?" Saetan replied.

"The Warlord Prince of Dhemlan."

Saetan set aside the books and looked at him. "You did the right thing. You didn't have sufficient reason to order an execution or to break Roxie and deprive her of the power she might have used to . . . persuade . . . a lighter-Jeweled male to have sex with her. I imagine some harsh things will be said about you by the aristo families in Doun—"

Lucivar snorted. "As if I give a damn."

Saetan nodded, as if he had expected that answer. "I also imagine, when word of this spreads, the Queens who rule the Blood villages in Ebon Rih are going to think long and hard about this. So are the War-lord Princes who live in the valley. You've drawn the line, Lucivar, and they're the ones who will be expected to help you enforce it." He paused. "I suggest you stay close to home for the next day or two."

"I'm not going to hide because I made a decision some of the Blood won't like," Lucivar snarled.

Saetan smiled. "You're not hiding, you're practicing domestic survival skills. If you leave Marian to deal with all the visitors I expect you'll have in the next few days, she'll be more than justified in kicking your ass."

TWENTY-ONE

Marian rushed into The Tavern, relieved to see Merry behind the bar. Even more relieved that the place hadn't begun to fill up with the people who stopped by for a midday meal.

"I need a small keg of ale," Marian said. Then she frowned. "Maybe two."

"Having a party?" Merry asked as she wiped down the bar.

"A party would be fun. This is—" Marian perched on a stool. "I'm not sure what this is."

"Word got out," Merry said, cocking her head. "You've been having visitors?"

Marian groaned. "It wasn't so bad yesterday. Several aristo Ladies from Doun called on Lucivar to assure him *they* hadn't done anything to deserve exile. Which makes you wonder what they *had* done. But today . . ."

"Last night, everyone who came into our place was talking about Roxie's exile." Merry reached for the coffee mug on the bar. "Good for us to be rid of the bitch. Good for Lucivar for doing it." She raised the mug in a salute. "Here's to the Prince of Ebon Rih."

"And how is our Lady Marian today?" Briggs said as he walked in from the back room.

"She needs two small kegs of ale," Merry replied.

"I'll add a couple of bottles of brandy to that," Briggs said. "The Prince might need something a bit stronger than ale by the time the day is done." He grinned. "Or you will."

Marian smiled weakly. There was more truth in that than Briggs knew. She'd baked yesterday and early this morning in anticipation of having a few visitors after Lucivar had told her about Roxie, but she hadn't anticipated so many. She'd already stopped at the bakery since there wasn't time to tend to the visitors and do more baking herself.

When the kegs and brandy appeared on the bar, she vanished them and jumped off the stool. "I'd better get back."

"I'm making steak pies to serve this evening," Merry said. "I'll make an extra and send it up to you. You'll have enough to do today without putting a meal together."

"Thanks," Marian said with a smile. She hurried out of The Tavern and flew home as fast as she could.

Hell's fire, Mother Night, and may the Darkness be merciful, Lucivar thought as he went to answer the door—again. How did Saetan tolerate days like this? A fist in the face had always gotten his message across well enough. Why did he have to *talk* to all these people?

And where was Marian? The aristo bitches from Doun had looked at her with barely concealed sneers, but the merchants and other family men who were showing up looked relieved when she greeted them and offered some refreshment. He made them nervous. She was someone they felt easy being around. Which is why he'd let her run herself ragged looking after them while they waited for an audience with him.

As soon as she got back, he was going to lock the door and they were going to sit down for a quick meal and an hour's peace. Until then . . .

When he opened the door, the Queen of Riada's Consort—and husband—walked in. A Summer-sky Prince, he'd been with his Lady for ten years now and was the father of her two children.

"Is the Queen upset about my decision?" Lucivar asked as he closed the door.

"No," the Prince replied. Then he smiled. "Although she's had her share of visitors today. No, I'm not here on my Queen's behalf."

Lucivar studied the man. He didn't know him well since he preferred a place like The Tavern to a dining house that catered to aristos, and the only time he'd attended dinner parties was when Jaenelle had been invited as well and needed him to be her escort.

"When Roxie leaves Ebon Rih, she'll no longer be your problem—or ours, for which I thank you. But a woman who would make false accusations about an Ebon-gray Warlord Prince is either stupid or trouble or both."

"We agree on that. I'm sorry to make her someone else's problem, but I couldn't justify doing more than getting her out of Ebon Rih."

"I understand that. There are ways to handle such problems." The Prince looked uncomfortable. "Sometimes a person takes a wrong turn and needs a new place where a smear on his, or her, reputation isn't reflected back from every person he meets."

Bitterness filled the Prince's eyes for a moment before a different memory warmed them again, making Lucivar wonder what kind of smear had brought the man to Ebon Rih for a fresh start.

"Sometimes that's all a person needs to find everything he was looking for," the Prince continued softly. Then he stiffened, as if suddenly realizing he'd said too much. "And sometimes a person won't change. A Lady can sleep with a different man every day of the year, and no one will say a thing because that is a Lady's privilege. At least, no one will say anything publicly. But a woman who is a user gets a reputation among the men, and when she leaves one hunting ground for another, word is quietly sent to warn the men there that her . . . affection . . . may not be sincere."

Lucivar nodded. He would have preferred blunt words to this diplomatic hedging, but he was Eyrien. "You have a solution?"

The Prince tipped his head in acknowledgment. "My brother serves as an escort in a Queen's court. She rules one of the larger cities on the coast of Askavi. A quiet word to him would spread to the other courts. If Roxie relocates to one of their cities, they'll know."

Lucivar thought about the young man he'd met on Roxie's street, a young man who would spend the next few years working hard to clean that smear off his reputation. "Do it."

Just then Marian rushed in from the kitchen, looking breathless and windblown—and beautiful.

"Lucivar, I— Oh. Good day, Prince."

"Lady Marian," the Prince replied, offering her a slight bow.

"Would you care for refreshments?"

Lucivar almost grinned at the exasperated look she gave him, could almost hear her thoughts: *Leave him alone for a few minutes, and he keeps an important visitor standing at the door.* She'd come a long way from the frightened hearth witch who had sat at his kitchen table last summer.

"Thank you for the offer, Lady, but I need to be getting back."

When the Prince left, Lucivar locked the front door and came back to the kitchen, rubbing his hands over his face. "I don't care who comes knocking, for the next hour you and I are going to have some peace."

"I brought back kegs of ale and some brandy," Marian said as she unbuckled the belt of her new cape.

"Give me a hug. That will do more for me than ale and brandy put together."

She looked at him, startled, then gave him an understanding smile as she walked into his open arms.

"Poor Lucivar," she said as she slid her arms around him. "You've had a beastly day, haven't you?"

He rubbed his cheek against her hair. "And it's not over yet." There was one visitor he was expecting who hadn't shown up yet. He was almost looking forward to that little discussion.

Marian heard the raised voices when she came out of the pantry with a jar of fruit to go with the steak pie. Feeling cowardly when she recognized Luthvian's voice, but not sufficiently ashamed of the feeling to enter the front room, she stayed at the edge of the kitchen where it was least likely she'd be seen. She didn't want to get in the middle of this— especially when she heard a viciousness in Lucivar's voice that made her shiver.

"Don't use that tone with me," Luthvian said.

"What tone?" Lucivar snarled. "I'm not a boy you can slap down, and I'm not a slave you can control. You don't like my tone, get out of my house."

Luthvian's voice gained a sharp, slicing edge. "You exiled an aristo witch simply because—"

"She was a bitch, a liar, and a user. She got away with it because she never quite crossed the line of forcing a male into her bed. Well, planning to accuse me of attempted rape crossed that line."

"You only have the word of a hearth witch that Roxie intended any such thing."

"A witch who was willing to open her mind to my Queen, knowing a lie would destroy her. Hell's fire, Luthvian! It doesn't matter if Roxie would have gone through with accusing me. Even if she'd had second thoughts about taking me on, she wouldn't have had second thoughts about trying that game with a male who wouldn't have known what to do once she'd gotten a Ring of Obedience on him."

"What would you have done?"

"Ripped the bitch apart. She wouldn't have lived an hour after she put a Ring on me."

Marian clamped a hand over her mouth to muffle her gasp. As the tense silence continued, she peeked around the corner and caught a glimpse of Lucivar as he paced away from Luthvian and turned back, framed by the archway. The look on his face . . . Warrior. Predator. He looked magnificent. And terrifying.

"You don't mean that," Luthvian said, her voice tight.

His laugh was sharp and bitter. "I saw hundreds of Roxies while I was a slave in Terreille. They didn't survive me. Do you know why they stopped trying to use me as a pleasure slave, Luthvian? Because I was so damned vicious, and every one of those bitches left the bed damaged in one way or another. The bedroom wasn't just a battleground for me; it was a killing field. I gloried in the spilled blood, the screams, the pain— because those bitches gloried in inflicting pain, in spilling blood, in hearing men scream."

"Stop it," Luthvian said.

"Why? Turning squeamish? I loathed everything Roxie was."

"She was a high-spirited aristo witch," Luthvian protested. "Maybe she'd become too obsessed with having you for a lover, but she's just—"

"Another Prythian. Another Dorothea. Another bitch like the ones who turned Terreille into a nightmare. If you're telling me *that's* what is festering in the aristo families in Doun, then there's going to be a purge and a bloodletting the likes of which Ebon Rih has never seen."

"You wouldn't."

"I don't bluff." A long pause. "Let it go, Luthvian. I let her live. Let that be enough."

Silence. Then the front door slammed.

Knees shaking, Marian crept into the kitchen. Setting the jar of fruit on the counter, she glanced over and saw Lucivar in the archway, watching her.

"You have an opinion?" he snarled. "Then say it."

She said the only thing she could think of, the only thing that mattered. "You aren't vicious."

He just smiled at her. "I'm a Warlord Prince, Lady. I was born vicious."

"Not like that," she said, hating that her voice quivered. "Not in bed."

She held her ground as he moved toward her, came close enough to touch her.

"Yes, I am," he said softly. "That's the way I was. That's the way I could be again." He shook his head as he raised his hand, his fingertips touching her hair. "I want to be your lover. I *chose* to be your lover. That makes all the difference. Being in bed with you is like soaring on a sweet wind. I chose to be your lover, Marian . . . just as you chose to be mine."

She threw her arms around him and held on, warmed by his embrace when his arms circled her. She gave herself a few moments to enjoy being with him before she asked, "Is this going to cause trouble between you and Luthvian?"

His lips brushed her temple. "There's always trouble between me and Luthvian. This is just another piece."

She nodded, not sure what to say to him. "There's steak pie for dinner. Merry brought it up a little while ago."

"Then why don't I open a bottle of wine and—"

He stiffened. When he stepped back from her, his eyes were hot with temper, on the borderline of wild. He bared his teeth and snarled softly.

Mother Night.

"Did you think you could hide it from me? Did you think I would have let those men into our home, would have left you alone with them when you're vulnerable?"

"I wasn't vulnerable," she protested. "It just started." And she hadn't thought he'd be able to catch the scent of moon's blood when there was barely a hint of it yet. Before he could start roaring, she spun around, opened a drawer, withdrew the six pieces of parchment she'd prepared as a joke, and held them out. "Here."

He took the pieces of parchment and looked at them, then frowned in puzzlement. "A certificate for fussing? What's—" He read it through. His eyes still held the heat of temper when he looked at her, but his mouth was curving into that lazy, arrogant smile. "This entitles me to twenty minutes of fussing with no snarls or grumbles from you?"

"Yes," Marian said warily, wondering if she should mention it was intended as a joke. A fluttery feeling filled her stomach when his smile got lazier, more arrogant.

He handed back one piece of parchment and vanished the other five. "I'll redeem this one now."

"What? But—"

"Uh-uh," he said, leading her over to a chair. "No snarls, no grumbles. Says so in your very own handwriting."

"But—"

His mouth covered hers. When he finally stepped back, whatever she'd been about to say didn't seem important anymore.

He laughed. "You should see your face. Such a grumpy little witch."

Well, she thought as she watched him put together their evening meal, at least she'd given him something to laugh about.

Sitting alone at her kitchen table, Luthvian poured another glass of wine and continued brooding.

Roxie was a bitch and a thorn in everyone's side. She couldn't argue with Lucivar about that. But she was an educated bitch from a good family. An aristo family. Lucivar just refused to see that *some* leniency had to be given for the Blood who ruled society and, more often than not, made up the courts that ruled in every other way.

She'd kept an eye on him since he'd become the Warlord Prince of Ebon Rih. He was her son, after all. Just as she knew his father had been keeping a close eye on him. But his father . . .

Luthvian gulped wine. Poured more. Better not to think of his father.

The point was, Saetan wasn't doing a thing to encourage Lucivar to associate with Blood who were his social equals. He should have been escorting the daughter of another Warlord Prince to dinner or the theater, should have been attending dinner parties where the guests were among the elite. Instead, he was still stopping at a tavern for an ale or a meal. And who did he escort to the theater? His housekeeper.

He was becoming too attached to the hearth witch. Oh, Marian had been useful enough cooking his meals and washing his clothes. And there was no arguing that his temper had mellowed a little since she'd started spreading her legs for him. But he wasn't treating her as a favorite servant or even a temporary lover. He was starting to treat her like a . . . wife.

And that wouldn't do. No matter what Saetan said, it simply would not do. She wasn't going to have some Purple Dusk witch from a noth-ing family dilute the SaDiablo-Yaslana bloodline. Marian didn't have the education, the culture, the background. She would never encourage Lu-civar to move in the social circles he should simply because she would never be comfortable in those circles. He'd never live up to his poten-tial. His children would be less than they should be.

He needed exposure to women who wouldn't set his back up the way Roxie did. Oh, not that Roxie would have been acceptable. A Rih-lander, a witch from one of the short-lived races, as Lucivar's wife? No. Not in a thousand lifetimes. But a dark-Jeweled Dhemlan witch from an aristo family? A woman like that would be perfect. Same coloring as an Eyrien but without those damned wings. The daughters from a union like that could become Priestesses, Healers, maybe even Black Widows. Maybe there would even be a Queen among them. And the sons would be something more than fighters, something more than arrogance and temper riding a cock.

Luthvian poured the last of the wine, studied the deep red color.

But Lucivar would never listen to her, would never yield to her wishes, would never even look at a different kind of woman while Marian was there making his favorite meals and keeping his cock sheathed.

Which meant she had to convince Marian it was in her own best interest to leave.

TWENTY-TWO

"They're lovely."

Marian turned away from the bed of spring flowers, wary of the friendly tone in Luthvian's voice. "Lucivar isn't here right now."

"I know." Luthvian opened the gate and stepped into the garden, looking around as if she'd never seen it before. "I came to see you."

"Why?" Marian pressed her lips together, struggling for enough composure to offer hospitality. Luthvian's opinion of her, disapproval of her, always pulsed in the air. So this unexpected warmth in the Black Widow's demeanor made her uneasy.

"You do care about Lucivar, don't you?" Luthvian asked, suddenly sounding anxious.

"Yes, I"—*love him*—"care for him very much."

"Then do what's right for him, Marian. Do what's best for him."

"I don't understand."

Luthvian looked distraught. "May I have something to drink?"

"Of course." She led Luthvian to the side entrance and down the domestic corridor to the kitchen. She never thought twice about Jaenelle using this entrance, but as Luthvian's presence seemed to gain weight behind her, she wished she'd gone around to the front door.

Tassle? Marian called. *Lady Luthvian is visiting.*

Sulkiness filled the link between them. *I will stay away.*

Luthvian wasn't fond of Tassle—probably because he referred to her as "Yas's bitch." Which, from Tassle's point of view, was true. It still didn't make things easy when the two of them were in the same room.

"I'll put a kettle on for tea."

"Thank you." Luthvian sank into a chair. She undid her cloak's fastenings but didn't take it off, a clear signal that she didn't intend to stay long.

Neither of them said anything until Marian brought the tea to the table. She watched Luthvian take a sip, then set the cup aside.

"Lucivar and I have our problems, but I only want what is best for my son," Luthvian said earnestly.

Marian nodded, not sure how to reply beyond that.

"And even though I've sometimes been harsh with you, I want what is best for you, too, Marian." Luthvian paused and pressed her lips together as if she were waging some deep internal battle. "Don't you see what's happening? You've made it too easy for him to play house."

"What?" Marian's cup clattered in the saucer, slopping tea.

"You're taking care of all of his physical needs, so he's not making any effort to find a wife."

"Wife?"

"Do you think this is easy for me?" Luthvian snapped. "Mother Night, woman, he comes from *the SaDiablo family*. They aren't going to accept anything less than an accomplished witch from an aristo family for Lucivar's wife."

"But— They like me."

"Of course they like you! You cook his meals, clean his home, give him regular sex that makes him easier to deal with. Why shouldn't they like you? But like is a far cry from accepting you beyond your role as housekeeper and bedmate. They know you're only a temporary pleasure for him. So why shouldn't they be friendly? But that's all you are, Marian. That's all you can be. You don't have the education, the accomplishments, or the family connections that would make you an acceptable mate for a man who can trace his bloodlines to the High Lord and Andulvar Yaslana."

Luthvian raked a hand through her hair and looked at Marian sadly.

"Even if he asks you to marry him, you'll always be the outsider, never quite be one of them. You don't really comprehend the power that family wields. When they start discussing spells and magic that is so far beyond you they might as well be dancing on the moon, what are you going to offer? A new recipe for nutcakes? When they're entertaining Queens and their courts, are you going to sit in the corner with your knitting? Don't you want a home that's really your own? Children who won't be measured by their father's potential and be found wanting? And what about Lucivar? Are you going to use sex to chain him to a woman who is less than he deserves?"

Tears thickened in Marian's throat. "I'm not chaining him with anything."

"Then let him go. Find a man who doesn't have obligations that you can never help him meet. Mother Night, Marian, I'm begging you. Let my son go." Looking defeated, Luthvian fastened her cloak and pushed away from the table. "If you truly love him, do this for him."

"I can't think," Marian choked back the tears. "I need to think."

"Then think," Luthvian said softly. "But if you wait too long, binding Lucivar to you will bring nothing but heartache."

Marian couldn't move. Could barely breathe. When she heard Luthvian leave, she pushed the cups aside, pillowed her head in her arms, and wept.

TWENTY-THREE

S tanding on the mountain where he could look down at his home, Lucivar brushed a finger across the two marriage rings in the jeweler's box. Something was wrong with Marian, had been wrong since yesterday. But she wouldn't talk to him, was shutting him out. Even in bed last night, her response had been discouraging enough that he'd given up after a few kisses.

A mood? The Darkness knew, females had them. But he felt her yearning toward him at the same time she tried to pull back. What did that mean?

Maybe that clash with Roxie had shaken her up more than he'd thought. Or maybe, after such a public display of her commitment to him, she was wondering about the strength of his commitment to her.

Only one way to find out.

Lucivar closed the ring box and vanished it. Then he spread his wings and glided down to the eyrie. As he went through the kitchen, he snatched a nutcake cooling on the metal racks, took a large bite, then paused and looked around. Were they having a party tonight that he'd forgotten about? She seemed to be cooking enough to feed ten people to the stuffing point.

He winced. A husband should remember if that many people were coming to dinner. Then he cheered up. Maybe she'd planned to invite some of the women from Riada to a female gathering—a couple of hours to eat and chat about . . . whatever it was women talked about when they booted men out of the room. Since he was usually gone for at least part of the day, she wouldn't necessarily have mentioned it.

He winced again. He hoped she hadn't mentioned it. Even if it had nothing to do with him, he should have remembered.

Maybe that's why she was moody. Nerves, most likely, about hosting her first gathering—which would make it clear to anyone who wasn't a fool that Marian was acknowledging her place as his Lady.

And what better way to celebrate a marriage announcement than with a party?

Grinning, he stuffed the last of the nutcake into his mouth and went out to the garden.

The lift in his own mood suffered a blow when he saw her gently touch the petals of one of the spring flowers. She looked so sad, so lost.

"Marian?"

She jumped at the sound of his voice. "Oh. I didn't think you'd be home."

"I want to talk to you about something."

He watched her pale as he walked toward her. Something was wrong here, something that pricked at him in warning, but he couldn't sense the source.

"What?" Her voice came out a tortured whisper.

He looked away for a moment. He'd thought this would be easy, just a formal step to acknowledge what was already between them.

"I'm in love with you," he said, watching her eyes, trying to read what he saw in them. "I want to make a life with you, have children with you if you want them, see the seasons turn with you. I want to marry you, want you to be my wife as well as my friend and lover. I want to be your husband."

She shook her head and took a step back.

He felt the sharp edge of rejection slice his heart. "Won't you at least consider it? We've done well together these past months and—"

"I can't." Marian turned away, her shoulders hunched as if he'd delivered a hard, unexpected blow.

"Why?"

"Because I'm not what you need," she said, her voice filled with pain. "I'm just a Purple Dusk hearth witch with little formal education, no accomplishments that count for anything—"

"Wait just a damn minute."

"—and I'd just be an embarrassment to a man who is the High Lord's son."

He took a step back, his head reeling. "You won't marry me because Saetan is my father? Hell's fire, woman. He adores you."

She shook her head fiercely. "I'm not going to diminish the SaDiablo line. I care about you, Lucivar. I care so much. I'll be your lover as long as you want me, but I won't marry you."

He took another step back. Then he laughed bitterly. "I'm good enough to bed but not good enough to marry? I don't think so, witchling. Fine. You don't want to marry me, that's your choice. You want to stay and keep working as my housekeeper, that's fine, too. But you'll move your things back to your own room before I return. I'm no one's toy, and without love, I'm no one's bedwarmer."

He leaped over the flower beds, lightly touched down on the stone wall, then launched himself skyward toward clean air—and away from a place that now filled him with pain.

"Lucivar," Marian whispered as she watched him slice the sky before he caught one of the Winds and disappeared.

What had she done? And why? She was doing it for him, wasn't she? Doing what was best. But . . . Her head felt stuffy, like it was full of cobwebs. So hard to think. But something wasn't right.

He'd been so hurt. He shouldn't have been hurt. Good enough to bed, but not good enough to marry? How could he think that? How terrible if he believed that. How could she leave while he was hurting so much?

She walked back into the eyrie and tried to settle herself with the familiar tasks of cooking and baking. She'd wanted to be sure there was plenty for him to eat that he wouldn't have to fuss over while he was looking for a new housekeeper. Wanted to be sure he was cared for before she . . .

I love him. I don't want to go. Why do I have to go?

She couldn't think properly. Something didn't feel right. But he hadn't demanded that she leave, so she had a little time to figure it out.

Luthvian stood on the edge of the flagstone courtyard, glad she'd shrouded herself in a sight shield before climbing the steps from the landing place. Lucivar would have detected her if he hadn't been so off balance, but Marian never would.

The compulsion spell had worked, but not well enough. The little hearth bitch was fighting it. If she'd been able to wrap the spell around Marian, everything would be done by now. But if Lucivar had sensed *any* kind of spell, he would have summoned his father to help him identify and break it, and Saetan . . . No, it wouldn't do to have Saetan become aware of that spell. So she'd wrapped the compulsion spell around her own voice, and her words had stuck to Marian like warm tar.

But not enough. Caution had forced her to keep the spell light. Too light, it seemed. Because it was clear to her that Marian would try to remain as Lucivar's housekeeper, and if the hearth witch was still here when the spell wore off completely . . .

No. She wasn't going to have her son married to a hearth witch.

It might look suspicious to show up so soon after Lucivar's departure, so she'd wait an hour and return to give the compulsion spell a little boost—one that would get Marian out of the eyrie . . . and out of Lucivar's life.

Merry threw a shawl around her shoulders. "Briggs, can you watch things for a little while?"

"Sure I can, but where are you going?"

She saw the worry in her husband's eyes. He had reason to worry. They both did. Lucivar had never walked into their tavern at opening time to gulp down three double whiskeys before he stormed out again, his eyes full of fury and pain. The Prince of Ebon Rih needed help, and there were only two people she could think of who could give it to him right now.

"I think Lady Angelline is staying at her cottage. I'm going to try to find her." And if she couldn't find Jaenelle, she'd go to the Keep. The Seneschal would know how to reach the Queen or the High Lord.

"Be careful, Merry."

"That I will." But as she left the tavern, she glanced up at the mountain where Lucivar made his home—and wondered what had happened there.

Lucivar strode into the room that had become Saetan's study at the Keep. Part of him wished he was still a child who could climb into his father's lap for comfort. He was too much of a warrior to ask for emotional comfort, so he settled for a fight that would let him vent the hurt inflicted by Marian's words.

"I asked Marian to be my wife," Lucivar said. He saw Saetan tense and wondered if Marian had been right after all. Would his father have been opposed to the marriage?

"You don't seem pleased about that," Saetan said in a neutral voice.

"She turned me down."

"Why?"

"Because I'm the High Lord's son." As soon as he said it, he realized he didn't want to fight after all—at least, not with words. But as he turned away from the desk and headed for the door, his own pain pushed him into making one more reckless verbal jab. "So you don't have to worry about the SaDiablo bloodline being diminished by a witch who hasn't got the education or the accomplishments to—"

The door slammed shut with a force that shook the room.

Lucivar spun around in time to see Saetan slowly rising from the chair behind the desk.

"You will not do this," Saetan snarled softly as he came around the desk. "You will not use me like this."

Wary now, his heart pounding because of what he saw in his father's eyes, Lucivar said, "Like what? I—"

That deep voice became thunder. *"You will not use me as a weapon against your own heart!"*

"I'm not. I didn't."

Saetan slipped into the Hayllian language. Words poured out in a hot river. Lucivar didn't understand most of it, but he caught a few phrases here and there, as well as the name Peyton.

I lanced an old wound, Lucivar thought with regret as a rage and pain he couldn't begin to match flooded the room. *I wouldn't have pushed at him if I'd known I'd open an old wound.*

"Father." No response. *"Father."*

The words stopped, but the rage still vibrated through the room.

"I didn't mean that. I'm sorry I said that." His own temper rose. "I'm not the one who used you as a weapon. And those excuses are nothing but shit." Since he couldn't get out of the room until Saetan let him go, he paced. "Just shit. Like that 'I'm just a hearth witch' crap she was spewing. I thought we'd gotten past that. Guess I was wrong." Beaten, he stopped pacing. "The truth is, she doesn't want an Ebon-gray Warlord Prince as a husband. She's willing to bed one, but not marry one. That has nothing to do with me being your son . . . and everything to do with me, with who and what I am."

He turned toward the door. "Let me go."

"Where?" Saetan asked too softly.

"Just away from people. Out on the land."

The door opened. He fled the Keep—and wondered what that blankness in Saetan's eyes meant.

Marian scrambled out of the way as Luthvian pushed past her into the eyrie's front room.

"You wouldn't listen, would you?" Luthvian growled. "Wouldn't heed the warning. Well, I hope you're satisfied, little witch."

"I did what you asked," Marian cried. "I told him I wouldn't marry him when he asked me this morning."

"But you intend to stay here, don't you, pouring salt on the wound? Keeping just enough of a tie so there's no clean break that will heal."

"No." She felt beaten, battered, unable to stand against the words.

"You stayed long enough for him to ask instead of resigning your position and getting out. So what happens to him now is on your head."

"What are you talking about?"

"He's gone to fight the jhinkas. Gone alone to face a savage race that hates Eyriens. And he'll throw himself into that fight with your rejection ripping at him, keeping him unbalanced while he tries to survive odds that are against even someone with *his* unusual strength and skill. If he dies . . ."

"No!" Marian cried. "He can't die. He can't."

"Everything has a price," Luthvian said ruthlessly. "If he dies, that's the price for loving *you*!"

Weeping, Marian sank to the floor.

"Go away, Marian. Disappear. If he manages to survive, your presence will only be a torment to him."

Lucivar dying? Because of her? She should go to the Keep, find the High Lord. No. He'd blame her for this. If Lucivar got hurt, he'd blame her. And why shouldn't he? Who else was there to blame?

Luthvian was gone long before Marian was able to stagger to the kitchen and splash cold water on her face. She'd pack. She'd go away. She didn't want to be a torment to the man she loved.

She looked around the kitchen.

But first she had to deal with all the food she'd cooked. It would spoil if she left it out, and if he was wounded, he would need the meals she'd—

Tears spilled from her eyes, and her head ached from that cobwebby feeling that had almost gone away. Still, she went about the business of doing everything she could for him before she disappeared from his life.

As the afternoon waned, Saetan paced, trying to push the past out of his mind so that he could consider the present.

Something wasn't right here. Something didn't fit. And his son's heart was bleeding because of it.

He called in his cape. Whipped it around his shoulders as he strode out of the room.

Something wasn't right. And he was damn well going to find out what it was.

When the front door of the eyrie crashed open, Marian dropped the plate. There wasn't time to think of the mess or broken crockery before Saetan stormed into the kitchen. He came to an abrupt halt when he saw her, his eyes filled with brutal intensity.

"Tell me why," he said too softly.

"I don't—" His power blazed in the room, making her feel cleaned out, hollow—and, strangely, as if she was starting to regain her balance after an illness.

"You love him. He loves you. So tell me why you're turning away from that love."

"It's because I love him!" Marian cried. But the words didn't seem quite right anymore. "I'm not what he needs."

"I'll tell you what he needs," Saetan roared. "A woman who loves him, who can accept him for who and what he is."

"I'm not good enough!"

Saetan stared at her. "The only way you wouldn't be good enough is if you didn't love him enough. So maybe you're right after all, Marian. I thought you had more backbone and heart. My error." He took a step back. "Good day, Lady."

It was the sneer in the way he said "Lady" that snapped something inside her. And she heard Lucivar's words again: *Don't let them win. . . . If you give up your wings, what else will you give up because someone tells you you're just a hearth witch?"*

"Lucivar," she whispered. Then, "High Lord!" She jumped over the broken plate and the spilled food and raced for the front door.

He paused on the threshold and turned to face her.

"You have to stop him," Marian gasped. "You have to help him. Please."

"Stop what?"

"He's gone to fight the jhinkas. He'll get hurt."

Saetan frowned, then turned away to look out the open door. "If he did, it didn't take him long. He's in Riada." He gave her a strange look, then held out his hand. "Come on. I'll take you to him."

She clasped his hand. It didn't matter what he thought of her. Nothing mattered as long as Lucivar was all right.

Lucivar strode down the main street of Riada, his temper on a choke chain, waiting to blaze. Being alone didn't comfort him, the land didn't comfort him. But being away had given him time to think.

Something wasn't right, and that "something" was the battleground.

He'd almost missed that, had almost turned away. Not anymore. If Marian didn't want to marry him, he'd have to accept it, but she'd have to do better than spew those piss-ass excuses before he walked away.

But before he went back home to corner his hearth witch, he'd coat his temper—and his nerves—with a couple more whiskeys.

As he approached The Tavern, Jaenelle and Merry burst out of the door. A moment later, Saetan dropped from the Winds and appeared in the street. With Marian.

She rushed toward him, then skidded to a stop. Her breathing hitched. Tears filled her eyes as she studied him from head to toe. Then her hands curled into fists, and when she opened her mouth . . .

"You stupid, idiotic . . . *male.*" Marian blinked back the tears. He was all right. No wounds. Not even bruises. He was all right.

She was so glad to see him she wanted to wring his neck.

"I love you too, sweetheart," Lucivar said in a very nasty tone of voice.

"How could you be so stupid?" she yelled. "How could you go off and fight jhinkas by yourself? I don't want to be a widow before I have a chance to be a wife."

"You don't want to be a wife, remember?" Lucivar snapped. "You made that quite clear this morning."

"I was confused. My head was feeling all cobwebby, and I couldn't think." From the corner of her eye, she saw Jaenelle and Saetan snap to attention and study her with narrowed eyes. "And before I could think straight, you were gone. How am I supposed to marry you if you go off and get yourself killed dead?"

"Dead is usually what happens when a person gets killed." Lucivar took a step toward her. "And what do you care anyway? You don't want to marry me."

"I do want to marry you!" She stamped her foot in frustration. "If there was a Priestess standing here, I'd marry you right this minute!"

"She offered to marry him," Merry said.

"In front of witnesses," Jaenelle added.

Lucivar pointed a finger at Marian and snarled, "I accept."

"And he accepted," Merry said gleefully.

"In front of witnesses," Jaenelle added. "How soon can the Priestess get here?"

A brief pause. "She says half an hour," Merry replied. "She needs to wash up a bit and change her clothes, then hitch up her pony cart."

"My cart's already hitched," a man called out. "I'll go and fetch her. That'll save some time."

Marian stared at Lucivar. Hell's fire, Mother Night, and may the Darkness be merciful. What had she just done? "I should— I—"

Jaenelle grabbed one arm, and Merry grabbed the other.

"No time for that," Jaenelle said as they dragged Marian through the tavern to the back room.

"You can clean up in our place," Merry said, tugging Marian up the stairs to the suite of rooms she and Briggs called home. "No need to go back to the eyrie."

"But—" Marian stammered.

"I'll dash up to the eyrie," Jaenelle said. "That green dress will look lovely as a wedding dress. And I'll bring the amber necklace Lucivar gave you at Winsol."

"We'll have to see what we can do for a wedding supper," Merry said to Jaenelle. "And I'll have Briggs nip over to the baker's to see if there's a cake left."

"I made lots of food today," Marian mumbled.

"Well, isn't that convenient?" Jaenelle said cheerfully. "I'll bring that, too."

"But—"

A hand pressed against her cheek. She looked into Jaenelle's sapphire eyes. Dark, soft power rose up beneath her, flowed through her, washing away the last of that cobwebby feeling—and the doubts along with it.

"Do you love him?" Jaenelle asked.

She offered the Queen of Ebon Askavi the truth. "With everything I am."

Jaenelle studied her for a moment. Then she smiled and said, "Welcome to the family, little Sister."

"Come along now," Merry said. "If you're not ready by the time the Priestess arrives, your man will start chewing holes in my bar."

A tug from Merry and a push from Jaenelle got her headed toward the bedroom where she would prepare for her wedding.

Lucivar stood in the street, watching as people scurried in and out of shops, shouting suggestions to each other while they prepared a wedding feast.

Saetan strolled over to join him, a glint of amusement covering vicious anger. "You were right, boyo. She does get feisty when she's riled."

"She wasn't thinking."

"Are you going to give her time to reconsider?"

"Hell's fire, no." Lucivar rubbed the back of his neck. "But where did she get the idea that I was going to go fight jhinkas?" Cobwebby. She'd said something about feeling cobwebby. He knew enough about the Black Widow's Craft—sweet Darkness, he was related to enough of them—that if she'd said anything like that to him this morning, he would have rushed her to the Keep for help.

He looked into Saetan's eyes and knew what lay beneath the anger.

"I told your mother that if she interfered again with what was between you and Marian, I would take her to the darkest corner of Hell and leave her there," Saetan said too softly.

For a moment, he couldn't think, couldn't breathe. No idle threat. Saetan didn't make idle threats.

"Let it go," Lucivar said. "I don't want blood spilled for my wedding." *But I won't forget this, Luthvian. I will not forget.*

Saetan looked away and nodded. When he looked back, he smiled. "Are you going to just stand there, or are you going to get dressed for your wedding?"

"Am I going to have to wear that fancy outfit I acquired when Jaenelle established the Dark Court?" Lucivar demanded.

"Definitely."

He sighed. "Thought so."

But he smiled as he raced through the sky toward home.

TWENTY-FOUR

Saetan lingered by the open tavern door. The evening air was chilly
this early in the spring, but it hadn't kept the party from spilling out
into the street once the tavern's main room got too crowded. People danced in the tavern—and they danced in the street. Ale and whiskey,
brandy and wine flowed along with the laughter and high spirits.

He winked at Prothvar as the Eyrien Warlord slipped into the room.
The sun hadn't set in time for Prothvar and Andulvar to make the wedding, and Mephis was still on his way here from the Hall, but the family
would gather and celebrate tonight.

"You know, don't you?" Jaenelle asked as she slipped her arm
through his.

"I'll take care of it, witch-child."

"In that case, I'm going to dance."

He watched her join the line of dancers, watched her say something
to Merry that had them both laughing so hard they missed the first few
steps of the dance. He hadn't been able to make those kinds of friendships, had stood too far apart from the people he ruled. Not by choice;
simply because he was who and what he was. But Lucivar, with his hot
temper and rough kindness, would have friends who cared about the
man. And Marian, with that fire and strength of will beneath her quiet
nature, would help him stay connected to the people he ruled.

"High Lord?"

He turned and found the Queen of Riada smiling hesitantly at him, her Consort beside her. "We don't have an invitation, but we'd like to offer the Prince and his Lady our warmest regards."

He smiled at them. "It's an open party. We'd be pleased to have you join us."

He watched the Queen and her Consort thread their way through the crowd. He saw Jaenelle glance their way and smile. Aristo manners didn't stand a chance against his daughter. Before those two knew it, they'd be dancing with shopkeepers and helping fill plates as if they did it every day.

Then he looked back at the door and saw her standing there, her eyes hot with suppressed anger. He'd sent her a message as a courtesy because she was Lucivar's mother. He'd deliberately sent it late as a kindness to his son—and to Marian.

"Luthvian." It was cold satisfaction to watch her anger change to fear as he walked up to her.

"So," Luthvian said. "You got your way after all."

"It wasn't a contest, Lady." At least, not for him. He stepped closer, lowered his voice until only she could hear. "I warned you, Luthvian. The only reason you aren't on your way to Hell is because Lucivar asked me to let it go. I'm going to honor that request—as a wedding present. But if you ever use a spell on Marian again—or try to cast one on Lucivar—I'll break you. I'll strip you of your Jewels and your power, strip you down until you have nothing left but basic Craft. And it will be done so fast, no one will be able to stop me."

She paled but said nothing.

"Now," Saetan said, fighting to keep his temper reined in. "Will you join us in celebrating your son's wedding?"

"There's nothing to celebrate," she said roughly. Then she turned and walked away.

Lucivar shifted to block Marian's view. The dark ripples of anger from Saetan and Jaenelle were sufficient warning to tell him who had arrived. He turned slightly so he could watch the door. After what he suspected was a brief, and futile, pissing contest with Saetan, Luthvian walked away.

★She wouldn't stay?★ he asked Saetan on an Ebon-gray spear thread.

★No, she wouldn't stay.★

★So be it.★ It stung that she wouldn't make the effort to wish him happy, but he wasn't surprised. She'd tried to drive Marian away, and she'd failed. That would be a sharp little bone in her throat for a long time to come. And the sad truth was, although she was his mother, she wasn't family.

"Lucivar?"

Before Marian had a chance to ask him what was wrong, a voice said, "So, Cousin. This is the Lady who captured your heart."

Lucivar grinned as Marian stared at the Red-Jeweled Eyrien Warlord standing before her. "Sweetheart, this is my cousin, Prothvar Yaslana."

"Oh, my," she squeaked.

Prothvar smiled. "I'm hoping my new cousin will honor me with a dance."

"Wait your turn, puppy," another male voice said. "This dance is mine."

He felt her tense, saw her eyes go wide as she stared at the older Eyrien Warlord Prince. "And this is my uncle Andulvar."

"The Demon Prince," she whispered.

Her knees buckled. He grabbed her under the arms and hauled her back up. And he saw the hesitation, and a hint of sadness, in Andulvar's eyes as the older man started to step back.

"The Demon Prince asked me to dance," Marian said, still wobbling a little. She leaned against his chest and looked up at him. "Do I look all right?"

She looked beautiful. "You have a smudge on your nose." Adorable, as she scrubbed at the nonexistent smudge. She was still a little wobbly when she gave Andulvar a brilliant smile and held out her hand.

"She's delightful, Cousin," Prothvar said as they watched Marian and Andulvar waltz.

"Yes, she is," Lucivar replied. *And she's mine.*

Which is why he cut in on his uncle halfway through the dance. "Mine," he said, giving Andulvar a hard tap on the shoulder.

"Possessive little puppy, aren't you?" Andulvar said, stepping aside.

"Damn right," Lucivar replied as he swept his hearth witch into the dance.

"That was rude," Marian scolded.

He grinned. "And your point is?"

She huffed—and struggled not to laugh.

He slowed the steps until they were doing little more than swaying in each other's arms. "Jaenelle suggested we spend a few days at her house in Scelt for a honeymoon."

"Oh, I wouldn't want to inconven—"

"She also said she would talk to the Queen of Sceval so that I could take you there to meet some of the unicorns."

"Unicorns? Really?"

"If you want. We can do anything you want. You can have anything you want."

"You," she said softly. "I want you."

Her words warmed every part of him. Warmed one part in particular.

He nibbled on her ear and whispered, "Are you going to let me fuss over you tonight?"

She pulled back. Her eyes danced with laughter as she bared her teeth and snarled at him.

His laughter filled the room. He scooped her up and spun her around. When he finally set her on her feet again, she clutched his jacket and swore at him.

He grinned at her as the people around them laughed and applauded. "That's my feisty hearth witch."

Zuulaman

A story from Saetan's past

1

Saetan set aside the latest letter from the Zuulaman ambassador, leaned back in the chair behind his blackwood desk, and rubbed his eyes. A half dozen meetings with the man and nothing had changed. The same complaints filled this letter as had filled the last three. He understood the concerns, even sympathized with them up to a point. But he wouldn't order Dhemlan merchants to buy coral and pearls exclusively from Zuulaman traders at a higher price than other Territories offered to sell sea gems of the same quality. He'd already checked on the complaints that Dhemlan ships were encroaching on the fishing grounds that belonged to the Zuulaman Islands. Hayllian ships were certainly plying the same waters and competing for catches, but the Queens who ruled the fishing towns in Dhemlan were quick to penalize any boat that fished beyond the Territory's established waters—just as they were quick to send the Warlord Princes who served them out to confiscate the catch of any boat that encroached on Dhemlan's fishing grounds.

Of course, he hadn't heard so much as a whisper of complaint about Hayll. Not yet, anyway. Sooner or later, the Zuulaman Queens would become less enamored with Hayll's Hundred Families—the aristo families that heavily influenced the Hayllian courts if they didn't rule them outright. He might be Hayllian by birth, might have lived his early years in the slums of Draega, Hayll's capital, but, thank the Darkness, he'd shed himself of that self-centered race centuries ago. For the most part. He had no interest in the Hundred Families, except to keep a watchful eye on their intrigues to be sure the people he ruled came to no harm because of them.

But that still left him with the problem of dealing with Zuulaman. He was certainly willing to sell them surplus grains, meat, and produce for a reasonable price that wouldn't beggar Zuulaman's people, but he wasn't willing to cut prices to the point that his own people suffered, especially when the islands still had enough arable land to feed their population, despite the fact that they made little effort to care for the land. Which was part of the problem. They overfished their waters, overplanted their farmland, pushed the islands' resources to the breaking point. Then the Zuulaman Queens complained that they couldn't sell their surplus, which rightly should have gone to feed their own people—or they complained that they had no surplus, and the pottery and other art forms that were distinct to their people didn't sell at the prices they wanted. Which wasn't surprising. No one but aristos with surplus income, or debts enough to ruin their families, could afford the asking price for most of what Zuulaman tried to sell.

Still, as the Warlord Prince of Dhemlan, it was his responsibility to deal with the Queens who ruled the other Territories in Terreille, so he would meet with the Zuulaman ambassador once more and hope that, this time, there would be some glimmer of understanding in the man's eyes when he explained why the trade agreements the Zuulaman Queens wanted were not acceptable.

As he reached for the letter to review its contents again, the door of his study opened, and his wife, Hekatah, hurried into the room as quickly as a woman three weeks away from childbirth could move.

"Saetan," Hekatah said as she lowered herself into the chair in front of his desk. "I just had the most distressing news from home."

This is home. But he bit back the words since it was as useless to think them as it would be to say them. Hekatah was a Red-Jeweled Priestess from one of Hayll's Hundred Families, and she looked at the Territory of Dhemlan in much the same way that she looked at her family's country estates—as something quaint and inferior . . . and valued only for what she could take from it.

"Is someone ill?" he asked politely, although he knew the reason for her distress.

"No, but Mother says you refused to give my father and brothers a loan. I'm sure she misunderstood something, because that accusation is utterly—"

"True."

She stared at him. "It can't be."

Her gold eyes filled with tears, and her mouth moved into that sexy, sulky pout that had pulled at his loins when he'd first met her and now always scraped against his temper.

"I'm sorry, Hekatah, but I won't give your family another loan." He'd informed her father of that fact a month ago. Since the bastard had delayed telling Hekatah, why couldn't he have waited a few more weeks until she had safely delivered the baby?

Her lips quivered. One tear rolled down her cheek. "But . . . why?"

"Because they didn't honor the agreement they made with me when I gave them a loan last year." When her only response was a blank look, he swore silently and struggled to be patient. "Last year, in order to save your family from financial and social ruin, I gave them almost two million gold marks to cover all of your father's and brothers' gambling debts. I paid close to a million gold marks to cover all the debts that were owed to all the merchants who would no longer allow anyone in your family to buy so much as a spool of thread or a handful of vegetables on account. And I also provided another million gold marks with the understanding that those funds would be put back into the estates so that the properties could be restored and once more provide an income. I made it clear that I required receipts to prove materials were being purchased for that purpose and that your father and brothers would receive no further financial help from me if they didn't fulfill their side of the bargain. I never received a receipt of any kind, and from what I can tell, absolutely nothing was done to benefit the estates and make them productive again. Since they squandered what they already received, that is the end of it."

"Maybe they did do something foolish with the money," Hekatah conceded with real, or feigned, reluctance before adding quickly, "But I'm sure they didn't believe you really meant it about not giving them another loan."

I'm a Black-Jeweled Warlord Prince, the strongest male in the history of the Blood. I'm the only male Black Widow in the history of the Blood. And I'm the High Lord of Hell. Despite the fact that I still walk among the living, I rule the Realm of the Blood's dead. How could your family not believe I meant what I said?

"It doesn't matter if they believed me or not," he said. "The decision stands."

She slapped the chair's arm. "You're being unreasonable. The Dhemlan people didn't complain the last time you raised the tithes to cover the loans. They won't dare whine this time, either."

Speechless, he stared at her and wondered if there was any point in explaining how deeply she'd just insulted him. Finally, he regained his balance sufficiently to reply. "I didn't raise the tithes, Hekatah. That was a personal loan, from me to your family."

Now *she* stared at *him.* "Our money? You used *our* money?"

"Of course. Why should the Dhemlan people have to pay for your family's financial imprudence?"

"So you took almost four million gold marks away from *us*?"

He shrugged. "I could afford it . . . once." And the timing for that last loan had pissed him off enough that he'd played their manipulative game with so much finesse Hekatah's family had never realized he was playing. "You could always give them a portion of your quarterly income."

"As if that pittance would do much good," Hekatah replied, her eyes filled with resentment.

"Thirty thousand gold marks a quarter is hardly a pittance," Saetan said with cutting gentleness. "Especially when you don't have to maintain a household"—he saw the jolt of nerves, quickly suppressed, which confirmed what he'd suspected—"and the only thing those funds have to cover are your personal expenses." He paused. "Or, if you prefer, I can release the principal I put in trust for you as a wedding gift, from which you receive that quarterly income, and you can give your family as much of it as you choose."

She said nothing. He hadn't expected her to.

She pushed herself out of the chair and stood before him, one hand resting on the large belly where his child moved inside her. It might have softened him enough to yield a little if he'd truly believed that gesture was a protective one rather than a reminder that she had power over something he wanted.

"I'm going to Hayll to offer my mother, and the rest of my family, whatever comfort I can," she said.

He choked back a protest, knowing she would use any concern he showed as a weapon against him. "Do you think that's wise?" he asked mildly. "You shouldn't be traveling so close to your time."

"I'm going to Hayll."

The challenge filled the space between them.

"I would appreciate it if you would send a message back to let me know you arrived safely," Saetan said.

Her shoulders slumped, her only acknowledgment that she had lost this battle of wills. Then she walked out of his study.

He waited there, his hands, tightly clasped, resting on the desk, while his mind, at times too facile for his own comfort, turned over nuggets of information and presented him with some unpalatable conclusions.

Last year, Hekatah's father had come to him for help in solving a "minor financial difficulty" shortly before Peyton's Birthright Ceremony, when the power a Blood child was born with was tested and confirmed, and the child received the Jewel that would be a visual warning of the depth of power that lived within that flesh as well as a reservoir for the power that wasn't used. It was also the time when paternity was formally acknowledged or denied. A man could sire a child, raise that child, love that child, but he had no rights to that child until the mother granted him paternal rights in a public ceremony that usually followed the Birthright Ceremony. It didn't matter if the child looked like the man in miniature, didn't matter if the woman had taken no lovers so there could be no question of who was the sire. If paternity was denied at that public ceremony, the man had no rights to the child. He could be cut out of the child's life in every possible way, becoming nothing more than the seed.

A public ceremony—and a decision that was never overturned. In many ways, a man who wanted children was held hostage by his heart until that ceremony. After that, the child was his, no matter what happened between him and the mother.

He should have wondered why Hekatah had wanted to get pregnant so soon after they'd married, should have wondered why she hadn't wanted a year or two just for the two of them to enjoy each other. But her true personality had already begun to crack the facade that had attracted him to her in the first place, so she couldn't afford to delay a pregnancy if she was going to keep the prize of a Black-Jeweled Warlord Prince whose wealth rivaled any of Hayll's Hundred Families and who ruled a Territory without having to answer to any Queen. At least, not a flesh-and-blood Queen that she could see or understand. She hadn't recognized his deep commitment to Witch, to the living myth, dreams made flesh. He had served Cassandra, the last Witch to walk the Realms. He had made a promise to serve the next one, no matter how long he had to wait for her to appear. *She* was the Queen he served, and he ruled both Dhemlan Territories, the one in the Terreille and the one in Kaeleer, on her behalf.

Hekatah hadn't recognized his commitment, and he hadn't recognized that she'd seen him as a way to fulfill her ambitions to become the most powerful Priestess in Terreille—or, possibly, all the Realms.

How convenient that she'd become pregnant with Peyton a few months before Mephis's Birthright Ceremony. How well-timed was her father's embarrassed admittance a year ago, when it was time for Peyton's Birthright Ceremony, that the family debts had become a difficulty. The bastard had mentioned too many times how distressed Hekatah was about the family's social status being tarnished by whining merchants who had so far forgotten their place that they'd gone to the Queen of Draega to complain about a "few" overdue bills.

He'd made sympathetic murmurs, but he'd understood the threat: If he didn't make some effort to reestablish her family financially, Hekatah might say something in haste when it came time to acknowledge Peyton as his son and grant him paternal rights to his child.

Hekatah's father and brothers were anxious to have their gambling

debts paid off since those were to other aristos and the invitations to social engagements had declined as those debts had piled up. Instead, Saetan had paid up the accounts with all the merchants and presented her
father with the receipts—and had insisted that he was simply too caught
up in the celebration of Peyton's Birthright Ceremony to deal with
"minor" gambling debts. He'd assured her father that those would be
taken care of after the ceremonies.

While they realized he might refuse to pay the gambling debts if
Hekatah said something in haste at the ceremony, it never occurred to
anyone in her family that his timing in paying off the debts that concerned them the most was as manipulative as their timing in asking for
financial help.

So his paternity of his younger son was granted, the debts were paid
off . . . and he gave himself a few weeks to consider if, with his sons safely
under his control, he wanted to remain married to a woman who expected absolute fidelity from her Warlord Prince husband while she indulged her taste for variety by having affairs with men from the minor
branches of Hayll's aristo families.

He'd almost accepted that his hopes for this marriage had been wish-
ful thinking and the self-delusion of a lonely man who, while receiving
plenty of bedroom invitations, had been craving love.

Then Hekatah had told him she was pregnant again. And, once again,
a child's life held his heart hostage. He didn't blame her for the pregnancy. He wanted another child, had willingly stopped doing anything
to prevent conception, and had let her decide when she was ready.

But the timing had just been a little too convenient to make him feel
easy, just as this request for another loan coming so close to when
Hekatah would be brought to childbed was a little too convenient.

He sighed. Hekatah would punish him for not agreeing to provide
the loan by staying with her family instead of being with him right now,
and Zuulaman . . .

He pushed away from the desk. Screw all of it. What was the point of
being the most powerful male in Terreille and shouldering the responsibility for a land and its people if he couldn't indulge himself once in a
while?

Leaving the study and moving through the massive structure he'd built as a symbol of his power as well as a family home, he bounded up the stairs and headed for the family wing. He opened a door and his sons, Mephis and Peyton, the two joys of his marriage, rushed forward to greet him.

"Papa!" Peyton said. "Look what we helped Daemon Carpenter make for us!"

"You helped him, did you?" Saetan said as he took a wooden ship from his younger son and gave it the careful inspection that was expected— and wondered if he should offer Daemon Carpenter hazard pay for whatever "help" had been given.

"Well," Mephis said, "we didn't actually help him make the ships, but we did make the sails."

Which explained the badly stitched canvas. But that was the difference between the two boys. Peyton tended to be fiery, dramatic, always leading with his heart, while Mephis thought things through as well as he could before acting, was a little less demonstrative, and more bitingly exact about details.

"That's helping," Peyton protested, scowling at his older brother. "Are you going to read us a story?" he asked, turning back to his father.

Saetan blew softly on the sail, using Craft to expand a puff of air into enough to fill the canvas. "No, I don't think so," he replied, handing the ship back to Peyton in order to inspect the one Mephis now held up for his approval.

Peyton's lower lip pushed out in a pout, but before he could start wheedling, Mephis gave him a hard elbow jab in the ribs.

"No," Saetan said slowly, "as commander of the fleet—"

"How come you get to be commander?" Peyton demanded. "Ow!" That because Mephis's elbow caught him in the ribs again.

"Because I'm bigger," Saetan replied. "As I was saying, as commander of the fleet, I think my stalwart captains should test their new ships on the Phantom Sea."

"Where?" Peyton asked.

"He means the pond," Mephis said out of the corner of his mouth. "Now, hush."

"Dangerous place, the Phantom Sea," Saetan said, his deep voice dropping into a croon while he continued to inspect Mephis's ship.

"Are there whirlpools, Commander?" Mephis asked.

Peyton frowned at his brother, still young enough that he had to work to catch up.

"Yes, Captain Mephis," Saetan crooned. "There are the Wailing Whirlpools and the Murky Mists. Challenges for even the most courageous sailors."

"Are there sea dragons, too?" Peyton asked, his eyes wide.

"What would the Phantom Sea be without sea dragons?" Saetan murmured.

"How'd we get sea dragons in the pond?" Peyton whispered to Mephis.

"Papa's going to make them for us," Mephis whispered back.

"Oooh." Peyton looked up at Saetan, his gold eyes sparkling with anticipation.

"If we're ready, gentlemen," Saetan said, handing the ship back to Mephis.

"And I suppose you're going to end up muddy to the knees and smelling like pond water," a female voice said.

Saetan turned to face the woman now standing in the doorway. He had no complaints about Lady Broghann, the Purple Dusk–Jeweled witch who was the boys' governess and teacher, but he was feeling a little too raw to accept a challenge from anyone, especially a woman.

Then he saw the humor in her eyes that balanced the stern tone of voice.

"I expect some mud will be inevitable," Saetan said solemnly.

"Yay!" Peyton said, only to be elbowed again by Mephis.

Puppy is going to be black-and-blue before he figures out when to keep quiet, Saetan thought.

"Now," Lady Broghann said. "Don't go drinking so much grog that you run aground."

"What's grog?" Peyton asked, starting to bounce with impatience.

"You would know if you had paid attention to the lesson about sailing," she replied.

While Peyton's face scrunched up in thought, Saetan turned away and coughed to clear the laughter from his throat.

Finally able to look suitably grim, he turned back to his captains. "Shall we go?" Then he noticed the boys' appearance. The trousers were worn to the point of looking shabby, and there was a long tear on the left sleeve of Peyton's shirt—neatly mended but still apparent. "Why are you wearing those clothes?"

"This is the attire of adventurous sailors," Lady Broghann said.

Curious, Saetan studied her. "According to . . . ?"

"My mother. I have three younger brothers."

And her younger brothers had a clever older sister.

"An unquestionable authority," Saetan said with a small bow.

"What's grog taste like?" Peyton asked, having circled back to something more interesting than clothes.

"It tastes like milk," Saetan replied.

"Sailors drink milk?"

"Short ones do."

While Peyton was working out why Mephis was snickering, Commander Saetan led captains Mephis and Peyton to the Phantom Sea, where they tested their ships against Murky Mists, Wailing Whirlpools . . . and sea dragons.

2

Hekatah stood at the window of her mother's private receiving room, rubbing her belly to soothe the whelp inside her while she stared at the back garden.

How much did Saetan know? Was the comment about not having to maintain a household simply a comment, or did he know about the little house she kept in Draega for the pretty toy-boys? It wasn't that she didn't enjoy sex with Saetan. He was an exquisite lover. How could a man who had been Witch's Consort for years not be exquisite in bed? But he wasn't as much *fun*. She couldn't play with him the way she could the toy-boys. So why shouldn't she enjoy a romp with a male she could dominate? Besides, it wasn't like she was doing anything wrong. Fidelity and sexual exclusivity were required of the male in a marriage, not the female. Males *served,* after all.

But Warlord Princes were a law unto themselves, and a Black-Jeweled Warlord Prince might not think the status of a wedding ring was sufficient reason to overlook his wife's lovers.

Her mother, Martella, entered the room, unhappiness and embarrassment rolling off her in waves.

"We had to go to a different butcher, so the Darkness only knows what the cook will set before us for the evening meal. And the bastard demanded payment before he'd hand over the meat!" Martella's mouth thinned to a petulant line. "I had to return the pearl brooch I'd bought last week in order to pay for the meat." She sighed as she joined Hekatah at the window. "Your . . . *husband* . . . is being difficult about assisting the family, isn't he?"

"He says he won't make another loan because the extra million gold marks he gave Father wasn't used for the estates as they'd agreed."

"How could it be?" Martella cried. "Your brothers wanted that new carriage and team of horses, and then there was that payment that the Queen demanded we make because that witch was broken when Caetor got a little too enthusiastic about enjoying himself."

"Didn't she tell him she was virgin?" Hekatah asked.

"Well, of course she did. But she wasn't anyone *important.* Nothing would have come of it if her family hadn't gone to the Queen and made a formal accusation. And they said it was *rape,* insisting the girl hadn't agreed to have sex. The Queen gave your father and Caetor a choice: They could pay all the Healer's expenses and make a settlement as compensation for breaking the girl and stripping her of her Jeweled power, or Caetor could stand before a tribunal of Queens to determine if the accusation of rape was justified. The only reason she offered a choice was because the girl is a nobody and Caetor is from one of Hayll's Hundred Families." Bitterness filled Martella's voice. "The question wouldn't have come up at all if we still had the wealth we deserve. But I suppose we can't expect your husband to understand aristo concerns."

Hekatah felt the verbal slice. Her family's opinion of her marriage was divided. "Saetan" was a common name among the lower social classes. Hell's fire! Even one of the footmen who worked at the family's house here in Draega was named Saetan. And "SaDiablo" wasn't even a twig on a branch of any of the Hundred Families. She'd searched when she'd considered him as a mate. Her mother and aunts had searched. He seemed to have come out of nowhere when he built SaDiablo Hall in Dhemlan and made the bargain with the Dhemlan Queens in both Terreille and Kaeleer to protect their people and lands in exchange for being the Warlord Prince of Dhemlan—*the* ruler of both Dhemlan Territories. Socially unacceptable, he was still a Black-Jeweled Hayllian Warlord Prince who had wealth and power—two things she coveted. So she'd studied him until she was certain how to approach her quarry. She'd worked hard to dazzle him, to intrigue him, to convince him that the Jewels he wore and the power he wielded were insignificant compared to her feelings for the man.

But the wedding ring hadn't brought her what she'd thought to get from the bargain. Despite what she'd said, she'd wanted to bend the strength of those Black Jewels to her will, had wanted him to wield all that dark power on her behalf. Instead, she'd gotten the man. A man who followed the Blood's code of honor, even though he was powerful enough to do anything he wanted and no one could oppose him. Of course, no one really knew what he could do with the Black Jewels. Telling people he was the High Lord of Hell was a nice fillip for a reputation of temper that had never actually been seen. Not that she believed it for a moment. After all, she *knew* the man.

No, Saetan wasn't aristo. Would never be aristo. Would never appreciate the wants and needs of any of the Hundred Families.

"There's still Zuulaman," Martella said. "The commission we'll receive from the new trade agreements with Dhemlan will help restore our status among the Hundred Families."

Hekatah rubbed her belly. She hadn't told her mother and aunts yet that Saetan was being stubborn about the new trade agreements. But Hayll was entitled to whatever Dhemlan could offer. After all, if Saetan hadn't made the bargain with the Dhemlan Queens, that Territory would have become the property of the Hundred Families.

Since he *had* interfered, they would have to get what was owed them another way.

She smiled at her mother. "I think it's time to give my husband more incentive to take the trade agreements with Zuulaman seriously."

3

Saetan dropped the papers on his desk and stared at the Ambassador. "Is this your Queen's idea of a joke?"

"It is the trade agreement between Zuulaman and Dhemlan," the Ambassador replied calmly.

"This is *shit,* and you know it," Saetan snarled. "Zuulaman expects the Dhemlan Queens to hand over the surplus from all the harvests as well as a percentage of the livestock, pay a tithe on every product made by the Dhemlan people, *and* add a 'market' fee for anything that comes from other Territories that is not bought through a Zuulaman merchant. Have you all lost your minds? The Dhemlan Queens will never agree to this."

"They will if you insist upon it. You rule here. You are the law here. If you sign the agreement, they have to comply or suffer the consequences."

He felt himself sliding down into the abyss, sliding down to where his inner web rested at the depth of power signified by the Black Jewels—the cold, glorious Black. At the same time, he knew he was rising to the killing edge, that state of mind that revealed a Warlord Prince for what he truly was—a born killer, a natural predator. The effort to keep his temper leashed made his body quiver.

"I made an agreement with the Queens of this Territory to protect their people and their land with everything that I am. Now you expect me to use that power as the whip that will force them to turn their people into chattel for Zuulaman's pleasure." Saetan shook his head. "There is nothing Zuulaman can offer that is worth this. You may tell your Queen, and the Queens who answer to her, that there will be no trade agreement with Dhemlan."

The Ambassador bowed his head. "I will leave you to consider the matter."

"There's nothing more to consider."

The Ambassador turned and walked to the study door. Then he paused. "I should mention that your wife is now a guest of the Zuulaman Queens—and will remain so until an agreement has been reached. The message I received also indicated that there was a miscalculation by the Dhemlan Healer as to Lady Hekatah's time. She may give birth any day now, if the birthing hasn't already begun."

"Do you know who I am?" Saetan asked too softly.

The Ambassador smiled. "You are an honorable man."

"Do you know who . . . and what . . . I am?" he asked again.

The Ambassador's smile faltered. "Hopefully, you are a man who realizes a small inconvenience to the Dhemlan people is worth less than the well-being of your wife and child."

Saetan waited until the Zuulaman Ambassador had left the Hall before he sank into his chair behind the blackwood desk.

Hell's fire, Mother Night, and may the Darkness be merciful. What had possessed Hekatah to leave Hayll and go to Zuulaman? Why would she choose to travel so near her time? She'd been aware of the difficulties he'd been having with the Queens who ruled those islands. Had she gone thinking she'd be an honored guest, that the Queens would try to sway her in the hopes that she, in turn, could sway him to agree to something that would be of no benefit to the people he ruled? Now she was a hostage—and their unborn child with her.

So tempting to declare war on the Zuulaman Queens. He wouldn't need to gather the Dhemlan Warlord Princes to do it. He wouldn't need anyone or anything but himself to annihilate the Zuulaman courts. But Hekatah was so vulnerable right now, unable to use her own power until after the birthing. They would kill her the moment they felt his presence anywhere near their islands.

He had to find another way. There had to be another way.

They had issued the challenge, drawn the line. Did any of them realize that, by doing so, they had invited him to step onto a killing field?

Did any of them realize what would happen if he did?

★   ★   ★

Andulvar Yaslana prowled the sitting room in Saetan's suite, too edgy and angry to remain still—and a little uneasy about the way Saetan *did* remain quietly at the window, watching Mephis and Peyton play in the enclosed garden bounded by the walls of the family wing. Anger needed sound and motion, unless it ripened to the point where it had a killing edge and needed to be quenched on a killing field. That was his kind of anger. Eyrien anger. But Saetan's stillness had a different quality to it. Always had, even before he'd made the Offering to the Darkness and came away from it wearing Black Jewels.

"What are you going to do?" Andulvar asked.

"Wait to see what Zuulaman wants," Saetan replied quietly.

"They made it clear enough," Andulvar growled as he picked up the trade agreements and dropped them back down on the table.

Turning away from the window, Saetan walked over to the table and stared at the agreements. "Either they really didn't think this through, or they intended something else all along and these agreements are just smoke."

"They're holding your wife hostage," Andulvar pointed out. And as far as he was concerned, Zuulaman could keep Hekatah. Saetan was better off without the bitch.

"My wife is a Red-Jeweled Priestess from one of Hayll's Hundred Families," Saetan said. "If they lay a hand on her, they'll not only have me to deal with but Hayll as well. Zuulaman is enamored with Hayll, so they won't do anything that will make the Hayllian Queens turn on them."

"There's still those agreements."

Saetan reached out and pushed the papers with one finger. "Which aren't worth a damn thing. Say I sign them on the condition that the agreements are handed over to Zuulaman at the same time that the baby and Hekatah are returned to me."

"Then Zuulaman gets what it wants."

"For a few hours. As soon as we were home, I'd send a message to the Dhemlan Queens that I was stepping down as the Warlord Prince of Dhemlan, giving up my claim to this Territory."

The words hit Andulvar like a fist in the belly. "You'd give up Dhemlan?"

"Everything has a price. These agreements are only for Dhemlan Terreille. I'd still have the Dhemlan Territory in Kaeleer."

"But . . . this is what you wanted."

An odd look crept into Saetan's eyes, gone before Andulvar could put a name to it.

"Ruling this Territory was a price equal to the protection I offered," Saetan said softly. "It was a price worthy of what I am. But I don't need it."

Andulvar rubbed the back of his neck. Damn politics. The Eyrien way was simpler—a blade and a battlefield, not these sly games played with words.

"Since the Dhemlan Queens didn't agree to this, the moment I step down, there are no trade agreements. Zuulaman gains nothing."

"They won't expect this."

"They should. If they've paid any attention to how I've ruled this Territory since the Queens here made their bargain with me, they should. Which means they never expected me to sign the agreements, but the greed and audacity of asking for so much will make their real goal seem more reasonable."

Saetan smiled a gentle, brutal smile.

Andulvar suppressed a shudder.

"So I'm waiting for them to name the ransom that will buy back my wife and child," Saetan said.

"Will you pay it?"

That odd look crept into Saetan's eyes again. "Yes, I'll pay it. And it will be the last thing Zuulaman ever gets from me that isn't paid for in blood."

4

Hekatah watched the children on the beach, laughing and shouting as they played some incomprehensible game. Whelps from a pissant race that thought it was Hayll's equal, that it could *ever* be Hayll's equal. But Zuulaman had its uses. Through them, several of Hayll's Hundred Families, including her own, would have their wealth replenished as soon as . . .

The bastard hadn't signed the agreements yet. And he should have. *He should have.* As soon as he'd been told *she* was being held, he should have abandoned the pretense of caring about the welfare of the Dhemlan people and signed the agreements. After all, she was his *wife*. She'd given him children.

A door opened, and the wailing that had been muffled by stout wood stabbed at her.

"The baby is crying," her aunt said as she entered the room.

As if it was necessary to tell her that when she could hear him clearly enough. "He'll stop."

"He's hungry."

Hekatah turned to look at the woman. It had been sensible to bring another family member with her, but she regretted letting her mother talk her into bringing this one. Divorced because she was barren and her husband had wanted to sire children the Families would acknowledge socially, this aunt still craved having a child of her own and was always eager to help any woman in the family take care of a baby.

Weak fool. Children were a bargaining chip, tools to achieve a goal. But once you granted the sire paternal rights, you had to wait centuries before the child was old enough to be really useful again. Of course, the existence of Mephis and Peyton had held her marriage together, had continued to supply her with *some* kind of income because as long as she remained married to Saetan he would make financial provisions for her.

But not enough. She'd expected to be the High Priestess of Dhemlan, with all the honor and rewards that came with being the leader of the Priestess caste. She *should* have been. If Saetan had balls for anything but the bed, he would have insisted that she be granted the title and the authority because she was his wife.

She wasn't anything in Dhemlan *but* his wife and a Red-Jeweled Priestess from Hayll, given the courtesy due her Jewels and caste but not accepted enough to hold some position of authority.

That would change. She'd make sure of it.

"The baby is hungry," her aunt said again.

Who cared if the brat starved or not?

Saetan would. He'd rather play with the boys than attend an important social function with her. Oh, he was always willing to escort her to functions, always presented her with the invitations that came from the Dhemlan courts and let her choose which ones she wanted to attend. But he preferred the boys' company to hers most of the time.

The bastard should have signed the agreements by now, but he valued his honor more than his wife.

He would have to be punished for that.

"Hekatah? Aren't you going to do something about the baby?"

She stared at her aunt, but in her mind she pictured the man she had married.

The solution was so simple. The agreements would be signed in no time.

All she had to do was break Saetan's heart.

5

The Hall still trembled from the explosive slamming of the door. Still echoed with the sibilant whisper of Black shields locking into place around the massive structure. Usually, there was no sound made when a shield was formed or triggered. He'd added that sibilance as a bit of flash and glitter, as a way to remind anyone who challenged him that he wasn't quite like them. Oh, he was Blood, yes, but not quite like them. Not since he'd made the Offering to the Darkness and walked away wearing Jewels no man had ever worn in the history of the Blood. Or maybe he'd never been quite like the rest of them, and that's *why* he wore the Black.

His hand wasn't steady as he held up the small, ornately carved box. He couldn't stop the tremors going through his body, a reaction to the shock. But his feelings were numbed by exquisitely brutal pain. He felt nothing except awareness that the pain had shoved him to the edge of a precipice. He knew the landscape beyond it. No trained Black Widow feared the misted, twisting roads so close to that edge. They learned how to stray over that border, walk those roads—and come back. But he held on to the precipice and, by doing so, held on to the self-control that leashed everything he was.

"Did they tell you what was in the box before they sent you here,

Ambassador?" Saetan asked. His voice, soft thunder, rolled through his study and over the man trying hard not to show fear.

"No," the Ambassador said, licking dry lips. "I was told to bring it to you immediately. That was all."

"Do you know what is in this box?"

The Ambassador shook his head. "I thought, judging from the size, it was a trinket of some kind, something your wife had worn to confirm she was a guest of the Zuulaman Queens. A ring, perhaps, or a pendant. Maybe a—"

"Finger," Saetan said too softly. "A baby's finger."

The Ambassador stared at him, looking sick. "No."

"Yes." Saetan smiled—and watched the Ambassador shudder. "So I'm going to tell you the new agreement between Dhemlan and Zuulaman. My wife and child will be returned to me at once. If there is no further harm done to either of them, I will forget Zuulaman exists."

As the words sank in, the Ambassador shook off his fear. "What kind of agreement is that?"

"A generous one," Saetan replied. "However, if anything more is done to either of them, it will be considered a declaration of war."

The Ambassador gaped for a moment. "You think Dhemlan will go to war—"

"Dhemlan will not go to war with Zuulaman." He paused. "I will."

"But—"

"You don't understand what I am. No one would do this who understood what I am."

The Ambassador closed his eyes. Once he'd regained his composure, he looked at Saetan and shook his head. "The Queens will accept nothing less than the trade agreements. Your wife and child will remain on our islands until the agreements are signed."

"You're making a mistake."

"I serve, Prince SaDiablo. I can only give you the words that were given to me."

"Then give my words back to them, Ambassador. And hope they appreciate what is at stake."

As the Ambassador bowed and left the study, Saetan drew the shields back into the stones of the Hall and released the Black lock on the front door. He set the small box down on the blackwood desk and stared at his baby's finger. Blood sings to Blood. One touch was all he'd needed to confirm that tiny finger was flesh of his flesh, blood of his blood.

The numbness that kept the pain at bay thinned, threatened to shatter. He held on to it, as he held on to the edge of sanity, ignoring the lure of the twisting, misted roads. It would be so easy to slip over the boundary into the madness the Blood called the Twisted Kingdom, especially when it beckoned to him, promising there would be no pain. Especially when he knew he wasn't able to step away from that edge right now and stand more firmly in the sane world.

With desperate care, he closed the lid on the box, poured himself a large brandy, and settled down to wait.

6

"It won't be enough," Hekatah said to the Zuulaman Queens who had assembled in the sitting room she'd been given. "It will upset him, shake him, but it won't be enough to make him yield and give us what we want."

"There hasn't been enough time for a message to come back from the Ambassador who's staying in that village near SaDiablo Hall," one of the Queens pointed out. "We can wait and see what—"

She shook her head. "We have to strike fast, have to strike hard before he has too much time to think. We have to—" *Punish him for valuing his precious code of honor more than his wife.* "—provide more incentive."

"What do you suggest we do?" another Queen asked.

Hekatah smiled. "Send the other box."

7

Andulvar strode through the great hall to the door of Saetan's study. The whole damn place had a hushed quality of people having taken shelter in the hopes of surviving a violent storm.

And there was a storm coming. He could feel it building below the depth of his Ebon-gray Jewels. Hell's fire! He'd been able to sense the edge of it from his eyrie in Askavi.

Which is why he'd caught the Ebon-gray Wind and ridden to the Hall, arriving at the first breath of dawn. Something was pushing Saetan to the breaking point, and he didn't want to find out what might happen when a Black-Jeweled Warlord Prince's control shattered.

Flinging open the study door, he walked into the room.

Saetan stood behind the blackwood desk, tears running down his face as he stared at an open box that sat in the center of the desk.

"They kept his head," Saetan whispered.

Andulvar moved forward. "What are you—"

He was a warrior, bred and trained. An Eyrien Warlord Prince who had never hesitated to step onto a killing field. But he took one look at what was inside that box and stumbled back two steps. "Mother Night."

Saetan's hand shook as he reached into the box and gently brushed a finger over a little leg. "What kind of people are they? What kind of people would do this to a baby?"

"Saetan . . ." Andulvar swallowed hard to keep his stomach down, then approached the desk.

"I didn't think they were capable of this. Even after they sent one of his fingers, I didn't think they were capable of this."

They what?

"I'm sorry," Saetan whispered, brushing a finger over another piece. "I didn't know they had no honor. I'm sorry. So sorry."

When Saetan looked up, Andulvar saw a strong man about to break—and wondered if Saetan was even aware of the rage growing beneath that grief.

"Andulvar . . ." Saetan's voice hitched. "Look what they did to my baby. Look—"

Andulvar grabbed him, pulled him into arms that held on with the strength of a friend's love as Saetan shattered on the jagged stones of grief. "Hold on to me, Brother. Hold on."

As Saetan clung to him, sobbing harshly, Andulvar forced himself to look at the jumbled pieces that had been a baby.

You fools. The Darkness only knows what will come of what you've done.

The sobbing finally stopped. Saetan stepped back, called in a hand-kerchief, wiped his face, and delicately blew his nose. His gold eyes were dulled by pain and grief.

Andulvar took a deep breath, then let it out slowly. "Why don't you go up to your room to rest? I'll take care of—"

"No." Saetan shook his head, vanished the handkerchief. "He's my son. I'll take care of him." After closing the lid on the box, he picked it up. "Would you send a message to the Zuulaman Ambassador and tell him to meet me here in three hours?"

"What are you going to do?"

Saetan swallowed hard. "Sign the damn agreements and get my wife back."

The world was full of soft shapes, gray shapes, meaningless shapes. He moved through it in silence as he walked out of the Hall and went to the tree. He often came to sit beneath it and read when he wanted some time alone. He often sat in its shade while keeping an eye on Mephis and Peyton when they played around the pond.

He sank to his knees, put the box down, and opened it.

No pain now. No feelings at all. Nothing but a terrible clarity. The mist had absorbed his grief, his rage. They were no longer inside him. Now, he was inside of them.

The baby was crying. Somewhere in the mist that turned the world into gray and ghostly shapes, the baby was crying.

He stripped off his shirt, laid it on the grass. Gently took the pieces out of the box and arranged them on the cloth.

"I'm sorry," he whispered. "I tried to do what was right for the peo-ple I rule. Tried to keep the promises I made. I didn't know the price would be so high." Tears filled his eyes. "You'll never know your broth-ers, you'll never sail a toy ship on the Ph-phantom Sea, but you won't be alone. You won't be forgotten. When I come here with them, I'll be here for you, too. That I promise you. For as long as I live, you will not be forgotten."

Carefully wrapping the shirt around the pieces, he used Craft to sink the bundle deep into the earth. When he was done, there was no mark on the ground to indicate the spot, no sign of a grave. It was as if his little son had never existed.

Except the baby kept crying.

He rose to his feet, vanished the box, and walked back to the Hall, empty of everything but a terrible clarity—and a growing storm that was hidden in the mist.

8

Andulvar stood back from the desk where Saetan sat. There was nothing on the desk except the trade agreements, a quill, and a small bowl made of black marble.

The Zuulaman Ambassador stood in front of the desk, clearly unhappy about being in a room with Warlord Princes who wore the Ebongray and the Black.

Andulvar didn't give a damn if the Ambassador was happy or not. Saetan had asked him to stay for this meeting, so he would stay. Besides, the glazed, sleepy look in Saetan's eyes worried him.

"You won," Saetan said quietly. He pushed up his left shirt sleeve and nicked his wrist with a long, black-tinted nail. Blood spilled into the marble bowl.

"What—" The Ambassador gave Andulvar a startled glance before focusing on Saetan. "What are you doing?"

"Your Queens killed my son," Saetan said as he used Craft to heal the nick. "They butchered a baby barely out of the womb. These agreements were bought with blood, so they will be signed in blood."

In silence, Andulvar watched Saetan pick up the quill, dip it into the blood, and sign the agreements. When he set the quill down, the Ambassador stepped forward and reached for the parchments.

One black-tinted nail came down, pinning the sheets of parchment to the desk.

"The agreements have been signed," Saetan said too softly. "You're a witness to that fact. So is Prince Yaslana. When I receive a message from

Lady Hekatah's father, and from the Lady herself, that she has been safely returned to her family's house in Draega, and is unharmed, I will bring these agreements to you. You're staying at the inn in Halaway, yes?"

"Yes," the Ambassador said, "but I don't think the Queens will agree . . ." He looked into Saetan's eyes . . . and shivered. "I will inform them that the agreements are signed. I'm sure you'll hear from Lady Hekatah very soon."

Saetan just smiled a gentle, terrible smile.

When the Ambassador left, Andulvar sighed and rubbed the back of his neck. "By nightfall, half the Queens in Dhemlan will hear about these agreements."

"It doesn't matter." Saetan's voice sounded queer and hollow, as if it were coming from far away. Then he roused, but the glazed, sleepy look was still in his eyes. "I'd like you to take Mephis and Peyton to Askavi. I need to know they're safe while I deal with Zuulaman."

Andulvar nodded, then studied the man who had been his closest friend for several centuries. "Will you be all right?"

"I'll take care of things. I'll take care of everything."

As Andulvar went up to the family wing to collect the boys, he didn't know which worried him more—the psychic storm he'd felt growing when he'd arrived that morning . . . or the fact that he couldn't sense any trace of it now.

9

Grief ripped into him, its jagged edges slicing his heart. He lost his precarious balance and tumbled through a landscape filled with knives and little arms that rose up from crevices in the stones like brown-skinned flowers. As he clung to a stone to keep from sliding further into the mist, the petals of one flower opened, became a tiny hand . . . with a missing finger.

A howl of rage and pain shook the landscape. Then silence.

Getting to his feet, he looked around. No landmarks he recognized, and he'd set no markers as guides to take him back to the border of that place called sanity.

He wasn't sure he wanted to find that place. It was quiet here, almost peaceful here, despite the flowers. But . . .

Mephis. Peyton.

He looked around again, saw two beacons shining above him. His markers. His anchors. Two reasons to go back.

But not yet. Here there was terrible clarity. Here there was quiet—except for the sound of a baby crying.

Saetan read the two messages again, not sure what he was searching for but certain he hadn't found it.

The message from Hekatah's father was a scrawled assurance that she'd arrived in Draega, distressed but unharmed, and would remain there until everything was settled with Zuulaman's Queens.

A similar message from Hekatah, with additional reminders that he was responsible for her safety, that her continued safety, and the safety of their two sons, depended on his fulfilling the agreements he'd made with Zuulaman.

As he read her message one last time, he knew what was missing. There was nothing about the baby. If she knew what had been done, there was no sign of grief. If she didn't know, there was no concern that she'd been allowed to leave without the child. Not one word about the loss of their newborn son. Not. One. Word.

He dropped the messages back on the silver tray his butler had placed on his desk. Called in a long, soft black jacket, slipped it on, adjusted his shirt cuffs and collar. Then he picked up the agreements and left the Hall.

While the Ambassador carefully looked over the agreements, no doubt to confirm that nothing had been altered after they'd been signed, Saetan looked around the room the man had called home for the past few weeks.

Two pieces of Zuulaman pottery were arranged on a table, along with a wooden flute and a book of the island's folk tales. He knew that's what the book contained because the Ambassador had given him a copy the first time the man had called to discuss the trade agreements. And on the wall was a framed, primitive sketch of a seashore.

"This takes care of it," the Ambassador said. "I believe this takes care of everything."

Not quite. The thought bloomed. Found the storm hidden in the mist. Echoed through that terrible clarity.

"If there's anything I can do to assist you in collecting the first shipment of goods . . ." The Ambassador frowned. "Prince SaDiablo?"

No word of regret. No mention of the child whose blood had bought those sacks of grain, those casks of wine, whose death had sentenced the Dhemlan people to buying pottery and sketches they didn't want.

Rage flowed through him, a cold, sweet poison.

Saetan looked at the Ambassador and smiled. "There is one thing you can do."

"I'm not available to anyone," Saetan said as he brushed past his butler.

"What if the Dhemlan Queens—"

"Not to anyone."

Down, down, down until he came to the corridor deep beneath the Hall that led to his private study. Only Andulvar knew about this study, with the small bedroom and bathroom attached to it. A private place for the times when his Craft demanded such privacy.

He pressed a spot in the study wall. A piece swung back, revealing another short corridor. After stepping inside, he closed the hidden door, then created a ball of witchlight to provide illumination as he walked down the corridor and entered the workroom. Setting the witchlight in a bowl on the large wooden table, he stripped out of his jacket and tossed it aside.

The baby kept crying.

He opened Black-locked cupboards. Took out the tools no other man owned and placed them on the table. When everything was ready, he carefully unrolled a spindle of spider silk and attached the thread to the wooden frame he'd placed in the center of the table.

The baby kept crying.

"Hush, little one," Saetan crooned. "Hush. Papa will take care of things. Papa will take care of everything."

10

"What do you mean he's not available?" Andulvar growled.

"We haven't seen him since he returned from seeing the Ambassador yesterday," the butler replied.

"But he's here?"

"We think so."

Andulvar shifted his weight, opened his wings slightly.

The butler swallowed nervously. "We thought he'd gone to the cellars to select a bottle of wine or some brandy, but when he didn't return, we looked for him."

And didn't find him. Which means I know where he's gone.

"When he reappears, tell him I want to speak with him."

"At once, Prince Yaslana."

Andulvar walked out of the Hall, cursing himself. He should have taken the boys to Askavi and come back here. Hell's fire, he should have taken them to Ebon Askavi and asked Draca and Geoffrey to look after them for a few days. They'd be safe at the Keep. *Nothing* could touch them at the Keep.

He should have come back here. Saetan wasn't stable. Anyone looking at the man could tell he was too close to sliding into the Twisted Kingdom.

But only a fool would go down to that private study without *some* idea of what he might find there.

So I'll give him the day to lick his wounds in private. Then I'll be a fool.

He spread his wings and prepared to launch himself skyward and catch the Winds to go back to Askavi. Then he hesitated, looked at the drive that became the road into Halaway. He couldn't reach Saetan right now, but there was one other person who could tell him if anything else had happened yesterday.

He clenched his teeth as the Warlord who owned the inn hurried along the corridor ahead of him.

"Haven't seen *him* since dinner yesterday," the Warlord said. "Sneers at every dish that's put before him, but he tucks into his food well enough.

Here it is. This is his room." He rapped on the door, waited a moment, then called in a ring of keys, selected a key, and opened the door.

Andulvar went in first, all his senses alert to some sound, some motion, a psychic presence that would indicate someone was in the room.

"Bastard," the Warlord said.

Bristling, Andulvar turned slowly, his hand itching to call in his Eyrien war blade. But the Warlord wasn't looking at him.

"He cleared out," the man said. "The bastard just cleared out without paying his bill."

Andulvar studied the room, noted the books on the bedside table, the clothes still hanging in the open wardrobe. "Are you sure?"

"Course I'm sure!"

"His things are still here."

"Not the things he brought from Zuulaman." The Warlord picked up the books, then set them back down before going to the wardrobe and riffling through the clothes. "He bought these clothes here in Dhemlan. Those books, too. My brother was in the bookshop the same day and saw the Ambassador buy them. But all the things he brought with him from Zuulaman are gone. Those bits of pottery and a book. There was a sketch on the wall, too. And the clothes."

A chill went down Andulvar's spine. There was no reason for the Ambassador to remain in Halaway now that the agreements were signed. No reason at all. And yet . . .

"Guess he didn't think the things that came from Dhemlan were worth enough to take back with him," the Warlord said with a trace of bitterness.

Andulvar left without saying another word to the innkeeper and flew back to the Hall. As he landed and started to walk toward the front door, three Warlord Princes dropped from the Winds and appeared on the landing web that was circled by the drive. Opal, Sapphire, Red. Even together, they couldn't challenge Ebon-gray and hope to survive, but it would be a vicious fight. He shifted, deliberately placing himself between them and the Hall's front door.

"We need to see Prince SaDiablo," the Red-Jeweled Warlord Prince said.

"He's not available," Andulvar replied.

The Sapphire swore quietly.

"We need to see him," the Red insisted. "We're here on our Queens' behalves to report some odd thefts that occurred last night."

"What kind of thefts?" Andulvar asked, feeling icy claws wrap around his spine.

"Reports came in from several Provinces in Dhemlan as well as Amdarh," the Sapphire said. "Items were stolen sometime during the night."

"What kind of items?"

The Red's smile had a bite but no humor. "If it came from Zuulaman, it's gone. There's no sign that anyone broke in to those homes and nothing else was taken."

"It's not just people's homes," the Sapphire said. "Merchants reported that anything they'd acquired from Zuulaman to sell is gone. Books, pictures, pottery. Doesn't matter."

"The Queens are wondering if some kind of spell had been woven into the items so that they'd vanish after a certain amount of time," the Red added. "They're wondering if we're going to end up buying the same books and bits of crockery over and over again."

Which confirmed that the Ambassador had made sure at least some of Dhemlan's Queens were aware of the trade agreements before he disappeared.

They waited now, watching him.

An ember of dread kindled in his belly, but he didn't let them see it. "I'll tell him."

He watched them walk back to the landing web. Waited until they'd caught the Winds to go back to their Queens. He looked up at the sky, judged the daylight. Still enough time before twilight, even though he'd be heading east.

He strode to the landing web, caught the Ebon-gray Wind, and headed for Zuulaman.

11

The baby stopped crying.

Saetan took a deep breath. Let it out slowly. His body ached right down to the bone. As he raised his right hand to brush back his hair, he noticed the ring. The Black Jewel looked dull. When had he drained it? And why? He brushed fingers over the Black Jewel that hung from a gold chain around his neck. That one, too, was drained. Only a few drops of power remained, just enough to keep the Jewel from shattering. He must have drained it. He was the only one who *could* drain it. But . . . why?

His vision kept going in and out of focus. One moment he could see clearly, the next the room looked muzzy and gray.

Food. Water. Sleep. He needed all of those things.

Slipping off the stool, he moved stiffly through corridors, swore quietly as aching legs climbed stairs. Dimly he realized his body was moving through the Hall up to his suite. Dimly he heard his voice, hoarse and strained, give orders to have food, water, and wine brought to his room. Dimly he was aware of stripping out of his clothes and stepping into the shower—a new variation of the Eyrien outdoor water tanks warriors used to clean themselves after a battle—and letting hot water pound against his skin while he braced himself against a wall.

Still lost in the mental twilight, he was also aware that he had climbed twisted roads within his own mind and now stood on one side of a familiar border. Still on the misted side of that border, where it was quiet. He wasn't ready to cross that line back to sanity. Not yet.

Food. Water. He consumed both, then realized he had no memory of getting out of the shower or putting on the long, warm robe that now wrapped his body. Didn't matter.

He held on long enough to climb into bed, even though the sun was still shining. He held on long enough to put a Red shield around the bed. Not as much protection as a Black shield, but it would do.

Then he surrendered to the sleep he needed before he could step across the border and leave the Twisted Kingdom.

12

Hell's fire! He should have reached the islands by now, should have sensed one of the landing beacons at the very least.

Dropping from the Ebon-gray Wind, Andulvar spread his wings and glided over the ocean. After a minute, he flew higher, swearing silently. Even if he'd misjudged and taken the wrong threads when he'd switched from radial to tether lines and back again, he couldn't be *that* far off. He *knew* where the islands were.

He went higher, then flew in a wide circle, searching. Searching. Six large islands and twice that many smaller ones. He should be able to see *something*.

He spiraled toward the water, calling himself a fool even while he did it. What did he think he'd see closer to the ocean that he wouldn't see higher up?

But he did see something. A bit of green floating on the swells. He glided toward it. Dipped down to snatch it.

The ember of dread that had settled in his belly kindled. His heart pounded as he exploded upward, away from the water, away from . . . What?

He circled back. Breathing hard and sweating, he hovered above the green.

Just a piece of a palm tree. Nothing to fear.

But he couldn't make himself get closer to it. Couldn't think about touching it.

He stared at it, floating on swells. He stared at the ocean. The big, empty ocean.

"Saetan," he whispered. "Saetan, what have you done?"

13

"What do you mean he's gone?" Hekatah said, wincing a little as she surged to her feet. "There are still settlements to discuss, arrangements to be made for our share of the profit from the first Dhemlan shipment."

"I know that," her mother snapped. "But I'm telling you the Zuula-man Ambassador is *gone*. The servants at the town house he keeps here don't know when he left or when he'll be back. But he took all his Zu-ulaman bric-a-brac with him." Her mouth thinned to a hostile line. "Are you *sure* your husband signed the trade agreements?"

"Yes, I'm sure." Hekatah's hands curled into fists. The Zuulaman Queens wouldn't dare try to cheat her and her family out of what was owed them. They wouldn't *dare*. "Send someone to Zuulaman. Find out what the Queens know about the Ambassador's sudden departure."

14

"There's something I have to show you," Geoffrey said, turning toward one of the archways that led to the stacks of books that were kept separate from the rest of the Keep's huge library.

Andulvar growled. "I don't have time for—"

"Make time."

He studied the man. Geoffrey had been the Keep's historian and librarian since long before Andulvar had been born. He was a Guardian, one of the living dead. He was also the last of his race—a race he never mentioned by name, never talked about. There was nothing that could touch a man like Geoffrey when he was inside the Keep. Nothing a man like him should fear inside the walls of Ebon Askavi.

But it was fear Andulvar heard underneath the temper in Geoffrey's voice. So he followed the Guardian through the archway and between the shelves of books until Geoffrey finally stopped walking and pointed.

"What do you see?"

Andulvar shrugged. "Empty shelves."

"Yes," Geoffrey said. "Empty shelves. Yesterday, those shelves held examples of Zuulaman's literature. Stories, poems, novels. Those shelves also held examples of pottery, held copies of songs as well as a flute and drum. They're gone now."

"I need to talk to someone from Zuulaman," Andulvar said, deciding against telling Geoffrey about the other stolen items that had come from Zuulaman—at least until his own business at the Keep was concluded. "Can you check the Registers and—"

"There aren't any Registers."

Andulvar swore. "There have to be. These people are *Blood*. Some of them *have* to be in the Registers. Even if they didn't officially register as they should, you would have made *some* notation about the Blood who wear darker Jewels."

"Yesterday, there were Registers for Zuulaman," Geoffrey said. "Now they're gone. As if they had never existed."

Beads of sweat broke out on Andulvar's forehead. "I'd like to talk to Draca."

Geoffrey nodded. "She's waiting for you."

Retracing his steps, Andulvar returned to the room that held a large blackwood table where scholars and other Blood could sit and read the books Geoffrey didn't permit to leave this part of the library.

The Keep's Seneschal was ancient . . . and didn't look quite human. She'd unnerved him the first time he'd met her when he came to the Keep as one of Cassandra's First Circle Escorts. She still unnerved him.

"I need to talk to one of the Zuulaman Blood," Andulvar said.

"They are gone," Draca replied.

"From Terreille, yes. But there must be some who are demon-dead. You could arrange this."

"They are gone," she repeated. "The Dark Realm wass purged of Zuulaman Blood."

Andulvar grabbed one of the chairs that surrounded the table to keep himself upright. "You purged Hell?"

"No."

"Then . . . ?"

"The Prince of the Darknesss. The High Lord of Hell." Draca stared at him. "Grief wass the hammer they ussed to break hiss control. Rage wass the forge in which he sshaped hiss power into a weapon."

"So there's no one left."

"There's no one left," Geoffrey agreed. He looked at Draca. "If Saetan did what we think he did, there isn't a shard of pottery, a scrap of cloth, or a line from a poem, story, or song left that came from the Zu-ulaman people. There isn't any trace of them in any of the Realms."

Including the islands they came from, Andulvar thought, feeling sick.

"It's as if they never existed," Geoffrey said.

Draca took a step toward Andulvar. "Ssaetan iss the ssame man today ass he wass a year ago, the ssame ass he hass been ssince he made the Of-fering to the Darknesss and wass gifted with the Black Jewelss. He iss the ssame man who hass been your friend for many yearss."

"But now I know what he's capable of doing if he's pushed too hard or too far," Andulvar said, shuddering.

"Yess," Draca replied gently. "Now you know."

15

The next morning, Andulvar walked into the informal receiving room at the same moment Saetan began descending the stairway that led to the family wing. They stopped at the same time and studied each other.

Andulvar felt a chill twist up his spine as he looked into Saetan's glazed, gold eyes.

"The boys?" Saetan asked.

"They're fine. I'll bring them back later today. I came now to see how you're doing." *To see if you're sane.*

"I—" Frowning, Saetan descended the rest of the stairs. He wasn't moving with his usual grace, and the hand that clutched the banister trembled. "Have I been ill?"

The glazed look gave way to puzzlement.

"How do you feel?" Andulvar asked, not quite sure how to answer the question.

"Hollowed out," Saetan replied, rubbing his forehead. "Like I've had a fever. Thoughts keep swimming through my head, but I can't put them together in a way that makes sense. Andulvar . . ."

He didn't see a Warlord Prince capable of destroying an entire race of people. He saw the man who had been his friend for centuries. He saw a man who was exhausted, a man so heartsick it *was* a kind of illness.

He held out his hand, certain that if Saetan accepted that hand, he would get his friend back. Saetan would regain his emotional balance, and the leash he used to protect the rest of the Blood from the full violence of what he was would be restored.

Then Hekatah burst into the room. The hand reaching for his fell away. The gold eyes glazed again, and in their depths swam something Andulvar had never seen before.

This is why the demon-dead call him the High Lord, Andulvar thought in despair. *This is why they fear him enough that he can rule the Dark Realm even though he's still among the living. It's too late. There's no going back. For any of us.*

"What have you done?" Hekatah screamed as she rushed toward Saetan.

Andulvar grabbed her arm, hauling her back out of reach. Not because he cared about *her,* but because he was afraid of what would happen if Saetan responded now.

"Darling Hekatah," Saetan crooned.

"What did you do?" she screamed again.

"I took care of things," he replied too softly. "I took care of everything." He turned and walked up the stairs. When he was halfway up, he stopped and looked back at her. "If you want other lovers, you don't want me as a husband. I've tolerated that game for the last time, Priestess. If it happens again, we'll be divorced before you have time to leave your lover's bed. As for him . . ." He smiled a brutal, gentle smile. "I'll take him to Hell. Your name will be the last thing he screams while the Hounds tear him apart."

Hekatah stared up at him. Then she made a dismissive gesture. "What did you do to Zuulaman?"

"Zuulaman? That's a word without meaning."

"It's a place, as you very well know."

Saetan shook his head. "It doesn't exist." He walked up the stairs and disappeared down the corridor toward his suite.

Since Saetan was no longer available, Hekatah rounded on Andulvar. "What did he do?" she demanded. "Did he put some kind of shield around the islands so no one can find them?"

"They're gone, Hekatah," Andulvar said quietly.

"We sent messengers to find out why the Ambassador left so suddenly but they couldn't find—"

"The islands are gone." Hell's fire! How many times would he have to say it before the bitch finally *heard* him?

Hekatah frowned at him. "What do you mean they're gone?"

"The islands don't exist anymore. The Zuulaman people don't exist anymore. Everything that ever came from them doesn't exist anymore."

She shook her head slowly. "Not possible. You can't destroy *everything* about a people that fast."

"You can't. I can't. But the Prince of the Darkness? The High Lord of Hell? He can. Oh, yes, Hekatah. *He can.*"

She kept shaking her head. "You don't believe that story about him ruling the Dark Realm. A living man can't rule the demon-dead, can't control them."

Andulvar released her arm and stepped back. "You believe what you choose. But when they butchered his son and sent the pieces to him, Zuulaman broke the chain he'd forged to keep the rest of us safe from what he is. I *know* what he is. So I *know* he's the High Lord of Hell."

Fear slowly filled her eyes. She staggered back a step. "I can't stay here. He's angry with me."

"He's still riding the killing edge," Andulvar said. "There's no room in him yet for something as small as anger. Not when the rage only needs a spark to rekindle and look for another killing field."

She shrank away from him.

"Why don't you go back to Hayll and spend a few more days with your family? Right now, there's nothing you can do to help him."

As she glanced up the stairs, her face turned a sickly gray. "Yes. I need—I don't feel well."

He watched her stumble out of the room. Then he went to the window and pulled back the curtains enough to watch her run to the Coach that was still waiting for her.

Stupid aristo bitch. He wondered if Saetan had sensed the Coach and realized Hekatah hadn't intended to stay. He wondered if Saetan cared. At least she was gone for a few more days and wouldn't stir things up.

I can't help you, SaDiablo, Andulvar thought as he let the curtain fall back into place. *She shattered the moment when I might have made a difference. But I can give you two reasons to step away from the killing edge . . . and come all the way back from the Twisted Kingdom.*

16

As he stared at the charred, broken remains of a tangled web, Saetan felt Andulvar's wary presence as the Eyrien entered the short corridor that led to this hidden workroom.

"The boys?" he asked when Andulvar stepped into the room.

"Upstairs in their playroom."

"The baby kept crying," Saetan said softly, keeping his eyes focused on the web. "Screams of pain. Shrieks of terror. He kept crying. When I made the pain go away, the terror go away . . . When the reason for those things ceased to exist, he stopped crying." He closed his eyes. He still felt hollowed out, knew he was still too close to the border of the Twisted Kingdom. But he had to ask. "They don't exist, do they? Zuulaman doesn't exist anymore."

"No," Andulvar said. "They don't exist anymore. Everything they were is gone."

He felt the weight of what he had done settle on his shoulders and knew he would feel that burden for the rest of his life. He was a strong man. He would carry that weight. But nothing would be the same because of it. He would never be the same because of it.

He turned and looked at Andulvar, noting how the Eyrien tensed and had to fight to keep from taking a step back.

"Are you afraid of me, Andulvar?"

A long pause. "Yes. I'm afraid of you." Another pause. "I'm still your friend. We've been friends too long for it to be otherwise. But what happened to Zuulaman has changed things. I need . . . some time."

"I understand." Saetan forced his lips to curve into a smile. "Prince Yaslana."

Andulvar didn't try to return the smile. "High Lord."

Saetan listened to Andulvar's retreating footsteps before he turned back to study the web.

Yes, they'd been friends too long to break completely. Centuries ago, they'd first met in a court, two Red-Jeweled Warlord Princes who came from cultures that had nothing in common. Despite that, or because of it, they had become friends. It wasn't the first time they'd parted on uneasy terms. It wouldn't be the last. But this time, it was different.

Are you afraid of me, Andulvar?

Yes. I'm afraid of you.

"So am I, my friend," Saetan whispered. "So am I."

Two hours later, after cleaning the workroom, locking away the tools of the Black Widows' Craft, and scrubbing himself while he silently wept, he opened the door to the playroom.

"Papa!"

Mephis and Peyton rushed toward him, then skidded to a stop. His heart broke when they hesitated to come near him.

Then Mephis said, "You should sit down."

Since his legs were shaking, that sounded like a good idea. Moving carefully, he made his way to the large stuffed chair near the hearth. As soon as he was settled, Peyton climbed into his lap. Mephis, always more cautious, leaned against the side of the chair, then brushed a hand against his shoulder.

"Were you sick?" Mephis asked.

"I . . . wasn't well," he replied.

"Was that why Uncle Andulvar took us to stay with him?" Peyton asked.

Wondering how long it would be before he and Andulvar sat at a table together to talk and argue as they'd done for so many years, he swallowed the lump in his throat and nodded. "Yes, that's why."

"Are you better now?" Mephis asked.

He reached up and curled his fingers around his son's hand. "Yes, I'm better now."

Mephis's hand tightened to hold on to his, surprising him.

They had been the beacons he'd followed to find his way out of the

Twisted Kingdom. He hadn't wanted to leave. There had been peace there after the baby stopped crying. There had been an absence of pain he knew he wouldn't find in the sane world. But he'd made the journey back because he needed to be with them, needed to be here *for* them.

His little Warlord Princes. The day would come when they realized who . . . and what . . . their father was. And things would change between them. But until that day came, they were his boys, his sons, his joy. He would protect them, no matter the price.

"Papa?" Peyton said. "Would you read us a story?"

He pressed his lips to Peyton's forehead, savoring the contact, just as he savored the feel of Mephis's hand in his. "Yes, my darlings. I'll read you a story."

Kaeleer's Heart

This story takes place after the events in
Queen of the Darkness

ONE

1

Rage filled him. Love drove him. He and Witch hit the Green web. He rolled, but he didn't have Lucivar's skill. They broke through close to the middle of the web. He kept rolling so that when they hit the Sapphire, they were close to the edge. He rolled the other way, wrapping her in the web's power.

They broke through the Sapphire, but they weren't falling as fast now. He had a little more time to brace, to plan, to pour the strength of his Black Jewels into fighting the fall.

They hit the Red, rolled, clung for a second before falling to the Gray. Only half the Gray strands broke immediately. He strained back as hard as he could. When the other half broke, he rolled them upward while the web swung them down toward the Ebon-gray. He pulled against the swing, slowing it, slowing it.

When the other side of the Gray broke, they sailed down to the Ebon-gray. The web sagged when they landed, then stretched, then stretched a little more before the strands began to break.

His Black Jewels were almost drained, but he held on, held on, held on as they floated onto the Black web.

And nothing happened.

Shaking, shivering, he stared at the Black web, not quite daring to believe.

It took him a minute to get his hands to unlock from their grip around her ankles. When he was finally able to let go, he floated cautiously above the web. Near her shoulder, he noticed two small broken strands. Very carefully, he smoothed the Black strands over the other colors that cocooned her.

He could barely see her, only just enough to make out the tiny spiral horn. But that was enough.

★We did it,★ he whispered. He looked up. He couldn't see his brother and father, but he knew they were still floating in the abyss, exhausted from their own part of this fight to save her. ★Lucivar! Priest! We did it!★

Then he looked at Witch—and horror filled him. In that moment of inattention, the Black web's strands had sagged, stretched, started to break. He lunged, trying to grab her. His fingertips brushed against her ankle, but no matter how hard he strained, he couldn't get any closer.

Her eyes opened. Even through the cocoon of webs, they glittered like fine sapphires.

"Daemon." Little more than an exhalation of breath, a sigh. "Daemon."

Then the strands of Black web broke, and she spiraled down into the Darkness and disappeared.

"No." Grief ensnared him, cocooned him in agony. "Noooo!"

Still trembling from the nightmare that had become a familiar companion over the past few months, Daemon Sadi braced his hands against the shower walls and let the hot water sluice over his bowed head.

He loved Jaenelle Angelline with everything in him, had waited all of his seventeen hundred years for the day when he would surrender to Witch and serve her, be her lover. He had dreamed of her, yearned for her, had endured the centuries of being used as a pleasure slave because he had to survive in order to find her. And now . . .

He was losing her. He didn't know what he'd done, or hadn't done, to cause her feelings for him to change, but he was losing her. There was sadness lurking in the depths of her sapphire eyes whenever he was with her, and with each passing day, she seemed a little more distant, a little more out of reach.

Daemon shook his head. He'd let doubt become a living cry of pain while the kindred were fighting to hold on to Jaenelle and heal her body, and those doubts had cost her dearly. He couldn't afford to let doubt surface again.

Soaping up a washcloth, he scrubbed himself fiercely, as if washing the sweat off his skin could also scour the nightmare from his mind and heart. When he finally shut off the water and toweled himself dry, his body was clean—and his heart still ached.

Going back into the bedroom of the master suite in his family's town house in Amdarh, Dhemlan's capital city, he looked at the bed and hesitated. No. He wouldn't take a chance of the nightmare coming back. Once in a night was more than enough. Besides, he could spend the hours before dawn going over the papers Marcus, his man of business, had delivered to the town house for his review.

During the years when he'd been lost in the Twisted Kingdom and the years he'd remained hidden while he regained his strength and patched together his sanity, Marcus had worked diligently on his behalf. Because of that, much of the wealth he'd accumulated over the centuries had been quietly transferred to investments in various Territories in Kaeleer. That diligence had served Marcus as well, establishing him as a businessman and making it possible for him to bring his wife and young daughter to Kaeleer without having to serve in a Queen's court. Now Marcus and his family also lived in Amdarh, where it was safe for a child to play in the park with her friends, where a woman could walk down the street and not fear the men she passed, where a man wouldn't have to wonder if he would be snatched and maimed for the amusement of a bitch's court.

Using Craft, Daemon turned on the candle-light near the chair and table where he'd left the large stack of papers waiting for his perusal. Between his personal assets and controlling the vast wealth of the SaDiablo family, he had enough work to keep him busy, enough work to fill the hours when Jaenelle . . .

He reached for the robe at the foot of the bed, then turned away empty-handed to stand in front of the freestanding mirror.

He had the light-brown skin, black hair, and gold eyes that were common to the long-lived races. But his face was beautiful rather than handsome and left women breathless; his deep, cultured voice with its sexual edge could cause a pulse to race; and his body, trim, toned and full of feline grace, made women, and more than one man, crave him. He was seduction in motion, a promise of pleasure to the woman who held his affection and loyalty—and a promise of pain to everyone else who thought to use him in a bed.

He was also a Black Widow, one of the Blood who could wield the Hourglass's Craft of dreams and visions . . . and poisons. His father had been the first male in the history of the Blood to become a Black Widow. He had been born one, and the venom held in the sac beneath the ring-finger nail of his right hand was deadly. Adding that to the fact that he wore Black Jewels made him the most powerful, and dangerous, male in the history of the Blood, second only to Saetan.

No. Not second. They had taken each other's measure, and they both knew the truth. He might be his father's mirror, but his power was a little stronger, a little darker. And whatever held his father in check from unleashing that power didn't hold him. With the right provocation, there was nothing he couldn't, and wouldn't, do.

Especially when it came to Jaenelle Angelline, the living myth, dreams made flesh, the Queen who had sacrificed herself and the tremendous power she'd wielded in order to cleanse the taint that Dorothea and Hekatah SaDiablo had smeared over the Blood in Terreille.

The Queen who was called Kaeleer's Heart.

She had stopped the war that would have devastated Kaeleer. The price had been vicious. Even though she had healed enough to come home, she had suffered so much during the first weeks when he'd brought her back to SaDiablo Hall. True, the pain had lessened as autumn gave way to the first breath of winter, but even now, when the winter days would soon give way to the promise of spring, she was still so fragile, still an invalid who could barely walk from bed to chair. She never spoke about shattering her Ebony Jewels, never spoke of the new Jewel, Twilight's Dawn, that had taken the place of what she had lost.

She didn't say much of anything anymore. At least, not to him.

"It's not over," he told his reflection. "You've kept your best weapons sheathed, old son. Maybe it's time to remind your Lady what you can offer a woman, remind her that you're hers for the taking. If you don't play this game out to the full and you lose because of it, you'll regret it for the rest of your life. It's not over until she asks you to leave, so give her a reason to want you to stay."

Turning away from the mirror, he slipped into the robe, poured a snifter of brandy, and settled in the chair to take care of the work that had brought him to Amdarh. If he could get through the business that required his immediate attention, he'd have time to take care of some personal errands in the morning before meeting with Marcus—and he'd be home with Jaenelle by tonight.

2

Daemon left the town house and strode down the sidewalk, his hands in the pockets of his wool coat, the collar flipped up to shield his neck from the bite of winter air. The walkways and streets were clear of snow, which made it easy to enjoy a brisk morning walk.

Personal errands first. As night gave way to dawn, he'd realized the only way to battle doubt was by feeding hope. He knew what he wanted more than anything else, and this would be a small step in the right direction.

The bookseller he patronized was his first stop, and the man barely had time to open his store before Daemon arrived. Today, browsing wasn't a temptation, so he simply looked at the books the man had set aside for him. Reading was Jaenelle's main entertainment these days, so every time he came to Amdarh on business, he made a point of stopping at the store. He selected three of the six books that had been set aside, but asked the bookseller to hold the others until he returned to the city in a fortnight. Buying them but not giving her all of them seemed dishonest, as if he were withholding a treat. Delaying the purchase gave him the pleasure of bringing her something new each time he had to leave the Hall on family business, and he needed to give her anything he could.

By the time he left the bookstore, there were plenty of people out and about Amdarh's shopping district. As he walked to his next destination, he greeted the men and women he'd met at aristo houses when he'd been invited to dinner or to a party. He'd made an effort to become acquainted with the Blood aristos in the city, especially the ones who served in Lady Zhara's court, since she ruled Dhemlan's capital. Except for Karla, the boyos and the coven who had made up Jaenelle's First Circle hadn't quite forgiven him for the games he'd played to keep them away from her while she created the spells that would protect them and Kaeleer. And he and Lucivar still weren't quite easy with each other. What he'd done in Dorothea's camp to protect his brother's wife and son was a still-healing wound between them.

He greeted two witches he'd met at a party when he was in Amdarh a few weeks ago buying gifts for Winsol. Baffled by the wary stares they gave him before returning the greeting, he shrugged it off as unimportant, his mind already focused on the shop at the end of the block.

"Good morning, Prince Sadi," Banard said as soon as Daemon walked into the shop. "I hadn't expected to see you here so soon after Winsol. Did the Lady like the pin?"

"Good morning," Daemon replied as he walked up to one of the glass displays that also served as a counter. "Yes, Lady Angelline was delighted with the unicorn pin."

A gifted craftsman who worked with precious gems and metals, Banard, a Blood male who wore no Jewel himself, had been commissioned over the years to create a number of unique pieces for darker-Jeweled Blood—including Jaenelle's scepter when she'd established her Dark Court.

"I have a commission for you," Daemon said. "One that requires your discretion for the time being."

Banard smiled. "Don't they all require discretion, Prince?"

"Yes, they do," he replied, returning the smile to acknowledge the truth of Banard's statement. "But this one needs a little more than most."

Banard just continued to smile.

Daemon hesitated, wondering if he was being premature. Didn't matter. If he ended up being a fool over this, so be it. "I want you to make two rings. One . . . I'm not really sure how I want it to look." Despite the fact that they were alone in the shop, he lowered his voice. "The other is a plain gold band."

"Do you know the ring size for this gold band?"

In answer, Daemon held out his left hand.

"Ah." Banard's smile widened. "Then this other must be a special ring for a special Lady?"

"A ring worthy of a lifetime."

Banard called in a velvet-lined ring case. Brass rings marched in neat rows from the largest, which would fit a man twice Daemon's size, to the smallest, which looked like it would fit only a small child.

"I made the rings for the Lady's Court," Banard said, his fingers moving above the rows of brass rings. "If I remember correctly . . ." He selected a ring and held it out.

Daemon slipped it on his finger. A perfect fit. Just as the Consort's Ring had been a perfect fit.

He removed the ring and gave it back to Banard, who returned the ring to its place and vanished the case.

"As for the other— "

Banard broke off as the shop's door opened and a woman stepped inside. She smiled at them, then moved to the display case that contained brooches.

"I'll give the matter some thought," Banard continued quietly. "Make a few sketches for you to look at the next time you're in Amdarh. Would that be sufficient?"

"That would be fine," Daemon replied, working to keep his voice from turning into a snarl. Something in the air. Something that honed his temper.

He turned his head and studied the woman. A lighter-Jeweled witch. Who was cloaked in an illusion spell. The kind of spell that could only be made through the Hourglass's Craft. *That's* what he sensed. But there was nothing . . . enhanced . . . about her appearance. She was attractive but hardly stunning. Perhaps she was disfigured in some way, from accident or illness. There were some things even the best Healer couldn't fix completely, so an illusion spell was sometimes used to hide a disfigurement.

Wondering if she had come from Terreille, and knowing the cruel and terrible things Dorothea and her followers had done to people, he felt a moment's pity for her and was glad the illusion spell gave her the courage to go out in the world.

"There is one thing I can show you," Banard said. "I just finished it yesterday." He retreated behind the curtain that shielded his workroom and the private showrooms, then returned quickly with a piece of folded black velvet. He set the cloth on the counter and revealed its contents.

Daemon picked up the bracelet. It was a double strand of white and yellow gold set with precious and semiprecious gems that matched the colors of the Jewels from the Rose to the Black.

"It's beautiful," Daemon said. And so appropriate since it reflected every color that made up Twilight's Dawn, the Jewel Jaenelle now wore. "A special gift for a special Lady."

"I was hoping you would think so," Banard said.

Grinning, he set it back on the velvet. "Wrap it up, and I'll take it with me."

"Oh. May I see it?"

The woman was standing near him, focused on the bracelet. There was a greediness in her eyes that made him want to lash out, to sweep the bracelet out of sight. But he thought of the illusion spell and the reasons she might have paid a Black Widow to create one. Beauty of any kind might be a new discovery for her.

He forced himself to step aside so she could get a better look at the bracelet, but he rested his hand on the counter close to the velvet, a subtle claim and a warning that she could look but not touch.

After a long study, she smiled and moved back to the counter with the brooches.

Wrapping the velvet around the bracelet, Daemon vanished it, promised to return in a fortnight, and turned to leave the shop. At the door, he looked back at the woman, but her attention was on the brooches, not on him. Shrugging off his uneasiness as a reaction to living in Terreille for most of his life, he headed back to the family town house, where he and Marcus would share a midday meal before getting down to business.

3

A few minutes later, Roxie left Banard's shop with a brooch safely tucked in her small carry bag. She strolled down the street, stopping to look into store windows, until she reached the horse-drawn cab waiting by the curb. As soon as she scrambled inside, the driver pulled into the stream of horse-drawn conveyances and Craft-powered coaches.

"Well?" Lektra demanded, twisting a curl around her finger.

"I think he noticed the illusion spell," Roxie said, feeling a little breathless now that their plan was truly in motion.

"Doesn't matter," Lektra replied. "There are plenty of reasons why people pay for illusion spells to change their looks. Besides, I was assured sensing an illusion spell isn't the same as seeing beneath it."

Lektra was the niece of a Queen who ruled a two-village District in Dhemlan, so she was known to many of the aristo Blood in Amdarh and couldn't afford to draw attention to herself right now—not if their plan was going to work. That was why Roxie had volunteered to get the information they needed. But Lektra had come up with the idea of paying a Black Widow to create the illusion spell so Roxie, a Rihlander originally from Ebon Rih, would look like a Dhemlan witch.

"I bought this," Roxie said, taking the brooch out of her carry bag.

"This will do nicely," Lektra said as she examined the brooch. "It's certainly pretty, and, most important, it has Banard's mark on the back."

"There were prettier ones," Roxie said.

"What do you care? You're not going to wear it."

"But—" Even if it wasn't the one she would have chosen if she could have spent anything she wanted, she'd still expected to keep it. After all, it was a brooch by Banard—something she could never afford for herself.

"What was Daemon doing there? What was he buying?"

"I think he commissioned Banard to make something special—probably for that stupid cripple, Jaenelle. But he *did* buy a bracelet. 'A special gift for a special Lady.' " As she described the bracelet, Lektra's gold eyes gleamed with delight.

"We can go to another jeweler and get a duplicate made," Lektra said excitedly. "It doesn't have to be exact, just have all the right elements, so when someone sees me wearing it, they'll think it's the one Banard made. And since Jaenelle Angelline isn't likely to be coming to Amdarh anytime soon, no one will know the difference."

"What about the brooch?" Roxie asked.

"While he was in Amdarh last time, Daemon attended several parties. There's always dozens of them just before the actual thirteen days of Winsol. Some of the theater folk attended one of them, and I heard Daemon spent some time with one of the actresses. Danced with her a couple of times. Even stood as her escort for dinner." Lektra pouted.

"So maybe he's not as chaste as everyone thinks."

"Don't be a fool. Of course he's chaste. Hell's fire! Any hint that he's been unfaithful to precious Jaenelle would have everyone worth knowing shunning him—which is the whole point, remember?" Lektra smiled. "That's why using this actress is the perfect starting point to freeing Daemon from Jaenelle's control. People *did* notice the attention he paid the bitch. If she receives a gift from a secret admirer—a 'special gift for a special Lady'—she's going to wear it, and she's going to tell people it's from a secret admirer. So all we have to do is mention that someone had seen Daemon in Banard's shop buying a 'special gift' and people will tie the knot between those two bits of information themselves."

Lektra tapped her lips with a fingertip and looked thoughtful. "Maybe I won't have another bracelet made after all. It will be so much nicer when Daemon takes me to Banard's shop to buy one for me."

"What do I get out of this?" Roxie muttered.

"You get to share the prize, just as I promised," Lektra said coolly. "And you get to pay the SaDiablo family back for the way Lucivar Yaslana treated you. And as my friend and guest, you get to attend parties and dances you'd never be invited to on your own—not to mention the lovers who come home with us."

Lektra's seconds, that's what she got. But what Lektra said was true: being exiled from Ebon Rih six years ago had cost her almost all her social status. It had gotten so bad in Askavi, no man wanted to dance with her, let alone do something more interesting. So she had moved to

Dhemlan, but it wouldn't have been any better if Lektra hadn't be-friended her.

So she put up with the reminders that she owed what social standing she had in Amdarh to Lektra's efforts on her behalf, and she put up with men who wanted Lektra but made do with her.

Now that Lektra's interest in Daemon Sadi had ripened into obses-sion, the Dhemlan witch needed her help, and that worked in her favor. Besides, if they won *this* prize, she wouldn't mind taking whatever crumbs were left over.

TWO

"Oh, Daemon. It's beautiful."

The delight in Jaenelle's sapphire eyes as she picked up the bracelet warmed him and gave him hope. There was so little these days that delighted her.

"Try it on." He took the bracelet and fastened it around her wrist, painfully careful not to touch the fragile skin—skin he wanted to caress, kiss, lick. The memory of how even the gentlest touch had left hideous bruises whenever he'd helped her move still made him ill. So he didn't let his fingers brush her skin as he fastened the bracelet, then eased back.

As she held out her arm to admire the bracelet, he no longer saw something beautiful. He saw the shadow the bracelet cast on her skin. Or was it something else?

He stiffened. "It's not too heavy, is it?" Fool. Idiot. It hadn't occurred to him when he bought it that having the metal resting against her skin would bruise her. And it should have occurred to him. When he'd brought her back to the Hall last autumn, she couldn't wear anything but the lightest-weight fabrics, couldn't have more than a sheet over her in bed. Anything more had left her covered in bruises—and had left him terrified that the constant effort to keep healing the bleeding under the skin would interfere with her overall healing—or even make it impossible for her to ever completely heal.

"No, it's not too heavy," Jaenelle said as she lowered her arm.

Daemon winced. By reminding her of how frail she was, he'd spoiled her pleasure in the gift.

When she looked at him, the delight that had been in her eyes was gone. *She* was gone. She still sat beside him on the couch, but there was a distance between them again that he didn't know how to bridge.

He looked at the table in front of him, and his heart sank a little more. The book he'd given her at Winsol lay on the table, the bookmark indicating she'd barely gotten halfway through it.

"The story doesn't appeal to you?" he asked, wondering if any of the new books he'd brought her would please her. Wondering if there was *anything* he could do anymore that would please her.

Jaenelle looked away, but not before he saw pain and sadness in her eyes. "I guess I've lost my taste for love stories," she said. Then she tried to smile. "I'm feeling a little tired. I think I'll get some sleep now."

He recognized a dismissal when he heard one. "I'll help you to bed," he said as he rose.

He waited until she slowly, painfully got to her feet. Then he used Craft to float her from the sitting room to the bedroom. With exquisite care, he removed the soft wool robe Marian had made for her and tucked the sheet and blanket she could now tolerate around her once she was settled in bed.

"Good night, sweetheart," he said. "I'll come to bed in a little while." *Unless you want me to stay. Please want me to stay.*

"Good night, Daemon."

Idly swirling the brandy in the glass, Daemon stared out the window of the bedroom that adjoined Jaenelle's. The Consort's room. Since she no longer ruled a court, technically he was no longer her Consort. Since he couldn't touch her, he wasn't technically her lover either.

Didn't matter. He was still her lover. Would always be her lover. He suppressed that thought before his body responded to it. After he brought her home and realized how frail she was, how little it would take to overwhelm the healing taking place inside her and have it fail, which would leave her permanently imprisoned in a body that wouldn't allow her to do more than exist, his desire for sex had vanished. Not surprising. Despite the centuries of being a pleasure slave, he'd been a virgin until he gave himself to Jaenelle. No other woman had aroused him, no other woman had filled him with hungry need.

That was still true. When he attended the dinners or parties in Amdarh, he danced with women because he enjoyed dancing. But none of them stirred any interest for her company beyond the dance. Only Jaenelle. Always Jaenelle.

He'd been content to let his desire sleep. So he wasn't sure what to think about the fact that, lately, he would wake in the night hard, hot, and aching, troubled by dreams of spreading Jaenelle's legs, of kneeling before her while his tongue and fingers stroked her to a climax.

Lately, the sound of her voice was enough to stir his cock—and her unhappiness was enough to wither desire. But not completely. Never completely. Between the erotic dreams and the nightmare of losing her, he hadn't had a decent night's sleep in weeks.

Prince?

Daemon turned and studied the Red-Jeweled Sceltie Warlord. Ladvarian's determination had gathered the kindred who had pored their strength, love, and unshakable belief that they, along with the Arachnian Queen who had spun the powerful healing webs, could rebuild Jaenelle's devastated body, could hold dreams to flesh and keep Kaeleer's Heart among the living. He had brought the Jewel that became Twilight's Dawn to the island that was ruled by the golden spiders who were the Weavers of Dreams. And he was the one who had finally allowed Daemon to come to the other island where the kindred had hidden, and cared for, Jaenelle after she rose from the healing webs.

You are unhappy, Ladvarian said.

Just tired, Daemon lied. *I haven't been sleeping well.*

Ladvarian hesitated. *Should we take Jaenelle somewhere else?*

No! Daemon struggled to remain calm while temper and fear raged through him. That the small dog could, and would, remove Jaenelle from his care wasn't lost on either of them. His inability to believe she would come back, his grief and longing filling the abyss day after day, had been the reason she had risen from the healing webs too soon. He was to blame for the suffering she'd endured when he'd first brought her back to the Hall. The kindred had been willing to overlook his failure to love without doubt, but they wouldn't overlook anything else that might interfere with Jaenelle's well-being.

No, he said again. *I'm grateful to have her here. I'm grateful to be with her.* And what he wouldn't admit to was the fear that if the kindred took her away, he might not be able to win her back enough for her to love him again.

She is healing, Daemon, Ladvarian said after another hesitation. *She is getting stronger.*

I know. But she would never be what she had been. It wasn't just her body that she'd crippled when she'd unleashed her power to save Kaeleer. She could no longer wear the Black or Ebony Jewels that had once signaled the enormity of her power, and no one really knew what to make of Twilight's Dawn since nothing like it had ever existed. Sometimes it felt similar to a lighter Jewel, sometimes he could feel a hint of Ebon-gray or Black when he was near her.

He didn't give a damn what Jewel she wore, but he, like the coven and boyos who had been members of her First Circle, worried that the loss of that power would affect her mental and emotional health, which, in turn, might damage her physical health.

Don't borrow trouble, old son. You've already got enough of it. Do everything you can to get her well again and deal with what her Jewels can—and can't— do another day.

Are you sleeping here? Ladvarian asked.

Here? Where he couldn't wake up and hear her breathing, where he couldn't have that immediate assurance that she was still with him? *No.*

As soon as Ladvarian trotted back to Jaenelle's room, Daemon stripped out of his clothes and shrugged into a robe that was a token gesture of modesty. He didn't need it for warmth. The warming spells he'd put on Jaenelle's suite of rooms and this one guaranteed she wouldn't catch a chill.

The fire burning low in the hearth was enough light to see by as he made his way to her bed, shrugged off the robe, and slipped under the covers. The bed, specially built and strengthened with Craft to accom-

modate Kaelas, the eight-hundred-pound Arcerian cat who had slept
with Jaenelle since she brought him home as an orphaned kitten, meant
he could sleep with her without fear of bumping her during the night
and causing an injury.

As he pulled the covers up, he heard the change in her breathing, felt
her roll onto her back.

"Go back to sleep, sweetheart," he said softly. "It's just me."

"Daemon." She sank back into the deep sleep her body demanded.

Propped up on one elbow, Daemon watched her sleep for a long
time. Had he heard longing in that one word?

He shifted closer to her. Then he reached out and touched the ends
of her golden hair. The kindred had used Craft to crop her hair very
short. A practical thing to do while they'd tended her body when she
was still connected to the healing webs. It had grown out enough to
look shaggy. It was also the one thing he could touch without fear of
hurting her.

So he brushed his fingertips over her hair, wishing she was healed
enough that he could brush his lips over hers, could slip his tongue into
her mouth and kiss her the way he wanted to kiss her.

Someday he would be able to kiss her that way again. Someday he
would be able to do a lot more than just kiss her.

He wouldn't allow himself to believe anything else.

THREE

Too restless to sleep, Lektra paced her bedroom. Roxie's scheme had to work. It *had* to. They would stir rumors and provide nuggets of information that, if strung the wrong way, would ruin a man's reputation. They would also be Daemon Sadi's most vocal defenders. In the end, when he was freed of his obligation to take care of that crippled invalid, he would feel grateful to the woman who had loved him enough to publicly defend him against the charges of infidelity.

And she did love him. She *did*. So why should that beautiful, virile man be trapped playing nursemaid to a woman who no longer had any use for him? Why should he spend the next few decades sitting by a sickbed, reading aloud to a lump of flesh? Or, worse, why should he have to hide his revulsion if Jaenelle Angelline still wanted something sexual from him?

She'd fallen in love with Daemon the first time she'd seen him over a year ago. He had come to Amdarh with Jaenelle to shop for Winsol gifts and attend a few parties before returning to SaDiablo Hall to celebrate Winsol with their family and Jaenelle's First Circle. It had made sense that he would have agreed to be Jaenelle's Consort. At the time, she'd been the Queen of Ebon Askavi—the most powerful Queen in Kaeleer. Every strong, ambitious male who had been trained for a consort's duties had wanted to wear the ring Daemon had worn on his left hand. But Daemon, beautiful Daemon, had won that coveted position.

And no wonder. He'd looked at Jaenelle as if no other woman existed—

or would ever exist. And when they danced together, every move he made was a prelude to the bedroom dance, a promise of what he could offer in private. Even when it was a dance that required several couples, you could see him bank that sexual heat when he turned to another partner, could watch it flare as soon as his hand touched Jaenelle's.

An exquisite male. The kind of male that made all the others seem lacking in some essential.

She would have waited for him to be free of his contract. After all, the five years he was required to serve in Jaenelle's court was nothing to someone who came from one of the long-lived races. Once his contract was completed, he would have been free to look elsewhere for a lover. She'd even tried to join the Dark Court so they could be together in some way. But the letter she'd received from the Steward made it clear there were no plans to expand the Dark Court to accommodate all the Blood who were offering to serve.

Then there was all that talk of a war between Kaeleer and Terreille, and news of fighting in other Territories. And then there was that unleashing of power unlike anything the Blood had ever experienced. When that power faded, the war was over, the Blood who had threatened Kaeleer were destroyed—and the Queen of Ebon Askavi was gone.

But not Jaenelle Angelline. Despite being hideously wounded, she'd survived somehow. Instead of grieving a few weeks for the loss of a Queen before moving on, Daemon was chained to a cripple who was still adored by the Queens and Warlord Princes who controlled the other Territories in Kaeleer.

He would never shake free of Jaenelle Angelline. So she would help cut the ties between the former Queen of Ebon Askavi and the Warlord Prince who, otherwise, would remain trapped for years, possibly decades. Oh, the Queens would snub him for a while, but in a year or two, they would realize it was better to have a Warlord Prince attached to a woman who could be what he needed. And while he would suffer a little because of the accusations of infidelity, she had no doubt, with the help of her family, she could restore his reputation.

And then he would look at her the way he had once looked at Jaenelle.

FOUR

1

"Let me see if I understand this," Jaenelle said.

Surreal turned away from the window. The gray day and the sleet that would make a mess of all the roads matched her mood, but she did her best to bury wounded feelings as she approached the couch where Jaenelle sat bundled in a nightgown and robe, her legs stretched out under a quilt.

She looks better, Surreal thought. Oh, far from well and still so fragile, but better than she'd looked a few weeks ago when Surreal had come back to the Hall to spend a few days with the family during Winsol.

"You and Falonar have decided to go your own ways," Jaenelle said with a patience that made Surreal wary.

She shrugged. "It was a mutual decision." *The bastard.*

"Uh-huh. So you packed your bags—"

"It was his eyrie," Surreal cut in. "I certainly didn't want to live there." *And I didn't want to watch him courting Nurian in ways he never thought to court me.*

"—and left Ebon Rih without telling Lucivar."

"Who would have strung Falonar up by the heels"—*or by the balls, which might have been interesting to watch*—"before having a little chat."

"No," Jaenelle said, "he would have waited for Chaosti to show up, and *then* he would have strung Falonar up by the heels." She paused. "Maybe by the heels."

Which just confirmed why Surreal had slipped away from Ebon Rih before Lucivar had time to notice. As the Warlord Prince of Ebon Rih dealing with a Warlord Prince who was his second-in-command, Lucivar would have been nasty and explosive. Chaosti, the Warlord Prince of the Dea al Mon and a kinsman on her mother's side, would have approached Falonar with the protective viciousness that made Warlord Princes such a deadly facet of Blood society.

Dealing with the male relatives she'd acquired since coming to Kaeleer was so much fun.

"And you entered the Hall through one of the side doors to avoid seeing Daemon, who's working in his study and would have met you before you got out of the great hall."

Feeling more wary by the minute, Surreal did her best to look indifferent. "No reason for him to get involved in this." *Sweet Darkness, please don't let him think this is any business of his.* "Besides, I don't need either of them getting all snarly and protective over something that was a mutual decision."

"So instead of mentioning this to either of them, you went to the Keep and told Saetan."

Surreal winced. "Well, I figured I should tell someone before leaving Ebon Rih."

"Uh-huh. So you told the High Lord of Hell, the patriarch of this family, the man from whom Daemon and Lucivar inherited the temper you were trying to avoid." Jaenelle pushed the quilt aside and swung her legs over the side of the couch to sit up straight. "Did I miss something?"

Unable to stand still, Surreal started pacing in a circle in front of the table that held the pot of coffee, cups, and sandwiches Beale, the Hall's butler, had brought in a few minutes after she'd knocked on Jaenelle's door.

"I thought he'd be reasonable," she snarled. "He's older and less . . . excitable." And Saetan *had* sounded calm and reasonable while she explained that living in an eyrie with Falonar had lost its appeal and she intended to spend a few days at the Hall before staying at the family's town house in Amdarh for a while.

"Did he hurt you?" Saetan had asked too softly.

Surreal snorted. "Uncle Saetan, sugar, do I look hurt?"

Watching his eyes glaze, she'd realized she'd made a serious tactical error. Which was why she'd caught the Gray Wind and headed for the Hall as fast as she could, hoping Jaenelle would have some advice about dealing with the rest of the family.

Jaenelle sighed. "All right. We'll deal with this."

Surreal watched Jaenelle's arm tremble as she lifted the coffeepot and poured two cups. When she reached for the cream and sugar, Surreal stepped forward.

"Want some help?"

"No."

Wondering about the whiplash of anger under the word, Surreal hesitated.

"Take your coffee and a sandwich," Jaenelle said, grabbing a sandwich off the plate and taking a bite.

"What's going on?" Surreal asked cautiously.

"You want Falonar to walk away from this intact?" Jaenelle countered. "Then take a sandwich. And hold on to that wall of sass and indifference you've erected in front of what you're really feeling."

Before Surreal could ask what coffee and sandwiches had to do with what she was, or wasn't, feeling, she felt the wash of dark power roll through the Hall. Ebon-gray and Black—immediately answered by another Black.

Hell's fire, Mother Night, and may the Darkness be merciful. All three of them—and all of them pissed off.

Grabbing a sandwich, Surreal took a bite and hoped she wouldn't choke.

"Come over here and sit down," Jaenelle said.

Feeling the three-pronged storm moving through the Hall toward them, Surreal sat on the end of the couch farthest away from the door. She gulped coffee to wash down the sandwich, then refilled both their cups after Jaenelle drained hers.

"Ready?" Jaenelle asked.

Shit shit shit. "Can I go back to being an orphan?"

Amusement lit Jaenelle's eyes. "Not a chance."

The sitting room door swung open. Saetan walked in, flanked by Daemon and Lucivar. Lucivar's gold eyes were lit with hot temper. Daemon's and Saetan's eyes had that chilling glaze. But the three of them stopped abruptly when Jaenelle smiled at them as if there was nothing in the world they could possibly be upset about.

"If you want coffee, you'll have to ask Beale to send up another pot," Jaenelle said, "but there are plenty of sandwiches left."

"No, thank you, witch-child," Saetan said, taking another step forward. He studied the woman who had been his Queen—and was still, and always, the daughter of his soul—before those glazed eyes focused on Surreal.

Looking past Saetan, Jaenelle focused her smile on Daemon. "Surreal's going to stay with us a few days."

"She's always welcome," Daemon replied. "This is her home, too."

Lucivar stepped away from the other men, his dark wings flaring, making him look bigger—and more formidable. "You left Ebon Rih in a hurry."

Surreal shrugged. "Just wanted to get away for a while. And frankly, sugar, your mornings start with a lot more noise than I want to deal with."

"Noise?" Jaenelle asked.

Surreal rolled her eyes. "The last time I was at Lucivar's eyrie around breakfast time, Daemonar was screaming because a wolf pup had chewed on his foot. Of course, the reason the pup had chewed on his foot was because *he* had been chewing on the puppy's tail."

"In other words, it was a typical morning."

"Precisely."

They both looked at Lucivar, who swore under his breath. "All right. Fine. Anything you want to tell me about Falonar?"

"No," Surreal replied.

Before Lucivar could argue, Saetan said, "Our apologies for intruding, Ladies. We'll let you get back to your own discussion."

Surreal held her breath as she watched Saetan and Lucivar leave the room—and noticed how Daemon lingered a moment, his eyes on Jaenelle, before he followed his father and brother. When the door closed behind him, she sighed with relief.

"Think they bought it?" she asked.

"No." Jaenelle set her cup on the table. "But it's understood that they have no justification for going after Falonar, so they'll leave him alone."

She set her own cup aside. "I owe you for this."

"Yes, you do." Jaenelle stared at the table. "Do you want to tell me why you really left Falonar and Ebon Rih?"

"Not really."

Jaenelle nodded. "Sometimes there's no specific reason," she said softly. "Sometimes things just don't work out between two people."

Are we still talking about me and Falonar? Surreal wondered. Remembering the way Daemon had lingered for a moment, she had an uneasy feeling Jaenelle was thinking of two other people.

2

She waited until Saetan and Lucivar had left the Hall before tracking Daemon to his study. It felt strange walking into that room and seeing another man behind the desk where Saetan had ruled Dhemlan for so many centuries. Even stranger to feel as if nothing had really changed.

"So," she said, settling into the chair in front of the desk. "Do you ever see any rooms in the Hall besides this one?"

"Occasionally," Daemon replied with a dry smile. "Brandy?"

"Sure." She watched him pour a snifter for her and top off his own before he used Craft to float hers over to her waiting hand. "Thanks."

Daemon leaned back in his chair, the snifter cradled in both hands. His Black-Jeweled ring glittered on his right hand. His left hand looked naked without the Consort's ring. Did he miss the feel of it on his finger? She'd noticed that Saetan still wore the Steward's ring, which the loss of his little finger made more noticeable. But she could understand why Daemon had set the Consort's ring aside. Saetan had withdrawn to live at the Keep, leaving his sons—Daemon, specifically—to handle the property owned by the SaDiablo family as well as the wealth acquired over Saetan's long, long lifetime. Daemon, on the other hand, was still very much in sight. He was no longer the Consort, since Jaenelle, while still a Queen, no longer ruled a court.

Of course, only a fool wanting to commit suicide would in any way imply that the absence of a ring made him any less Jaenelle's Consort.

"What are your plans?" Daemon asked quietly. "Or haven't you thought that far ahead?"

"Know anyone who needs an assassin?"

He choked back a laugh. "In Kaeleer? Hardly."

She saw the question in his eyes. "If I'd wanted him dead, Sadi, Falonar wouldn't be breathing. You know that."

His gold eyes stayed locked on hers as he took a sip of brandy. "Point made. Besides, I'm surprised you put up with him this long."

That startled her. "Why?"

"Too much of that Eyrien arrogance for you to swallow for long."

"You have a brother who has even more of that Eyrien arrogance," she pointed out.

"You want to sleep with him?"

"I'd eat worms first. Live." Since the image made her a little queasy, she took a healthy swallow of brandy. "Not that I don't like him," she added. "Maybe even love him a little in a sisterly way . . . when he's not being a stubborn prick about something."

"Hmm, all of five minutes a month."

She grinned. "If you add it up." The grin faded. "What about you?"

He rolled the snifter between his hands and studied the way the brandy followed the motion. "We're doing all right. He's . . . wary. Can't blame him for that. But he'll stand. If I need him, he'll stand."

And you and Jaenelle?

"Anyway," she said, "I thought I'd spend some time in Amdarh, if you have no objection to me using the town house."

"It's the family's town house. You're family." He hesitated for a moment. "I have to go to Amdarh in a few days. If you're willing to wait, we can go at the same time. I have a box at two of the theaters, if you'd like to see a play—and wouldn't mind some company."

I think you're the one who needs some company. Shit, Sadi, what's going on here?

"Fair enough." She set the snifter on the blackwood desk, stood up, and stretched. "I'd better see what Graysfang is up to. He's of the wolfie opinion that I enjoy drying him off and brushing him when he comes in wet and muddy. Don't know why."

"He's male. He's getting petted. This is hard to understand?"

The words were said lightly, but there was an undertone of anguished yearning.

Not knowing what to say, she left the study. But she thought about it on and off for the rest of the day. She watched the two of them through-out dinner. And when she was staring at the ceiling late that night, with Graysfang curled up beside her, snoring softly, she came to a decision.

All right, Sadi. I'll keep the peace while we're at the Hall. But once we get to Amdarh . . . The Blood in Terreille had good reason to call you the Sadist. If I have to dance with that side of your temper to find out what in the name of Hell is wrong between you and Jaenelle, then that's what I'll do. But one way or another, you're going to talk to me.

And if she couldn't get anything out of him, informing the patriarch of the family that there was serious trouble between Daemon and Jaenelle would get some results. One way or another.

FIVE

1

Jealousy coiled around Lektra's heart as she watched Daemon settle the lovely woman in the seat beside him. He *never* invited anyone to sit with him when he came to the theater. *Never.*

"Who is she?" Lektra asked, struggling to hide the feeling of betrayal that welled up at the sight of Daemon with another woman. He should be keeping other women at arm's length until he could be with *her*.

Lord Braedon, the Warlord who had agreed to be her escort tonight with gratifying eagerness, looked across the theater to the box opposite theirs. "Who? Oh. That's Sadi's 'cousin.'"

Tavey, Lektra's cousin on her father's side, snickered and leaned forward a little to see around Roxie, who was sitting on Lektra's right. "Convenient, isn't it?"

"Meaning what?" Lektra snapped.

"I heard she used to be a whore," Roxie replied primly.

"A high-priced one, from what *I* heard," Tavey said. "Wonder if she and Sadi had a standing arrangement when they both lived in Terreille."

"I doubt there was much standing," Braedon said blandly.

Shocked, Lektra stared at her escort. "Do you mean Dae— Prince Sadi and that woman used to . . . ?"

Braedon shrugged. "It's *possible* she's really related in some way to the

SaDiablo family. But if a man needed to be very discreet about getting certain . . . needs . . . met, having a 'cousin' who could stay under the same roof without anyone thinking twice about it would make it much easier."

"Especially an 'experienced' cousin," Tavey said, snickering again.

"You're both being ridiculous," Lektra said, remembering she was supposed to be Daemon's defender.

"Is she wearing a bracelet?" Roxie said, then hunched her shoulders as if she'd said something she shouldn't have.

"Who's going to notice a bracelet when you can notice other things?" Tavey asked, cupping his hands close to his chest.

Lektra bit back a snappish remark about making such gestures in public. Tavey was a Yellow-Jeweled Warlord who was devotedly loyal to her, which made up for him not being very bright. He also had a thirst for gossip that accounted for his never having a contract renewed when the family managed to get him accepted in a court.

"Well," Roxie said, sounding reluctant, "I'd heard Prince Sadi had bought a bracelet from Banard. A 'special gift for a special Lady.' "

"Thought it was a brooch," Tavey said, frowning.

"There was an actress showing off a brooch that had been sent by a secret admirer," Braedon said. His eyes flicked from the stage to Sadi's box and back again. "You don't think—"

"No, I don't," Lektra said firmly. "Everyone knows Prince Sadi is devoted to Jaenelle Angelline."

"Who hasn't been seen in months," Braedon murmured.

"Oh, hush," Lektra said. "The play will start in a few minutes. I'm looking forward to seeing it." Her eyes flicked to the box opposite hers as she added softly, "I'm definitely looking forward to it."

2

Surreal watched Daemon remove two items from the wooden box he'd called in as soon as they were settled in their seats, at first with idle curiosity, then with growing apprehension.

"Is that a tangled web?" she asked. She knew he was a Black Widow. Hell's fire, she'd lived with him for several years while he was struggling to come back from the Twisted Kingdom and then rehone his Craft skills.

"Of a kind," Daemon replied as he used Craft to set the frame holding the tangled web on air where it couldn't easily be seen by other people attending the play. Behind the tangled web, he set a faceted, oval crystal. "I started with the kind of web the Hourglass uses to see dreams and visions and adapted it for a specific purpose."

"Which is?"

He grinned, but there was an acknowledgment in his eyes of why she was asking the question—and why she was wary of the answer. Daemon rarely announced his intentions when he went hunting, and she'd often wondered how many of the Blood he'd destroyed in the Terreillean courts were aware of what had killed them until the last moment when that slash of Black power burned out their own power, finishing the kill.

"By using a spell I worked out and channeling through the web, I can retain the play in the crystal so that it can be played again."

"Like the spelled music crystals retain a musical performance?"

Daemon nodded. "But this one holds what is seen as well as what is heard."

Surreal studied the web and crystal again, this time with keen interest. "That's brilliant! But . . . why?"

He hesitated. "Jaenelle is still too fragile to come to Amdarh to see a play . . . so I bring the plays to her."

Emotion that felt appallingly sentimental welled up in her. She punched it down. "Does she enjoy the plays?"

Now he smiled ruefully. "I hadn't quite worked out all the snags in the spell the last time I tried it. There was a . . . lag . . . between when the actor said his lines and the words were heard. She found it entertaining, but not in the way I'd intended."

Surreal laughed. "Anything I can do to help?"

"This spell doesn't work independently. At least not yet. So I need to stay focused on the play."

She heard the warning under the words. "That explains why you

Black-locked the door." And why he'd told her he preferred to attend the theater alone when she'd asked him earlier if he ever invited anyone to join him as a guest. She'd been thinking of Marian, Lucivar's wife, but the chill in the air when he'd replied made her wonder how many offers he'd had for company whenever he came to Amdarh.

It also told her how much of a concession he'd made by inviting her to join him tonight. And how he trusted her to let him do what he'd come here to do.

As the house lights went down, Daemon made himself comfortable and focused his eyes on the stage.

The play was entertaining, but Surreal found Daemon more interesting to watch, even though she, too, kept her eyes fixed on the stage. How much of the play did he actually notice since he kept looking at the center of the stage to see the whole of it instead of shifting his gaze to follow the action when it moved closer to one wing or the other? Or would he finally enjoy it when he replayed it for Jaenelle? Although she doubted his attention would be on the play at that point.

When the first act ended and she offered to fetch some refreshment, his quick agreement surprised her—until she made her way through the crowd to the curved bar at one end of the theater's lobby and ordered two glasses of sparkling wine. The number of women who had given her a cool appraisal as she passed made her wonder how many of them were trying to find out how deep Daemon's attachment to Jaenelle still ran.

From their point of view, she understood the interest. Daemon was no longer officially Jaenelle's Consort. Few beyond the family and Jaenelle's former First Circle would know he'd committed himself to Jaenelle years before he ever became her Consort. They wouldn't know what he'd done—and suffered—to try to save an extraordinary child who became the most powerful Queen in the history of the Blood. What they saw was a beautiful, sensual male who came from one of the most powerful, and wealthiest, families in Kaeleer, and was a Black-Jeweled Warlord Prince in the bargain.

He'd be a prize for any woman who could win him.

She shuddered at the thought of any woman trying to win him away from Jaenelle.

"That's a lovely bracelet."

Surreal glanced over at the Warlord who had squeezed in beside her to wait for his order. "Thank you."

"Is it a design by Banard?"

Something about his interest wasn't quite right, but she couldn't figure out what it was about him that made her want to spill his guts all over the floor. So she hooked her long black hair behind one delicately pointed ear—and saw his eyes widen at the evidence that she wasn't solely from any of the long-lived races.

"No," she said, "it's Dea al Mon."

Nerves danced in his eyes at the mention of the Children of the Wood—a race who fiercely protected their Territory and seldom let anyone who crossed their border walk out again—but he worked to keep his smile easy.

"Then you must be Lady Surreal," he said. "I've heard of you."

You didn't hear enough, sugar. If you'd heard about more than my "public" profession, you wouldn't be crowding me.

She smiled at him, called in a silver mark and put it on the bar when the server gave her the glasses of sparkling wine, and turned to leave. The woman directly in her path stared at her with hostile jealousy for a moment before moving aside.

She dismissed the look without a second thought as she worked her way back up to the box. She'd seen enough of those looks when she'd been a whore in Terreille.

Maybe that accounted for the odd feeling she got from the Warlord and his interest in the bracelet. Maybe he'd just been trying to find out where he could buy something similar and was nervous about his Lady seeing him talking to another woman. Besides, there was something about the woman in the moment when their eyes met that practically shouted "possessive bitch" to someone who'd spent her life quickly sizing up rivals, enemies, and prey.

Not her problem, she thought as Daemon opened the door enough for her to slip back into the box. Noticing the unhappiness lurking in his eyes before he took the glass she offered, she almost said something, but the house lights began fading as a warning that the second act was about to begin.

No, the Warlord and the bitch weren't her problem—not when she had a bigger, and more dangerous, one sitting beside her.

3

Surreal waited until they'd enjoyed the appetizers at the dining house Daemon had chosen for their after-theater meal.

"Do you want to talk about it?" she asked quietly.

"The play?"

"No, about what's going on between you and Jaenelle that's making you so unhappy."

"Leave it alone, Surreal," he said, his voice turning icy and razor-edged.

She shook her head. "Can't, sugar."

"Do you want to talk about Falonar?" he countered.

She hissed.

"Exactly." Smiling, he raised his wineglass in a salute. Then he looked down at his plate—and sighed. "I'll talk if you will."

Hell's fire. The least said about Falonar to any male in her family the better. But . . . "I have your word you won't do anything to him? *Anything?*"

She didn't like the fact that he thought about it for several seconds before inclining his head in agreement.

Pushing her plate aside, she folded her arms on the table. Not a lady-like posture, but it let her lean closer to him. It occurred to her that they could have this entire conversation on a psychic thread to keep it silent and private, but it felt necessary to give the words the weight of sound.

"I'm not what he wanted," she said, feeling the sting of the truth.

"He doesn't want a beautiful, intelligent, talented woman?"

Realizing Daemon meant what he'd said eased the sting a little. She tried to smile. "He wants a Marian. Not *Marian,*" she added quickly, seeing the instant chill in Daemon's eyes. "The things that intrigued him enough initially for him to offer to share his eyrie with me were the same things that eventually stuck in his throat. Hell's fire, Sadi, I'm not going to apologize for what I've been."

"He couldn't get past the fact that you used to be paid for sex?" Daemon asked too softly.

"Since he wasn't offering to be anything more than my lover, that didn't bother him. Well, not much. And he certainly appreciated my . . . skills." She sighed. "No, what rubbed the wrong way was my skill with a knife—and the fact that an assassin doesn't worry about sticky details like letting the prey know he's about to be turned into carrion."

"You were a competitor."

She sat back as the dishes vanished and the server brought the main course. She savored the taste of a perfectly cooked filet before going back to a subject that would ruin her appetite.

"I was a competitor," she agreed. "Falonar could be indulgent about the Eyrien witches learning to use weapons to defend themselves because none of them will ever have enough skill to be a rival to him. And they were only learning because Lucivar insisted on it, not because they wanted to. But I wanted to improve skills I already had—and killing is what I do."

"And since Falonar wears a Sapphire Jewel and you wear the Gray, he wasn't stronger than you in that arena," Daemon said. "There are plenty of men who have lovers who wear darker Jewels than they do."

"Falonar wants a woman who looks at him and sees a protector, a defender. He wants someone who needs his strength, someone whose talents are . . . gentler."

"Who is she?" Daemon asked as he dipped a piece of lobster into the bowl of clarified butter.

Surreal studied him warily. "I didn't say there was someone in particular."

Daemon just smiled and continued eating.

She concentrated on her own meal for a few minutes. Then she sighed. "Nurian. She's a Healer."

"And she's Eyrien."

"I don't know how deep Falonar's feelings about her run, but I'm pretty sure she's in love with him. Over the winter, things changed between him and me. Lots of sex and not much else. Some snide comments about my snipping off balls because I wanted a pair of my own. And for the record, I'd rather have the discomfort of moontimes than carry what you've got between your legs."

He just raised an eyebrow.

"Moon's blood only throws me offstride three days out of a month. A cock makes a man potentially stupid at any hour of any day."

"You have such faith in the male gender," he said blandly.

"I made a good living because cocks make men stupid," she countered, picking up her glass to sip her wine.

"And Falonar's cock kept pointing in Nurian's direction?"

She clamped a hand over her mouth to keep from spraying wine all over the table. "Now that's a picture," she said when she finally managed to swallow. "No, it wasn't that obvious. Mostly because I was in the way," she added softly.

Daemon nodded. "A Gray-Jeweled witch who is skilled with a knife . . . and is also related to Lucivar."

"I think Falonar couldn't figure out how to step back."

"Probably afraid that if you didn't rip his balls off, Lucivar would."

"Exactly."

"So you told him things weren't working between you and packed your bags."

She shrugged. "Seemed the only thing to do."

"Did you love him?"

She hesitated, then shook her head. "I felt . . . special . . . for a little while. I've had sex with hundreds of men over the centuries, but I've never had a lover. I'm feeling bruised, but I'm not heartbroken over it."

Dipping the last piece of lobster into the butter, Daemon held it out to her. "Someday you'll find a man worthy of you."

She looked into his eyes, scared that she'd see some underlying message. What she saw was the warm affection of an older brother. She took the bite from his fork.

Easing back, she enjoyed the warmth for a moment before saying, "Your turn."

He set his fork on his plate with painful care. Then he picked up his wine and studied it.

"I'm losing her," he said softly. "I don't know what I'm doing wrong, but . . . I'm losing her."

Surreal stiffened. "What you are talking about?"

His voice dropped to a whisper. "Maybe I'm no longer what Jaenelle wants."

"Wait," she snapped. "Just wait." She studied the misery in his eyes. "You really believe that."

"She isn't comfortable being around me anymore."

Surreal shook her head. "I agree something isn't right between you, but, Daemon, I'm sure it isn't that."

"You were only at the Hall a few days."

"Which was long enough to know you're going down the wrong path if you think Jaenelle doesn't love you anymore."

He closed his eyes, shutting her out, but not before she saw the pain and desperation he was choking back.

She reached across the table and took his hand. Worry spiked through her when his fingers curled around hers in a fierce hold, a sure sign he was looking for reassurance.

"She won't talk to me," he said. "I don't know what to do."

"I do."

He opened his eyes, disbelief warring with hope.

"I'm willing to wager a year's income that her feelings haven't changed," Surreal said. "And I *know* yours haven't changed. So maybe the reason she can't talk to you is because you have a cock."

"I've always had a cock," he said dryly.

"Right. And there are things you might admit to another man you'd never admit to a woman. And there are things a woman might say to another woman that she would never say to a man—especially a man she loves."

"And your point is?"

"You're going to be in Amdarh a few more days, right?"

"I do have some things to take care of."

"Fine. You go tend to things, and I'll go back to the Hall and have a little chat with Jaenelle."

"What makes you think she'll talk to you?"

I'm not going to give her a choice. Which wasn't something she intended to ever tell Daemon, so she gave him a sassy smile. "Because I know the opening line to this little play." She eased her fingers out of his grip and patted his hand. "Trust me. And signal the server to bring over the dessert tray."

"Did you see the way he fed her that bite of lobster?" Roxie said, sighing. "That's like something from a love story. He's sooo romantic."

Tavey frowned. "If you wanted to taste some of my dinner, why didn't you say so?"

Watching Daemon, Lektra wanted to smash all the plates and glasses on the table. How could he betray her like that? How could he sit there, *in public,* and fawn over a *whore. She* was the one who was working to free him from that useless cripple, Jaenelle. He shouldn't be playing with another woman. He shouldn't even be *thinking* of another woman. It was so . . . sluttish. When he was hers, she'd make sure he severed all association with that bitch, Surreal.

Her hands curled into fists as she watched Surreal take his hand.

How *could* he be so lost to propriety that he'd let a woman touch him like that? He might as well stand on the table and announce he was going to drop his pants for his "cousin" as soon as they got behind closed doors.

If they even waited that long.

Selfish bastard.

Well, she'd still have him because she loved him. Besides, he was beautiful and was, no doubt, magnificent in bed. But he was obviously more ripe to belong to another woman than she'd realized, so she was going to have to fan the flames and ruin his reputation faster, and more thoroughly, than she'd intended if she wanted to be sure he didn't accept another offer from a woman who just wanted to use him.

Yes, she had to save him before he tumbled into any other bed but hers.

SIX

The next morning, rumors seeped through Amdarh's marketplace as the servants who worked in aristo households gathered to take care of the day's shopping. Arguments broke out between those who declared they weren't surprised by the news that Daemon Sadi had abandoned the pose of still being the faithful, devoted lover of the former Queen of Ebon Askavi and those who hotly denied there could be any truth to Prince Sadi taking a lover, let alone escorting her to such a public place as a theater.

But they all took those rumors back to their respective houses to chew over with their fellow servants.

By midday, the stories trickled through the shopping district. Some merchants worried that the aristo Blood, especially those who served in Lady Zhara's court, would take their business away from any shop that was patronized by Prince Sadi. Other merchants, who counted several members of the SaDiablo family as regular customers, paled at the news—and wondered how much of Amdarh would be left if Lucivar Yaslana found out about his brother's supposed betrayal of the Queen they'd both served.

By evening, the rumors had reached the ears of the aristo Blood and were the main topic during the evening meals. Some defended Prince Sadi, saying he would never insult Jaenelle Angelline by taking a lover while she was still living with him at the Hall. Some defended him by insisting he wasn't breaking any vows by taking a lover, that Jaenelle was now nothing more than a family member who required care, and no matter what their relationship had been, it was no longer of a nature that demanded celibacy from a Warlord Prince. Others argued that, even if taking a lover could be excused under the circumstances, holding hands with her in a dining house was hardly discreet.

No matter what anyone thought of Daemon Sadi's behavior, they all pitied Jaenelle Angelline, who had sacrificed her body and her Jewels in order to save Kaeleer and was now being abandoned by the only man she'd ever cared for enough to take as a lover.

SEVEN

1

Surreal walked into Jaenelle's sitting room and came to an abrupt stop when she saw the shoes scattered around the room. Jaenelle stood in the middle of the room, holding a pair of soft leather house shoes. Color brightened her face, and her eyes sparkled.

"Look," Jaenelle said excitedly. "I can call in my shoes."

Pity squeezed Surreal's heart, but she smiled as she walked over to Jaenelle. "Well, that's . . . wonderful." Or would be if Jaenelle was a child learning basic Craft.

"Isn't it?" Jaenelle dropped the shoes, then held out her hands. A moment later, a pair of boots hovered in the air. She took the boots and grinned. "I decided it was time to find out what I can do with Twilight's Dawn."

A year ago you could do things the rest of the Blood couldn't even dream of doing, Surreal thought sadly as she looked at the shoes. *And now you're excited about being able to do basic Craft. Ah, sugar.*

Trying to think of something to say that would be encouraging, she looked into Jaenelle's eyes. It took everything in her not to stumble back a step or two.

No delight in those sapphire eyes now. There was strength there, power there. Those eyes were cold, feral, and filled with deadly anger.

Then Ladvarian trotted into the room, and Jaenelle looked away.

Witch, Surreal thought as she fought to hide a shiver of fear. She hadn't expected to see that look in Jaenelle's eyes ever again—and wasn't sure what to think about seeing it now.

Ladvarian sniffed the shoes on the floor, then looked at Jaenelle. ★Why is Surreal calling in your shoes?★

"She didn't," Jaenelle said quietly, dropping the boots. "I did."

★You called in your shoes?★

Jaenelle shrugged, a quiet sadness draining the color from her face, leaving her looking ill and frail.

★You called in your shoes!★ Ladvarian's tail wagged madly while he danced in place. ★You could never do that before!★

Jaenelle smiled reluctantly. "No, I never could."

That admission startled Surreal. Ladvarian was right. Jaenelle never *could* call in her own shoes. It was a standing joke in the family and the First Circle that Jaenelle could move an entire library of leather-bound books without any effort at all but couldn't call in something to put on her feet.

Ladvarian shot upward, hovering on air so that he was face-to-face with Jaenelle. ★The kindred will still fetch your shoes during the moon-days when you can't use Craft, but the rest of the days you can call in your own shoes,★ he said happily.

Jaenelle smiled as her hands cupped the Sceltie's furry face. "Yes, I can."

★And you won't have to wear the wrong shoes because we didn't pick the right ones.★

Well, Surreal thought, that explained why Jaenelle's shoes hadn't always matched the rest of her outfit.

"I never said you chose the wrong shoes," Jaenelle said softly.

★You didn't tell us because you love us.★

Jaenelle rested her forehead against the dog's. "Yes, I love you."

Surreal swallowed the lump that was suddenly lodged in her throat. Shit shit shit. Hadn't she learned anything from seeing the kindred's unshakable loyalty and belief in Jaenelle? She had felt pity and had spoiled Jaenelle's pleasure in successfully performing a bit of Craft.

Ladvarian was simply delighted—and had recognized that Jaenelle wasn't regaining a piece of skill that was lost, she was exploring new ground.

I have to tell Kaelas! Ladvarian bounded out of the room.

"By tonight, all the kindred who were part of the Dark Court will know you can call in your shoes," Surreal said dryly.

Jaenelle grinned. "Do you think it will take that long?" Then the grin faded. "I thought you were going to stay in Amdarh."

"I came back to talk to you." She took a deep breath and let it out slowly—and hoped she wouldn't see that cold, feral anger leap into Jaenelle's eyes again. "What's wrong between you and Daemon?"

"Nothing you can mend."

Surreal reached out, her fingertips just brushing the sleeve of Jaenelle's robe. "Talk to me. Mother Night, Jaenelle, the man is eating his heart out because he doesn't know why you're pushing him out of your life."

Jaenelle turned away. "For his sake." Her voice was a pained whisper. "So he isn't trapped into staying with a woman he no longer wants just because everyone else expects him to remain loyal."

"Trapped, my ass," Surreal snapped. *"You're who he wants. You're who he needs."*

"He wanted and needed what I was," Jaenelle snapped back. "But what I am now?" She shook her head.

"Do you still love him?"

"It doesn't matter what I feel."

"Of course it matters! You love him. He loves you. Why are you throwing him out of your life?"

"Look at me!" Jaenelle shouted, jabbing a finger toward her chest. "I'm healed, Surreal. Completely healed. But he can't bring himself to touch me, can't even bear to hold my hand. Why should he be chained to someone who repulses him when he's s-so damn beautiful it hurts just to look at him and remember what it was like when he w-wanted . . ."

Shocked, Surreal just stood and stared. Then she shook her head. She didn't doubt Jaenelle believed what she said, but that didn't tally up with what Daemon believed.

"Does he know you're completely healed?" Surreal asked. "And by completely, you do mean *completely*?"

A gleam of anger flashed in Jaenelle's eyes again. "I don't need his pity any more than I need yours."

"So you haven't told him."

"And have him feel obligated to service his former Queen?" Jaenelle smiled bitterly. "I don't think so."

Surreal raked her fingers through her hair. Hell's fire, Mother Night, and may the Darkness be merciful. If Daemon found out that *this* was why Jaenelle was pulling away from him, he'd explode six times over. And *that* was only if he retained a measure of self-control.

Dropping her hands to her hips, she sighed. "All right, sugar. Strip. Let's see what we've got to work with."

Jaenelle stared at her. "What?"

"You heard me. Strip."

Doubt filled Jaenelle's eyes. "I don't think—"

"Good, since you're not thinking straight anyway. Come on. You don't have anything I don't see in the mirror every day."

More hesitation.

"Fine," Surreal said, turning around. "I won't watch." *And it will give me time to brace myself in case there are any nasty surprises.*

Silence. Then, finally, the sound of clothes being removed.

"All right," Jaenelle said.

Surreal turned around. Stared. Frowned. Circled slowly to study Jaenelle from the back before continuing the circle until they were facing each other again.

"All right," she said, "I'll play the game. What's wrong with you?"

Jaenelle's mouth dropped open. *"Look at me."*

"I am. What's wrong with you?"

"I'm—"

"Skinny. You were always slender, but now you're skinny." Surreal tipped her head to one side. "Despite that, you've got a decent pair of tits and a nice ass."

Jaenelle just gaped at her.

She growled in frustration. Jaenelle had picked a lousy time to become sensitive about her appearance. "You need to eat more to fill out a bit, need to start working out to build up and shape your muscles again. Lucivar can help with that."

"He won't," Jaenelle said, looking away. "I asked him. He said no."

"He's going to help. Trust me." Surreal picked up the robe and handed it to Jaenelle. "As for the rest, we're going to Amdarh tomorrow."

"But—"

"I heard of a new place that opened a few months ago. Pure female indulgence. Manicures, pedicures, massages, the works. We can even stay there, so we don't have to bundle all the appointments together. The place even has shops." She held up a hand before Jaenelle could grumble about shopping. "And you're going to get your hair trimmed so that it has some style."

"I was growing it out," Jaenelle protested, one hand reaching up protectively.

"Which doesn't mean you have to look shaggy," Surreal countered. "And, yes, some new clothes. Something that fits. Not a lot since you'll grow back into your former wardrobe, but enough to cover different activities until then." She paused. "And then, once you look like you again instead of a stray wearing hand-me-downs, you'll go to the town house and see Daemon. And you'll tell him in direct, simple words that you are completely healed."

"Then what?"

If you can't guess how Daemon will react to that . . . She shrugged. "Then you'll know the truth, one way or the other."

Jaenelle sighed. "So what do we do today?"

Surreal gave her friend a knife-edged smile. "I'm going to have a chat with Lucivar."

2

Smiling, Surreal waved Lucivar into Daemon's study. She put a Gray lock on the door as she closed it, and by the time he turned to face her, she'd called in her crossbow and had it aimed below his belt.

He studied her for a moment, then growled, "What's this all about? You asked me to come here, so I'm here."

"Yes, you are," Surreal replied, still smiling. "And now I'm going to talk, and you're going to listen. If you don't listen, I'll shoot you with this little crossbow arrow."

"Quarrel."

She shook her head. "We're not going to quarrel. I'm going to talk, and you're going to listen—or I'll pin your balls to the wall." She didn't have any chance of actually hitting him. She wore Gray; he wore Ebon-gray. The moment he sensed the Gray lock on the door, he'd put an Ebon-gray shield around himself. There was nothing she could do that would get an arrow through that shield, but the threat warned him that she wasn't going to let him dismiss what she had to say.

Lucivar shook his head. "It's called a 'quarrel' or a 'bolt,' not a 'little crossbow arrow.' "

"But—" Her face flushed. *Falonar, you son of a whoring bitch.*

"I guess Falonar didn't mention that when he agreed to teach you how to use a crossbow," Lucivar said, giving her a thoughtful look, as if a few pieces of a puzzle had just fallen into place.

"Doesn't matter."

"What does matter?"

"Jaenelle."

He took a step toward her, then stopped and looked at the crossbow. "Is she all right?"

"She needs to start training again to rebuild her strength. You're going to help her."

"No."

"Yes."

"No!" Swearing viciously, he turned away and paced, giving her searing looks every time he turned in her direction.

"Lucivar?" Surreal said quietly. "How long are you going to keep her an invalid? How long are you going to block her from being strong enough to stand on her own again?"

He charged toward her, stopping before she was within reach. "You bitch! How dare you?"

She lowered the crossbow. "I dare because I love her too."

He stared at her, fury in his eyes. "She's too frail."

"She's not as frail as you think." She saw hope, confusion, fear. "I understand that you're afraid of doing anything that might hurt her. I really do. But she needs you, Lucivar. She needs your help to regain what she lost."

Pain now as he looked away. "Not everything she lost."

"No, not everything." She vanished the crossbow and took a step toward him. "She learned how to call in her shoes today."

He snapped to attention, surprising her. "Jaenelle called in her shoes? She could never do that before." He walked over to the desk and leaned back against it. After staring at the floor for a long moment, he sighed. "All right. I'll take her through a warm-up. We'll see after that."

"I'm surprised you gave in so easily," Surreal said, joining him at the desk.

He shrugged. "Marian's been muttering similar things over the past few days."

"You married a smart woman."

His only response was a grunt. Then he turned his head and studied her. "Are you coming back to Ebon Rih, or do you want to stay here for a while?"

"Actually, I had my eye on the town house in Amdarh. I've missed city living." When she came to Kaeleer, she'd ended up signing a contract to serve the Prince of Ebon Rih, so, technically, Lucivar could demand that she go back to Ebon Rih with him.

"If that's what you want," Lucivar said.

"Well, I don't really want to watch Falonar make kissy faces at Nurian."

Temper flared in his eyes, confirming that Falonar hadn't wasted any time declaring his interest in the Eyrien Healer. "I can take care of that."

Being related to Warlord Princes was such a joy. "I'll tell you the same thing I told Daemon. If I'd wanted him dead, he wouldn't still be among the living."

"Twisting his cock off wouldn't kill him."

Surreal laughed. "That's what I like about you, Lucivar. You're so subtle."

He gave her a grudging smile before he pushed away from the desk.

"Unlock the damn door so I can see Jaenelle and decide if I should be pissed off with myself for being wrong or with you for being right."

She released the Gray lock on the door, watched him walk out—and hoped.

Seeing Jaenelle's hesitant pleasure as he handed her the Eyrien sparring stick bruised Lucivar's heart.

Are you sure you're not clipping her wings instead of helping her learn how to fly again?

Had Marian been right about that? Had they placed Jaenelle in a cage because they were so afraid of letting her do anything that might harm that terrifyingly frail body? They'd done it for the best of reasons, and certainly out of love, but a cage was still a cage.

"Partnered warm-up," he said, taking his position in front of Jaenelle. "Go easy. Don't push. When you feel tired, we'll stop."

He mirrored her slow movements, always watching, always assessing. She remembered the moves, but couldn't complete any of them. Not fully. Choppy motion where there had once been fluid grace. She began panting by the time they'd gone through the first third of the warm-up. By the halfway point, her arms and legs shook from the effort to shift from one move to the next.

Then one end of her stick hit the floor, and she used its support to stay on her feet. Refusing to look at him, she shuffled to the couch and sank down on the cushion at one end.

"So," she said. "You were right."

He took her stick, vanished it along with his, then crouched in front of her. "No, I wasn't." He waited until she looked at him. "Do you remember when you went into the Twisted Kingdom to mark a trail for Daemon to follow? Your body was already strained from healing the landens who had been trapped by a jhinka attack, and by the time you got back to the Keep after finding Daemon, you'd made a mess of yourself."

"I remember," she whispered, staring at her hands.

"As soon as you were able to stand on your own, we started working to rebuild your muscles and your strength."

"What's your point?" She looked weary, defeated.

He placed one hand lightly over hers. "You didn't get half as far that first time as you did today. So the point, Cat, is I'm sorry. I wanted you to come back to us so much, it got in the way. I clipped your wings instead of helping you learn how to fly again."

"So you'll be my sparring partner again?"

He smiled. "We'll get there. I'll come back tomorrow."

She made a face. "Can't tomorrow. Surreal and I are going to Amdarh for what she calls a female indulgence."

"You're staying at the town house?"

Jaenelle shook her head. "Surreal says it's easier to be pampered if we stay at that . . . whatever it is. Besides, Daemon's at the town house right now."

So? He didn't ask because there was something odd about her tone. Something . . . nervous. And Daemon had become edgy over the past few weeks—and subtly territorial in a way that made all the male servants at the Hall wary of drawing his attention. "Then let me know when you get back."

He stayed at the Hall long enough to assure Surreal he'd start working with Jaenelle once the two women got back from their female indulgence, whatever that meant, then caught the Winds and headed for Ebon Rih. But before he went home, he stopped at the Keep to have a little chat with his father.

EIGHT

1

Baffled by the worried glances he'd gotten from the servants and too restless to stay inside, Daemon left the town house shortly after breakfast, walking aimlessly until the shops opened. Then he headed for the bookshop where he could fill an hour or two browsing. Since love stories had lost their appeal, maybe he could find something else Jaenelle would find intriguing—and find something for himself that would catch his interest enough to keep him occupied while he waited for some word from Surreal.

After she left for the Hall yesterday morning, he'd summoned Marcus and had exhausted the energy and patience of his man of business by reviewing every possible business transaction that might come up in the next few weeks. If Surreal succeeded in finding out what was troubling Jaenelle, if she actually managed to fix the problem so that Jaenelle wanted his company again, he wasn't going to allow anything to intrude on his time with his Lady.

But he needed to keep busy until he heard from her—or from Jaenelle. Maybe he'd contact Lucivar and invite him to dinner. Or go to the Keep and spend a few hours with his father. He'd been choking on his fear of losing Jaenelle but had said nothing to anyone except Surreal. Now . . . Maybe he should get another male's opinion? But Lucivar would be too blunt and probably have the unfortunate effect of honing a temper that didn't need honing. Saetan, however, might be able to offer an insight into Jaenelle's emotional retreat . . . or even an assurance that it was a stage of healing and would pass. Maybe . . . Maybe even talking to Saetan about the nightmare that kept plaguing him might help, although lately, the erotic dreams were giving him more physical and emotional discomfort.

Shaking off those thoughts, he entered the bookshop and smiled at the owner—and wondered why the man's eyes cooled at the sight of him and the usual smile of greeting looked forced.

"Prince Sadi." The shopkeeper sounded like he'd swallowed glass. "You've come for the books I was holding for you?"

"Yes—and a few others," Daemon replied, starting to turn away from the counter to browse the shelves. He'd give the love stories to Marian. She and Jaenelle often exchanged books, so he knew she'd enjoy them.

"Very well."

The reluctance in the shopkeeper's voice stopped Daemon and had him turning back to study the man.

He doesn't want me here, Daemon thought, stung by the unexpected reaction to his presence.

Feeling a hint of ice brush the edge of his temper, he walked to a part of the shop where the shelves hid the shopkeeper from view. For the sake of past, and possibly future, courtesy, it was better to keep his distance until the desire to shred the shopkeeper's skin passed. After all, the man could be upset about something that had nothing to do with him.

Dismissing the shopkeeper for the time being, he began perusing the shelves of fiction, skipping over the love stories and straightforward adventures, and finally stopping at a section that looked interesting.

Pulling a book from the shelf, he read the first page and choked back a laugh. By the time he got to the fourth page, he was leaning comfortably against the shelves and grinning. The heroine was a Blood female named Tracker, a musician by trade, whose companion was a Purple Dusk Sceltie Warlord named Shadow. The village they lived in was clearly modeled on the village of Maghre, and the Warlord who ruled the village and requested their assistance in solving a mystery. . . .

Did Khardeen know about these stories? He'd send Khary a brief note this evening. It would be a good way to respond to the note he'd received from the Warlord of Maghre last week. Khary's note had been nothing more than a few sentences about horses, but he'd understood the significance of the note coming to him rather than Jaenelle. His actions during the time Jaenelle needed to create her spells to save Kaeleer had broken the friendships that had developed between him and the other males in Jaenelle's First Circle. Since then, they'd all been coldly civil with him. Khary's note was the first sign of any willingness to try to repair those friendships.

Closing the book, Daemon checked the shelves and found two others by the same author that featured Tracker and Shadow. He took those, too. Even if the mystery part of the story didn't end up being sufficiently compelling, the author's understanding of human-kindred relationships was certainly entertaining.

As he crouched to look at another book, he heard two women, speaking in low, urgent tones, walk up to the other side of the shelves.

"It's true, I tell you," one woman said.

"I don't believe it," the other replied, sounding oddly defiant. "And accusing a man of infidelity without proof is irresponsible."

"He was seen, *in public,* with the bitch he's bedding. How much more proof do you need?"

"I'd heard she was his cousin."

"Her being one thing doesn't exclude her being the other."

A hesitation. "No. I'm certain this is all a dreadful misunderstanding. You only had to look at him last winter to see he was in love with his Queen. He wouldn't betray her *now.*"

"We'll see," the first woman said darkly.

Her companion sighed. "Did you want a book from this section?"

"No, I just wanted to get away from the shopkeeper to finish telling you what I'd heard. The way he kept shushing us was most annoying—and peculiar. I don't usually come to this shop, and I'm not sure I will again."

"Then let's go. I already have my selections."

When he no longer sensed the women's presence in the shop, Daemon stood up and took his books to the counter. As he waited for the shopkeeper to return from another part of the shop, he thought about what he'd overheard.

Poor bastard. An accusation of infidelity could rip a man's life apart. Marriage was the prized partnership—a commitment of the heart rather than a contract for the body and sexual skills. Being branded unfaithful could not only cost a man his marriage, he could lose his children as well. A few hurtful words could destroy everything that mattered to him.

"Prince." The shopkeeper approached the counter, gray-faced and trembling.

"What's wrong?" Daemon asked. "Are you ill?"

"No." The man swallowed hard. "Is this everything?"

Since the man didn't want any assistance, at least from him, Daemon waited until the price of the books was tallied and added to his account. Then he initialed the account, vanished the books, and left the shop.

As he walked to Banard's shop, bafflement shifted into irritation as male acquaintances he passed on the street avoided looking at him or responding to a greeting and the women gave him hostile stares before pointedly looking away, making it clear they didn't want any connection with him. When he walked into Banard's shop, the three people already there, including a Priestess who served in Lady Zhara's court, turned away from the display cases and walked out without saying a word.

"What in the name of Hell is wrong with everyone today?" Daemon snarled as he approached the glass display case that served as a counter.

"You've come for the rings?" Banard asked.

"Yes, I've come for the rings."

Banard cupped his hands over the display case. When he lifted his hands, two velvet-lined ring boxes rested on the glass.

Everything else was forgotten as Daemon picked up what he hoped would be Jaenelle's wedding ring. Simple and fluid, it held a sapphire flanked by rubies.

"It's perfect," he murmured, setting it back in its box before examining the other ring. Just a plain gold band. No etching in the gold or fancy embellishments. He didn't need those things, didn't want those things. All he wanted, *everything* he wanted, was what that ring would stand for when Jaenelle put it on his finger.

Closing both boxes, he vanished them and smiled at Banard.

Banard didn't return the smile. "Some distressing rumors have spread throughout Amdarh."

Hearing a warning under the words, Daemon inclined his head. "I believe I heard a bit of it this morning. Do you think it's true?"

"No."

Banard's certainty surprised Daemon, but before he could phrase a question, the jeweler added, "You wouldn't have asked me to make those rings if the rumors were true."

For a long moment, he just stared at Banard, unable to make sense of the words. Then cold rage flowed through him, sweet and deadly.

"Thank you for telling me," Daemon said too softly.

As he walked back to the town house, he took mental note of every person who shunned him and every person who made a point of acknowledging him. He saw everything . . . and he saw nothing because the city had faded behind a soft mist that held a terrible clarity.

2

Arms linked, Surreal and Jaenelle strolled to the registration desk at the far end of the two-story atrium that was decorated to feel tranquil and lush—and was a clear signal that pampering Ladies was a serious business.

"Mother Night," Jaenelle said, looking around with wide eyes. "Are there really enough female indulgences to take up a place this size?"

"You'd be surprised," Surreal replied, biting back a smile when Jaenelle groaned. The place was built on a much grander scale, but it reminded her of Deje's Red Moon house in Chaillot, Terreille—and made her wonder, since there were guest rooms, if there were a few accommodations that weren't advertised. Not that sex was on her list of indulgences right now. Not for herself, anyway. "We'll get settled in our suite, then I'll make the appointments for our pampering."

"Maybe just—"

"No."

"But—"

"You'll love it. Trust me."

Jaenelle gave Surreal a narrow-eyed stare. "You think painting your toenails is normal."

"And your point is?"

Sighing, Jaenelle slipped her arm out of Surreal's and turned away from the registration desk just as a trim man returned to the desk from the other direction.

"Good morning, Ladies," he said, giving them a warm smile.

Returning the smile, Surreal gave him her name—and watched hostility flash across his face before he managed to hide it behind a neutral mask.

"I am sorry, Lady Surreal, but there are no rooms available."

You're not sorry at all, you spineless little prick. "I made a reservation, which was confirmed. Check your book."

"There's no need. I assure you—".

"Don't fret about it, Surreal," Jaenelle said quietly, turning back to face the registration desk—and the man. "If an error was made, we can stay at the family town house. There are other shops in Amdarh, and I'm certain this establishment isn't the only place that has people skilled at trimming and styling hair."

She wasn't sure which was more fascinating—the way Jaenelle bloodlessly gutted the little prick with a few words or the way the little prick scrambled to rectify his error when he recognized the golden-haired woman standing in front of him.

A minute later, Surreal tucked the key into her pocket, linked arms with Jaenelle to provide support without being too obvious, and headed for their suite of rooms.

"He didn't want us here," Jaenelle said quietly.

"Oh, he was thrilled to have *you*," Surreal replied. *I'm the one he looked at as if I was shit on his shoes. Now why is that, I wonder?*

The ground-floor suite had its own small, heated pool off the sitting room as well as two bedrooms with private bathrooms. At least the little prick was smart enough to give them one of the best suites.

"Why don't you rest for a bit while I go make the appointments?" Surreal said as she walked to the door.

"Are you going to take care of things, Surreal?"

Thinking Jaenelle hadn't heard her, she turned—and saw the look in Witch's eyes. And understood Jaenelle wasn't talking about appointments.

She smiled. "You can count on it."

She grabbed the first official-looking person she met, swung the other witch into a tiny alcove, and had the tip of her favorite stiletto tucked under the woman's chin before her prey had a chance to react.

"Listen up, sugar," Surreal said softly. "My cousin has spent months recovering from brutal injuries. Now that she's well enough, I brought her here for the kind of pampering I heard you specialize in. You understand me so far?"

"Y-yes," the witch stammered.

"Wonderful. So here's the deal. Whatever problem you have with me, you bury it while she's here, and you give her the best you've got. Because if you do anything to spoil this first outing, I'm going to tell her father, her brother, and her lover that you made Jaenelle very, very unhappy. By the time those three are finished expressing their displeasure, I sincerely doubt there will be anything in this place big enough to qualify as a pebble. Is that clear enough?"

The woman nodded.

"Good. I'm going to set up some appointments and give you a little time to pass the word." Surreal vanished the stiletto and stepped back into the corridor. "And, sugar? Jaenelle's male relatives aren't the only ones who are dangerous."

"My toes will be rose?"

"You'll love it. That polish will complement the sapphire jacket and trousers I saw in one of the shops we passed on the way to this room. We'll go there next so they'll have time to make any alterations by this afternoon."

"But . . . rose toenails? Who's going to see them?"

Daemon will when he's nibbling his way down your legs.

But there wasn't any reason to mention that right now.

★   ★   ★

"Mud? They're going to put *mud* on my face?"

"You'll love it."

"Whenever the kitties and I played stalk and pounce and we ended up muddy, everyone frowned about it."

Surreal grunted softly. Only Jaenelle referred to Jaal and Kaelas, a full-grown tiger and an eight-hundred-pound Arcerian cat, as "the kitties"—or voluntarily played games with them to keep their predatory skills honed.

"So why is this mud different?" Jaenelle grumbled.

Stretched out on the other table, Surreal turned her head and opened one eye. "It's expensive."

Whispers rose and fell, an ebb and flow of sound as they went to their various appointments throughout the day. They pretended not to notice the way conversations stopped when they entered a room, pretended not to see the uneasy glances. It wasn't the fun, relaxing experience Surreal had wanted it to be, but it served its purpose. By late afternoon, Jaenelle's hair was trimmed and styled, her nails—all of them—were painted, and they'd found enough clothing in the shops to suffice as a wardrobe for a few weeks.

Now, waiting for Jaenelle to return from the dressing room, Surreal studied a display of shawls. Two of them had the right colors to blend nicely with Jaenelle's new clothes and provide extra warmth if it was needed.

Her lips twitched. Well, extra warmth when Daemon wasn't wrapped around his Lady.

"I heard you were here," a voice said.

Turning, Surreal studied Zhara, who was staring at her with an expression that was close to dislike but hadn't quite crossed that line. "And you're here, too. Busy place."

Interesting, Surreal thought as Zhara moved closer. *She doesn't want to talk to me, doesn't want to get close to me, but something is pushing her.*

"I've heard some disturbing rumors," Zhara said.

"Really? Are you going to share them, or are you going to be another bitch whispering behind her hand?"

Temper flared in Zhara's eyes. "Remember who you're talking to."

"You're the Queen of Amdarh. And I'm a witch who wears Gray Jewels. If push comes to shove, sugar, you're a corpse. So you want to tell me in plain words what's bothering you, or do you want to keep dancing around in the shit?"

"There's a rumor that Daemon Sadi . . . that he . . ."

"What about Daemon?" asked a midnight voice.

Reading the discomfort and embarrassment in Zhara's eyes before they both turned to face Jaenelle, Surreal suddenly had a good idea of what kind of rumors were going around. Hell's fire, Mother Night, and may the Darkness be merciful. There were better ways of committing suicide than starting a rumor like that about a man the Blood in Terreille had called the Sadist.

Of course, pissing off Witch wasn't a great idea either. Especially when that deadly anger was back in Jaenelle's sapphire eyes.

"What about Daemon?" Jaenelle asked again, as if Zhara's expression hadn't told her plainly enough the reason for the whispers that had followed them all day.

"I—I'm sure the rumors aren't true," Zhara said.

Jaenelle's smile was razored ice. "So am I."

"Where are you going?" Surreal asked as Jaenelle headed out of the shop.

"I'm going to talk to Daemon."

She didn't try to stop Jaenelle, and she didn't offer to go with her. She didn't want to be around either one of them during that discussion.

"Well, that was fun," she said, looking at Zhara. "You planning to do anything else today to create a firestorm in the city? I was thinking of doing something dull like reading or sleeping, but if you've got your heart set on starting a gut-spilling slaughter, I'm willing to play."

"What are you talking about?" Zhara snapped.

You don't know who . . . and what . . . he is, Surreal thought. She shook her head. "Never mind." *It's too late anyway.*

3

Daemon prowled the town house's sitting room. He would have preferred walking through the city to being caged in this room, but he
couldn't tolerate one more cold look, one more silent condemnation.

The hurt went deep. The fear went deep. But the rage went much,
much deeper.

Damn them all to the bowels of Hell. He'd tried to fit in. Knowing
the Queens in Dhemlan would be wary of a Black-Jeweled Warlord
Prince, he hadn't worn the Black when he came to Amdarh. At least, not
in public. He'd been courteous and civil, had done all the proper things
a man was permitted to do when he was in an established relationship—
and *only* the things a man was permitted to do. What had that courtesy
and civility gotten him? At the first slur to his reputation, they'd con-
demned him of thinking more of his cock than the woman who had
given everything she had to defend and protect all of them.

Jaenelle should have let them all die, should have let them all choke
in the twisted, vicious cruelty Dorothea had spawned in Terreille before
Witch had cleansed the taint of Dorothea and Hekatah out of the Blood.
She should have—

"Is this the response of a Warlord Prince, to tuck his tail between his
legs and hide in his lair instead of standing up for himself?"

That wonderful, chilling midnight voice shivered over him. Despair
clawed his heart, leaving it bleeding, as he turned around.

Mother Night. *Jaenelle.*

She was still painfully thin, but standing there, dressed in a rose silk
shirt and soft sapphire jacket and trousers, she looked like the woman
he'd known and loved before she'd torn both of their lives apart to save
Kaeleer. She looked like the Queen of Ebon Askavi, strong and powerful, despite the fact that it was Twilight's Dawn and not a Black or Ebony
Jewel hanging from the gold chain around her neck.

And her eyes . . . Feral. Angry.

Witch. The living myth. Dreams made flesh.

He wanted to kneel before her, wanted to surrender everything he was
and could ever be, wanted to offer his life in any way she would have him.

But she'd obviously heard the rumors. She knew what was being said about him. That's what had brought her here. Someone's vicious lies had created a chasm between them, and if he didn't find a way to bridge that distance, if he lost her now . . .

Despair and fury twisted together, became a roar of pain. *"I have not been unfaithful!"*

"Do you think I don't know that?" Jaenelle replied. "I know you, Daemon. I *know* you. Even if there had been no hope of me healing, you would have stayed with me, celibate and faithful."

"Of course I would have. I love you." The bitterness under her words frightened him, but the fury was turning cold and sharp.

"I know." Jaenelle looked away, adding, "Maybe it would have been better if that weren't true."

"Meaning what?" he asked too softly, taking a step toward her.

"If you were capable of infidelity, it would be easier to believe you were staying with me because you wanted to stay and not because you felt you had to stay."

"What in the name of Hell are you talking about?"

"I'm talking about you . . . and me." Pain flickered in Jaenelle's eyes before she looked away. "I know I don't look . . . that a man wouldn't be attracted . . ."

"Damn you." He didn't think about it. He grabbed the back of a stuffed chair and let his rage flow.

The chair exploded. Startled, Jaenelle stumbled back a step.

Daemon smiled bitterly. He'd instinctively created a bubble shield to contain the debris so that nothing sprayed over the room, so that not even the smallest sliver would strike Jaenelle and possibly harm her.

But that release was enough to shift ice to heat, so he snapped the leash that held his temper. "Is that why you've been pushing me away? Because of how you *look*?" He moved away from her, needing whatever distance he could get within the confines of the room as the insult churned through him. "I waited for you my whole life. Yearned for you my whole life. After Tersa told me you were coming, I spent *seven hundred years* searching for you in the court of every Queen who had bought my service as a pleasure slave. I searched in every Territory in

Terreille that was within reach of wherever I'd been sent. For you. For Witch. For dreams made flesh. I never gave a damn what you might look like—tall, short, fat, thin, plain, beautiful, ugly. Why would I care what you looked like? The flesh was the shell that housed the glory. It was a way to connect with you, please you, be with you. Even if I couldn't be your physical lover, there are other ways to be a lover, and I know them all. So don't stand there and tell me what I feel for you depends on *how you look!*"

"Doesn't it?" Jaenelle snapped, her voice shaking with anger and hurt. "I'm healed, but you still can't bring yourself to touch me, can't even hold my hand—"

"Do you think it's because I don't want to?" Daemon roared. "*I can't* touch you!" His breathing hitched, surprising him, as the guilt he'd tried to lock away broke through. "It made me sick when I realized that no matter how careful I was, I couldn't touch you without hurting you, that even the lightest brush of my fingers left bruises smeared on your arms and hands, that when I helped you sit up in bed, there would be dark bruises in the shape of my hands on your back and shoulders. Every time I touched you, I hurt you, drained more of your strength because there was something else you had to heal."

"That's not—" Jaenelle paused. Then she sighed. "In the beginning, that was true. Everything was so . . . frail . . . it didn't take much to cause damage. But I did heal. It's been months since I've been that fragile."

He heard the words, but pain drove him now, forcing him to say what he'd hoped he'd never have to admit. "You suffered. Every moment you were awake, every move you made . . . you suffered." He still couldn't bear thinking of how much worse it had been when she'd first risen from the healing webs. How had Ladvarian, Kaelas, and the rest of the kindred who had cared for her endured watching her suffer?

Tears filled his eyes. "I understand why you want me out of your life. Sweetheart, I do understand. But I'd hoped you could forgive me."

Jaenelle's anger faded, but the hurt was still there. "Forgive you for what?"

"You suffered . . . because of me. You rose up from the healing webs too soon . . . because of me."

Horror began filling her eyes. "Daemon . . ."

The tears fell. He choked back a sob. "They told me you would come back, but I didn't believe them. Couldn't believe them. I wanted you so much, needed you so much . . . and you came back too soon. Because of me."

"That isn't true. The healing webs had done all they could and—"

"Liar." He waited, but she didn't deny it. She couldn't—and they both knew it. "You could have stayed longer in the healing webs, could have given your body more time to mend. But you never could withstand a plea for help from someone you cared about. And a cry of pain from me?" He shook his head. "You would have answered that cry no matter what it cost you. You paid the price for my doubts, and there was nothing I could do to make it up to you."

"Daemon . . ."

"Do you want to try another lie and tell me you didn't hear me calling to you in the abyss?" he asked bitterly.

Jaenelle's hands curled into fists. "Yes, I heard you. How could I *not* hear you? Begging. Pleading. I could feel you breaking under the pain."

"So you rose out of the healing webs too soon and then discovered the flesh was barely able to survive despite how much healing had already been done."

"Yes, I rose too soon—and then there was no going back. After that, the healing had to be done from within—and done in a way that only I had the skill to do. But it wasn't just you, Daemon. Did you think you were the only voice calling to me, pleading with me to come back? *You were one voice among hundreds.* All of them wanting me to return. I could feel Lucivar's and Saetan's yearning, the coven's grief, the boyos fear that, without me there as a connection for all of them, the Shadow Realm would splinter again, that most of the kindred would retreat from human contact again. And the kindred . . . They didn't want to let go of the dream either, and they held on with everything in them. All of you calling, pleading, hoping that love could do what shouldn't have been possible. Hell's fire, Daemon. I'm a Healer. I know better than you ever will what happened to this flesh when I got hit with the backlash of power still left in those webs I'd created. I *knew* the healing would be hideous and painful, and that after everything was done that could be done, I might not have anything better than a shell that would exist but never really be able to live." Jaenelle's eyes filled with tears. "But sometimes," she added, her voice breaking, "love is worth whatever price must be paid."

Daemon turned away. He should have felt relieved that it wasn't his fault—at least, not his alone. But her words had numbed him. No pain now, no anger. Nothing. "So you loved them enough to come back."

A long silence. Then Jaenelle said, "No. I came back for you."

He looked at her, not quite trusting enough to hope . . . or believe. But the emotional pain in her eyes now was more devastating than any physical suffering he'd seen.

"I came back for you," Jaenelle said, tears streaming down her face. "Because you were worth the price."

His heart ached as emotions flooded him. Pain. Pleasure. And the love. Oh, yes, the love. "Jaenelle." His legs trembled as he took the few steps that separated them. He raised his hand, intending to brush away the tears, but he was still afraid to touch her.

Jaenelle closed her eyes and took a few breaths before she looked at him. "I don't know if it will ever be better than this, but I'm healed, Daemon. Completely healed."

He stared at her, trying to decipher what she was telling him. His heart pounded hard enough for him to feel the beat against his chest as his fingertips touched her cheek. Fever raged through him, settling between his legs. His mouth watered as he brushed a finger over her lips. He wanted his tongue there, slicking her mouth until he slipped inside to stroke her tongue. And after that he wanted to stroke . . .

Healed. *Completely healed.*

"Are you sure?" he asked.

Jaenelle nodded. "I'm completely healed. I have been for weeks now."

And she hadn't told him? Or had she tried in some hesitant way and he hadn't heard because he'd been caged by the memories of her being so frail?

Weeks. She'd been healed for weeks—which is when he'd begun having the erotic dreams, when his hunger for sex had reawakened. His body had known she was ready for him.

"Are you sure?" he whispered. Same words. Different question.

"I'm sure," she whispered back.

His lips brushed hers, softly, carefully. One hand cupped the back of her head while the other trailed down her spine, urging her to relax against him. As he deepened the kiss, he savored the feel of his tongue caressing hers.

The taste of her. The smell of her. The feel . . .

He eased back in order to brush his lips over her cheek. "You're wearing too many clothes," he whispered. The tip of his tongue traced the curve of her ear, making her shiver. "They're lovely clothes, but they are very much in the way right now."

"We need . . . to talk," Jaenelle gasped as he licked the pulse in her neck.

"We will," he promised, drifting back to her mouth to give her a long, sinking kiss. "In an hour . . ." Even through layers of clothing, her nipple hardened as he rubbed his thumb over it. ". . . or two."

Then she wrapped her arms around his neck and pressed against him, changing his desire into something close to desperation. "Tomorrow," he said, his voice part snarl, part groan. "We'll talk about anything you want tomorrow."

Not giving her time to disagree, he picked her up and headed out of the sitting room, maintaining enough control to use Craft to simply open the door rather than rip it off the hinges. As he walked into the entrance hall, he gave his startled butler, Helton, a searing look. "The Lady and I are not at home. To anyone. Is that clear?"

"That is very clear, Prince," Helton replied. "Shall I inform the cook that you will be dining upstairs this evening?"

"I'll let you know when to send up a tray," Daemon replied, taking the stairs two at a time.

"Someone might think you're in a hurry," Jaenelle murmured.

The bedroom door flew open as they reached it and slammed shut behind them, the locks clicking into place.

Private now, with the bed only a step away, the fury of lust eased back to the steady blaze of desire.

"Oh, no," he crooned, setting her on her feet so that he could unbutton the sapphire jacket. "This is going to be a long . . . slow . . . banquet." He slipped the jacket off her shoulders, slid it down her arms. "And I'm planning to enjoy every single morsel."

Since that seemed to stun her, he took advantage of her lost wits to unbutton the rose silk shirt and slide that off her. The camisole beneath it was a paler rose and sheer enough to veil her breasts without really hiding them. So he let her keep it on a little longer while he enjoyed the feel of stroking her through the material until her skin warmed under his hands. Then he vanished the camisole, and there was nothing between his hands and her skin.

"Daemon." His name ended in a moan as he gave her breasts a fleeting caress before opening her trousers and sliding them, and the whisper of material beneath them, down her legs. After vanishing her shoes and thin socks, he coaxed her into bed.

Walking around to the other side of the bed, he shrugged out of his jacket, letting it slide to the floor. It had been awhile since he'd stripped with the intention of having a woman hot and willing to let him do whatever he wanted by the time he slid between the sheets, but the look in Jaenelle's eyes told him plainly enough he hadn't lost his touch.

She reached for him as soon as he got into bed, but he had other plans.

"Roll over," he said, a hand on her shoulder guiding her to stretch out on her belly.

"What?" Confused, she obeyed.

He started with her neck and worked down. What his fingers didn't touch, his mouth tasted. By the time he'd licked his way down her spine, she was moaning. By the time his teeth gently scraped her calves, her skin was so sensitized to his touch, he didn't need more than warm breath to excite her.

Turning her over, he stroked her inner thighs and smiled at the painted toenails. Next round, he was going to have to admire them more closely. But judging by her glazed eyes and flushed skin, she was reaching the point where much more would become too much.

"Come here, sweetheart." Rolling on his back, he settled her over him, sheathing his cock between her legs before coaxing her to stretch out over him. He wrapped his arms around her to keep her still.

"Daemon."

Wildly aroused by the hint of snarl in her voice, he kept his kisses viciously soft.

"Let me do this, sweetheart," he whispered as he licked her throat. "It would destroy me if I hurt you now, so let me do this."

"Do what?" She sounded breathless, almost too aroused.

In answer, he used Craft to create a phantom touch, something he'd never done with her before because he'd wanted to give her his body—and because he'd never used that phantom touch except to hurt someone . . . especially when he pleasured her. Now he wanted to use everything he was and everything he knew to please Jaenelle, so his hands stroked her back and his tongue kept hers busy while phantom fingers caressed the sweetness between her legs until her body bucked within his gently restraining arms, milking him as he sent her on that last wave of pleasure.

Limp and quivering, she sprawled over him. "Mother Night," she gasped.

Brushing his lips against her forehead, Daemon just smiled and used Craft to pull up the covers. It might be spring, but it was still cool during the day, and the nights got cold. He wanted her to stay warm—in every way.

He waited until her heartbeat and breathing quieted. Still inside her, he was already swelling to fill her again, so he slid his hands down to gently knead her ass while a featherlight phantom touch played with her.

She finally raised her head. "Would you teach me how to do that?"

"Do what?" he purred.

"You know perfectly well what."

"Oh, you mean this?" He increased the phantom touch enough to have her gasping as pleasure pulsed through her.

"Ooooohhhh, yes, that."

"Not yet. We'll save that for dessert. Right now, I don't want you thinking about anything except what I'm doing between your legs."

He used phantom hands to restrain her movements, but he let her ride him until she took them both over the edge.

She was sound asleep moments after she stretched out beside him.

Tucking her against his chest to keep her warm, he breathed out a sigh of pleasure—and slipped into a deep, dreamless sleep.

4

Catching her lower lip between her teeth, Roxie shifted on the cab's seat to find a comfortable position while she continued to watch the town house across the street. A few minutes after she'd arrived, another horse-drawn cab had pulled up to the town house, and a woman who looked somewhat like Jaenelle Angelline had gotten out of the cab and entered the SaDiablo residence.

But it *couldn't* have been Jaenelle. For one thing, she wasn't supposed to come to Amdarh. For another, she wasn't supposed to be that . . . healthy. She was *supposed* to hear the rumors from some well-meaning acquaintance who had scurried to SaDiablo Hall to convey the news, but she wasn't supposed to come here and confront Daemon. What if he managed to talk Jaenelle out of breaking whatever ties remained between the two of them? What if he was doing a lot more than talking to convince Jaenelle to keep him?

No. Even that beautiful body, hot and ready for sex, wouldn't be enough reason for a woman to forgive a man for breaking faith with her in *that* way.

Of course, that didn't mean a woman wouldn't enjoy him before tossing him out of the house.

Two hours. If it *was* Jaenelle who had arrived at the town house, she should have left long before now—even if Daemon *had* tried sex as a distraction from the accusations of infidelity. After all, even a man who'd spent centuries as a pleasure slave couldn't spin out sex for *two hours*.

Could he?

The cab door suddenly opened, tearing her from that intriguing thought. She gasped and pressed herself against the back of the seat before she realized it was the driver standing there and not a member of the Sa-Diablo family.

"Day's ended," the driver said roughly, giving her a less-than-friendly look. "If you want me to drop you somewhere on my way home, I'll do that. Otherwise, you can pay me for the time my horse has been standing and step out of my cab."

"I'm not ready to leave," Roxie said, putting the kind of aristo haughtiness in her voice that usually made merchants and other kinds of tradesmen back down.

"I am." The driver held out his hand and stared her down. "Of course, I could always go across the street and knock on the door of that town house you've been watching. Someone there might be interested in knowing that a witch has been keeping watch of who comes and goes."

Before she could rail at him for threatening her, a horse-drawn cab pulled up in front of the town house. When it went on, Surreal SaDiablo stood on the sidewalk, looking at the cab Roxie occupied.

The whore didn't worry her, but it was more attention than she wanted today. "Very well," she said as she called in her leather wallet and named a place that was close to the dining house where she was meeting Lektra.

She was outraged when the driver told her his fee, but that bitch Surreal was still watching them, and it would take so little effort for the driver to cause trouble. She handed over the marks.

The driver looked at the marks, then at her before he vanished his fee and climbed up to the driver's seat.

Roxie breathed a sigh of relief as the cab headed for the theater district. Thank the Darkness she'd used the illusion spell today and looked like a thousand other Dhemlan witches. While she wasn't the only fair-skinned witch in Amdarh, the driver had studied the illusion's face a little too long for comfort, so it was good he couldn't tell anyone who had *really* been watching the town house.

As she watched the cab drive away, Surreal rolled her shoulders to release the tension. She couldn't say why seeing the driver talking to his passenger had caught her attention—or why it had made her uneasy.

Shaking her head, she climbed the steps to the front door and walked into the town house. She'd barely gotten far enough into the entrance-way to close the door before Helton rushed up, blocking her.

Hell's fire. If the servants had heard the rumors—and believed them—things were going to get nasty.

"Lady Surreal," Helton said. "The Prince and the Lady are not at home this evening."

"Really?" Since she could feel Daemon's presence, why the lie? Then she noticed the gleam in Helton's eyes. "Ah. Where did they dine while they weren't at home?"

"The Prince has not yet requested that dinner be sent up, Lady."

"I see." She looked at the staircase and grinned. Oh, she hoped it meant what she thought it meant.

She called in the small trunk she'd brought from the Hall. "When Lady Angelline is available, please see that she gets that trunk. It has the new clothes she purchased today. I think she'll need them." Her grin widened. "Eventually."

Helton returned the grin before regaining his professional demeanor. "I'll see to it personally."

Dancing down the steps, she stood on the sidewalk, not sure what to do with herself. Standing in the middle of the street dancing and whooping would be fun but would require an explanation she didn't want to give.

So she turned around with the intention of heading back to her rented suite for an indulgent dinner—and stifled a shriek as a large shape moved toward her.

Lucivar studied her for a moment, then shook his head. "If you're not going to pay attention to your surroundings to the point where you don't sense someone standing this close to you, you damn well better shield to protect yourself from an attack."

"I'm not likely to be attacked in Amdarh," Surreal snapped. But she glanced across the street to where that cab had stood. She shook off the hint of uneasiness and focused on the Warlord Prince in front of her. "What brings you to Amdarh?"

"Figured I'd better talk to Daemon," Lucivar replied, moving toward the town house's steps.

Surreal jumped in front of him. "Trust me, sugar. You don't want to do that. Not tonight. Daemon isn't interested in talking to anyone tonight."

Lucivar studied the town house door. "Where's Jaenelle? Aren't you doing some female thing today?"

"We were. We did. Now . . ." Surreal looked pointedly at the town house. "Jaenelle's not interested in talking to anyone either."

"You're telling me it'll be worth my balls if I walk in there and interrupt something?"

"At the very least."

Lucivar grinned. Then he looked at her. "So where are you staying tonight?"

"Jaenelle and I had a suite at the female place, but it looks like I'll have it to myself tonight."

"They have any rooms there where you can get something to eat?"

Oh, shit. "They do, but the place is really . . . female."

"No males there at all?"

Remembering all the looks and whispers she'd endured that day, she gave in to the urge to be pure bitch. "Yeah, there are males. We can get dinner there if you want. And since Jaenelle won't be using it, you're welcome to the other bedroom." She paused. "Besides, we need to talk. There's some trouble here."

"Fine. Let's go."

"We'll probably have to walk to the corner to find a cab," Surreal said, walking past him.

His snort of laughter warned her, but before she could react, he clamped one arm around her waist and launched them skyward. Since her back was pressed to his chest, she didn't have many places to grab while he flew way too close to the treetops, so she settled for swearing as creatively as possible.

"Shut up," Lucivar said, "or you'll end up with bugs in your teeth."

"What?"

Roaring with laughter, he spun them a few times before gliding down to the sidewalk and backwinging to land lightly in front of the "female place."

"You son of a whoring bitch," Surreal snarled. The sidewalk tilted, and she grabbed the arm he offered. "Just for that, I hope being in this place a few hours makes your balls shrivel up."

He just snorted and escorted her to the registration desk.

"Am I supposed to sign in or something?" he asked.

"You can do whatever you want." Surreal grabbed the desk. The atrium wasn't moving, but she still didn't quite trust her legs. The same little prick who had signed her and Jaenelle in that morning was still on duty—and eyeing Lucivar.

"We do request that any . . . company . . . visiting with our guests sign in," he said, setting a leather-bound guest book on the desk and offering a pen.

Taking the pen, Lucivar dipped it in the inkwell and signed his name. "I'm not company, I'm family."

It was the man's sneer, there and gone in a moment, that pricked Surreal's temper.

"What would you do if someone misinterpreted the reason for you being here?" she asked Lucivar.

He studied her. "I'm here to have dinner with a member of my family, and since your suite has a spare bedroom and I need a place to sleep tonight, I'm staying there. What's there to misinterpret? That's simple enough."

"Not everyone sees what's obvious—or true."

His gold eyes narrowed. Then he shrugged. "That's easy enough to deal with. If people turn my spending an evening with my cousin into something it's not, I'll just rip out their lying tongues."

Her jaw dropped, and she was very glad she was holding on to the desk. "Don't you mean you'd cut out their tongues?"

"No, I said what I meant."

She thought about the difference—and shuddered.

His hand closed over her arm. Then he led her toward one of the archways that provided access to the rest of the establishment.

"So where do we find dinner?" Lucivar asked.

"That way." She noticed her hand was trembling. Hell's fire. She was a Gray-Jeweled witch and an assassin. But he was . . . "You're family, and

I love you, but I gotta tell you, Lucivar, sometimes you are a scary son of a bitch."

"Yes, I am." He stopped at the doorway of one of the dining rooms. "But if what went on back there has anything to do with the trouble you want to tell me about, then there's something the Blood in Amdarh haven't learned yet."

"What's that?"

Lucivar studied her long enough to make her stomach tighten. Then he said softly, "That I'm not the Warlord Prince they should be afraid of."

NINE

1

Daemon woke slowly, gradually becoming aware that his hand rested on a soft, smooth thigh, and someone's fingers were gently combing through his hair.

"You're so beautiful."

He opened his eyes and smiled at Jaenelle, who was sitting up in bed, watching him. Feeling more content than he'd felt in a long time, he caressed her thigh before lifting his hand to brush across her ribs and continue on to her back.

"You can thank my father for that. I didn't have anything to do with it," he replied.

She didn't smile, didn't respond. Just watched him.

Remembering what they still had to talk about, uneasiness began coiling around his contentment.

"What do you want, Daemon?" Jaenelle asked.

"You. Just you."

Her sapphire eyes changed. Became haunted, ancient. He hadn't seen that look in almost a year—since the day he'd gone to Hayll to play out a vicious game to keep Dorothea and Hekatah distracted while Jaenelle prepared to unleash her immense power to cleanse the taint of those two bitches out of the Blood. His heart beat painfully as he looked into those haunted eyes, knowing it was no longer Jaenelle who watched him.

"What do you want?" Witch asked.

Daemon swallowed the lump in his throat. "A wedding ring," he said, his voice roughened by longing—and a fear that he might still lose the one person who meant everything to him. "I want the wedding ring you promised I'd wear after I got back from Hayll."

She went so still he wasn't sure she was still breathing. Then her eyes changed again.

"I'm not the same as I was when that promise was made," Jaenelle said.

He couldn't stop himself from looking at the Jewel she now wore. Twilight's Dawn was a Jewel unlike any other, which made it extraordinary. But it wasn't the Ebony Jewel she used to wear. It wasn't the Black that had been her Birthright. As unique and mysterious as Twilight's Dawn was, it still represented a loss of the power she once wielded. And that *did* make her different, but . . .

He sat up to face her. Brushed his fingertips over her face. "No, you're not the same—except in the ways that truly matter."

"Do you really believe that, Daemon?"

Can you accept the difference? That was the question under the question.

"Yes, I really believe that." *And I can accept the difference.*

A sheen of tears brightened her eyes as she smiled. "Then let's do it. Let's get married. Today."

Now! Excitement, fierce in its intensity, flooded through him before common sense intervened. He rested his forehead against hers and forced himself to consider the ramifications of following desire.

"We can't." He pulled back enough to see the uncertainty, and a hint of hurt, on her face. "Sweetheart, there's nothing I'd like better than to marry you today, but we can't."

"Why not?"

He sighed. "For one thing, the coven and the boyos would never forgive me if they weren't invited to your wedding." *Her* wedding. Things were still too shaky between him and the rest of the humans who had made up her First Circle that they would give a damn whether or not they came to *his* wedding. "If we're going to avoid hurt feelings, we have to have a formal wedding. That means sending out invitations, talking to Mrs. Beale about preparing a wedding feast for the guests. It will take a few weeks." And the Darkness only knew what other rumors might be spread about him in that time.

Jaenelle echoed his sigh. "You're right. But . . ."

The look on her face made him giddy . . . and a bit terrified.

"We could have a private wedding today, just for us, and then have a formal wedding in a few weeks," she said.

"You mean a secret wedding?" *Yes!* But common sense, which he was really beginning to resent, intruded once more. "There isn't a Priestess in Kaeleer who would be willing to marry us in secret and risk the wrath of the Queens who rule Kaeleer—not to mention Lucivar and Saetan."

She took his face in her hands. "Daemon," she said, her voice full of laughter, "I've just discovered something about you. As much as you know and as much as you've experienced, you can still be naive about some things."

His mouth hung open, and no brilliantly phrased words came out.

After giving him a smacking kiss on the forehead, Jaenelle got out of bed and headed for the adjoining bathroom. "If we leave within the hour, we can get there by this afternoon."

"Where?"

"Since we'll have to rent a Coach here in Amdarh to ride the Winds to the Hall, contact Ladvarian and tell him to have one of our private Coaches ready so we aren't home long enough for anyone to ask questions. And tell him not to bring anyone except Kaelas."

"Why do we have to bring *him*?" Daemon grumbled as he got out of bed and slipped on a robe.

Jaenelle paused at the bathroom door. "Daemon? Where are you planning to sleep for the next decade?"

Hell's fire. "Fine. All right. I'll tell the Sceltie to bring the cat."

She just smiled and closed the bathroom door.

Great. Wonderful, Daemon thought as he left their room to use the bathroom down the hall. She had a point about placating those two. If

Ladvarian's feelings were hurt by being excluded, the Sceltie could make his life very difficult. And Kaelas had a few points of his own. They were called teeth and claws. Pissing off an Arcerian cat who was a Red-Jeweled Warlord Prince and who already resented that a human male was claiming a piece of Jaenelle's bed wasn't the best way to begin his new position as a husband.

As he adjusted the water in the shower, he contacted Ladvarian on a psychic spear thread and delivered Jaenelle's instructions—and felt grateful the dog didn't ask any questions since he didn't have any answers.

That done, he stepped into the shower and quickly washed while he considered if he was amused or insulted by Jaenelle's "discovery."

Growing up under Dorothea's control had stripped him of innocence at a very early age, and there was little, if anything, of a twisted, vile nature that he hadn't experienced. The Darkness only knew all that he'd done, but one thing he knew with absolute certainty: He was *not* naive.

2

Surreal stared at Helton. "They left?"

"Immediately after breakfast," Helton replied.

"Did Prince Sadi say where he and Lady Angelline were going?" Lucivar asked.

"He did not, Prince Yaslana. Nor did he leave instructions on how to reach him. He did say he and the Lady would be returning, but he did not say when."

Surreal blew out a breath and looked at Lucivar, who shrugged.

"Would you like some breakfast?" Helton asked. "Or perhaps coffee served in the sitting room?"

"Coffee's fine," Surreal said. She walked into the sitting room and waited until Lucivar closed the door before she kicked a footstool.

"You pissed off about something, or are you reacting to this room?" Lucivar asked, moving around the room as if he were looking for a trap he knew was there but couldn't see.

"What about the room?" she snapped.

"The hot anger still lingering in it." Lucivar studied a spot on the carpet. "The cold rage underneath the anger."

Surreal stopped her own prowling to see what had caught his attention. "Where's the chair?"

"What?"

"There was a stuffed chair in that spot. At least, there was when I was here this winter to do some shopping for Winsol."

Lucivar crouched, his hand moving slowly just above the carpet. Then he pulled a sliver of wood out of the carpet and held it up.

He didn't have to say anything.

She closed her eyes. "Mother Night, Lucivar. Did I do something stupid by coaxing Jaenelle into coming to Amdarh?"

Rising, he tossed the sliver into the fireplace. "You didn't know about the rumors."

"Where do you think they've gone?"

Lucivar turned slowly. His Ebon-gray Jewel glowed. He paused, then clearly broke whatever link he'd been trying to make. "Daemon's not responding, but he's west of here. Heading for the Hall, I think."

Daemon was the only person Surreal knew who could make Lucivar wary. That Sadi wouldn't respond to his brother made her nervous.

A light knock on the door preceded Helton, who brought in the tray that held a dish of pastries as well as the coffee. It would have been natural, even expected, for one of them to ask him about the chair's absence.

Neither of them asked. They kept silent until Helton left the room.

Then Lucivar sighed and raked his fingers through his hair. "What are you planning to do?"

Surreal poured coffee for both of them. "I'll stay here for a few days, do some shopping, see if I hear anything interesting. What about you?"

"I think I'd better go to the Keep and inform the family patriarch about what's happening," Lucivar replied, taking his cup of coffee.

"Well, that should perk up Uncle Saetan's day."

He snorted. "Yeah. He's going to be thrilled."

3

"Is there anything you can do?" Lucivar asked, finding no comfort in the way Saetan sat so silent and still.

Finally, Saetan sighed. "I gave up my claim to Dhemlan last year when I decided to remain here at the Keep. The Queens there no longer have to answer to me."

"But they know you. They'll listen to you. Hell's fire, Father. Things are shaky enough between Jaenelle and Daemon. If these rumors—"

"I beg your pardon?"

He felt that whiplash of icy temper and winced. "You've visited them at the Hall often enough," he hedged. "Surely, you've noticed . . ." Oh, shit.

Saetan shook his head. "My apologies, Lucivar. I have no right to lash out at you for saying something I don't want to hear. Daemon came too close to sliding back into the Twisted Kingdom when he thought Jaenelle died. If he loses her now . . . I'm not sure what would happen."

"You know what will happen," Lucivar said. "You were in that camp in Hayll. You know what it's like to dance with the Sadist. He played out a game with illusions, but with the right provocation, he's capable of doing things like that. He's capable of doing *anything*. You know that."

"Yes, I know that," Saetan replied too softly. "After all, he is his father's mirror."

For a moment, Lucivar couldn't breathe. The deliberate reminder that a place called Zuulaman no longer existed was a caution about dealing with the man who sat on the other side of the desk—and a warning about the other man who wore Black Jewels. After all, Daemon was the reason he didn't fear Saetan. When it came down to it, the Sadist could be a more elegantly vicious enemy than the High Lord of Hell would ever dream of being.

"What do we do?" Lucivar asked.

"We wait." Saetan paused, then added, "And we hope."

4

He was naïve. It was the only explanation for why he was standing in a meadow on a spring afternoon feeling overdressed and feet-deficient.

Of course, being flanked by a huge cat and a small dog while enclosed by a circle of unicorns could make any man feel . . . out of step.

Then the unicorns shifted, making an opening in the circle. Jaenelle stepped through the opening, flanked by Moonshadow, the Queen of Sceval, and her mate, Mistral, the Warlord Prince of the unicorns. Behind them came the Priestess, who had agreed to do her best to say words that would be meaningful to humans while she stood as witness to the "mating" of Kaeleer's Heart to Prince Daemon Sadi.

Thank the Darkness, none of them expected him to consummate the marriage in front of these witnesses.

Jaenelle's eyes brimmed with amusement as she took her place beside him. On his left.

He didn't think about it. He simply stepped back and shifted until he stood on her left, the subordinate position. Her startled expression told him she didn't know what to think about that move, since he now out-ranked her and was entitled to stand on the right. But his choice had nothing to do with the Jewels she now wore and everything to do with who, and what, she still was. Her place wasn't at his side; his place was at *her* side. And always would be.

Before her uncertainty could be sensed by the unicorns around them, Mistral reared. Then, looking at Daemon, he flicked his tail and snorted before moving to one side.

Jaenelle pressed her lips together.

★You'd have no use for me if I was hung like that,★ Daemon told her on a psychic thread.

She changed her muffled laugh into a series of coughs, causing Ladvarian to declare it was still too cold for the Lady to be outside much longer.

So Moonshadow tossed her head, the sun gleaming on her spiral horn, and all the unicorns pricked their ears as the Priestess took her place in front of the two humans.

Jaenelle, the Priestess said, *this human stallion stands before you, wanting to be your mate. Will you accept him?*

"I will accept him," Jaenelle said. She called in the gold band Banard had made. Even though he'd given it to her for this ceremony, Daemon stared at it as if he'd never seen it before.

His left hand trembled when she slipped the ring on his finger, adding, "I offer this token to let everyone know Daemon is now my mate."

Daemon, the Priestess said, *the Lady is willing to have you as her mate. Do you promise to be her friend and . . .* She looked at Ladvarian, who, Daemon guessed, was helping the mare with human concepts. *. . . lover? Do you promise to protect her from enemies?*

"I promise," Daemon replied. He called in the sapphire ring and slipped it on Jaenelle's finger. "Let this token be a symbol of my commitment to honor, cherish, and protect, to be friend, lover, and husband." He lifted her left hand and brushed his lips across her knuckles. "This I promise . . . with everything I am."

When he drew her into his arms and kissed her, he forgot about standing in a meadow, forgot about who was watching, forgot everything but her . . .

. . . until a young voice close to his hip said, *Are they going to mate now?*

Since his libido was rising a little too eagerly, he started to step back—and got stabbed in the ass by a little unicorn's horn.

"It could have been worse," Jaenelle said as he led her back to the Coach and the picnic Ladvarian had procured from somewhere.

"How?" Daemon said, grateful he was just bruised, not punctured.

"You could have been facing the other way."

Before he could decide if he wanted to be an intelligent husband or a snippy bastard, she kissed him, and when her tongue slipped into his mouth, he decided being an intelligent husband was the far better choice.

Wrapping his arms around her, he sank into the kiss, soaring on the feel of her body brushing against his.

She scraped her teeth over his chin. "Did you notice that Ladvarian chose the Coach that has a bed?"

"I noticed."

She licked his throat. "Do you think you can perform your duties as a husband, or are you too wounded?"

Since she was pressed against him, the answer was rather evident, but he said, "Oh, I think I can manage."

5

"I appreciate your having us to stay tonight," Daemon said as Khary refilled the brandy snifters. In Scelt, the Blood still held with that quaint custom of the men and women separating after dinner for a while so that each group could chat with their own gender. So he and Khary had remained in the dining room while Jaenelle and Morghann had gone to the sitting room.

"Well, you could say we were expecting company," Khary replied, a twinkle in his blue eyes. "Especially since Ladvarian came pelting up to the house earlier today, saying he needed a picnic in a hurry and could we have you and Jaenelle to dinner and put you up for the night."

Daemon tried not to wince. "We could have stayed at Jaenelle's house."

"Now, that you couldn't. The staff put most of the furniture under dustcovers after Wilhelmina moved to her own cottage. This way, the house can be put to rights before your next visit." Khary gave Daemon an expectant look.

He smiled. "I have some business in Amdarh that requires my immediate attention, so we'll be going back to Dhemlan in the morning, but we're planning to come back here after the wedding for at least part of the honeymoon. And now that Jaenelle is completely healed, I expect we'll be dividing our time between here and the Hall."

Khary rolled his snifter between his hands. "Wilhelmina said you settled a generous income on her."

Daemon shrugged. "She's Jaenelle's sister. The family could afford it."

"Ah."

As they drank their brandy, the silence took on the weight of anticipation. Of course, there had been a feeling of anticipation since he and Jaenelle arrived at the home of the Queen of Scelt and the Warlord of Maghre. Morghann and Khary had greeted the news of their intended marriage with enthusiasm and hearty well-wishing, but as the evening wore on, Daemon couldn't shake the feeling that Khary especially was waiting for something.

"Perhaps we should join the Ladies for coffee," Daemon said, pushing away from the table.

"If you're trying to keep it a secret, you should stop playing with the ring," Khary said quietly.

He'd intended to pretend ignorance, which would have been a lie, but he looked into Khary's eyes and realized they stood on a point of no return. Whatever conclusions Lord Khardeen had reached about what had happened last spring, and why, had been reason enough for him to offer a hand in friendship again. But if that offer of friendship was repaid with a lie, it would never be offered again—and Khardeen had enough weight with the rest of the boyos to bring him back into that circle of friendships . . . or leave him outside of it forever.

Daemon held out his left hand and dropped the sight shield he'd placed on the gold band to keep it hidden. "How did you know?"

Khary leaned forward to admire the ring. Then he grinned. "Did the same thing with mine when I first got it. Couldn't quite believe it was really there." He rose and gave Daemon's shoulder a friendly squeeze. "So that's what you were doing in Sceval this afternoon."

Feeling awkward, and not liking it, he shrugged. "We wanted to get married. But we are going to have the formal wedding."

"Damn right you are." Khary studied him. "Is there a reason for keeping this secret?"

Daemon felt himself going cold and fought against it. This wasn't the time or place for that sweet, deadly rage. But soon. Soon. "There's some . . . trouble . . . in Amdarh. It could shift to Jaenelle if our marriage became public knowledge." He wasn't sure when that realization had bloomed, but he trusted his instincts. "I'll take care of it."

"If you need help, you'll let me know?" Khary asked.

He nodded.

"Well, then." Khary rubbed his hands together. "Why don't we join the Ladies?"

Jaenelle's amused, guilty look when he and Khary entered the sitting room told him she'd had no better luck keeping their secret from Morghann than he'd had keeping it from Khardeen.

Khary looked at the two women and grinned. "So. Are we going to talk about the wedding that *will* take place or the one that *did* take place?" His eyes shifted to Daemon. "Because we were wondering why you were having so much trouble sitting through dinner."

Jaenelle snorted.

Daemon sighed, and muttered, "I backed into a unicorn."

Morghann burst out laughing. "Oh, we've *got* to hear the details."

So Khary and Morghann heard the details, and the evening ended with laughter—and the warm sense that he was back among friends.

TEN

1

Daemon drove the Coach back to Dhemlan. He didn't have much choice, since Ladvarian, who had driven the Coach to Sceval, had announced that he and Kaelas would meet them at the Hall. He usually didn't mind driving, but he'd anticipated talking Jaenelle into tucking into bed for the journey. And they would have gotten *some* sleep.

Still, it was pleasant to have her with him in the driver's compartment. Except for the time they spent in bed, it was rare for them to be together without the presence of kindred, court, or family.

But looking at her, he noticed the dark smudges beneath her eyes . . . and the way she shivered despite being wrapped up in her winter cape.

"Why don't you stretch out on the bed and get some sleep?" he suggested.

"No, I'm fine."

She might be completely healed, but she hadn't regained her physical stamina. He could see the toll the past two days had taken on her.

Scooping her out of the other chair, he returned to his chair and settled her on his lap.

"You're driving," Jaenelle said. "You have to pay attention."

"I'll pay attention," he promised, wrapping his arms around her. She was right. The psychic pathways through the Darkness made it possible for the Blood to travel faster than they could otherwise, but inattention while riding the Winds could be fatal, and guiding even a small Coach demanded extra care. "Just rest. We'll be back at the Hall a little after midday."

Jaenelle rested her head against his shoulder. "I thought we were going to Amdarh."

He hesitated a little too long.

She raised her head and looked at him, too much knowledge in her eyes.

"I'll take care of things in Amdarh," he said.

"No."

She'd been born a Queen. Even though she no longer ruled a court, she was still a Queen—and she was still *his* Queen. He couldn't prevent the instinctive desire to yield when Jaenelle gave him a direct command, but living in Kaeleer for the past year had shown him that males could, and did, dig their heels in and oppose the Queen they served when a command might put her at risk.

"I won't come to harm," he began.

"You've already been harmed," she snarled.

His temper strained at the leash. "So far, whoever is playing this game has used nothing but words. Once the announcement of our intended marriage is made—"

"The game may turn physical. I'm aware of that."

"I can take care of myself."

"But you don't think I can. Not having my full strength physically doesn't make me weak."

But you're not as strong as you used to be—and we don't really know how strong you are. "I'm aware of that."

When she squirmed, he tightened his hold, thinking she was trying to move away from him. But she only freed her left hand from the folds of the cape and held it up.

"What does this ring mean, Daemon?"

"My promise to honor, cherish, and protect."

"Besides that."

He studied her face, trying to discern what she wanted him to say.

"Partnership," Jaenelle said quietly. "You went to Hayll and played out a vicious game to distract Dorothea and Hekatah because that's what I needed you to do. And it cost you. Don't think I'm not aware of how much it cost you, Prince."

"That was different." Remembering the emotional cruelty he'd inflicted on his family in order to keep them from physical harm made his chest tighten, made it hard to breathe.

"Yes, it was different," Jaenelle said. "This isn't about serving in a court. This isn't about saving a Realm from being shattered by war. This is personal. Someone is going after *you*. And whether you like it or not, you are not going to play out this game alone."

Jaenelle would protect anyone she loved, no matter the price. If he refused to let her help, she would go off on her own to find whoever was playing games with his life. At least if they stayed together, he could protect her while she was trying to protect him.

"All right, partner," he said. "What did you have in mind?"

She frowned. "I'm not sure yet. But we'll think of some way to find the source of the rumors being spread about you." Then she looked at him through her lashes. "So, who's going to tell Mrs. Beale she's got a month to plan a wedding feast?"

Hell's fire. Mrs. Beale was a marvelous cook. She also had what he considered an unnatural relationship with her meat cleaver. Since he'd inherited SaDiablo Hall, he had gained a finer appreciation of why his father had stayed away from anything to do with the kitchen unless cornered. The woman was downright scary at times.

The fact that she and Beale, the Hall's butler, were happily married was something he tried not to think about because it made him wonder things about Beale he'd rather not wonder.

"If we both went to Amdarh, we could just write her a note," Jaenelle said.

He looked at Jaenelle. She looked at him.

"Good idea," he said.

That settled, she snuggled against him and slept for the rest of the journey.

2

High Lord?

Ladvarian's suppressed excitement made Saetan's nerves twang, but he continued warming a glass of yarbarah as if he had no concerns. "Lord Ladvarian. What brings you to the Keep?"

There's something you should know. But it's a secret.

Comfortably settled in a window seat, Saetan watched as twilight faded the colors in the small garden beyond the room Draca had given him to use as a study.

The daughter of his soul and the son of his blood had married yesterday. He'd told Ladvarian he was delighted, and he was. But in the privacy of his own heart, he could acknowledge a nip of hurt that he hadn't been asked to witness that bond. A father's wish to share the important moments in his children's lives.

And yet, he understood the reason behind this secret wedding. It didn't matter that Jaenelle was no longer the Queen of Ebon Askavi. Her decision to take a husband would create ripples throughout Kaeleer. Even if the guest list was contained to the Blood who had made up the First and Second Circles of the Dark Court, it would take weeks to plan the celebration that would follow the simple ceremony. For two people who wanted, or needed, to make a formal commitment to each other *now*, waiting in order to plan a party would have been intolerable.

Especially for Daemon. Because Daemon Sadi's loyalty began and ended with Jaenelle Angelline. The fact that someone was trying to give Jaenelle a reason to break all ties with him indicated the Blood in Dhemlan still didn't realize the kind of man they were dealing with. And that frightened him. The only thing restraining the power and temper of a Black-Jeweled Warlord Prince was a woman whose own power was, as yet, undetermined. If the rumors spreading through Amdarh and, by now, through the other courts in Dhemlan, provoked Daemon into striking out indiscriminately, there was no one, including himself, strong enough to stop him.

The bloodbath could be horrific.

So it was prudent of Jaenelle to marry Daemon in a way that required little fuss to give him the assurance that he wouldn't lose her.

Saetan scrubbed his hands over his face and sighed. With things balanced so precariously right now and so dependent on Daemon's state of mind, he just wished he had the answer to the question the coven, the boyos, and even Lucivar had been asking over the past few months.

If the kindred had truly succeeded in holding onto Jaenelle so that she would heal and come back to all of them, why had she come back different?

ELEVEN

1

L ektra dropped her cup, oblivious of the tea seeping into the white tablecloth as she twisted around to stare at the two women seated at the next table in the dining house.

"I—I beg your pardon," Lektra stammered. "I didn't mean to overhear your conversation, but . . . Daemon Sadi *is getting married*?"

The woman Lektra recognized as the Priestess in Zhara's First Circle nodded. "Lady Angelline and Prince Sadi came to Lady Zhara's court this morning and announced they were going to marry in a month."

"But I . . . I thought Lady Angelline was an invalid." Lektra gripped the back of her chair so the other women wouldn't see her hands shaking.

Looking puzzled, the Priestess shook her head. "I don't know where you heard that, but she's not an invalid, although she looks like she's still recovering from her injuries." She paused. "There were some disturbing rumors about Prince Sadi's fidelity, but he was very solicitous with his Lady, doing and saying everything one would expect of an ardent lover."

"Perhaps doing and saying it too well?" the Priestess's companion asked.

The Priestess gave her friend a sharp look. "He was concerned for her well-being—as he should be."

Lektra forced herself to smile and turn away just as a waiter hurried to her table to vanish the soiled tablecloth, replace it with a clean one, and bring her another cup of tea. As much as she wanted to hear about her unfaithful lover's performance while he'd been visiting Zhara's court, it wouldn't do to make anyone wonder about her interest.

She picked at the meal she'd ordered, no longer taking pleasure in the food, too aware of the women at the other table. Finally, feeling too ill to continue pretending, she paid for her meal and hurried out of the dining house, wanting nothing more than the sanctuary of her own home.

2

"What's wrong with that bitch?" Lektra snarled as she paced her sitting room. "Doesn't she have any pride? She *must* have heard that he's been unfaithful to her. She should have severed whatever ties still hold him to her."

Roxie, curled in one corner of the sofa, selected another chocolate from the large box on the table. "Have you *seen* her?" She made a disgusted sound. "Even if he *was* unfaithful and having sex with six other women every day, she wouldn't let Daemon go if he's still willing to service her. What other man would want her?"

"But he's going to *marry* her!" Lektra's hands clenched. "He's supposed to want *me*. He's supposed to love *me*." How dare he disappoint her when she was counting on having the strongest, most beautiful man in the Realm as her lover? How could he even think of staying with Jaenelle when *she* loved him so desperately?

Roxie frowned. "Maybe we can give *him* a reason to walk away from *her*."

Or maybe it's time to take a more direct approach to the problem. "I'm going out," Lektra said, hurrying toward the door. Her Summer-sky Jewels were strong enough for what she had in mind. And with luck, there would be some tragic news for people to discuss over dinner tonight.

3

Wrapping one arm around Jaenelle, Daemon tucked her closer to his right side as the horse-drawn cab headed out of the shopping district.

Jaenelle said, "We could—"

"No."

"But—"

"Enough."

She studied him with narrowed eyes. "You've got that bossy I'm-a-Warlord-Prince-so-I'm-right tone in your voice."

"No, I've got that I'm-a-Warlord-Prince-who-is-your-adoring-loving-husband tone in my voice."

"Sounds like bossy from where I'm sitting."

"Must be the acoustics in the cab." He smiled as he kissed her frown-wrinkled forehead. "Sweetheart, you're exhausted. We've paid a courtesy call to Zhara and been seen in several shops today. That's enough. You need to rest." He paused. "Hell's fire, *I* need to rest."

She considered that for a moment. "What did you have in mind?"

Several things, but he'd take them in order. "Tucking into the sitting room for the rest of the afternoon. If you're a good little witch and nibble on some food to make up for what you didn't eat at midday, I'll read to you."

"That's bribery," Jaenelle grumbled.

"And your point is?"

"It's a good bribe."

Daemon grinned, then looked out the window when the cab stopped. "Streets are crowded today."

"What else is on your mind?"

He sighed. Of course she'd noticed his preoccupation at the last two shops they'd visited. Taking her left hand in his, he dropped the sight shield on his wedding ring for a moment. The brief sight of it warmed him, soothed him.

"Maybe we should let this go," he said quietly, rubbing his thumb over the back of her hand.

"Someone tried to ruin your reputation and isolate you socially from the rest of the Blood," Jaenelle pointed out.

"Someone wanted you to turn away from me. You didn't. Nothing else matters." The cab started forward. "I don't give a damn if the Blood in Amdarh accept me or not."

"If someone wants you enough to hurt you—"

The driver cried out. The horse screamed and bolted.

Daemon had enough time to throw a Black shield around both of them before the horse veered sharply. The sound of wood snapping . . .

"Air!" Jaenelle shouted.

. . . then the cab tipped, crashing on its side before continuing a sickening flip with unnatural speed until it smashed against walls of power.

The inside of the cab was a dazzle of colors—Green, Rose, Summersky, Purple Dusk, Red, Sapphire.

As the cab came to rest, Daemon blinked to clear his vision. The colors danced around them a moment longer before they faded—and he realized they were floating in the middle of the cab. He had automatically created a tight, defensive shield that would have protected them from invasive harm, but they would have been thrown around the inside of the cab. Jaenelle's bubble shield had provided a better cushion.

Shattered glass and thrusting spikes of broken wood littered the cab's roof, which was now beneath them.

He wasn't aware he'd risen to the killing edge, wasn't aware of the freezing rage flooding him until Jaenelle said quietly, "Leash it, Prince. They just want to help."

He stared at her, working through what she was telling him, what she was demanding from him. He wanted to rip flesh from bone, wanted to crush the minds surrounding the cab. He wanted to wash Amdarh's streets in a river of blood.

"Daemon," Jaenelle said.

"For you," he crooned. "Only for you."

With effort, he chained the desire to strike out with lethal intent as the cab door opened, revealing worried male faces. The air bubble shrank around them. In the space of a heartbeat, he dropped the Black shield around them and reformed tight shields around each of them. Then he shifted until he could crouch among the shattered glass and shards of wood and help the Warlords reaching into the cab to guide Jaenelle, still floating on air, through the door.

As Daemon emerged from the cab, he noticed how the males had formed a protective circle around Jaenelle, noted the distress and anger in all of their faces.

"Where's the driver?" he asked too softly.

"Over there," a Warlord said, pointing to another cluster of males.

The males near the driver backed away as he approached. He looked down at the man sprawled in the street, testing with a delicate psychic probe.

Physically dead but not burned out.

He put a Black shield around the driver and vanished the body, ignoring the startled exclamations of the other men. The Warlords surrounding Jaenelle watched him with fear in their eyes.

Jaenelle just watched him.

Her presence was the tiny spark of warmth in a world that had gone sweetly, deadly cold. So he held on to that spark while he led his Lady to one of the carriages offered for their use—and he held himself in the eye of a storm that he would either dissipate . . . or unleash on Amdarh.

Keeping her inner barriers tightly shut to prevent anyone picking up on her frustration and fury, Lektra, along with several other women, stood on a street corner and watched the Warlords ease Jaenelle Angelline from the broken cab. She walked away, knowing she'd be sickened by the sight of Daemon fawning over that pale bitch.

It should have worked. *It should have.* Even if Jaenelle wasn't as much of an invalid as she'd thought, being tossed around in a tumbling cab should have injured *something.* But the bitch didn't even have a *scratch.*

Of course, she hadn't seen Daemon emerge from the cab.

She turned back, barely able to stop herself from running. It hadn't occurred to her that *Daemon* might get hurt. She'd expected him to shield himself and be safe. But what if he'd shielded Jaenelle instead? What if he was still in the cab with a broken leg or a broken back or . . .

She reached the corner in time to glimpse Daemon helping Jaenelle into another carriage. Staggering back a few steps, she braced a hand against the nearest building. He wasn't hurt. Her beautiful love wasn't hurt.

But he still wasn't free to be her beautiful love, and if she couldn't find some way of preventing him from marrying that used-up bitch, it could be decades before he could be with his *real* love.

Maybe Roxie was right. Maybe she'd gone about this from the wrong direction. *No* woman would give up Daemon Sadi. But since Jaenelle Angelline didn't have any status anymore to attract a strong male, maybe the thing to do was give Daemon a reason to walk away from Jaenelle.

4

Feeling the cold rage wash over the town house, Lucivar stepped into the small entrance hall and shivered. A moment later, Surreal rushed down the stairs.

"Mother Night," she muttered. "We're going to dance with the Sadist, aren't we?"

"Yeah, it looks like we are." What had provoked Daemon into cold rage? Lucivar looked at Surreal. "Maybe you should get out of here."

She shook her head. "Two people distracting him are—"

"Twice as many targets for him to splatter over the walls."

"He doesn't splatter," she snapped. "He's not that merciful when he's this pissed off."

She was right. Unfortunately.

A minute later, they heard a carriage pull up in front of the town house.

Taking a deep breath and blowing it out, Surreal opened the front door. Her shock hit Lucivar with the force of a fist. He gave himself a moment to acknowledge his stomach-churning fear before he locked it away. He couldn't afford to show even a hint of fear. Not if he had to deal with the Sadist.

"Hell's fire!" Surreal flung the door wide open and stepped back. "What happened?"

"A carriage accident," Daemon replied as he carried Jaenelle into the house.

"Cat!" Lucivar leaped forward, but Daemon's glazed, sleepy eyes stopped him from actually touching Jaenelle.

"I'm fine," Jaenelle said.

"I'll settle the Lady upstairs," Daemon snarled. "Then we'll talk. In the meantime, contact Gabrielle and ask her to come as quickly as possible. We need a Healer."

Lucivar stepped aside to give Daemon a clear path to the stairs. "There are Healers in Amdarh."

"None that I trust," Daemon replied. He climbed the stairs and disappeared down the hallway that led to the suite he shared with Jaenelle.

"Oh, shit," Surreal said as she shut the door. "If he considers all the Blood in Amdarh as an enemy, someone is going to die."

"Let's try not to be among the corpses," Lucivar growled. "You stay here. I'll contact Chaosti." He walked into the sitting room and closed the door. Ebon-gray to Gray, he could make the psychic reach to the Warlord Prince of the Dea al Mon.

Chaosti. He waited a few moments, then called again.

Lucivar?

We need Gabrielle here in her capacity as a Healer.

Hesitation. *How much do you need her?*

What?

Another hesitation. *We confirmed yesterday that Gabrielle is pregnant. If she uses more than basic Craft . . .*

She'll miscarry.

Everything has a price, Chaosti whispered.

Lucivar closed his eyes, understanding the question behind the words. If she was truly needed, Gabrielle would come and use whatever power was required for a healing, knowing it would destroy the baby she carried.

No, Lucivar said. *We'll find some other way.*

We could come to Amdarh, just to be there, Chaosti offered.

No. Stay away from Amdarh.

There's trouble?

He felt the change in Chaosti and recognized a Warlord Prince's predatory nature rising to the fore. *Nothing we can't handle.* Which was true in its own way. No one was safe while Daemon was cold, so why ask a friend to step onto a potential killing field? *Stay home and take care of your Lady . . . papa.*

Chaosti's pleasure filled the link between them. Then he asked, *Have you spoken to your brother lately?*

He's here in Amdarh.

Silence. Then Chaosti said, *Take care of yourself, Lucivar.*

I'll try to stay off the killing field.

He broke the link and walked out of the sitting room just as Daemon came down the stairs and Surreal opened the front door to admit Zhara and another witch.

"I heard about the accident," Zhara said. "I brought my Healer to offer what help we can."

"No," Daemon said too softly.

Daemon, Gabrielle is pregnant, Lucivar said on a spear thread.

Those glazed eyes stared at him for too long before Daemon focused his attention on the two witches.

The Healer tried to smile. "Why don't I just have a look at Lady Angelline and—"

Daemon's snarl filled the small entrance hall.

"We *do* have a qualified Healer in residence," Surreal said. "I'll go up and ask Jaenelle if she needs another Healer. You just stand there and . . . breathe . . . until I get back." She eased around Daemon and bolted up the stairs.

Don't do anything to provoke him, Lucivar thought, watching ice coat the windows on either side of the door. The entrance hall was so cold he could see his breath, and Zhara and her Healer were shivering.

Daemon just stood there, his hands in his trouser pockets, staring at Zhara and the Healer.

Surreal raced down the stairs. "Jaenelle says she has a few sore muscles. Nothing worse than that. Not even a bruise. She's fine, Daemon. She really is. I'm going to help her into a hot bath to soak a bit while you cool off." She looked around the entrance hall. "Or warm up." She started back up the stairs, then turned. "Oh. Jaenelle also said you promised to read to her. She told me to remind you."

Saying nothing, Daemon walked into the sitting room.

Surreal dashed up the stairs, leaving Lucivar with Zhara and the Healer.

Zhara's eyes glittered with anger. "If Prince Sadi thinks the respect the Dhemlan Queens have for his father means he can act any way he—"

"Shut up and get out," Lucivar snarled, keeping his voice low enough not to carry to the sitting room. "He doesn't trust you, and right now, he'll kill anyone he doesn't trust." *Even me.*

"I am Amdarh's Queen, and—"

"You don't know who you're dealing with. You. Don't. Know. But I'm very much afraid you're going to find out. So get out while you can— and hope you're still among the living when this is done."

Zhara's light-brown skin turned gray. "What are you talking about?"

Lucivar swore. "He's a Warlord Prince. Someone tried to hurt his Queen. What do you *think* is going to happen?"

"It was an accident."

"You believe that if you want to. You seem willing to believe a lot of things lately."

Before Zhara could reply, they all heard the quiet clink of glass against glass. She glanced toward the sitting room—and the two women left with more speed than dignity.

Lucivar closed the front door, then leaned against it for a moment. He didn't want to walk into that sitting room, but someone had to dance with the Sadist, and it looked like it was going to be him.

Taking a deep breath, and hoping he wasn't about to make Marian a widow, he walked into the sitting room and closed the door.

"Brandy?" Daemon asked as he filled a snifter halfway.

"Sure." Lucivar walked toward his brother, watching for any sign that things would turn lethal. Daemon *sounded* calm, but that didn't mean a damn thing.

Daemon poured brandy into another snifter and handed it to Lucivar.

"I was willing to let it go," Daemon said softly. "I told myself it was just words. Some petty bitch sees a male she wants and goes after him in one way or another. How many times had we watched that game played out in Terreillean courts over the centuries?"

"Too many," Lucivar said, wishing he could test the brandy for poison—and knowing the insult would probably get him killed. "Hell's fire, when that little Rihlander was planning to trap me a few years ago, I exiled the bitch."

"Just exile? Did you have a weak moment, Prick?" Daemon's smile was still on the chilling side, but not quite on the killing edge anymore.

Lucivar shrugged. "At the time, killing her would have caused more problems."

Daemon nodded and took a large swallow of brandy. "If this game had stayed focused on me, I would have let it go. Jaenelle didn't believe the rumors, and I don't give a damn what anyone else thinks." He looked away. "And I thought, if it got physical, I would be the target."

"You were in that carriage, too."

"But I'm not the one who was supposed to get hurt. It happened fast, Lucivar. We'd been using that same cab all afternoon. Anyone following us would have had time to put a spell on it—or at least prepare the spell for a fast strike. The way the cab rolled . . . It was too fast, too violent. Had to be Craft-enhanced. Which means someone hoped Jaenelle would be hurt."

"In order to have you." He could see it too clearly. A shield would have protected her from broken glass or wood, but being thrown around in a rolling cab could have resulted in a damaged neck or spine. Jaenelle could have been crippled, perhaps forever, just when she was starting to reclaim her life.

"In order to have me," Daemon agreed.

"So what are we going to do?"

"Whoever caused the accident killed the driver but didn't finish the kill. I have him. After he makes the transition to demon-dead, he may be able to tell me something."

"You have plenty of experience in finishing the kill and none when it comes to dealing with someone newly demon-dead."

"So?"

"Why not take the cab driver to the one person who *does* know how to deal with the demon-dead?" Lucivar took a swallow of brandy. "If you don't tell Father about what happened today, he's going to kick your ass. You know that."

The room went cold. "Do you think he can?"

Hell's fire. *No.* "Jaenelle is his Queen, too, Bastard. If she's in danger, he needs to be told."

The temperature in the room eased closer to normal.

"I don't want to leave Jaenelle," Daemon finally said.

"Then I'll take the driver to the Keep."

"All right."

"And after we find out whatever the driver knows?"

Daemon watched the brandy as he gently swirled the snifter. "Jaenelle wants to help me find whoever is behind the rumors. I'm not happy about that, but I understand the need. If I try to keep her away from everything that might hurt her, I'll smother her—and I'll lose her. She won't stay if she's thought of as less than what she was."

"She is less than what she was." Lucivar shrugged, ignoring the skitter of nerves down his spine at the way Daemon looked at him. "But she'll never discover what she can do if we keep standing in the way."

"Exactly." Daemon sighed. "There's a party in three days. One of those mind-numbing affairs. So Jaenelle and I will play out a little game at the party. Maybe we'll even find out something. Either way, I think I can convince her that she played out her part and should go back to the Hall."

"A mind-numbing party," Lucivar muttered. "Sounds like fun."

Daemon's eyes and smile finally warmed. "I'm delighted you think so, since you'll be there, too."

Lucivar swore. "Why do I have to be there?"

"Because if someone there goes after Jaenelle and somehow manages to get past me, I want to know they'll have to go through you in order to hurt her."

"Done." He set the snifter on the table. "You'd better include Surreal in this party. If you piss her off, she'll threaten to pin your balls to the wall."

Daemon grinned. "She does have a way of expressing her opinions, doesn't she?"

"That she does. So what happens after the party?"

The grin changed into a viciously gentle smile. Daemon set the snifter down and turned his right hand palm up so Lucivar could see the snake tooth slide out of its channel beneath the ring-finger nail.

"After that," Daemon said, "I'm going hunting."

TWELVE

1

Daemon shrugged into his black jacket and adjusted the cuffs of his white silk shirt. He didn't want to go to this party, didn't want Jaenelle anywhere near the aristo Blood who would be crowding the rooms. But her plan to try to draw out whoever was behind the rumors sounded safe enough, especially with Lucivar and Surreal in attendance.

That didn't mean he liked it. And he wasn't sure he could do it.

To distract himself, he silently rehearsed the phrase in the Old Tongue that he'd painstakingly pieced together over the past few weeks. He'd learned a few phrases of the Blood's ancient language over the centuries from scholars who still had some knowledge of those fluid words, but nothing he'd known had come close to what he wanted to say. Something private. Something erotic. Something he could whisper to Jaenelle to tell her what she meant to him.

Unfortunately, there were only two people in all of Kaeleer who were fluent in the Old Tongue. He couldn't ask Jaenelle to help him translate the phrase since he wanted to surprise her, and Saetan . . . Well, no matter how sophisticated the relationship, no matter how adult the people involved, there were some things a son just couldn't ask his father.

So he'd struggled with the books he'd found in Saetan's private study deep beneath the Hall, books that were filled with the grammar and vocabulary of that old language. What they didn't tell him was how to pronounce those words.

Maybe he could talk Jaenelle into giving him a few lessons while they were on their honeymoon. After all, he was going to offer to teach her a few things, too.

A quiet click. The bathroom door opened.

He turned to face her as she entered the bedroom. He'd seen desire mingled with the heat of lust in other women's eyes, and had hated them for it because they saw only the body, wanted only the bedroom skills he'd had no choice in learning. But seeing those feelings in her . . .

A different kind of heat flowed through him, and all those bedroom skills finally had a purpose.

"You look beautiful," he said as he crossed the room and held out his hand.

"So do you." She blushed.

Watching the color wash over her cheeks made him hungry.

Drawing her into his arms, he nuzzled her temple. "What would you like to do on our honeymoon?" The look she gave him made him grin. "Besides that."

Her blush deepened.

He eased back enough to trace a finger over the gold chain that held Twilight's Dawn. "I was thinking we could see what skills you might have now with a different Jewel."

A touch of wariness filled her eyes. "Craft?"

"I was thinking more along the lines of cooking."

Her eyes widened. "Cooking? But I can't cook."

His fingers followed the chain back up to her neck. "You couldn't before. But you couldn't call in your shoes before, either."

"I don't know, Daemon."

The words were doubtful, but her expression was eager.

His hands caressed her back. His lips brushed her cheek. "We could start with something simple. A roast."

"A roast," she repeated, as solemn as any student learning her first difficult spell.

"We start with a choice cut of meat." His hands caressed her hips, her ribs, gave her breasts a teasing brush before circling back up to her shoulders. "Rub it gently with herbs to season it and bring out the flavor." Since her head had tipped back, exposing her throat, he took the invitation and left a trail of delicate kisses from her throat to her ear. "Then we give it heat, but carefully, slowly, so the juices rise and tremble on the surface to be savored."

"Are you sure we're talking about cooking?"

He licked her ear, enjoying the little tremors going through her.

"My legs are weak," she said, sounding breathless.

He froze, fighting against the panic that the strain of the past few days had been too much for her. But before he could think of a careful way to ask, she added, "When your voice gets that purr in it and you kiss me like that, my legs get weak."

His body relaxed in one way, tightened in another. He brushed his lips over hers. "We could skip the party, stay home, and"—the tip of his tongue touched her bottom lip—"discuss the merits of basting."

She stared at him. "I'm supposed to be annoyed with you. How am I going to be annoyed with you?"

"By remembering the second part of the evening's entertainment."

"What's that?"

"The kiss-and-make-up part." He smiled as phantom tongues delicately licked her nipples.

She wobbled, then held on to him to stay upright. "Mother Night."

"Ready?" he purred.

"For what?"

She sounded nervous. He never wanted her to fear him, but nervous . . . Oh, he knew *exactly* how to play with a light case of nerves.

Since he could think of a dozen answers to her question—and only one of them would get them out of the bedroom—he stepped back enough to guide her toward the door.

"For the party, of course."

"The party. I remember."

He grinned. Strange to feel savagely volatile and lighthearted at the same time. "Let's collect Surreal and Lucivar and go play party games."

2

Surreal scanned another room full of milling people. It felt like every aristo in Amdarh was stuffed into this house. "Parties like this were more fun to attend when I was a whore."

Standing beside her, Lucivar also scanned the room. "Why?"

"Watching all the prissy bitches trying not to act scandalized that I was there was almost as entertaining as watching the men I'd slept with sweat over what I might say to the prissy bitches. Now that I'm considered part of an aristo family, these little evenings aren't as interesting."

"You're not 'considered' part of an aristo family," Lucivar growled. "You *are* part of an aristo family."

"Whatever."

"We've been here an hour. You don't have to stay."

"I'm not here for the food or the entertainment. Thank the Darkness."

She didn't catch most of the low, snarling response except for the words "moon's blood."

"It's the fourth day," she said with insulting precision. "I can wear my Jewels again."

"The males here don't know that," he snapped. "They'll just pick up the scent. You might as well hang a sign around your neck that says, 'I'm vulnerable. Hurt me.'"

She gave him a razor smile. "Exactly. Any male who looks at me and sees 'prey' is a man I want to have a private chat with."

He gave her a long, assessing stare. She knew that look. This was Lucivar assessing a warrior's potential to step onto a killing field and be able to walk away from it once the fight was done.

"You have your knives with you?" he asked.

"I used to be an assassin as well as a whore, remember? Yes, I have my knives."

"Are they honed?"

"Yes, they're honed. Would you like me to test one on you to prove it?"

He just stared.

Surreal sighed. Since he was Eyrien, a Warlord Prince, and a relative, getting pissy with Lucivar about weapons was pointless. She decided to change the subject. "What's wrong with Daemon and Jaenelle? They were snuggly in the carriage on the way to this party, and now . . ." She frowned. "Now Daemon has this look on his face—"

"His court mask."

The sudden tension in Lucivar's body and the wariness in his voice made her uneasy. "His what?"

"That's the way he always looked in the Terreillean courts when he was a pleasure slave. Cold. Bored. His face was a mask that revealed nothing of what he was really thinking. It was a look that said, 'You can touch my body, but you'll never touch *me*.' "

That distracted her. "He actually let the bitches touch him—and they lived?"

"I didn't say they lived," Lucivar replied grimly.

Surreal shivered and went on to the second part. "Then there's Jaenelle. One moment everything is fine, and the next it's like she almost believes the rumors."

"Hell's fire," Lucivar said. "This is the game. Daemon told me they were going to try flush out whoever was behind the rumors. This is how they're doing it."

She thought it over, and her stomach churned at the possibility. The last time she'd been involved in one of Daemon's "games," the Sadist had scared the shit out of everyone in that Hayllian camp.

"It's a game," Lucivar repeated. "He knows his role—Mother Night, he's played it enough times over the centuries."

"And Jaenelle is pretending to waver between refusing to believe the rumors and wondering if there's some truth to them?"

"That's my guess." He sighed. "Come on. We'd better find them."

"I prefer watching the Sadist's games from a distance."

But when Lucivar threaded his way through the crowd to reach the ballroom, she swore under her breath and followed him.

Lektra pulled her cousin Tavey into a small alcove where she could keep an eye on the ballroom and still talk with relative privacy. Watching Daemon fawn over Jaenelle was beyond intolerable, and if he continued playing the ardent lover so publicly, all her efforts to free him would be ruined. So she had to do something *now*. It was unfortunate that she didn't have time to find a male who could make the lie believable, but she had to hope that the shock of the claim would make Daemon react without thinking.

"This is what I want you to do," she said. Tavey's eyes widened as she told him.

"But he's a Warlord Prince," Tavey said, his voice rising until she shushed him.

"Exactly. By Protocol, if he's told to walk away, he *has* to walk away."

"But doesn't *she* have to tell him to go?"

"*She'll* never tell him. So you have to."

"But I don't even know her!"

"Shush!" Lektra looked around to assure herself no one was paying attention to them. "That doesn't matter. *He* won't know that." She paused and made her lips quiver. "Tavey, if you don't do this for me, my love will never be free, and if he ends up having to marry *her*, I'll be so miserable I—I don't think I'll be able to stand living anymore."

"Don't say that, Lektra. Don't." Tavey squeezed her hands. "I'll do it. I promise."

She sniffled and gave him a brave smile. "I won't forget this. And once Daemon and I are married, I'm sure he'll use his family's influence to get you a position in whatever court you want."

"Wouldn't mind having a month or so with Sadi's 'cousin.' "

"You want the whore? You can have her. I've already made plans for getting her out of the way for a while to insure she's not a distraction. There's no reason why she can't provide you with some company while she's staying in the country."

"Is something wrong?" Daemon asked as he escorted Jaenelle around the edge of the ballroom.

"I'm trying to look petulant," she replied. "Don't I look petulant?"

"You look like you have gas."

"*Daemon.*" She choked back a laugh.

His lips twitched. This party was turning out to be more fun than he'd anticipated. Oh, not the party itself, but playing out this game with Jaenelle was definitely entertaining. It had been easy enough to slip behind that cold, bored expression that had served him so well in the Terreillean courts. Problem was, the mask kept slipping. *They* kept slipping, forgetting their roles of suspicious woman and discontented man. Dancing with her for the first time in months was too delicious a feeling to spoil with a game.

But he'd agreed to play this out, so that's what he would do.

"Are we still scheduled to have a public quarrel?" he asked, slipping an arm around her waist once they found an open space where they could watch the dancers.

"Yes, we are, because I'm upset with you." Jaenelle frowned as she looked at him. "Why am I upset with you?"

"So that we can spend hours tonight doing the kiss-and-make-up part of this pretend quarrel," he purred, using Craft to change the sexual heat that, even leashed, poured out of him into psychic seduction tendrils that gently coiled around her while phantom hands stroked the inside of her thighs.

"Mother Night," she gasped.

Suddenly she was leaning hard against him, letting him support her.

"Feeling a bit weak in the legs?" he asked too innocently.

Her laughing snarl turned into a warm smile when she noticed the man swiftly approaching them.

Handsome, graceful and lean, with a mane of brown hair artfully disheveled, the man had fair skin, which meant he wasn't native to Dhemlan, and green eyes that were focused on Jaenelle. An Opal-Jeweled Warlord Prince. A rival.

Daemon hated him on sight.

"My darling," the man said, pressing his lips to the back of the hand Jaenelle held out to him.

"Prince Rainier," Jaenelle replied, still smiling.

"I'm wounded," Rainier said.

Not yet, but you will be, Daemon thought.

"My favorite Lady finally makes an appearance at a party and hasn't asked me to dance," Rainier continued. "But that's all right. I'm content just to flirt with you."

I'll see you in Hell first.

Rainier gave him an amused glance before focusing on Jaenelle again. "Would you mind telling your lover that I'm allowed to flirt with you?"

"Of course you're allowed to flirt with me," Jaenelle said, her voice filled with laughter. "After all, you never mean it." She paused. "On the other hand, if you were flirting with Daemon . . ."

"Pointless," Rainier said, grinning, "since it's *so* obvious that he's taken. But . . ." Releasing Jaenelle's hand, he smiled at Daemon. "May I have this dance?"

Hot fury. Cold rage. Suddenly it was easy to slip into the game. He'd assumed the person behind the rumors was female—an assumption he shouldn't have made.

"If my Lady has no objections," Daemon crooned. Out of the corner of his eye, he noticed Lucivar and Surreal entering the ballroom. As soon as he moved away, they'd stay close to Jaenelle.

"Do you mind?" Rainier asked, glancing at Jaenelle.

She looked baffled. "No, I don't mind."

"Shall we?" Smiling, Rainier offered an arm.

Daemon didn't take the arm—too much temptation to rip it off—but he turned and matched his stride to the Warlord Prince beside him until they reached the dance floor.

The music started. A waltz. He wondered if Rainier had arranged that.

"Who leads?" he asked.

"I asked, so I lead."

The man could dance. Daemon heard startled gasps, noticed other couples stumble to a halt and move out of the way. But those were distant things. His focus—and his temper—were fixed on Rainier.

"Before you decide in favor of killing me, I should mention that I'm Second Circle," Rainier said.

That statement almost threw him off balance. It was possible. Jaenelle's court had been so informal, he'd never met anyone beyond her First Circle. "You mean you *were* Second Circle. The Dark Court no longer exists."

"Hmm. Yes. I'm no longer Second Circle just like you're no longer the Consort."

They whirled around the dance floor, perfectly matched, studying each other.

"I'll think you'll find, Prince Sadi, that those who serve Jaenelle don't give a damn that there's no longer formally a court. The Dark Court still exists because she still exists. We still serve—and you're still the Consort."

"What's your game, Rainier?"

"Figured I'd better help you two by providing a distraction. You're doing a lousy imitation of a quarreling couple. You're having too much fun. I'm thinking you're trying to draw out whoever started those rumors. So this should catch someone's interest."

The man had a point. They certainly had the attention of everyone in the room. "How did you end up in the Second Circle?"

Rainier grinned. "I was the coven's dance instructor. The fifth or sixth one the High Lord hired. I wasn't much older than the girls and had no credentials except a knowledge of, and love for, dancing, but he told me if I could last the hour with them I had the position."

"And you lasted the hour."

Rainier nodded. "The Heart of the Realm was in that room. If the personalities and power of the coven didn't scare the shit out of a man, there was no better place to be. There's still no better place to be."

He had a feeling Rainier was more than a dance instructor, but the man wasn't a rival, and a skilled ally could prove useful right now. "Do you know court dances?"

"I adore court dances."

"My lead." Daemon sent a psychic command to the head musician.

When the music changed, he and Rainier broke the steps of one dance and flowed into the other as smoothly as if they'd been partners for years.

Hand to hand. Turning. Circling. Gliding. Watching each other. Restrained sensuality swelling to the point of bursting. He saw the hint of fear in Rainier's green eyes as the web of desire he was spinning through the dance became a snare for the unwary.

"Mother Night," Rainier whispered hoarsely. "You must be a mean bastard when you want to hurt someone."

Daemon smiled a cruel, knowing smile, and crooned, "But you'd let me hurt you, wouldn't you?"

The sudden tremble in Rainier's hand was answer enough.

As the dance ended, Daemon leaned in, trapping their hands between their bodies, bringing lips close to lips. "That's why they called me the Sadist."

Something was scraping his temper, some feeling in the room that reminded him too much of the Terreillean courts, something that had him teetering a heartbeat away from the killing edge.

But that *something* wasn't the man staring into his glazed eyes. This male belonged to his Queen and shouldn't be harmed.

With effort, he pulled back the seduction tendrils, eased back physically. "Thank you for the dance."

"My pleasure." Rainier cleared his throat. "It's been an education."

They walked back to where Jacnelle and Surreal stood. No one in the ballroom spoke, no one moved. Even the musicians were silent for a long moment before the music began for the next dance, and the room was once more filled with movement and murmurs.

Jaenelle watched him approach, her face flushed, her eyes wide.

Was she repulsed by seeing him dance with another man? What was she thinking? He wanted to reach out, mind to mind, but he didn't dare. Not when his temper was being held back by a frayed thread.

As he stopped in front of her, Rainier still beside him, he saw her throat muscles working to swallow.

Looking dazed, Jaenelle said, "It's awfully warm in here. Is it warm in here?"

Surreal snorted as she studied him and Rainier. "Sugar, we passed warm and leaped straight to blazing."

"Oh. Good. It's not just me."

Surreal gave him a wary look and linked her arm through Jaenelle's. "I imagine everyone is feeling a bit warm right now. Let's go out on the terrace and get some air."

"Air is good," Jaenelle said, wobbling a little. "Air is . . . good."

He said nothing as the two women made their way to the glass doors that led out to the terrace.

Rainier cleared his throat. "It's been . . . um . . ." He shook his head and walked away.

Daemon stayed where he was, watching Lucivar approach, seeing wariness in his brother's gold eyes. Rainier had been given the lightest taste of what it was like to dance with the Sadist, but Lucivar *knew*. And Lucivar was afraid.

But being afraid never stopped him from issuing a challenge with all the Eyrien arrogance in him.

"Quite a dance," Lucivar said.

"It had its moments."

"Rainier is a good Warlord Prince."

"He's a dance instructor?"

"Among other things."

Which confirmed his sense of the man. "Who trained him?"

"I helped him hone what he'd already learned."

Which meant Rainier wasn't just a natural predator, he was also a well-trained killer.

"Daemon . . . Jaenelle and Rainier are just friends."

"I know. It isn't him. But there's something in this room . . ." He shook his head. "I'm going to find someplace to be alone for a few minutes. I need a few minutes."

Lucivar stepped aside, letting him pass. With a bit of hunting, he found a small, secondary parlor near the ballroom. By the look of it, this was where visitors who weren't "important company" were entertained. Which meant right now it was quiet and empty, and that was what he needed to bring himself back from the point of going cold.

Lektra grabbed Tavey's arm. "Do it now. He's by himself."

"You want me to talk to him alone?"

"Well, you can't do it when *she's* nearby, and she's been clinging to him all night. This may be your only chance." And after watching him dance with that other Warlord Prince, she'd go mad if she couldn't have Daemon soon.

Tavey looked scared, but he never could refuse her for very long. So he left the ballroom to deliver his little speech.

By the end of the evening, her beautiful love would be free to be with the one woman in the whole Realm who truly deserved to have him.

*   *   *

Hearing the parlor door open, Daemon slipped his hands into his trouser pockets to hide his wedding ring. He'd spent the past few minutes just staring at it, taking comfort in its presence. He'd almost regained his balance, but he wasn't quite far enough away from the killing edge yet. He needed to find Jaenelle and tell her he couldn't go through with their public quarrel. He couldn't afford to have anything prick his temper right now.

As he turned toward the door, he caught sight of himself in the mirror above the fireplace. His gold eyes were still glazed—the prelude to cold rage.

"You don't want to be here," he snarled softly as the Yellow-Jeweled Warlord slipped into the room and closed the door. "You really don't want to be here."

"I—" The Warlord swallowed hard. "I'm asking you to do the right thing."

"And what is the right thing?" He glided toward the door, forcing the Warlord to sidle farther into the room to avoid getting close to him.

"We—We're in love. We want to be together."

"Who is 'we'?"

"Jaenelle. Me. We're in love. But she hasn't wanted to say anything because . . ."

"Because?" Daemon asked too softly.

"She's afraid of you." The Warlord blurted out the words. "She doesn't want to be with someone like you anymore."

"Someone like me." The words sliced his heart, inserted a tiny sliver of doubt. Then he rubbed his left thumb against his wedding ring.

If Jaenelle had fallen in love with someone else, she might not have told him until she felt capable of dealing with him. But she *never* would have married him, because she understood the nature of Warlord Princes better than anyone else could.

"*You* may be in love," Daemon said, "but—"

"We're lovers."

His brain shut off, snuffing out control, shattering the illusion of civilized behavior. As he descended to the level of the Black, the cold, glorious Black, every thought, every feeling funneled through the lethal rage of a Warlord Prince.

Ice glazed the mirror over the fireplace, formed a crust over the carpet. In the moments when he and the Warlord stared at each other, he created a bubble shield and an aural shield, both ready to snap into place in a heartbeat. Then he rose from the abyss, his Black power delicately surrounding that weaker mind, preventing the Warlord from reaching anyone through a psychic thread.

"So," Daemon crooned as he drew his left hand out of his pocket and rubbed a finger over his chin, "just when did you sleep with my wife?"

Horror filled the Warlord's eyes as he stared at the plain gold band.

The aural and bubble shield snapped up around the Warlord at the same moment Daemon's Black power smashed through all of the man's inner barriers.

The Warlord's mouth opened in a scream of terror and pain, but no sound filled the room. He tried to run—and crashed against the shield that contained him.

Daemon gave his prey a few moments to stare at death before he ripped into the Warlord's mind—and found all the answers he needed.

One flash of the Black. The Warlord's torso burst open, his guts spilling out. Ribs snapped as they were ruthlessly spread open. The heart burst out of the body to hang, impaled, on a shattered rib.

Another flash of the Black. Witchfire filled the Warlord's skull—and it *burned*. As the Warlord hit the floor, the skull broke open. Hot ash spilled out on the ice-covered carpet. Steam rose as the ice melted, soaking the carpet enough to keep it from catching fire.

One last flash of the Black drained the Warlord's Jewels and burned out all of the man's psychic power, finishing the kill.

Daemon studied his work with a critical eye—and smiled a cold, cruel smile.

Lucivar flung the parlor door open and rushed into the room, pulling up fast when he saw the body on the floor. His gorge rose, but he braced himself for whatever would come. He knew what that glazed, sleepy look in Daemon's eyes meant, what that smile meant. The Sadist had gone cold, and there was *no one* strong enough to control him.

Daemon glided up to him—and waited.

"Annoyed about something?" Lucivar asked.

"Not anymore." Stepping around him, Daemon walked to the door and stopped. "Shall we go? I have an appointment to quarrel with my Lady."

No. Sweet Darkness, no. Lucivar moved to the door. "You don't have to quarrel with Jaenelle."

"What my Queen wants, my Queen will have."

Knowing better than to argue, Lucivar walked out of the parlor. Daemon followed him. The door closed behind them.

"Don't worry, Prick," Daemon said. "It won't be much of a quarrel."

Daemon walked away. Lucivar hesitated, then turned back to the parlor. Better to get rid of the corpse before someone else found it.

But when he reached for the doorknob, a feeling of revulsion swept through him, making his skin crawl. Stepping back, he studied the door. Stepping forward, the feeling swept over him again.

Craft. Daemon had done something in the moment when he walked out the door that guaranteed no one would willingly open that door until the spell wore off. Which meant Daemon wanted the body to be found—but not until he was ready to have it found.

"Well, bitch . . . or whoever you are," he whispered. "You wanted to play with the Sadist? Looks like you'll get your chance."

Turning away from the parlor, Lucivar hurried back to the ballroom. He couldn't stop what would happen, but he'd do whatever he could to protect Jaenelle and Surreal.

Daemon glided back to the ballroom. He had to find Jaenelle and get them both out of this house. He was a danger to everyone around him right now. The kill had cleared his mind enough to give him back a fragment of control, but not enough for him to be sure he wouldn't leave these rooms strewn with corpses.

Unfortunately, Jaenelle was waiting near the door, waiting for her cue to begin the quarrel.

"Where have you been?" she asked, handing her glass of sparkling wine to Surreal.

Hell's fire, Mother Night, and may the Darkness be merciful. It stabbed at him that her power was so much less that she hadn't been able to tell that he'd descended to the Black, that he was struggling not to go cold again.

He walked past her, not quite knowing what to do. He didn't want to quarrel with her. *Couldn't* quarrel with her. If he said anything that hurt her . . . Mother Night, he'd destroyed entire courts in Terreille when his temper had been riding this edge. If he hurt her, his control would snap completely, and the killing wouldn't stop until he'd exhausted his body and his power.

"Where have you been?" Jaenelle raised her voice enough to have conversations throughout the ballroom stutter to a halt.

He pivoted to face her, enough space between them to explain the raised voices. As he looked into her eyes, relief swept through him so fiercely he felt light-headed. She *knew*. Whatever her reasons for going through with this "quarrel," she knew he was too close to the killing edge and would take care not to push him back into a lethal rage.

He saw Lucivar walk into the ballroom, saw Surreal hand over Jaenelle's glass of sparkling wine. Hoping those two would have the good sense to stay out of this, he focused on Jaenelle, who, along with every-one else in the room, was waiting for his answer.

"I wasn't with another woman, if that's what you're asking," he snarled.

He felt a flash of frustration from her as she tried to find some way to respond to his words that wouldn't hurt either of them.

Balling her hands into fists, she shouted something at him. The fact that Lucivar choked on the wine confirmed the words were Eyrien, but he didn't know what she'd said. Which gave him a clue how to provide the tone of a quarrel without wounding.

Unfortunately, there was only one phrase he could think of that no one else would understand. So he bared his teeth and said the words he'd in-tended to say out of love, in the heat of passion. Words in the Old Tongue.

Her eyes widened in shock. She clamped a hand over her mouth to muf-fle the mewling noises. Then she whirled and rushed out of the ballroom.

Startled by her response, he hesitated. *Play out the game, old son.* Struggling to look irritated and slightly disgusted, he shook his head and left the ballroom to find Jaenelle.

She'd made it as far as the conservatory, where large ferns shielded her, giving her some privacy. He approached quietly, pained to see her shoulders hunched and her hands over her face. She gasped for air between sobs.

"Jaenelle," he said, brushing a hand over her shoulder—and bracing himself for her rejection of his touch. Mother Night, she sounded close to hysterical.

She lowered her hands and looked at him.

She *was* close to hysterical . . . because she was laughing so hard she could barely stay on her feet.

"I—I—I eat cow brains?" she gasped.

Shocked, his mouth fell open. "What? You do?"

"N-n-no. *You* do."

He gripped her upper arms to keep her upright. "What? No, I don't."

"Th-that's what you said. 'I eat cow brains.' " She collapsed against him, howling with laughter.

That was so far removed from what he'd intended to say it was embarrassing—and he could imagine how much worse it would have been if he'd whispered those words in the middle of hot lovemaking. "That wasn't— It wasn't what I thought I said." Feeling his face heat, he wrapped his arms around her and pressed her face against his chest to muffle her laughter.

"Oh, g-good." She gulped air and made an effort to regain some control. "What did you mean to say?"

Oh, no. He wasn't about to embarrass himself *that* much. "Never mind." He paused. "So what did you say to me?"

"Oh. Well."

"Come on, fair is fair." He tugged on her hair. "What did you say?"

"I said you had the feet of a pig and smelled like a goat." She burst into laughter again.

Daemon sighed. "Well, we certainly descended fast enough to barnyard mudslinging, didn't we?"

"We did. Oh, we did."

Her laughter broke his temper better than anything else could have. "Let's get out of here."

She gulped and wiped the tears from her face. "I'm not sure I can."

He picked her up. "Just keep your face turned away. I'll get us to the carriage."

"Are you going to look all snarly and fierce?" she asked, fighting against another burst of laughter.

He rolled his eyes. "I'll do my best." And if he didn't get them away from here in a hurry, they were both going to be rolling on the floor, laughing like fools.

After contacting the carriage driver they'd hired for the evening, he strode out of the conservatory—and almost ran into Surreal. The look in her eyes told him she was primed for a fight. She couldn't take him, but he respected her as an adversary—and she'd fight him until he killed her if she thought Jaenelle needed the protection.

"I'm taking her home," Daemon said. "She's hysterical."

"I am," Jaenelle bubbled. "I really am." She turned her head to look at Surreal.

"Yeeesss, I can see that," Surreal said, narrowing her gold-green eyes.

Because he didn't want Surreal to worry about Jaenelle, he shifted his bundle of witch, drawing her attention to his hands. Then he dropped the sight shield around his wedding ring for a moment.

Brushing past Surreal, he said, "I'll send the carriage back for you and Lucivar."

"You do that," Surreal muttered.

No one else tried to stop him, no one else even dared speak to him as he walked out of the house and settled his Lady in the carriage. Jaenelle might find his fierce and snarly look amusing, but the rest of the Blood at the party finally began to realize he was a male they should fear. And very soon, they would understand why.

Surreal stood just inside the conservatory, wanting a few moments alone to ponder.

Had she really seen what she thought she'd seen? Sadi . . . wearing a *wedding ring*? He and Jaenelle. *Married?*

"Surreal?" Lucivar stepped into the conservatory.

"He took her home. She was hysterical."

Grim worry filled Lucivar's eyes. "Hysterical?"

"She was laughing so hard, I don't know what else to call it."

The grimness faded but the worry remained.

Wanting to ease the worry, she said, "So what did Jaenelle say that made you snort wine out your nose?"

He rubbed the back of his neck. "I'm not sure I should repeat it."

She tipped her head to one side. "You tell me what she said, and I'll tell you what I just found out."

So he told her, and when she managed to stop laughing, he growled, "What did you find out?"

She took his left hand and tapped a finger against the gold band. "Daemon's wearing one of these." She wasn't sure how she expected Lucivar to respond, but she *hadn't* expected his concern to increase. "What's wrong?"

He stared over her shoulder. "Do you know the only thing more dangerous than a Warlord Prince? A married Warlord Prince who has someone playing games with his life that could threaten his marriage."

Suddenly nothing was amusing. Provoked, Daemon was dangerous enough. Pushed to defend something, or someone, who truly mattered to him . . .

She shuddered. "What do we do?"

"I don't know. I really don't know."

"Let's split up. Maybe we can learn something that will help end this."

Lucivar shook his head. "Daemon may already have all the information he needs."

Shit. She had a good idea what *that* meant. "I'm going to the ladies' lounge and freshen up. I'll meet you at the front door. I think I'd rather wait for the carriage outside."

He headed back to the ballroom to talk to Rainier, and she headed for the lounge. It had struck her as odd that a private home would have a "lounge" until she discovered the owners often "loaned" out the downstairs rooms for a "monetary gift." She didn't know why they couldn't just say they rented out their ballroom, but the lounge made sense, and right now, she was glad to have the privacy.

After taking care of personal needs, she sat down on a padded bench and closed her eyes.

"Are you feeling all right?"

Damn. She must be more tired than she thought. She hadn't even heard the woman enter.

She opened her eyes and studied the woman who stood nearby, looking concerned. The face looked vaguely familiar, but she was certain she'd never met the other witch. She was also certain there was something about the woman that wasn't quite . . . right. Something that put her on edge. Something that made her want to call in a knife.

She smiled and wrinkled her nose. "Just cramps," she lied. "Sometimes they're wicked mean."

"I know the feeling. Let me get you something to drink."

"No, that's all right." She shifted on the bench, prepared to get up and leave.

"It's no trouble. Really."

Suppressed excitement in the voice. A feverish glint in the eyes.

The witch opened the lounge door and whispered something to someone outside. Then she closed the door and leaned against it.

Bitch. Surreal felt fairly certain she'd just met the source of Daemon's problems, but considering Daemon's mood and Lucivar's worry *about* Daemon's mood, she'd prefer being absolutely certain before she said anything to either of them. And there was still the question of why anyone would be foolish enough to play with a Black-Jeweled Warlord Prince.

It didn't take long before someone knocked on the door. The witch opened it, and another Dhemlan witch Surreal didn't recognize slipped into the room, carrying a glass.

Same suppressed excitement. Same feverish glint in the eyes.

The first witch took the glass from her companion, then handed it to Surreal. "Drink this. You'll feel better in no time."

Yeah. Cramps aren't a problem when you're dead, Surreal thought. As soon as the other woman let go of the glass, she used Craft to probe the liquid and the glass itself. No poisons. But there *was* something in the sparkling wine. She didn't recognize the drug, but she could sense its presence. Probably meant to knock her out for a while. But why knock *her* out?

Obvious. They wanted her out of the way for some reason. Of course, if she was unconscious, she wouldn't be hard to kill.

Refuse the drink and put these two bitches on alert—maybe make them nervous enough to bolt—or drink it and hope she wasn't doing something stupid? Because if they *did* end up killing her, Lucivar would help her make the transition to demon-dead just so he could spend a decade or two yelling at her, and the High Lord . . . Uncle Saetan would be *sooo* pissed.

She studied the two women and saw a kernel of suspicion in the eyes of the witch who had first approached her. So she took a sip, figuring she could get enough of a sense of what the drug was without it disabling her.

She figured wrong. That one sip made the room lift and drop with stomach-churning speed. Her fingers went numb. The glass dropped to the floor. Her vision faded.

She made one attempt to contact Lucivar on a psychic thread, but even that was already beyond her ability.

"Ah, shit," she muttered before she tumbled off the bench.

Lektra suppressed the urge to give her rival a hard kick in the ribs. Or in the face. After all, she'd promised Tavey he could have the whore for a while, so it wasn't fair to damage the bitch beforehand. And it *was* possible that the SaDiablo family would be upset if anything . . . permanent . . . happened to Surreal. But they could hardly complain about a whore spreading her legs for one more man. Besides, it wasn't like Tavey would be *paying* for the sex.

"Let's get her out of here," Lektra said.

Roxie opened the lounge door, peeked out, then signaled. A moment later, a Sapphire-Jeweled Warlord slipped into the room.

Lektra didn't like the man. Rough manners, rough temper. Roxie had found him somewhere, and the payment that had been promised had been enough to make him put aside any qualms about being an "escort" for an unwilling witch.

"Take her to the country house as arranged, and keep her there until I say otherwise," Lektra said.

"Gets boring in the country," he growled.

"I'm sure you'll find something to do," she replied, glancing pointedly at Surreal.

He smiled—and she sincerely hoped she'd never see him again. Of course, once she and Daemon were married, she'd never have to worry about men like *him*.

She watched him pull Surreal up off the floor. A moment later, he left the lounge, wrapped in a sight shield to avoid anyone inquiring about his presence at an aristo party—or about the woman slung over his shoulder.

"We'd better leave," Lektra said. "Have you seen Tavey?"

"Not since earlier this evening, when he left the ballroom," Roxie replied.

Tavey should have come back to report Daemon's reaction to their conversation. She'd seen her beautiful love carry that pale bitch out of the party. She hadn't liked that. He should have asked his brother to take *her* home. No matter. He wouldn't have to cater to Jaenelle Angelline much longer.

"If we don't meet up with him on our way out, Tavey will have to make his own way home," Lektra said.

With Roxie discreetly staying in the background, Lektra made her way to the front door, slipping into the ballroom and making a point of being seen talking to Lady Zhara, who had arrived late—and also giving herself and Roxie a reason to avoid walking past Lucivar Yaslana on the chance that he might recognize Roxie by her psychic scent, despite the illusion spell.

As soon as he strode away from the front door, they hurried out and went home.

Swearing under his breath, Lucivar headed for the ladies' lounge. Hell's fire! How long did it take a woman to piss anyway?

He flung the door open and walked in, not caring if he walked in on a woman pulling down her pants or pulling them up. But the lounge area was empty, and the toilet wasn't occupied.

Damn her. Where did she—

Turning to leave, he spotted the glass on the floor near a padded bench. Crouching, he studied it. Most of the liquid had seeped into the carpet, but the few drops left in the glass were enough.

Surreal! His temper flared. *Surreal!*

No answer. Not even an irritable flicker that would have helped him pinpoint a direction.

Rainier.

Yaslana?

Have you seen Surreal?

Not since I danced with her earlier. Is there a problem?

I'm not sure yet. See if you can find her. I'm going out to widen the search.

Rainier hesitated. *Are you going to contact Prince Sadi?*

Now Lucivar hesitated. *No. Not yet.*

He left the party and spent hours soaring over Amdarh, searching, hunting, calling.

No answer. No way to find her.

As night gave way to the first hint of dawn, he flew back to the family town house. Daemon knew Surreal better than the rest of them. It was time to call him into the hunt.

CHIRTEEN

1

Aroar of fury and frustration that sounded like Lucivar in a mood rattled Surreal's mind, jolting her awake. Her head pounded, and her stomach felt queasy. And that pissed her off.

Moving slowly, she rolled to her side and opened her eyes. The soft predawn light revealed enough to confirm she was in an unfamiliar room. A pillow under her head and a sheet beneath her hand told her she was in a bed. And her psychic senses told her she wasn't alone.

Pushing herself upright, she swung her legs over the side of the bed—and swore silently as the bed seemed to lift and dip under her. Apparently, her body hadn't worked through all the effects of the drug, which was still playing nasty games with her sense of balance.

A chair creaked. A large body moved to a lamp on the table near the window. The sudden flare of light as he used Craft to engage the candle-lights made her squint.

"They said you wouldn't wake up until sometime this afternoon," he said, giving her a mean smile. "Glad that's not the case. It was getting boring, just watching you sleep."

Since the skirt of her gown was shoved up to the tops of her thighs, she figured his self-restraint had more to do with not wanting to soil his cock with moon's blood than using an unconscious woman for sex.

She knew his type, had seen enough men like him when she was a child living in the meanest streets of a city in Terreille, whoring to earn enough to buy a day's food and, maybe, some shelter for the night.

"Just so you don't go getting any ideas, Greenie, there's a Sapphire shield around this room and a Sapphire lock on the door. So you don't go anywhere unless I say you can."

Greenie? She'd never advertised she wore the Gray when she'd worked in the Red Moon houses in Terreille, and while she hadn't made it a secret since coming to Kaeleer, there weren't many of the Blood beyond those who had been in Jaenelle's First Circle and the ones who lived in Ebon Rih who knew she wore a Jewel darker than her Birthright Green.

Which meant there might be a few other things the bitch who arranged this didn't know about her.

"What— What do you know about me?" she asked. The shakiness in her voice was due to the drug her body was still shaking off, but it made her sound afraid and, right now, that suited her just fine.

"I know you're a Green-Jeweled witch who's caused some trouble for a fine aristo Lady, who paid me a generous sum to make sure you don't cause her any more trouble. And I've heard you were an expensive whore who only worked out of the best Red Moon houses until you came to Kaeleer and managed to talk yourself into an influential family." He stared at her mouth and leered. "Or maybe you did something besides talk to convince them you'd be handy to have around."

Bastard. Her legs wobbled when she stood up, but she steadied quickly as the last of the drug, meant to subdue a Green-Jeweled witch, was burned off by a body that was a vessel for the Gray.

She walked up to him, keeping her gait unsteady. "What do you want?"

His big hands clamped on her shoulders, pulling her against him. "You be good to me, and I'll be good to you."

"I can be good." Her right hand curled in preparation for calling in her stiletto. "Sugar? There's one thing your Lady forgot to mention."

"What's that?" he asked as one hand groped her breast.

The stiletto was in her hand and through his ribs before he realized she'd moved. His eyes widened.

Surreal bared her teeth in a smile. "I earned more as an assassin than I ever made as a whore." She rammed the stiletto into him up to the hilt, piercing his heart.

He hit the floor with a hard *thud*.

Surreal yanked the blade out of him, cleaned it on his shirt, then vanished it. Her "housekeeping" completed, she studied him.

"I think it takes a few hours to make the transition to demon-dead, but it would be best to make sure you don't wander off before we have a little chat," she told him. Not that he could hear her. Yet.

Calling in her Gray Jewels, she broke his Sapphire shield and lock, replaced them with Gray, and left the bedroom to see if she could find the tool she needed.

2

★Daemon.★

Daemon stirred, then snuggled closer to Jaenelle.

★Come on, Bastard. Wake up.★

Lucivar. Hell's fire. Just because the man was usually up before the sun didn't mean everyone wanted to be.

But he got out of bed, pulled on a robe, and slipped into the hallway. "What is it?" he asked, his voice rough from sleep. Then he noticed that Lucivar looked furious and exhausted. That woke up all his fighting instincts. "What is it?"

Lucivar raked his fingers through his hair. "Surreal is missing."

The three of them sat at one end of the dining table, the remains of a small, hastily made breakfast in front of them.

"If she was drugged, we'll find her as soon as she wakes," Jaenelle said after Lucivar related his search—and his failure to find Surreal.

"If they didn't kill her," Lucivar snarled.

"Then we'd better start looking."

"No," Daemon said. He poured them all more coffee. "I want you to go back to the Hall."

A feral anger that excited and chilled him came into Jaenelle's eyes.

"She's my family, too," Jaenelle said in a voice that warned him he was close to crossing a line he might never be able to cross back over.

He laid a hand over hers, needing her to understand. "I know she is, but they've already tried to hurt you, and if they're confident they're strong enough to take on a Gray-Jeweled witch, they aren't going to hesitate to go after you."

"They?" Jaenelle asked too softly.

"I know who's behind this. I'll take care of it."

"Alone."

"Yes. Alone. This began with an obsession with me, so it's mine to deal with. But I need to know you're safe. I *need* that, Jaenelle. Please."

She stared at him a long time. Then she drew her hand away from his and pushed her chair back. "Very well, Prince. I'll go back to the Hall, and you do what you have to do. But once that's done, you and I will talk." She walked away from the table.

"Jaenelle." He waited until she turned to face him. "This has nothing to do with the Jewels you wear."

"If I still wore Ebony, would you ask me to go back to the Hall?"

"Yes. Because this is mine to do."

"We'll talk, Prince," she said after giving him a long, thoughtful look. Then she left the dining room.

Lucivar winced. "She's never cheerful in the morning. You know that."

"I know." He also knew that this "talk" would determine whether or not he still wore a wedding ring.

Lucivar cleared his throat. "So. When were you going to tell me that you and Jaenelle were already married?"

He suddenly felt awkward, and that surprised him. So he kept his eyes on his cup. "We just wanted to get married."

"I understand that. The celebration coming is more for everyone else than the two of you." Lucivar paused. "But if you'd asked, I would have been there."

"For Jaenelle," Daemon said.

"For Jaenelle," Lucivar agreed. "And for you."

Daemon looked up and met Lucivar's eyes—and saw things he hadn't been sure he'd ever see again. Love. Understanding. Acceptance.

And for you. Those three words healed the last of the rift between them.

"Thank you," Daemon said, his voice husky.

Lucivar reached across the table. Daemon locked hands with his brother. They didn't say anything. They didn't need to.

Finally, reluctantly, Daemon eased back. "I'd like you to take Jaenelle to the Hall. I'll ask Father to come to the Hall to free you up in case there's more than one battlefield. I don't think it will come to that, but . . ."

Lucivar nodded. "I'll contact Marian and ask her to come to the Hall to keep Jaenelle company." He waited a beat. "What about Surreal?"

"I'll find Surreal."

Lucivar pushed away from the table. "In that case, let's get this done."

3

Daemon waited until Lucivar and Jaenelle were on their way to the Hall before trying to contact Surreal. The staff had cleaned off the dining room table and brought him a fresh cup and another pot of coffee.

Pouring a cup, he sent a call on a Gray psychic thread, aimed toward a mind he knew well. *Surreal?*

What?

The surly tone relieved him enough to make him smile. *Are you all right?*

I'm . . . fine.

Where are you?

Country house. Don't think it's that far away from Amdarh.

Are you sure you're all right? You sound breathless.

Damn . . . ax . . . is dull.

Daemon raised an eyebrow. *Do I want to know what you're doing with an ax?*

Have you had breakfast?

I've eaten.

Then you don't want to know.

He sipped his coffee while he considered how to respond to that.

In a few hours, I might have some information for you, Surreal said.

I know who's behind the rumors.

Well . . . shit. A pause. *Guess I'll finish this anyway.*

Do you need help?

Do you?

No.

Then I'll take care of my business, and you take care of yours. I'll be back in Amdarh late tonight.

Taking a last sip of coffee, Daemon left the dining room. Since Surreal didn't need his help, he'd take care of the next errand.

4

After he and Saetan had settled in comfortable chairs in one of the Keep's smaller sitting rooms, Daemon got to the point.

"I have business to take care of in Amdarh. Until it's done, I would appreciate it if you would stay at the Hall—at least for part of the time."

"To protect Jaenelle?" Saetan asked softly.

Daemon nodded.

"What about Lucivar?"

"He'll be there. So will Kaelas and Ladvarian. But . . ."

"But?"

Daemon looked into his father's golden eyes. "But they aren't you."

Saetan inclined his head. "Understood."

No questions about his business, no comment about why an Arcerian cat and an Eyrien Warlord Prince wouldn't be sufficient protection. There was no need. He was, after all, his father's mirror.

"Anything else?"

Daemon hesitated. Who else could he ask? "I— There was something

I wanted to say to Jaenelle . . . in the Old Tongue. But it didn't come out as I intended."

Saetan raised an eyebrow. "What did you say?"

Daemon hesitated, then said the words.

" 'I eat cow brains'?" Saetan burst out laughing.

Since there was nothing else he could do, he sat back to wait out his father's amusement. So he waited. And waited. And waited.

Finally, he sighed. It could have been worse. There could have been witnesses. No matter what else was said about him, he did *not* want to be known as the man who had reduced the High Lord of Hell to giggles.

"I'm sorry," Saetan gasped. Calling in a handkerchief, he wiped his eyes. "I can imagine the response to that."

"I'm sure you can," Daemon said dryly.

With effort, Saetan regained his composure. "So, what were you trying to say?"

Daemon took a deep breath, let it out slowly—and told him.

Great. Wonderful. He'd not only made the High Lord giggle, he'd made the man blush.

"I see." Saetan cleared his throat. "I'm . . . not sure that *can* be said in the Old Tongue. Let me think about it and see if I can come up with something that would let Jaenelle know she—"

"Is everything," Daemon finished quietly. "She is everything."

Saetan smiled. "Yes. She is everything."

FOURTEEN

1

Shivering, Lektra called in a shawl and wrapped it around herself. So cold. So terribly cold. But no one else seemed to notice except Roxie, who had retreated to her room.

Tavey was dead. Viciously murdered. Lady Zhara's Master of the Guard had come earlier that morning to tell her the body had been found—and to ask questions. Even through her shock and dismay, she'd realized the Master didn't care who had killed Tavey. After all, there was no law against murder among the Blood. No, he'd come to the town house as a courtesy—and to find out if Tavey's death foreshadowed a danger to his Queen.

She couldn't tell him what he wanted to know, and she wasn't about to tell him anything else. What could she say? She didn't actually *know* Tavey had talked to Daemon. And why would her beautiful love kill a man who was offering him a way out of an unwanted marriage? Besides, Daemon had been trained to be a lover, not a warrior.

So it had to have been someone else, someone who didn't want Daemon free of his ties to Jaenelle Angelline.

A warrior. Like Lucivar Yaslana. Maybe Daemon had already left the parlor by the time Tavey got there. Maybe Tavey had found Lucivar in the parlor and had blurted out his little speech, thinking that telling Daemon's brother was easier than telling Daemon himself. But Lucivar was an Eyrien warrior. Brutal. Savage. Roxie had told her over and over how mean Lucivar had been to her, threatening to kill her once he got tired of bedding her, forcing her to flee her home and family in Ebon Rih so that *he* could marry some hearth witch nobody.

Yes, Lucivar Yaslana wouldn't have thought twice about killing Tavey. After all, killing was what he did. Why not force Daemon into continuing to play nursemaid so that *he* wouldn't have to take care of Jaenelle?

She walked over to the window, intending to look out, but something shuddered through her, making her back away.

There was something outside, waiting for her. Something dangerous. Something deadly. Something cold.

Shivering violently, Lektra hurried to the other side of the room, away from the windows, away from whatever was out there.

As long as she stayed inside, she was safe. Whatever it was couldn't get in, couldn't harm her. As long as she stayed inside.

Wrapped in Black shields that prevented the rest of the Blood from detecting his presence, Daemon watched the town house across the street. Lady Lektra's town house. Easy enough to find the root of all the rumors once he'd known where to look—and if it hadn't been for the Warlord at the party last night, he never would have looked in her direction. He'd probably seen her at a party or some other public gathering, maybe had even danced with her, a transient partner in one of those country dances. But he didn't remember her. The face he'd pulled from the Warlord's mind meant nothing to him.

Lektra's friend, however, did have a connection to him. Or, at least, to his brother. How unfortunate for her.

Smiling, Daemon walked away. His prey wouldn't go anywhere. The spells he'd wrapped around the town house would make sure of that. Whenever Lektra or Roxie got near a window or door leading outside, they would feel certain something deadly waited for them beyond those doors and windows . . .

Which was true.

. . . and they were safe as long as they remained inside.

Which was not true.

But he would let them have the illusion of safety for a few more hours. Because some games were best played in the dark.

2

Saetan knocked on the workroom door, then opened it enough to poke his head into the room. "I'm looking for a witchling. Seen any about?"

Turning away from the worktable, Jaenelle gave him a dazzling smile. "Papa! What brings you to the Hall?"

"Nothing in particular," he replied, walking toward the worktable. "I just wanted to see . . . how . . . you were . . . doing." He stared at the rosebush rising up from a bowl on the table. "Mother Night, witch-child. It's beautiful."

Jaenelle looked at the rosebush and grinned. "I'm pleased with it."

Saetan circled the table to get a better look at the illusion she'd created. But he tried to touch one of the roses just to be sure it *was* an illusion. She'd always been able to create illusion spells that could fool the eye, and it seemed she hadn't lost that ability. But something felt different about this spell.

"Can you show me how you did this?"

She looked at the various jars and small bowls on the table and nodded. "I have enough ingredients to make several more."

So she showed him how to build a rosebush out of powders made from pastel chalks, dried rose petals, thorns, and a few other things. He mentally noted what she did and how much of each ingredient she used, but most of his attention was on Twilight's Dawn.

Whenever he'd seen it before, the Jewel she now wore looked like a Purple Dusk accented by other colors. Now, as she worked through the illusion spell, he watched it change. When she began working on the leaves, the center of the Jewel became dominantly Green, then shifted to Rose with a strong touch of Red while she created the flowers.

He didn't know why it was changing like that, didn't know how it *could* change like that.

It played havoc with his ability to measure her strength against his own because hers kept sliding. One moment he would have sworn the woman beside him was a Rose-Jeweled witch. The next moment, her power resonated with his Birthright Red. It was as if she were dancing on webs of power, and the threads she plucked shone the brightest.

Webs of power. Lorn had created webs of power to help prevent Witch, the living myth, from plunging back into the Darkness after Jaenelle unleashed her Ebony power to save Kaeleer. And Lorn had given Ladvarian the Jewel that was called Twilight's Dawn.

Fingers snapping in front of his face startled a snarl out of him.

"Hell's fire, witch-child."

"Well, you haven't heard anything I've said for the past minute or so," Jaenelle said. "I didn't want you to come back from wherever your mind had wandered and find me gone."

"Gone?" His heart leaped as memories of webs of power shattering in the abyss filled his mind. "Where are you going?"

We can't lose her now. We can't. She is everything. She is still everything.

Jaenelle studied him for a long moment, her sapphire eyes seeing too much. But she gave him a daughter's tolerant smile. "First I'm going to wash up. Then I'm going to join the others for the midday meal. Which I already told you."

"My apologies, witch-child. You're right. My mind was elsewhere."

"I noticed. Are you going to join us? Khary and Morghann are here, as well as Lucivar and Marian."

"No, I'd like to stay here and play around with your powders if you don't mind."

Jaenelle kissed his cheek. "Please yourself."

"What about you, witch-child?" He looked into her eyes. Still beautiful, still ancient. But he couldn't shake the feeling that he had disappointed her in some way. "Are you pleased?" She knew him well enough to know he wasn't asking about the illusion spell.

"I lost nothing I regret losing," Witch said softly. "I am what I want to be."

He watched her walk out of the room. There was a message under her words, something she wanted him to understand but didn't want to tell him outright.

Turning back to the worktable, he set her rosebushes to one side. Maybe figuring out one puzzle would help him figure out the other.

"Am I interrupting? I could come back later."

An hour of frustration hadn't made him cheerful, but he forced himself to smile at Marian, who hesitated in the workroom's doorway. "Yes, you're interrupting, and I'm grateful."

Marian walked over to the worktable. "Oh, dear. Is it that bad?" She looked at the dark, twisted, misshapen lump that rose out of the bowl and winced. "I guess it is that bad." She hesitated. "Jaenelle did that?"

"No, Jaenelle created those." Saetan pointed at the rosebushes.

Marian's mouth fell open. She hurried around the table to get a better look. "Oh, these are lovely. If you rubbed some rose oil on the rim of the bowl for scent, you wouldn't know for sure these aren't real until you tried to touch them." She studied the rosebushes. "I wonder how long the spells last."

"Why?"

"Well, if the spells lasted a while, people could decorate a room with one of these illusions and have a potted rosebush in a room that wouldn't support a real plant—or even have roses in a climate that wouldn't be suitable for real ones."

He smiled with real warmth and fatherly affection. Jaenelle, the living myth, could create such an illusion, but Marian, the practical hearth witch, could think of a way to use it.

Marian walked around the table to stand beside him. "So what is that?"

They looked at the misshapen lump in the bowl.

Saetan sighed. "My attempt to reproduce the illusion." Then he studied Marian, an idea springing up. "Is there something you need to do right now?"

"No," she said cautiously.

"Would you be willing to help with an experiment? We'll need Morghann, too."

"All right. I'll call her."

He set aside his failed spell, called in another bowl, then made sure the two witches would have everything they needed. By the time Morghann hurried into the workroom, he was ready.

"But we don't know how Jaenelle created that illusion spell," Morghann said after he'd explained what he wanted them to do.

"I know how she did it," Saetan said. "I'll talk you through the steps, but I want the two of you to do the actual spell."

They didn't understand, but Morghann and Marian followed his instructions, Morghann using her Green Jewel and Marian alternating between her Birthright Rose and her Purple Dusk Jewels.

When the last ingredient was added and the last part of the spell invoked, the two women laughed in delight as the rosebush rose out of the bowl. The illusion wasn't as big as the ones Jaenelle created, and it didn't fool the eye quite as well, but the spell had worked.

He wasn't sure if that pleased him or chilled him.

"So just what was it you were trying to find out, Uncle Saetan?" Morghann asked.

"The two of you can reproduce the illusion spell Jaenelle created," he said quietly. "I can't."

Marian frowned. "But . . . you're stronger than either of us. Why can't you do it?"

"Because I wear the Black, and the Red is my Birthright Jewel." He studied their illusion. "Power can't be diluted. It's not just that I have a deeper well of power than someone who wears a Jewel lighter than mine, my power is also more potent."

Morghann nodded. "Something you could do with one drop of Red power I could do with three or four drops of Green—and Marian could do using more of her Purple Dusk strength. But that's how it is. Three people doing the same spell will create the same thing, but how much power they have to use and the potency of the spell will depend on their Jewel strength."

"But not in this case." Saetan tipped his head to indicate the rosebush. "I couldn't reproduce the spell using an equivalent amount of power that should have matched the Rose, Purple Dusk, and Green that

Jaenelle used. You two could reproduce it because your power has the right potency."

Marian frowned. "Then . . . how did Jaenelle create the illusion spell in the first place?"

"I don't know." *But I'm going to find out.* "Tell Lucivar I'll be back as soon as I can." He headed for the door, his mind already focusing on how to ask the questions that would provide some answers.

"Where are you going?" Marian asked.

Saetan paused in the doorway and looked back at the two witches. "I'm going to visit an old friend."

3

Saetan descended the stone stairs. He'd gone down this staircase many times during the years when Jaenelle had been the Queen of Ebon Askavi. Since returning to the Keep to live, he made this descent at least twice a month because he understood loneliness, and an hour's company now and then was all he could offer this ancient being.

The double doors at the bottom of the stairs swung open. Torches set in the walls flared to life as he walked to the other end of the huge chamber where the dragon's head came through an opening in the wall.

Unable to stop himself, he looked at the simple throne and the shattered scepter that lay on the seat exactly where Draca had set it after telling the First Circle that the Queen of Ebon Askavi was gone and the Dark Court no longer existed. Did seeing those reminders of what was lost ever bother Draca or her mate, the legendary Prince of the Dragons? Or did they think of it as a memorial for a Queen who had been the most powerful witch in the history of the Blood?

He looked away—and saw the dragon's large golden eyes were now open and watching him.

"Lorn," he said.

Ssaetan.

"I need answers."

You have assked no quesstionss, Lorn replied, sounding amused.

Saetan didn't feel amused. "What is Twilight's Dawn?"

★It iss the Jewel for Kaeleer'ss Heart.★

Frustration welled up inside him. "But what *is* it? How can one Jewel act like it's *many* Jewels? How did you create it?"

★I didn't. You did.★

Saetan stared at Lorn.

★Father. Brother. Lover. You created Twilight'ss Dawn.★

Webs of power stretching across a chasm somewhere in the abyss. Him, racing up to intercept Witch as she plummeted toward those webs, Lorn's warning that if she smashed through all the webs they would lose her ringing in his head. Catching her, smashing through the White, the Yellow, the Tiger Eye webs while he fought to slow her descent. Lucivar, taking his place, rolling Witch in the Rose web as they smashed through it. Rolling her in the other webs, beginning to slow the descent while wrapping her in a cocoon of power. Daemon, taking over at the Green web, fighting to stop the fall, fighting to hold on to the person who held his heart. Finally coming to rest on the Black web.

A Jewel formed by layers of power? A Jewel that had, somehow, retained those distinct layers? Extraordinary, to be sure . . . but still less than her Birthright.

"We didn't know," Saetan said quietly, deep sorrow weighing on his heart. "If we'd realized, maybe there was something we could have done differently."

★Your tassk wass to hold the dream to the flessh. You did what needed to be done,★ Lorn said.

"But we changed her."

★You changed nothing, Ssaetan. Sshe iss who sshe hass alwayss been.★

He shook his head. "If that were true, Jaenelle would still wear the Black. She lost that."

★Sshe losst nothing.★

"How can you say that? It *is* a loss!" Saetan raked his fingers through his hair. "If I broke my Black Jewel, broke my power back to the Red, I would adjust. I would have to relearn some things, but I would adjust, like a person who loses a limb adjusts to the loss. But I would always remember what I had."

That iss you. That iss not Jaenelle.

"Who had even more to lose!"

Who grievess the losss, High Lord? Lorn snapped. *You or Jaenelle?*

Stung, Saetan took a step back, straining to hold his temper. "Are you saying I'm selfish because I want her to be everything she was? That Daemon and Lucivar and the coven and the boyos are *selfish* because we regret what she lost in order to save us and Kaeleer?"

The chamber grew cold. *The kindred undersstand. But they ssee ssome thingss more clearly than humanss do.*

They stared at each other, anger and frustration swelling on both sides.

Then Lorn sighed. *Look up, Ssaetan.*

Reluctantly, he obeyed.

The torches lit the lower part of the chamber, but where the light began to fade, he saw the colors of twilight—rose and bright blue deepening to sapphire and red and dark lavender, which gave way to night black.

Twilight'ss Dawn, Lorn said softly. He closed his eyes, a clear sign of dismissal.

More frustrated and uncertain than when he entered the chamber, Saetan walked back to the double doors. As he reached them, Lorn said, *Look with your heart, Ssaetan. You already know the ansswerss.*

But he didn't. He *didn't*. And it was clear Lorn wouldn't tell him anything more.

The kindred understood? Maybe it was because they had seen something he hadn't.

It was dangerous, but there was one other place he could look for answers, one other . . . person . . . he could ask.

Not giving himself time to consider what might happen if things went wrong, he left the Keep, caught the Black Wind, and headed for the island ruled by the Weavers of Dreams.

4

"Well," Surreal said cheerfully, "look who's back among the living. Not that you actually *are* among the living anymore, but why quibble?" Looking down at the Warlord on the floor, she bared her teeth in an insincere smile. "At any rate, your brain is working again—at least as much as it ever did."

"Bitch," the Warlord snarled.

"Right on the first guess."

Struggling to sit up, the Warlord got a good look at his naked torso. "You filthy *bitch*! You cut off my cock!"

"And your balls. Not to mention your arms and legs. So relax, sugar. You're not going anywhere just yet."

Using Craft, Surreal lifted a chair and settled it near the Warlord.

"And just so there's no further misunderstandings, the Green are my Birthright." She tapped the Jewel hanging from a gold chain around her neck. "I wear the Gray."

His Sapphire Jewel glowed as he tried to strike her with a bolt of power. She slapped the power back at him with interest—and heard his rib cage snap in several places.

He lay still, taking shallow breaths. Being demon-dead, he didn't actually need to breathe, but she imagined it took a little while for the brain to stop trying to do what it had once needed to do.

Sitting in the chair, she leaned forward, resting her arms on her thighs. "Here are your choices. You can tell me everything you know about why I ended up here, and in return, I'll finish the kill, freeing you from what's left of a dead body."

He started swearing.

"Or," she continued, raising her voice to compete with his, "I can haul your sorry carcass up to the Keep, dump you on the High Lord's desk, and tell him you not only abducted his niece, you also worked for the bitch who tried to physically harm his daughter and ruin his son's reputation. You can imagine how well Uncle Saetan is going to respond to that."

He probably would have paled if he was still capable of doing that.

"Un—Uncle Saetan?"

You really weren't paying attention to much beyond your fee, were you?
"Prince of the Darkness. High Lord of Hell. Patriarch of the SaDiablo
family. Since he has over fifty thousand years of experience in ruling the
Dark Realm, your being demon-dead isn't going to get in his way when
it comes to hurting you. So who are you going to talk to, sugar? Me or
Uncle Saetan?"

I wanted information about the bitch who hired him, not his life story, Surreal
thought an hour later. Still, given his choices, she appreciated why the
Warlord had wanted to be thorough.

She'd finished the kill as she'd promised, burning out what was left of
his power and freeing his spirit to return to the Darkness. And thinking
about the pack of Hell Hounds that had obeyed her mother and were
now left without a mistress to look after them—assuming those animals
actually needed someone to look after them—she wrapped cold spells
around the torso and the other pieces, caught the Winds, and rode to the
Keep.

Draca, the Keep's Seneschal, accepted her offering without comment,
and offered, in return, a guest room where she could clean up and have
a meal. She accepted both, glad of the opportunity to wash thoroughly
and change into fresh clothes, and pleased when Draca sent along a selection of books with the meal. Choosing one, she decided to settle in
for a few hours. Maybe Uncle Saetan would be back by then and she'd
have a chance to talk to him before she headed back to Amdarh.

5

There was no official landing place on the island, since visitors were seldom welcome—and anyone unwelcome usually didn't survive. But he
did sense a residual power he could home in on. Hoping he would land
in a safe place, Saetan dropped from the Black Wind, wrapped himself in
Black shields, and closed his inner barriers as tightly as possible.

A moment later, he appeared in the center of a small clearing. The trees and bushes around the clearing were veiled with webs, some old and tattered, others looking freshly spun.

As powerful as he was, he felt the whispery tugs from those tangled webs, luring him to open his mind, just a little, and slip into a dream from which he might never return.

He closed his eyes and fought against the lure—and wondered how the kindred Ladvarian had gathered here to help heal Jaenelle had managed to keep their minds intact. Or had the golden spiders refrained from spinning those tangled webs during those weeks?

I am the High Lord. He sent the thought rolling over the land. *I need to talk to the Weaver of Dreams. It concerns Jaenelle.*

He waited, slowly becoming aware that all the whispery tugs had faded until only one remained. Strong. Powerful. But not threatening. Just a thread to follow.

He followed a path out of the clearing. More of a game trail, actually. The kindred must have used the clearing as their landing place, must have created this trail as they traveled from one part of the island to another.

He moved carefully since he wasn't sure what would happen if he stumbled and brushed against one of the tangled webs close to the trail. He couldn't judge how far he'd walked, but his bad leg ached by the time he reached the caves and the thread of power drew him inside.

Witchlight glowed in niches in the cave walls. Was it for his benefit or did the spiders need the light as well? As he passed from one chamber to the next, the floor rocked beneath him, and the air became golden and veiled. No longer sure if he was still in the real world or caught in a dream, he stopped moving.

Here, a soft voice called. *Here.*

Light filled another chamber. Since he was watching where he set his feet, the dark stain that covered most of the chamber floor was the first thing he saw when he reached the entrance.

And the Blood shall sing to the Blood. And through the blood.

Jaenelle's power, and her pain, rose up from the blood that had seeped into the stones, choking him. He sank to his knees. His hand touched the stain.

Feelings flooded him, but, thankfully, no images. Still, he recognized the feel of Ladvarian, the Sceltie's feet planted on the blood-washed stone as the dog braced for the battle of helping to heal a body devastated by a backlash of power.

He didn't know how long he knelt there while feelings of love, courage, and stubborn determination washed through him. No human could have done what the kindred had done. No human could have believed as they had believed. Had he ever thanked Ladvarian, Kaelas, and the other kindred for their gift of courage and love? He couldn't remember.

Pulling his hand away from the stain, he regained enough self-control to wipe the tears from his face and look around the chamber.

The tangled web that covered one part of the chamber left him breathless. The large golden spider clinging to the wall near one end of the web scared him to the bone.

This is Kaeleer's Heart, the Arachnian Queen said.

Gathering his courage, he stood and moved closer to the web.

Living myth Dreams made flesh. Witch.

Hundreds of threads made up this web. The wishes and longings of all those dreamers. Lifetimes of longings. Generations of wishes. All woven together to create one extraordinary woman capable of touching all the races in Kaeleer, human and kindred, giving them a way and a reason to connect with each other.

You ask about Jaenelle, the spider said.

He kept his voice quiet, barely above a whisper. "Why is she different? I mean no disrespect, but if you truly were able to re-create the web that formed that dream and made it flesh, why did she come back to us different?"

She is not different, the spider replied. *She is still Kaeleer's Heart.*

"But not the same. If she were truly the same, she would be able to wear a Black Jewel."

Kaeleer does not need the Queen. Her task is done. But Kaeleer still needs the Heart.

Saetan closed his eyes, not even sure why he couldn't let this go.

Jaenelle was alive, and she seemed happy. Why couldn't he let this one difference go?

"Answer this one question, and I'll never ask again. Is this the same web? Can you tell me, with no doubt, that this is the same web that originally shaped that dream?"

The spider didn't answer.

Saetan opened his eyes and stared at the Arachnian Queen. "Is it the same web?"

It is not quite the same web, the spider admitted reluctantly. Walking on air, she moved above the web until she reached a place where three thick strands formed a triangle. *Because of that.*

He stared at that triangle, his heart pounding. He was one of those strands, one of those dreamers. Father. Brother. And the Lover, who was the father's mirror. Within that triangle, one delicate thread ran from the apex to the center of the base. One fragile strand with a tiny bead of blood attached to it.

If he broke that thread, would Jaenelle be everything she had been?

He took a step forward, lifted his right hand . . . and felt a thrum of power far, far, far below him.

The light in the chamber changed, refocused on that triangle and the single strand. The tiny bead glittered in a way a drop of blood never would.

And suddenly he knew what he was looking at—a tiny chip of an Ebony Jewel.

The Weaver of Dreams said, *There was another dreamer.*

6

Saetan sat on the window seat in his study at the Keep, staring at the evening sky, a glass of yarbarah dangling from his fingers. As much as he adored her, he was glad Surreal had left the Keep before he returned. Right now, he needed some time to himself before he returned to the Hall.

There was another dreamer.

What is Twilight's Dawn?

It iss the Jewel for Kaeleer'ss Heart.

There was another dreamer.

Sshe iss who sshe hass alwayss been.

I lost nothing I regret losing. I am what I want to be.

Lorn was right. He should have looked with his heart to find the answers. If he had, he would have realized there was one person who had no regrets, who felt no grief about the power that had been lost. Was, in fact, enjoying her "diminished" strength.

There was another dreamer.

One tear spilled over, not from sorrow this time but from joy.

He raised the glass of yarbarah in a salute. "To you, witch-child."

FIFTEEN

1

No one saw him, heard him, felt him as he entered Lektra's town house and climbed the stairs. He paused on the landing. He'd spent the day learning about his prey, so it was simple enough to sense which woman huddled in which bedroom.

Turning away from Lektra's room, Daemon walked down the corridor. As he passed through the door of Roxie's bedroom, he placed aural and psychic shields around the room that would keep this conversation private.

She was curled up in a chair, reading a book—something he doubted she usually did for entertainment. She wasn't aware of him as he watched her, as he breathed in her scent.

An illusion spell could hide what a person looked like, but it didn't change her psychic scent. When he'd seen her in Banard's shop the day he bought the bracelet for Jaenelle, he'd felt pity for the witch who needed an illusion spell to hide a disfigurement.

Tonight, pity—and mercy—were words that had no meaning for him.

"So," he said pleasantly as he dropped the Black shields that had kept him hidden from her, "since you couldn't have my brother, you decided to play games with me."

Roxie sprang out of the chair, dropping the book. "I—I don't know what you're talking about."

"Roxie, darling, of course you do. Lucivar exiled you from Ebon Rih when you tried to force him into your bed. I know all about you. Or enough about you. I made it my business to find out. But I really don't care what games you played with Lucivar. I want to know why you decided to play games with me."

Roxie pouted. "Lektra wants you. I just helped her."

"By spreading lies about me, by watching me when I was in Amdarh so you could build those lies on a foundation of truth?" Smiling, he crooned, "Did you also help Lektra with the carriage accident that could have injured Jaenelle?"

"No!" Panic laced her voice, filling him with pleasure. "I didn't know about that! Not until she got back to the town house."

"Ah." Daemon sent wisps of a seduction spell into the room—just enough to dull the sharpest edges of her fear. "Everything has a price, darling. It's time to pay the debt for your part in these games."

"I suppose you're going to tell Zhara to exile me from Amdarh."

Smiling, he glided across the room until he stood in front of her. "Exile? Oh, no. That was Lucivar's choice." He held out his right hand.

As the seduction spells coiled around her, her eyes gleamed with speculation. She slipped her hand into his, then sighed with pleasure when he raised her hand and brushed his lips across her knuckles.

Roxie licked her lips. "So you're not going to exile me?"

"No, I'm not. Because there is one small detail you didn't take into account." He licked the back of her hand as his fingers shifted to her wrist.

"What's that?" she asked, sounding breathless.

"I'm not my brother."

His nails stabbed her. His snake tooth pricked her wrist, and he pumped half of his venom into her before he released her and stepped back.

She stared at the wounds on her wrist, then looked at him, stunned.

"As I said, darling, everything has a price."

He watched her die—and it was a hard death.

Hearing the click of a lock, Lektra spun around and stared at Daemon Sadi, who was leaning against her bedroom door. She pressed a hand against her chest, as if that would control the sudden pounding of her heart. "How did you get in? My butler didn't announce you."

"I didn't want to be announced," he replied.

"You came for me." She breathed out the words, hardly daring to believe. Her beautiful love was here. He had realized who *really* loved him and had broken his ties with Jaenelle in order to be with *her*.

He walked toward her. "Yes, I came for you."

There was something cold about his smile, something mocking in his deep voice, but she didn't care about that because his gold eyes were already glazed with passion.

She flung herself at him, intending to throw her arms around him, but he stepped aside at the last moment. She staggered, off balance, and almost fell.

"Don't touch me," he snarled softly.

"But—" Confused, she pushed her hair away from her face. "Then why are you here?"

"I came to give you what you want from me. I came to give you what you deserve from me."

A low-backed stuffed chair drifted across the floor, then turned until it faced her freestanding mirror.

"Sit down," Daemon said.

She could almost feel his voice on her skin, as if it were some intoxicating lotion he was pouring over her. She couldn't defy it, couldn't disobey that voice. It scared her a little that she couldn't rouse herself enough to make her own demands. Not demands. Requests. She would never make demands. Not with him.

As she moved to obey, he said, "Not in the seat. On the back of the chair."

Being low enough and wide enough, she often perched on the back of that chair, but now she felt self-conscious as she climbed into position and saw her reflection in the mirror.

Daemon stepped up behind her. "What do you see?"

She gave him a coy smile. "I see my lover."

"And I see a woman so obsessed with a man she tried to harm a
∘n."

Her pleasure at having him in her bedroom vanished. "Is that why you're here? Because of stupid Jaenelle?"

For a moment, his face became a cold mask carved out of fine wood. Then he smiled. "You're right, darling. Jaenelle has no place in this room. This is between you and me."

His hands caressed her arms beneath her nightgown. He wasn't actually touching her—he couldn't take his eyes off the woman in the mirror any more than she could stop watching him—but she felt his hands caressing her arms. Then another pair of hands caressed her breasts—and another pair lightly stroked the insides of her thighs.

"How—" she gasped. But she couldn't form the question because a pair of lips brushed over hers. Two mouths closed over her nipples, licking and suckling. And another mouth . . .

Moaning, she arched her back and rested her head on his shoulder. This was so delicious, she never wanted it to stop, never wanted it to end.

Gently, relentlessly, those hands caressed her, those mouths licked and suckled . . . until the pleasure became an unbearable craving for his *real* hands, his *real* mouth.

"Touch me," she gasped, ripping open the nightgown to reveal her breasts. "I need you to touch me."

"Not yet," he whispered. "Not yet."

It didn't stop, didn't end. The pleasure went on and on until she began weeping from the need for release.

"Daemon . . . *please.*"

His right hand curled around her neck, and the warmth of that hand was ten times better than the feel of those phantom hands and mouths.

Feeling intensified until the pleasure became excruciating. As she finally crested, she felt a sharp prick in her neck, which somehow only added to her climax. The fierce release gradually eased to warm waves of pleasure, and finally faded to a delicious glow.

Still watching her, Daemon stepped away from the chair.

Gasping, Lektra stared at the flushed, wild-eyed woman in the mirror. A woman thoroughly satisfied by her lover. *Brutally* satisfied. And now . . .

Feeling strangely heavy and numb, she twisted on her perch to face him. "Now you—" It took her a moment to understand what she was seeing—and what she wasn't seeing. "You—You're not aroused."

"Why would I be?" he replied, sounding bored and cold. So terribly cold.

"It didn't excite you to make love to—"

"I serviced you like I serviced the bitches in Terreille who tried to play games with me. Love had nothing to do with it."

She slid down into the seat. Her legs didn't feel right. Neither did her arms. And she couldn't quite draw a full breath.

"You don't mean that," she panted. "You love me, and I love you."

"I don't know you—and you don't know me."

"But—" She pushed herself out of the chair and tried to walk over to him, but her legs wouldn't hold her. She collapsed on the floor. "There's something wrong with me."

"Everything has a price." Holding out his right hand, he flexed his ring finger. "The price for playing with the Sadist is pain."

She watched the snake tooth slide out beneath the long, black-tinted nail. "You—you *poisoned* me?"

He looked at her and smiled a cold, cruel smile. "Yes."

Remembering the prick she felt, she tried to reach up and touch her neck. "You poisoned me . . . while . . . I . . . was—"

"Coming. Yes."

"Why?"

"Because of your obsession with me, you tried to hurt Jaenelle. So you will be the lesson for any other bitch who thinks she can have me if she eliminates the competition. Just between you and me, darling, if I have to kill every witch in Amdarh to assure no one tries to hurt Jaenelle again, I'll do it and have no regrets. You're all expendable, and she is . . . everything."

Lektra stared at him, fighting for each small gasp of air. Pain danced through her limbs, setting her nerves on fire. She would have screamed if she could have drawn enough breath.

"Daemon . . . help me."

"I will," he promised. "Before you draw your last breath, I'll finish the ᵗⁱ. At least you won't have to face the High Lord and endure this kind ⁿ a second time."

As her lungs failed and her vision faded, she tried to see her beautiful love one last time. And even though he stood in front of her, the only thing she saw as the cold Black rage ripped through her was those glazed, sleepy eyes and that cold, cruel smile.

After he finished the kill, Daemon studied the room. The Blood had a saying: The walls remember. Wood and stone could hold strong emotions, and a skilled Black Widow could draw out those feelings and replay a ghostly image of what happened in a room.

At another time in his life, he would have walked away from this room, would have, most likely, added a few seduction spells that would have been triggered by drawing the memories out of wood and stone. Whoever had come to watch the events leading up to Lektra's death would have felt those phantom hands, those phantom mouths. They would have stood there, helpless to escape, knowing how the previous seduction ended.

It wouldn't have killed them, but the message would have been clear: anyone who tried to play games with his life or someone he loved would die.

But there was Jaenelle to consider, and he didn't want this game paraded before the rest of the Blood. He felt soiled enough being near Lektra and Roxie. So he would leave enough of a warning for the witches in Amdarh. As for the rest . . .

He could deal with that easily enough.

2

Surreal stood across the street and watched the town house burn. She'd spent the evening wandering the nearby streets, passing by the town house often enough to keep an eye on things. Because Sadi had said Lektra was his business, not hers, she'd kept her participation to a passive watch.

So she'd been nearby when witchfire suddenly filled two of the upstairs rooms. She didn't run to the town house to pound on the door and alert the servants. There was no need. The Sadist had his own kind of justice, and the fire remained in those two rooms until the last servant had fled. Then the witchfire took the town house, roaring up to twice the structure's height, a beacon for the rest of the Blood in Amdarh.

They'd come running, but witchfire was fed by power, and there was nothing they could do to extinguish a fire fed by the Black. The water wagons were brought out, and the roofs of the neighboring town houses were doused, but the fire remained confined. He would have made sure of that before he walked away.

"Here," Lucivar said, joining her. He handed her a steaming mug of coffee. "It's damn cold to be standing around."

"Is it this cold a couple of blocks away?" she asked, taking a sip of coffee.

"No."

He'd arrived in Amdarh just as the rest of the town house went up, so they'd found each other easily enough. He, too, would have recognized the fire as a signal—and a warning.

After taking a sip from his own mug, he called in a bundled napkin, used Craft to balance it on air, then flipped open a corner.

Surreal grabbed one of the rolls filled with meat and cheese. She took a big bite, washed it down with coffee, then asked, "Where did you get these?"

"Dining house down the street a little ways. They were still open when the fire started, so they stayed open to keep serving food and drink."

"At least someone will profit from the evening." Finishing the first roll, she checked the napkin bundle, pleased to see two more stuffed rolls. Lucivar was going to share fairly—and just in case that wasn't what he had in mind, she took another roll and bit into it.

"And let's hope this is the only thing in Amdarh that burns tonight," Lucivar growled, using the mug to point to the carriage and riders slowly moving up the street.

The carriage stopped. Zhara stepped out and was immediately surrounded by her guards.

"He doesn't have any reason to go after her, does he?" Surreal asked.

"Not that I know of," Lucivar replied.

Someone pointed them out. Zhara and her circle of guards pushed their way through the crowd. On Zhara's command, the guards stepped aside so the Queen of Amdarh could face Surreal and Lucivar without looking over a wall of male bodies.

"Is Daemon Sadi responsible for this?" Zhara demanded.

Lucivar took a long swallow of coffee before answering. "Yeah, he is."

"Did he also kill Lord Tavey?"

"Sadi killed a Warlord?" Surreal asked.

"At the party the other night," Lucivar replied. "He was fairly neat about it—in a messy sort of way."

"I'm so glad I didn't know that."

"Stop it, both of you," Zhara snapped. "You find this all amusing? It's likely Lady Lektra and her friend were caught in that fire."

"They wouldn't have been alive when the fire started." Surreal shrugged. "What do you want us to say, sugar? The little bitch played a game with the Sadist—and she lost."

Zhara went very still. "What did you call him?"

Lucivar vanished his mug. "In Terreille, they called him the Sadist—with good reason. If you want to push at him for going after a witch who spread those rumors about him and tried to hurt Jaenelle, you go right ahead. You'll live just long enough to regret it."

The fire went out. One moment it was still blazing, the next it was gone.

"Oh, shit," Surreal said softly.

There was plenty of light from the houses on this side of the street to see him coming. That gliding walk, that feline grace. The waves of cold that had the rest of the Blood scrambling to get out of his way.

"Zhara," Lucivar said very quietly, "don't be a fool."

Daemon got close enough that Surreal could see his eyes were still glazed, and his lips were curved in that brutal, chilling smile. He was still in a cold rage, still riding the killing edge. If anyone pushed him now . . .

Lucivar shifted, drawing Daemon's attention.

"Still pissed off?" Lucivar asked.

"Not anymore," Daemon replied. "At least, for now." Those glazed eyes fixed on Zhara. "But if anyone from Dhemlan ever tries to hurt my Queen again, I'll kill you all."

As Daemon turned and walked away, Zhara slowly sank to the ground.

Not hurt, Surreal decided, just . . . shocked. Seeing Daemon as the Sadist for the first time had that effect on most people.

Lucivar wrapped a hand around her arm and pulled her away. "He'll head back to the family town house now to have the quiet he needs to step back from the killing edge. We should be there."

She didn't want to be anywhere near Daemon right now, but Lucivar was right. Even if there was nothing they could do for Sadi, they could stand as a buffer between him and the rest of the Blood until the cold rage passed.

"Do you think he could do that?" Surreal asked. "Do you think something could provoke him enough that he'd really kill everyone in Dhemlan?"

Lucivar muttered, "He's his father's mirror." Then he added, "Let's hope we never have a reason to find out."

SIXTEEN

Daemon waited until the following evening before he returned to the Hall. After a long night's sleep, the cold rage had thawed, but he hadn't been able to sheath his temper quite enough to face the "talk" with Jaenelle. So he'd stayed in his room most of the day, letting Surreal and Lucivar deal with the visitors who timidly knocked on the town house door.

He'd known the moment Zhara had stepped into the town house. Even Lucivar's efforts to shield him from the other visitors' shrill emotions hadn't been enough to keep him from sensing Zhara's spikes of fear. His warning had been found: two bodies, completely untouched by the witchfire that had consumed everything else in Lektra's house. As powerful as he was, his venom didn't offer a kind death, and the fact that he'd made sure there was no way to mistake how they'd died had chilled the aristo Blood in the city. So now the Queen of Amdarh knew what so many witches in Terreille had learned, although usually too late: The Black-Jeweled Warlord Prince who was called the Sadist had no mercy for anyone he considered an enemy. They wouldn't forget the warning because he wouldn't let them forget. The Black Jewels would be in evidence whenever he walked through the streets of Amdarh, and the Blood would understand that their continued survival depended on Jaenelle's compassion, not his. As long as she held the leash, the Sadist would yield to his Queen. If anyone tried to break that leash . . .

But there *was* someone who might break that leash—and she was waiting for him on the other side of the sitting room door.

When he walked into the room, he saw her standing at the window. It was too dark to see the garden, so he wondered what held her attention.

"Is it done?" Jaenelle asked.

"It's done."

"The debt is paid to your satisfaction?"

"It's paid." He couldn't sense her mood, and that frightened him. "Jaenelle—"

She held up her left hand, commanding silence. He felt sick relief when he saw she still wore her wedding ring.

"I am what I am," he said.

Nodding, she turned to face him. "A Black-Jeweled Warlord Prince who grew up in a brutal training ground. That shaped what you are when you become a weapon. But that's only one side of you. The other side is a warm, caring man with a sharp sense of humor and more tolerance for the foolishness of others than you'll ever admit to having. I can accept the Sadist as well as Daemon Sadi. The question is, can you accept me?"

"I do." He took a step toward her. "I always have."

Jaenelle shook her head. "I'm no longer stronger than you. I no longer wear a Jewel that eclipses your power."

"I know that." He raked his fingers through his hair. "You lost—"

"Nothing. Until you can accept *that,* you'll keep stumbling over *this.*" She tapped a finger against Twilight's Dawn. Then she held out her hand. "There's something you need to see."

He slipped his hand into hers. One moment they were standing in their sitting room. The next moment, he was standing in a mist-filled place in the abyss. He'd been in the Misty Place twice before—and he wondered why Jaenelle had brought him here now.

The mist retreated, forming a circular boundary. Almost circular. ʼraight ahead of him there was clear ground.

ʼaenelle?*

ʼnswer. Since there was something she wanted him to see, he

moved forward cautiously until he came to the edge and could look down into a vast chasm.

But it was the huge, spiraling web filling the chasm that took his breath away. Anchored to the Misty Place, it curved until it touched the other side of the chasm, then curved again, gently spiraling, going so deep into the abyss he couldn't see the end of it.

As he studied it, trying to understand, he felt a shiver of power far, far, far below him at the same moment he heard the quiet click of hoof on stone. Turning, he saw her step out of the mist. Here, her true nature wasn't hidden beneath human flesh. Here, she looked like what she was—a living myth, dreams made flesh. The same face and a mostly human body, but a tiny spiral horn rose from her forehead, her fingers had retractable claws, and she stood on delicate hooves instead of human feet. Witch.

She watched him with those ancient sapphire eyes. And waited.

Turning back to study the web, he suddenly understood what he was looking at—a web made out of power. Somehow, the Ebony-Jeweled power she used to wield was being transformed into this web instead of filling a vessel of human flesh. Since it was tied to the Misty Place, surely there was a way for her to regain that power if she—

He remembered Jaenelle as a child—a girl who felt the distance between herself and other people because of the Black power that was her Birthright, a girl whose family had never accepted her because she was different. He thought about the Queen who could have destroyed them all if that had been in her nature, a Queen so strong her power was a deep chasm that separated her from the rest of the Blood—even someone as strong as a Black-Jeweled Warlord Prince.

You didn't want it, he said, staggered by the strength of that conviction.

No, Witch said, *I didn't want it. Why would I want power so great I could destroy the Realms but couldn't do what almost every Blood child can do because I was so powerful?* She looked away, and added softly, *I never wanted a formal court, never wanted to rule, never wanted more power than I already had with the Black. But I made the Offering to the Darkness and formed my court to prevent the Dark

Council from destroying the kindred and taking their lands. I needed that power to defend Kaeleer and be a weapon to stop a war, but I never wanted it for myself.*

He moved closer to her, wanting to hold her, wanting to offer comfort, but he wasn't sure she would accept it yet.

How did you do it? he asked. *How did you separate the power that was part of the dreams that made you without destroying who you are?*

She let out a pained little laugh. *I dreamed I wasn't so different from the rest of the Blood—a dream I've had all of my life. That desire was strong enough that the Weaver of Dreams added it to the web . . . and this is the result.*

Daemon studied Witch, who looked sad and vulnerable. People had turned away from her before because she was so powerful. Now she wondered if the friends she loved might always feel uncomfortable with the fact that she *wasn't* so powerful. He didn't think the coven and the boyos would turn away from her, and once they realized she still was who and what she had always been, and was truly happy, they wouldn't care what Jewel she wore.

Wrapping his arms around her, he fit his body to hers. *This is really what you want for yourself, isn't it? An extraordinary ordinary life.*

Yes, it is.

Then that's what I want for you. He kissed her softly. *For both of us.* Closing his eyes, he kissed her again.

When he shifted to nuzzle her neck, she said, "Are you sure, Daemon?"

He opened his eyes and raised his head. They were back in the sitting room.

"I want to be with you for as many years as life grants us," he said. "I want to be the warm, caring man you see in me and let the Sadist sleep."

Jaenelle brushed his hair back. "He'll never really sleep. The Sadist is a part of who you are, and he'll always be there, just under the surface— d that's the way it should be."

never loved her more than he did at that moment when her ac quieted the volatile nature of a Warlord Prince.

Scooping her up, he held her close to his chest. "What do you say to locking the doors, going to bed, and making love for the rest of the night?"

"Is that going to be the extraordinary or ordinary part of our life?" she asked, laughter and love dancing in her sapphire eyes.

He grinned. "Both."

SEVENTEEN

Too edgy to stay still, Daemon prowled the room that opened onto the flagstone terrace at the back of the Hall. It wasn't unusual for a man to have pre-wedding jitters, even if he *was* already married to the woman he loved. Besides, how many men had their marriage vows witnessed by fire-breathing dragons and man-eating cats?

Although, he probably shouldn't have snarled at Jaenelle when she suggested that he take off his wedding ring so that she could give it back to him. Guests be damned, he wasn't giving up his ring.

"Would you like some brandy?" Saetan asked, his bland tone accenting his amusement.

"No," Daemon snarled.

"A sedative?"

"No."

"A whack upside the head?"

Daemon glared at his father. "You're finding this too amusing."

"Oh, I think I'm entitled," Saetan replied dryly.

Suddenly feeling as if the ground was about to get yanked out from under him, Daemon stopped moving.

"Anything you want to tell me?" Saetan asked.

"No," he said, feeling wary.

"In that case, since the guests are all assembled and Jaenelle will be any moment, let's go out and get you married. Again."

Daemon winced. "It's not that we didn't—I mean, I *meant* to tell you before—Ah, Hell's fire."

Saetan laughed. "It's just as well you *are* married already. If your nerves don't settle, you're going to be useless tonight."

"Thank you. I so appreciate your confidence in me."

Saetan's amusement faded. "I do have confidence in you, Prince. More than you realize." He walked over to the glass doors.

"Wait." He crossed the room to stand next to his father. "There are a couple of things I wanted to tell you." He hesitated, not sure how to begin. "Lady Zhara came to see me last week, on behalf of all the Queens in Dhemlan. They asked me to rule as the Warlord Prince of Dhemlan." He snorted softly. "I suspect they're asking out of fear rather than any real desire to have me rule . . ."

"But?"

Daemon looked out the door. The Queens who ruled the other Territories were out there, laughing and talking. The strongest Warlord Princes in the Realm were out there. All of them were connected to each other by the woman who was Kaeleer's Heart. Just as he was connected to all of them because of her.

"But that was your place," he said.

"That is correct. It *was* my place." Saetan paused. "Is it going to be yours? Are you going to accept?"

"I told Zhara I would consider it, but I wouldn't make any decision until after Jaenelle and I returned from our honeymoon."

"Are you going to accept?"

He took a deep breath, then let it out slowly. "Yes, I'm going to accept. It . . . feels right."

Saetan rested a hand on Daemon's shoulder. "I think it is the right choice. For you—and for Dhemlan. Just don't expect Jaenelle to be cheerful whenever she has to dress up for a formal occasion."

"She's already explained that."

After giving Daemon a sympathetic pat, Saetan stepped back. "What's the second thing?"

This was harder. If Jaenelle had wanted everyone to know why she no longer wore Ebony Jewels, she would have told her friends and family.

Maybe it was fear on her part that if they knew it was possible for her to be *exactly* like she'd been, they'd want it so much, she'd give in to their desire instead of holding on to her own. But Saetan needed to know. At least, enough to let go of any regrets.

"It's about Twilight's Dawn," Daemon said carefully.

"A Jewel for Kaeleer's Heart," Saetan replied just as carefully.

"She is what she wants to be."

"And has lost nothing she regrets losing?"

Daemon nodded. A cautious dance of words, so that neither of them would break faith with their Queen. "She's dreamed of having an extraordinary, ordinary life. Wearing Ebony Jewels, she could only have half of that. With Twilight's Dawn, she'll have all of it."

"Do you know that for certain, Prince?"

"Yes, High Lord. I know that for certain."

They smiled at each other.

"There is one more thing," Saetan said, calling in a folded piece of parchment and handing it to Daemon. "It isn't what you had originally intended, but I think it will do."

Daemon unfolded the parchment and studied the words in the Old Tongue.

A light brush against his inner barriers. He opened the first barrier, and his father's deep voice rolled through his mind as Saetan spoke those fluid words.

Suddenly he was a child again, listening to that voice teaching him phrases in the Old Tongue in exactly the same way. He thought he'd learned the language from the scholars, but they'd only awakened the memories of what he'd learned from the man standing before him.

He said the words over and over, until he wasn't sure if he was hearing his father's voice or his own.

Another light brush against his mind, and Saetan withdrew.

Folding the parchment, Daemon tucked it in his jacket pocket. "What does it mean?"

" 'You are my breath, my life, my heart.' " Saetan smiled. "Does that ...ough?"

...ung his eyes. "That says everything."

Saetan kissed him. "Your Lady is waiting for you."

They opened the glass doors and walked across the terrace, side by side. Then Saetan stepped back and he was alone, walking the rest of the way across the grass to where his finest dreams waited for him to begin the next season of their lives.

Anne Bishop is a winner of the William L. Crawford Memorial Fantasy Award for *The Black Jewels Trilogy*. She lives in upstate New York. Visit her Web site at www.annebishop.com.